Thorssen had not been content with just inspecting the machine I had almost forgotten. With his hands grasping the metal bars, he was leaning over that unspeakable blackness. . . .

Suddenly my knees gave way with panic. Like the light from a snuffed-out candle, Thorssen disappeared from sight!

I was too horrified and numbed to do much intelligent thinking. I could have saved my own skin if I had. Hypnotized by the unholy machine, I scrambled up to it and clung to the bars even as Thorssen had. Whatever made me think I could succeed where Thorssen's steel muscles had failed, I don't know. I peered into that blackness, thinking insanely I could discover some trace of him.

The blackness was impenetrable, and that feeling of instability stole over me again, only doubly strong this time. I felt my grip on the bars melting, a horrible dizziness set in. . . .

Then, like Thorssen, I was sucked into those awful depths!

—from WINGS OF THE LIGHTNING LAND,
    by James MacCreigh

TO
US

ALL OF US

SCIENCE FICTION: THE GREAT YEARS

Edited by

CAROL & FREDERIK POHL

ace books

A Division of Charter Communications Inc.
1120 Avenue of the Americas
New York, N.Y. 10036

ACKNOWLEDGMENTS:

... *And Then There Were None*, copyright 1951 by Street & Smith Publications, Inc., reprinted by permission of the author and the author's agents, Scott Meredith Literary Agency, Inc., 580 Fifth Avenue, N.Y.C. 10036.

The Liberation of Earth, copyright 1953 by Columbia Publications, Inc. Reprinted by permission of the author.

Old Faithful, copyright 1934 by Street & Smith Publications, Inc. Reprinted by permission of the author and his agent, Forrest J Ackerman.

Placet Is a Crazy Place, copyright 1946 by Street & Smith Publications, Inc., reprinted by permission of the agents for the author's estate, Scott Meredith Literary Agency, Inc., 580 Fifth Avenue, N.Y.C. 10036.

Wings of the Lightning Land, copyright 1941 by Fictioneers, Inc. Reprinted by permission of the author.

The Little Black Bag, copyright 1950, in U.S.A. and Great Britain, by Street & Smith Publications, Inc. Reprinted by permission of Robert P. Mills, Ltd., 156 East 52d Street, N.Y.C. 10022, agents for the estate of the author.

A Matter of Form, copyright 1938 in the U.S.A. and Great Britain by Street & Smith Publications, Inc. Reprinted by permission of the author.

First Ace printing: January, 1973

Printed in U.S.A.

CONTENTS

INTRODUCTION THE FIRST

When I began reading science fiction I was ten years old. It was my parents' fault. They had taken me to one of those Sunday visit things where there was no one my own age in the house, and nowhere to go outside, and the only thing I could find to read was a magazine called *Amazing Stories Annual*. (That sounds like it ought to come out once a year, but in fact that was the only "annual" they ever published; it sold well enough so that Hugo Gernsback, its publisher, decided to bring it out every three months, thus becoming *Amazing Stories Quarterly*. Since he was already publishing Amazing Stories itself once a month, that made sixteen times a year he amazed the customers—but somehow I had missed the monthly magazine, so all this was new to me.)

Almost the whole magazine turned out to be devoted to a single story, a marvelous tale called *The Master Mind of Mars* by a fellow named Edgar Rice Burroughs. It was a John Carter story, but that didn't mean anything to me then: I'd never heard of John Carter. I'd never heard of Edgar Rice Burroughs, either, in spite of all the Tarzan movies (who but a literary nut or another writer ever remembers a writer's name?). I'm not entirely sure I'd ever heard of Mars. It didn't matter. I loved it, every word. I ate it up. Iconoclastic, impassioned, penetrating—to me it was all those things, though not, naturally, framed in those words but rather: wow, how long have they been writing stuff like *this?* "Tur Is

Tur!" roared the besotted Martian worshippers in the temple, and I saw at once how brilliantly Burroughs was destroying the idiot hypocrisy of organized religion. I had formed a taste for pungent satire from Voltaire's *Candide*, which my mother had given me under the impression it was a fairy tale, but I hadn't known where else that kind of thing could be found until I discovered Burroughs.

And it was not just satire, it was incisive thinking. Social thinking: how much better organized than ours, I found, the Barsoomian city-states were. Scientific thinking. In Burroughs's Martian cities even the streetlights were better than ours. They didn't waste illumination where it wasn't needed. They sent their rays out in a boomerang circle, so that they lit the front of you, slid around your sides and lit them, passed and lit the back of you, and then returned economically to the lamp from which they had issued, to be radiated once again. How smart of Burroughs, I thought, and why didn't we have streetlights like that on Flatbush Avenue?

Well. That was a while ago. I know now why we don't have lights like that—because we can't; it violates, among other laws, the law of entropy. But I still find marvels in science fiction. I have gone on finding those marvels for more than forty years.

The marvels are not exactly the same ones any more. Things happen; times change. Science fiction itself has changed somewhat, in a direction that is sometimes described as "maturity". Now some three hundred colleges and universities teach courses in science fiction; I've taught some myself. Large companies and management groups import sf writers to consult with them on the shape of the future; I've done that, too. Scholars devote their lives to disentangling the bibliographies and influences of sf writers. We are, in a word, respectable now.

We were not always that way, certainly not in those

8

days of the 30's and 40's and 50's, when some of the people I knew tore the covers off the sf magazines when they carried them in public. We were crude, brash and— a word that I will come back to in a minute—vulgar.

I have very mixed emotions about the changes that have happened to science fiction. Some of this maturity is clearly good. The kind of sf that is being written today is in literary ways far superior to the product that filled the pulps a generation ago. It is more smoothly, often more elegantly written. There is still passion and danger and suffering in it, but its characters suffer as you and I do—which is to say, often wretchedly, more often out of our own inadequacies and despairs than under the onslaught of a Rigellian worm-creature.

It has, in fact, become fashionable to look down on the old pulp magazine days with some scorn and contempt. And yet, what was it that made sf worth reading? It wasn't today's stories, however beautifully they are written and maturely they are conceived. It happened before today's stories were thought of, before most of today's writers had ever put words on paper. It happened twenty years ago and more.

It was, in fact, those very stories of the old pulp days that made science fiction great in the first place.

The word "pulp", of course, is a pejorative term. Pulp magazines were the cheapest magazines there were, in physical details and in literary quality. "Pulp" as an adjective carries with it the flavor of lousy, skill-less writing hacked out at the rate of five thousand words a day (and paid for at the rate of a quarter of a cent a word) by literary whores who gave themselves wherever the money was. Baseball stories and science fiction; crime shockers and air-war adventures; Western gunplay and drippy love stories for pre-pubescent females. This was the range of the pulps, and it is true that a good many of the writers wrote it all, interchangeably.

It is also true that a good many of the most prolific pulpsters had no discernible way with words at all. I know; I spent four years editing pulps for the old Popular Publications, Inc. All kinds. I still remember with pain the ordeal of trying to put some of those stories into English. We all tried, all of us ill-paid editors in the pulps; we didn't very often succeed. Most of what we published was garbage, and we all knew it.

But among the garbage, immaculate and untouched by their settings, were jewels. Not all "pulp" writers followed the money, and not all of the ones who did were bad writers. In science fiction particularly (and in one or two other categories, like detective stories and general adventure fiction) there were stories which were worth reading. They were not always elegantly written, but they had something uniquely their own.

What many of these writers had was the trait the literary critic, Leslie Fiedler, calls "vulgarity". Science fiction has lost a lot of its vulgarity, Fiedler thinks, and he believes that that loss is serious.

So do I, for what Fiedler means by "vulgarity" is the willingness to sacrifice style and polish to a purpose, the purpose being the conveying of a kind of wonder and excitement that could not be made to exist in any other way.

In this book you will find some "vulgar" stories. They are what seem to me the kind of stories that made the Great Years great.

This is, let me see, the twentieth or thirtieth anthology that I've had (or shared) the editing of. In some ways it was the most difficult, because it presented a special problem. I did not select these stories by reading through every old sf magazine in print; I selected them in the first place from memory—from remembering the pleasure they had given me when they first came out, and remembering the pleasure that they gave me still, decades later. I read them again to make sure that I still liked them, and that was how I came to the first rough selection of possible stories.

But choosing stories on that basis involves a great risk. I can only describe that risk by saying that it reflects the decay of the world. Summers aren't as long as they used to be, snowfalls are not as beautiful. Back when I read these stories for the first time I was a lot younger than I am now, and a lot more impressionable. How much of the joy I got from, say, *Skylark Three* came from the actual words Doc Smith wrote on the page . . . and how much from the fact that I was a bouncy, enthusiastic thirteen-year-old? Do these remembered great stories still stand up for a modern audience? And how would it be possible for me to say ever whether they do or not?

This problem so concerned me that I decided to invite a collaborator to help on this anthology. What I needed, I reasoned, was someone who knew a great deal about science fiction, whose literary taste was good, whose intelligence was high . . . but who had not read any of these stories before.

Such a person is hard to find. I did not despair. In my travels I cover a lot of ground and meet a lot of people who know science fiction well. I made up lists of possible collaborators, and one by one crossed them off . . . until, at the end, it was clear that there was only one obvious perfect choice; and that is the one who shares the by-line of this volume with me.

I consider myself lucky to have her as a collaborator on this book . . . but far luckier to have had her as a collaborator on countless other things, over the more than twenty years since we were married.

I will now let her speak for herself.

—Frederik Pohl

INTRODUCTION THE SECOND

When Fred came to me, months ago, and said out of the blue, "How would you like to collaborate on an anthology with me?" I shrieked, "Who, me? You must be kidding. I don't know enough about science fiction to collaborate on an anthology."

"That's just the point," he said calmly. "I know enough for both of us, but I need someone who hasn't read everything. I want you to read some *old* stories *now* for the first time, without any built-in sentiment about the old days. All you have to do is read the ones I like, and tell me which of them you like."

"Now that you put it that way, it is an offer I cannot refuse," I said, and shortly thereafter Fred appeared in the bedroom doorway, staggering under what looked like several tons of tatty, ragged old magazines.

"Happy reading," he said brightly. "When you finish these I'll bring down the next batch."

I picked up the first magazine, and the cover fell off in my hands. I took a deep breath—which was a mistake; there is a very odd smell to old pulp paper, dust and chemicals—and began to read.

It was like taking a fix for the first time. It was addicting. It also explained something. For twenty years most of our best friends have been science-fiction writers, and now I can understand, for the first time, why Fred and so many of my closest friends have been carrying this monkey on their backs for so many years. Reading science fiction is great fun!

Selecting the stories for the anthology turned out to be harder than I had expected. It wasn't just a matter of finding stories I liked. I liked far more than we had room to print. The final selection was painful.

But we made it, and I think you will find these stories very good. Happy reading!

—Carol Pohl

Red Bank, New Jersey
October, 1972

John W. Campbell edited *Astounding/Analog*, under either title one of the great seminal influences in the science-fiction field, for more than a third of a century, until the day of his death in the summer of 1971. He published fine stories of many kinds, but there was one special kind of story which touched his own grin muscles: the story of hard-headed individualists triumphing over bureaucratic ineptitude. Eric Frank Russell's *. . . And Then There Were None* is the archetype of those stories: not just one stubborn hero but a planetful of them, out-Randing Ayn Rand. It doesn't require much of an introduction. If you ever liked any part of *Analog/Astounding*, you'll like this story. Almost everyone does.

... AND THEN THERE WERE NONE
By Eric Frank Russell

The battleship was eight hundred feet in diameter and slightly more than one mile long. Mass like that takes up room and makes a dent. This one sprawled right across one field and halfway through the next. Its weight made a rut twenty feet deep which would be there for keeps.

On board were two thousand people divisible into three distinct types. The tall, lean, crinkly-eyed ones were the crew. The crop-haired, heavy-jowled ones were the troops. Finally, the expressionless, balding and myopic ones were the cargo of bureaucrats.

The first of these types viewed this world with the professional but aloof interest of people everlastingly giving a planet the swift once-over before chasing along to the next. The troops regarded it with a mixture of tough contempt and boredom. The bureaucrats peered at it with cold authority. Each according to his lights.

This lot were accustomed to new worlds, having dealt with them by the dozens and reduced the process to mere routine. The task before them would have been nothing more than repetition of well-used, smoothly operating technique but for one thing: the entire bunch were in a jam and did not know it.

Emergence from the ship was in strict order of precedence. First, the Imperial Ambassador. Second, the battleship's captain. Third, the officer commanding the ground forces. Fourth, the senior civil servant.

Then, of course, the next grade lower, in the same order: His Excellency's private secretary, the ship's second officer, the deputy commander of troops, the penultimate pen pusher.

Down another grade, then another, until there was left only His Excellency's barber, boot wiper and valet, crew members with the lowly status of O.S.—Ordinary Spaceman—the military nonentities in the ranks, and a few temporary inkpot fillers dreaming of the day when they would be made permanent and given a desk of their own. This last collection of unfortunates remained aboard to clean ship and refrain from smoking, by command.

Had this world been alien, hostile and well-armed, the order of exit would have been reversed, exemplifying the Biblical promise that the last shall be first and first shall be last. But this planet, although officially new, unofficially was not new and certainly was not alien. In ledgers and dusty files some two hundred light-years away it was recorded as a cryptic number and classified as a ripe plum long overdue for picking. There had been considerable delay in the harvesting due to a superabundance of other still riper plums elsewhere.

According to the records, this planet was on the outermost fringe of a huge assortment of worlds which had been settled immediately following the Great Explosion. Every schoolchild knew all about the Great Explosion, which was no more than the spectacular name given to the bursting outward of masses of humanity when the Blieder drive superseded atomic-powered rockets and practically handed them the cosmos on a platter.

At that time, between three and five hundred years ago, every family, group, cult or clique that imagined it could do better someplace else had taken to the star trails. The restless, the ambitious, the malcontents, the eccentrics, the antisocial, the fidgety and the just plain curious, away they had roared by the dozens, the hundreds, the thousands.

Some two hundred thousand had come to this particular world, the last of them arriving three centuries back. As usual, ninety percent of the mainstream had consisted of friends, relatives or acquaintances of the firstcomers, people persuaded to follow the bold example of Uncle Eddie or good old Joe.

If they had since doubled themselves six or seven times over, there now ought to be several millions of them. That they had increased far beyond their original strength had been evident during the approach, for while no great cities were visible there were many medium-to-smallish towns and a large number of villages.

His Excellency looked with approval at the turf under his feet and plucked a blade of it, grunting as he stooped. He was so constructed that this effort approximated an athletic feat and gave him a crick in the belly.

"Earth-type grass. Notice that, captain? Is it just a coincidence, or did they bring seed with them?"

"Coincidence, probably," thought Captain Grayder. "I've come across four grassy worlds so far. No reason why there shouldn't be others."

15

"No, I suppose not." His Excellency gazed into the distance, doing it with pride of ownership. "Looks like there's someone plowing over there. He's using a little engine between a pair of fat wheels. They can't be so backward. Hmmm!" He rubbed a couple of chins. "Bring him here. We'll have a talk, find out where it's best to get started."

"Very well." Captain Grayder turned to Colonel Shelton, boss of the troops. "His Excellency wishes to speak to that farmer." He pointed to the faraway figure.

"The farmer," said Shelton to Major Hame. "His Excellency wants him at once."

"Bring that farmer here," Hame ordered Lieutenant Deacon. "Quickly!"

"Go get that farmer," Deacon told Sergeant Major Bidworthy. "And hurry—His Excellency is waiting!"

The sergeant major, a big, purple-faced man, sought around for a lesser rank, then remembered that they were all cleaning ship and not smoking. He, it seemed, was elected.

Tramping across four fields and coming within hailing distance of his objective, he performed a precise military halt and released a barracks-square bellow of, "Hi, you!" He waved urgently.

The farmer stopped, wiped his forehead, looked around. His manner suggested that the mountainous bulk of the battleship was a mirage such as were five a penny around these parts. Bidworthy waved again, making it an authoritative summons. The farmer calmly waved back and got on with his plowing.

Sergeant Major Bidworthy employed an expletive which—when its flames had died out—meant, "Dear me!" and marched fifty paces nearer. He could now see that the other was bushy-browed and leather-faced.

"*Hi!*"

16

Stopping the plow again, the farmer leaned on a shaft, picking his teeth.

Struck by the notion that perhaps during the last three centuries the old Earth language had been dropped in favor of some other lingo, Bidworthy asked, "Can you understand me?"

"Can any person understand another?" inquired the farmer, with clear diction. He turned to resume his task.

Bidworthy was afflicted with a moment of confusion. Recovering, he informed hurriedly, "His Excellency, the Earth Ambassador, wishes to speak with you at once."

"So?" The other eyed him speculatively. "How come that he is excellent?"

"He is a person of considerable importance," said Bidworthy, unable to decide whether the other was being funny at his expense or alternatively was what is known as a character. A good many of these isolated planet-scratchers liked to think of themselves as characters.

"Of considerable importance," echoed the farmer, narrowing his eyes at the horizon. He appeared to be trying to grasp an alien concept. After a while, he inquired, "What will happen to your home world when this person dies?"

"Nothing," Bidworthy admitted.

"It will roll on as usual?"

"Of course."

"Then," declared the farmer, flatly, "he cannot be important." With that, his little engine went *chuff-chuff* and the wheels rolled forward and the plow plowed.

Digging his nails into the palms of his hands, Bidworthy spent half a minute gathering oxygen before he said, in hoarse tones, "I cannot return without at least a message for His Excellency."

"Indeed?" The other was incredulous. "What is to stop you?" Then, noting the alarming increase in Bidworthy's color, he added with compassion, "Oh, well, you may tell him that I said"—he paused while he thought it over—"God bless you and good-by!"

Sergeant Major Bidworthy was a powerful man who weighed two-twenty pounds, had hopped around the cosmos for twenty years, and feared nothing. He had never been known to permit the shiver of one hair—but he was trembling all over by the time he got back to the ship.

His Excellency fastened a cold eye upon him and demanded, "Well?"

"He won't come." Bidworthy's veins stood out on his forehead. "And, sir, if only I could have him in my field company for a few months, I'd straighten him up and teach him to move on the double."

"I don't doubt that, sergeant major," soothed His Excellency. He continued in a whispered aside to Colonel Shelton. "He's a good fellow but no diplomat. Too abrupt and harsh-voiced. Better go yourself and fetch that farmer. We can't sit here forever waiting to find out where to begin."

"Very well, your excellency." Colonel Shelton trudged across the fields and caught up with the plow. Smiling pleasantly, he said, "Good morning, my man!"

Stopping his plow, the farmer sighed as if it were another of those days one has sometimes. His eyes were dark brown, almost black, as they looked at the other.

"What makes you think I'm *your* man?" he inquired.

"It is a figure of speech," explained Shelton. He could see what was wrong now. Bidworthy had fallen foul of an irascible type. Two dogs snarling at one another. Shelton went on, "I was only trying to be courteous."

"Well," meditated the farmer, "I reckon that's something worth trying for."

Pinking a little, Shelton continued with determination. "I am commanded to request the pleasure of your company at the ship."

"Think they'll get any pleasure out of my company?" asked the other, disconcertingly bland.

"I'm sure of it," said Shelton.

"You're a liar," said the farmer.

His color deepening, Colonel Shelton snapped, "I do not permit people to call me a liar."

"You've just permitted it," the other pointed out.

Letting it pass, Shelton insisted, "Are you coming to the ship or are you not?"

"I am not."

"Why not?"

"Myob!" said the farmer.

"What was that?"

"Myob!" he repeated. It smacked of a mild insult. Colonel Shelton went back.

He told the ambassador, "That fellow is one of these too-clever types. All I could get out of him at the finish was 'myob', whatever that means."

"Local slang," chipped in Captain Grayder. "An awful lot of it develops over three or four centuries. I've come across one or two worlds where there's been so much of it that one almost had to learn a new language."

"He understood your speech?" asked the ambassador, looking at Shelton.

"Yes, your excellency. And his own is quite good. But he won't come away from his plowing." He reflected briefly, then suggested, "If it were left to me, I'd bring him in by force, under an armed escort."

"That would encourage him to give essential information," commented the ambassador, with open sarcasm. He patted his stomach, smoothed his jacket, glanced down at his glossy shoes. "Nothing for it but to go speak to him myself."

Colonel Shelton was shocked. "Your excellency, you can't do *that!*"

"Why can't I?"

"It would be undignified."

"I am aware of it," said the ambassador dryly. "Can you suggest an alternative?"

"We can send out a patrol to find someone more cooperative."

"Someone better informed, too," Captain Grayder offered. "At best we wouldn't get much out of one surly hayseed. I doubt whether he knows a quarter of what we require to learn."

"All right." His Excellency abandoned the notion of doing his own chores. "Organize a patrol and let's have some results."

"A patrol," said Colonel Shelton to Major Hame. "Nominate one immediately."

"Call out a patrol," Hame ordered Lieutenant Deacon. "At once."

"Parade a patrol forthwith, sergeant major," said Deacon.

Bidworthy went to the ship, climbed a ladder, stuck his head in the lock and bawled, "Sergeant Gleed, out with your squad, and make it snappy!" He gave a suspicious sniff and went farther into the lock. His voice gained several more decibels. "Who's been smoking? By the Black Sack, if I catch—"

Across the fields something quietly went *chuff-chuff* while balloon tires crawled along.

The patrol formed by the right in two ranks of eight men each, turned at a barked command, and marched off noseward. Their boots thumped in unison, their accouterments clattered and the orange-colored sun made sparkles on their metal.

Sergeant Gleed did not have to take his men far. They had got one hundred yards beyond the battleship's nose when he noticed a man ambling across the field to his right. Treating the ship with utter indifference, the newcomer was making toward the farmer still plowing far over to the left.

"Patrol, right wheel!" yelled Gleed. Marching them straight past the wayfarer, he gave them a loud about-turn and followed it with the high-sign.

Speeding up its pace, the patrol opened its ranks to become a double file of men tramping at either side of the lone pedestrian. Ignoring his suddenly acquired escort, the latter continued to plod straight ahead like one long convinced that all is illusion.

"Left wheel!" Gleed roared, trying to bend the whole caboodle toward the waiting ambassador.

Swiftly obedient, the double file headed leftward, one, two, three, hup! It was neat, precise execution, beautiful to watch. Only one thing spoiled it: the man in the middle maintained his self-chosen orbit and ambled casually between numbers four and five of the right-hand file.

That upset Gleed, especially since the patrol continued to thump ambassadorwards for lack of a further order. His Excellency was being treated to the unmilitary spectacle of an escort dumbly boot-beating one way while its prisoner airily mooched another. Colonel Shelton would have plenty to say about it in due course, and anything he forgot Bidworthy would remember.

"Patrol!" hoarsed Gleed, pointing an outraged finger at the escapee, and momentarily dismissing all regulation commands from his mind. "Get that yimp!"

Breaking ranks, they moved at the double and surrounded the wanderer too closely to permit further progress. Perforce, he stopped.

Gleed came up, said somewhat breathlessly, "Look, the Earth Ambassador wants to speak to you—that's all."

The other said nothing, merely gazed at him with mild

21

blue eyes. He was a funny-looking bum, long overdue for a shave, with a fringe of ginger whiskers sticking out all around his pan. He resembled a sunflower.

"Are you going to talk with His Excellency?" Gleed persisted.

"Naw." The other nodded toward the farmer. "Going to talk with Zeke."

"The ambassador first," retorted Gleed, toughly. "He's a big noise."

"I don't doubt that," remarked the sunflower.

"Smartie Artie, eh?" said Gleed, pushing his face close and making it unpleasant. He gave his men a gesture. "All right—shove him along. We'll show him!"

Smartie Artie sat down. He did it sort of solidly, giving himself the aspect of a statue anchored for eons. The ginger whiskers did nothing to lend grace to the situation. But Sergeant Gleed had handled sitters before, the only difference being that this one was cold sober.

"Pick him up," ordered Gleed, "and carry him."

They picked him up and carried him, feet first, whiskers last. He hung limp and unresisting in their hands, a dead weight. In this inauspicious manner he arrived in the presence of the Earth Ambassador where the escort plonked him on his feet.

Promptly he set out for Zeke.

"Hold him, darn you!" howled Gleed.

The patrol grabbed and clung tight. His Excellency eyed the whiskers with well-bred concealment of distaste, coughed delicately, and spoke.

"I am truly sorry that you had to come to me in this fashion."

"In that case," suggested the prisoner, "you could have saved yourself some mental anguish by not permitting it to happen."

"There was no other choice. We've got to make contact somehow."

"I don't see it," said Ginger Whiskers. "What's so special about this date?"

"The date?" His Excellency frowned in puzzlement. "Where does that come in?"

"That's what I'd like to know."

"The point eludes me." The ambassador turned to Colonel Shelton. "Do you get what he's aiming at?"

"I could hazard a guess, your excellency. I think he is suggesting that since we've left them without contact for more than three hundred years, there's no particular urgency about making it today." He looked at the sunflower for confirmation.

That worthy rallied to his support by remarking, "You're doing pretty well for a half-wit."

Regardless of Shelton's own reaction, this was too much for Bidworthy, purpling nearby. His chest came up and his eyes caught fire. His voice was an authoritative rasp.

"Be more respectful while addressing high-ranking officers!"

The prisoner's mild blue eyes turned upon him in childish amazement, examining him slowly from feet to head and all the way down again. The eyes drifted back to the ambassador.

"Who is this preposterous person?"

Dismissing the question with an impatient wave of his hand, the ambassador said, "See here, it is not our purpose to bother you from sheer perversity, as you seem to think. Neither do we wish to detain you any longer than is necessary. All we—"

Pulling at his face-fringe as if to accentuate its offensiveness, the other interjected, "It being you, of course, who determines the length of the necessity?"

"On the contrary, you may decide that yourself," said the ambassador, displaying admirable self-control. "All you need do is tell—"

"Then I've decided it right now," the prisoner chipped in. He tried to heave himself free of his escort. "Let me go talk to Zeke."

"All you need do," the ambassador persisted, "is to tell us where we can find a local official who can put us in touch with your central government." His gaze was stern, commanding, as he added, "For instance, where is the nearest police post?"

"Myob!" said the other.

"The same to you," retorted the ambassador, his patience starting to evaporate.

"That's precisely what I'm trying to do," assured the prisoner enigmatically. "Only you won't let me."

"If I may make a suggestion, your excellency," put in Colonel Shelton, "let me—"

"I require no suggestions and I won't let you," said the ambassador, rapidly becoming brusque. "I have had enough of all this tomfoolery. I think we've landed at random in an area reserved for imbeciles and it would be as well to recognize the fact and get out of it with no more delay."

"Now you're talking," approved Ginger Whiskers. "And the farther the better."

"I'm not thinking of leaving this planet if that's what is in your incomprehensible mind," asserted the ambassador, with much sarcasm. He stamped a proprietory foot on the turf. "This is part of the Earth Empire. As such, it is going to be recognized, charted and organized."

"*Heah, heah!*" put in the senior civil servant, who aspired to honors in elocution.

His Excellency threw a frown behind, then went on: "We'll move the ship to some other section where brains are brighter." He signed to the escort. "Let him go. Doubtless he is in a hurry to borrow a razor."

They released their grips. Ginger Whiskers at once

24

turned toward the still-plowing farmer, much as if he were a magnetized needle irresistibly drawn Zekeward. Without a word he set off at his original mooching pace. Disappointment and disgust showed on the faces of Gleed and Bidworthy as they watched him go.

"Have the vessel shifted at once," the ambassador instructed Captain Grayder. "Plant it near a suitable town—not out in the wilds where every hayseed views strangers as a bunch of gyps."

He marched importantly up the gangway. Captain Grayder followed, then Colonel Shelton, then the elocutionist. Next, their successors in due order of precedence. Lastly, Gleed and his men.

The gangway rolled inward. The lock closed. Despite its immense bulk, the ship shivered briefly from end to end and soared without deafening uproar or spectacular display of flame.

Indeed, there was silence save for the plow going *chuff-chuff* and the murmurings of the two men walking behind it. Neither bothered to turn his head to observe what was happening.

"Seven pounds of prime tobacco is a heck of a lot to give for one case of brandy," Ginger Whiskers was protesting.

"Not for my brandy," said Zeke. "It's stronger than a thousand Gands and smoother than an Earthman's downfall."

The great battleship's second touchdown was made on a wide flat one mile north of a town estimated to hold twelve to fifteen thousand people. Captain Grayder would have preferred to survey the place from low altitude before making his landing, but one cannot maneuver an immense space-going job as if it were an atmospheric tug. Only two things can be done so close to a planetary surface—the ship is taken up or brought

25

down with no room for fiddling betweentimes.

So Grayder bumped his ship in the best spot he could find when finding is a matter of split-second decisions. It made a rut only twelve feet deep, the ground being harder and on a rock bed. The gangway was shoved out; the procession descended in the same order as before.

His Excellency cast an anticipatory look toward the town, registered disappointment and remarked, "Something's badly out of kilter here. There's the town. Here's us in plain view, with a ship like a metal mountain. A thousand people at least must have seen us even if the rest are holding seances behind drawn curtains or playing pinochle in the cellars. Are they excited?"

"It doesn't seem so," admitted Colonel Shelton, pulling an eyelid for the sake of feeling it spring back.

"I wasn't asking you. I was telling you. They are not excited. They are not surprised. In fact, they are not even interested. One would almost think they've had a ship here before and it was full of smallpox, or sold them a load of gold bricks, or something like that. What is wrong with them?"

"Possibly they lack curiosity," Shelton offered.

"Either that or they're afraid. Or maybe the entire gang of them are crackers. A good many worlds were appropriated by woozy groups who wanted some place where their eccentricities could run loose. Nutty notions become conventional after three hundred years of undisturbed continuity. It's then considered normal and proper to nurse the bats out of your grandfather's attic. That, and generations of inbreeding, can create some queer types. But we'll cure 'em!"

"Yes, your excellency, most certainly we will."

"You don't look so balanced yourself, chasing that eye around your pan," reproved the ambassador. He pointed southeast as Shelton stuck the fidgety hand

26

firmly into a pocket. "There's a road over there. Wide and well-built by the looks of it. Get that patrol across it. If they don't bring in a willing talker within reasonable time, we'll send a battalion into the town itself."

"A patrol," repeated Colonel Shelton to Major Hame.

"Call out the patrol," Hame ordered Lieutenant Deacon.

"That patrol again, sergeant major," said Deacon.

Bidworthy raked out Gleed and his men, indicated the road, barked a bit, and shooed them on their way.

They marched, Gleed in the lead. Their objective was half a mile and angled slightly nearer the town. The left-hand file, who had a clear view of the nearest suburbs, eyed them wistfully and wished Gleed in warmer regions with Bidworthy stoking beneath him.

Hardly had they reached their goal than a customer appeared. He came from the town's outskirts, zooming along at fast pace on a contraption vaguely resembling a motorcycle. It ran on a pair of big rubber balls and was pulled by a caged fan. Gleed spread his men across the road.

The oncomer's machine suddenly gave forth a harsh, penetrating sound that vaguely reminded them of Bidworthy in the presence of dirty boots.

"Stay put," warned Gleed. "I'll skin the guy who gives way and leaves a gap."

Again the shrill metallic warning. Nobody moved. The machine slowed, came up to them at a crawl and stopped. Its fan continued to spin at low rate, the blades almost visible and giving out a steady hiss.

"What's the idea?" demanded the rider. He was lean-featured, in his middle thirties, wore a gold ring in his nose and had a pigtail four feet long.

Blinking incredulously at this getup, Gleed managed to jerk an indicative thumb toward the iron mountain and say, "Earth ship."

27

"Well, what d'you expect me to do about it?"

"Cooperate," said Gleed, still bemused by the pigtail. He had never seen one before. It was in no way effeminate, he decided. Rather did it lend a touch of ferocity like that worn—according to the picture books—by certain North American aborigines of umpteen centuries ago.

"Cooperation," mused the rider. "Now there is a beautiful word. You know what it means, of course?"

"I ain't a dope."

"The precise degree of your idiocy is not under discussion at the moment," the rider pointed out. His nosering waggled a bit as he spoke. "We are talking about cooperation. I take it you do quite a lot of it yourself?"

"You bet I do," Gleed assured. "And so does everyone else who knows what's good for him."

"Let's keep to the subject, shall we? Let's not sidetrack and go rambling all over the map." He revved up his fan a little, then let it slow down again. "You are given orders and you obey them?"

"Of course. I'd have a rough time if—"

"That is what you call cooperation?" put in the other. He shrugged his shoulders and indulged in a resigned sigh. "Oh, well, it's nice to check the facts of history. The books *could* be wrong." His fan flashed into a circle of light and the machine surged forward. "Pardon me."

The front rubber ball barged forcefully between two men, knocking them sidewise without injury. With a high whine, the machine shot down the road, its fanblast making the rider's plaited hairdo point horizontally backward.

"You goofy glumps!" raged Gleed as his fallen pair got up and dusted themselves off. "I ordered you to stand fast. What d'you mean, letting him run out on us like that?"

"Didn't have much choice about it, sarge," answered one, giving him a surly look.

"I want none of your back-chat. You could have busted a balloon if you'd had your weapons ready. That would have stopped him."

"You didn't tell us to have guns ready."

"Where was your own, anyway?" added a voice.

Gleed whirled round on the others and bawled, "Who said that?" His irate eyes raked a long row of blank, impassive faces. It was impossible to detect the culprit. "I'll shake you up with the next quota of fatigues," he promised. "I'll see to it—"

"The sergeant major's coming," one of them warned.

Bidworthy was four hundred yards away and making martial progress toward them. Arriving in due time, he cast a cold, contemptuous glance over the patrol.

"What happened?"

Giving a brief account of the incident, Gleed finished aggrievedly, "He looked like a Chickasaw with an oil well."

"What's a Chickasaw?" Bidworthy demanded.

"I read about them somewhere once when I was a kid," explained Gleed, happy to bestow a modicum of learning. "They had long haircuts, wore blankets and rode around in gold-plated automobiles."

"Sounds crazy to me," said Bidworthy. "I gave up all that magic carpet stuff when I was seven. I was deep in ballistics before I was twelve and military logistics at fourteen." He sniffed loudly, giving the other a jaundiced eye. "Some guys suffer from arrested development."

"They actually existed," Gleed maintained. "They—"

"So did fairies," snapped Bidworthy. "My mother said so. My mother was a good woman. She didn't tell me a lot of tomfool lies—often." He spat on the road. "Be your age!" Then he scowled at the patrol. "All right, get out your guns, assuming that you've got them and know where they are and which hand to hold them in. Take orders from me. I'll deal personally with the next one along."

He sat on a large stone by the roadside and planted an expectant gaze on the town. Gleed posed near him, slightly pained. The patrol remained strung across the road, guns held ready. Half an hour crawled by without anything happening.

One of the men said, "Can we have a smoke, sergeant major?"

"No."

They fell into lugubrious silence, watching the town, licking their lips and thinking. They had plenty to think about. A town—any town of human occupation—had desirable features not found elsewhere in the cosmos: lights, company, freedom, laughter, all the makings of life. And one can go hungry too long.

Eventually a large coach came from the outskirts, hit the high road, and came bowling toward them. A long, shiny, streamlined job, it rolled on twenty balls in two rows of ten, gave forth a whine similar to but louder than that of its predecessor, but had no visible fans. It was loaded with people.

At a point two hundred yards from the roadblock a loudspeaker under the vehicle's bonnet blared an urgent, "Make way! Make way!"

"This is it," commented Bidworthy, with much satisfaction. "We've got a dollop of them. One of them is going to chat or I leave the service." He got off his rock and stood in readiness.

"Make way! Make way!"

"Bust his bags if he tries to bull his way through," Bidworthy ordered the men.

It wasn't necessary. The coach lost pace and stopped with its bonnet a yard from the waiting file. Its driver peered out the side of his cab. Other faces snooped farther back.

Composing himself and determined to try the effect of fraternal cordiality, Bidworthy went up to the driver and said, "Good morning."

"Your time-sense is shot to pot," observed the other. He had a blue jowl, a broken nose, cauliflower ears, and looked the sort who usually drives with others in hot and vengeful pursuit. "Can't you afford a watch?"

"Huh?"

"It isn't morning. It's late afternoon."

"So it is," admitted Bidworthy, forcing a cracked smile. "Good afternoon."

"I'm not so sure about that," mused the driver, leaning on his wheel and moodily picking his teeth. "It's just another one nearer the grave."

"That may be," agreed Bidworthy, little taken with that ghoulish angle. "But I have other things to worry about, and—"

"Not much use worrying about anything, past or present," advised the driver. "Because there are lots bigger worries to come."

"Perhaps so," Bidworthy said, inwardly feeling that this was no time or place to contemplate the darker side of existence. "But I prefer to deal with my own troubles in my own time and my own way."

"Nobody's troubles are entirely their own, nor their time, nor their methods," remarked the tough-looking oracle. "Are they now?"

"I don't know and I don't care," said Bidworthy, his composure thinning down as his blood pressure built up. He was conscious of Gleed and the patrol watching, listening, and probably grinning inside themselves. There was also the load of gaping passengers. "I think you are chewing the fat just to stall me. You might as

31

well know now that it won't work. The Earth Ambassador is waiting—"

"So are we," remarked the driver pointedly.

"He wants to speak to you," Bidworthy went on, "and he's going to speak to you!"

"I'd be the last to prevent him. We've got free speech here. Let him step up and say his peace so's we can get on our way."

"*You*," Bidworthy informed, "are going to *him*." He signed to the rest of the coach. "And your load as well."

"Not me," denied a fat man, sticking his head out of a side window. He wore thick-lensed glasses that gave him eyes like poached eggs. Moreover, he was adorned with a high hat candy-striped in white and pink. "Not me," repeated this vision, with considerable firmness.

"Me, neither," endorsed the driver.

"All right." Bidworthy registered menace. "Move this birdcage an inch, forward or backward, and we'll shoot your potbellied tires to thin strips. Get out of that cab."

"Not me. I'm too comfortable. Try fetching me out."

Bidworthy beckoned to his nearest six men. "You heard him—take him up on that."

Tearing open the cab door, they grabbed. If they had expected the victim to put up a futile fight against heavy odds, they were disappointed. He made no attempt to resist. They got him, lugged together, and he yielded with good grace, his body leaning sidewise and coming halfway out of the door.

That was as far as they could get him.

"Come on," urged Bidworthy, displaying impatience. "Show him who's who. He isn't a fixture."

One of the men climbed over the body, poked around inside the cab, and said, "He is, you know."

"What d'you mean?"

"He's chained to the steering column."

"Eh? Let me see." He had a look and found that it was

32

so. A chain and a small but heavy and complicated pad-lock linked the driver's leg to his coach. "Where's the key?"

"Search me," invited the driver, grinning.

They did just that. The frisk proved futile. No key. "Who's got it?"

"Myob!"

"Shove him back into his seat," ordered Bidworthy, looking savage. "We'll take the passengers. One yap's as good as another so far as I'm concerned." He strode to the doors and jerked them open. "Get out and make it snappy."

Nobody budged. They studied him silently and with varied expressions, not one of which did anything to help his ego. The fat man with the candy-striped hat mooned at him sardonically. Bidworthy decided that he did not like the fat man and that a stiff course of military calisthenics might thin him down a bit.

"You can come out on your feet," he suggested to the passengers in general and the fat man in particular, "or on your necks. Whichever you prefer. Make up your minds."

"If you can't use your head you can at least use your eyes," commented the fat man. He shifted in his seat to the accompaniment of metallic clanking noises.

Bidworthy did as suggested, leaning through the doors to have a gander. Then he got right into the vehicle, went its full length and studied each passenger. His florid features were two shades darker when he came out and spoke to Sergeant Gleed.

"They're all chained. Every one of them." He glared at the driver. "What's the big idea, manacling the lot?"

"Myob!" said the driver, airily.

"Who's got the keys?"

"Myob!"

Taking a deep breath, Bidworthy said to nobody in

particular, "Every so often I hear of some guy running amok and laying 'em out by the dozens. I always wonder why—but now I know." He gnawed his knuckles, then added to Gleed, "We can't run this contraption to the ship with that dummy blocking the driver's seat. Either we've got to find the keys or get tools and cut them loose."

"Or you could wave us on our way and go take a pill," offered the driver.

"Shut up! If I'm stuck here another million years I'll see to it that—"

"The colonel's coming," muttered Gleed, giving him a nudge.

Colonel Shelton arrived, then walked once slowly and officiously around the outside of the coach, examining its construction and its occupants. He flinched at the striped hat whose owner leered at him through the glass. Then he came over to the disgruntled group.

"What's the trouble this time, sergeant major?"

"They're as crazy as the others, sir. They give a lot of lip and say, 'Myob!' and couldn't care less about His Excellency. They don't want to come out and we can't get them out because they're chained to their seats."

"Chained?" Shelton's eyebrows shot upward. "What for?"

"I don't know, sir. They're linked in like a load of lifers making for the pen, and—"

Shelton moved off without waiting to hear the rest. He had a look for himself and came back.

"You may have something there, sergeant major. But I don't think they are criminals."

"No, sir?"

"No." He threw a significant glance toward the colorful headgear and several other sartorial eccentricities, including a ginger-haired man's foot-wide polka-dotted bow. "It is more likely that they're a bunch of whacks

34

being taken to a giggle emporium. I'll ask the driver."
Going to the cab, he said, "Do you mind telling me
your destination?"

"Yes," responded the other.

"Very well, where is it?"

"Look," said the driver, "are we talking the same
language?"

"Huh?"

"You asked me if I minded and I said yes." He made
a gesture. "I do mind."

"You refuse to tell?"

"Your aim's improving, sonny."

"Sonny?" put in Bidworthy, vibrant with outrage.
"Do you realize you are speaking to a colonel?"

"Leave this to me," insisted Shelton, waving him
down. His expression was cold as he returned his attention to the driver. "On your way. I'm sorry you've been
detained."

"Think nothing of it," said the driver, with exag-
gerated politeness. "I'll do as much for you some day."

With that enigmatic remark, he let his machine roll
forward. The patrol parted to make room. The coach
built up its whine to top note, sped down the road, and
diminished into the distance.

"By the Black Sack!" swore Bidworthy, staring purple-faced after it. "This planet has got more punks in
need of discipline than any this side of—"

"Calm yourself, sergeant major," advised Shelton. "I
feel the same way as you—but I'm taking care of my
arteries. Blowing them full of bumps like seaweed won't
solve any problems."

"Maybe so, sir, but—"

"We're up against something mighty funny here,"
Shelton went on. "We've got to find out exactly what
it is and how best to cope with it. That will probably
mean new tactics. So far, the patrol has achieved noth-

ing. It is wasting its time. We'll have to devise some other and more effective method of making contact with the powers-that-be. March the men back to the ship, sergeant major."

"Very well, sir." Bidworthy saluted, swung around, clicked his heels, and opened a cavernous mouth. "Patro-o-ol! . . . right form!"

The conference lasted well into the night and halfway through the following morning. During these argumentative hours various oddments of traffic, mostly vehicular, passed along the road, but nothing paused to view the monster spaceship, nobody approached for a friendly word with its crew. The strange inhabitants of this world seemed to be afflicted with a peculiar form of mental blindness, unable to see a thing until it was thrust into their faces and then surveying it squint-eyed.

One passer-by in midmorning was a truck whining on two dozen rubber balls and loaded with girls wearing colorful headscarves. The girls were singing something about "one little kiss before we part, dear." Half a dozen troops lounging near the gangway came eagerly to life, waved, whistled and yoohooed. The effort was wasted, for the singing continued without break or pause and nobody waved back.

To add to the discomfiture of the love-hungry, Bidworthy stuck his head out of the lock and rasped, "If you monkeys are bursting with surplus energy, I can find a few jobs for you to do—nice dirty ones." He seared them one at a time before he withdrew.

Inside, the top brass sat around a horseshoe table in the chartroom near the bow and debated the situation. Most of them were content to repeat with extra emphasis what they had said the previous evening, there being no new points to bring up.

"Are you certain," the Earth Ambassador asked Captain Grayder, "that this planet has not been visited since the last emigration transport dumped the final load three hundred years back?"

"Positive, your excellency. Any such visit would have been recorded."

"If made by an Earth ship. But what about others? I feel it in my bones that at sometime or other these people have fallen foul of one or more vessels calling unofficially and have been leery of spaceships ever since. Perhaps somebody got tough with them, tried to muscle in where he wasn't wanted. Or they've had to beat off a gang of pirates. Or they were swindled by some unscrupulous fleet of traders."

"Quite impossible, your excellency," declared Grayder. "Emigration was so scattered over so large a number of worlds that even today every one of them is underpopulated, only one-hundredth developed, and utterly unable to build spaceships of any kind, even rudimentary ones. Some may have the techniques but not the facilities, of which they need plenty."

"Yes, that's what I've always understood."

"All Blieder-drive vessels are built in the Sol system, registered as Earth ships and their whereabouts known. The only other ships in existence are eighty or ninety antiquated rocket jobs bought at scrap price by the Epsilon system for haulage work between their fourteen closely planned planets. An old-fashioned rocket job couldn't reach this place in a hundred years."

"No, of course not."

"Unofficial boats capable of this range just don't exist," Grayder assured. "Neither do space buccaneers, for the same reason. A Blieder-job takes so much that a would-be pirate has to become a billionaire to become a pirate."

"Then," said the ambassador, heavily, "back we go to

my original theory—that something peculiar to this world plus a lot of inbreeding has made them nutty."

"There's plenty to be said for that notion," put in Colonel Shelton. "You should have seen the coach load I looked over. There was a mortician wearing odd shoes, one brown, one yellow. And a moon-faced gump sporting a hat made from the skin of a barber's pole, all stripy. Only thing missing was his bubble pipe—and probably he'll be given that where he was going."

"Where was he going?"

"I don't know, your excellency. They refused to say."

Giving him a satirical look, the ambassador remarked, "Well, that is a valuable addition to the sum total of our knowledge. Our minds are now enriched by the thought that an anonymous individual may be presented with a futile object for an indefinable purpose when he reaches his unknown destination."

Shelton subsided, wishing that he had never seen the fat man or, for that matter, the fat man's cockeyed world.

"Somewhere they've got a capitol, a civic seat, a center of government wherein function the people who hold the strings," the ambassador asserted. "We've got to find that place before we can take over and reorganize on up-to-date lines whatever setup they've got. A capitol is big by the standards of its own administrative area. It's never an ordinary, nondescript place. It has certain physical features lending it an importance above the average. It should be easily visible from the air. We must make a search for it—in fact, that's what we ought to have done in the first place. Other planets' capitol cities have been found without trouble. What's the hoodoo on this one?"

"See for yourself, your excellency." Captain Grayder poked a couple of photographs across the table. "There are the two hemispheres as recorded by us when coming in. They reveal nothing resembling a superior city. There isn't even a town conspicuously larger than its fellows or possessing outstanding features setting it apart from the others."

"I don't place great faith in pictures, particularly when taken at long distance. The naked eye sees more. We have got four lifeboats capable of scouring the place from pole to pole. Why not use them?"

"Because, your excellency, they were not designed for such a purpose."

"Does that matter so long as they get results?"

Grayder said, patiently, "They were designed to be launched in space and hit up forty thousand. They are ordinary, old-style rocket jobs, for emergencies only. You could not make efficient ground survey at any speed in excess of four hundred miles per hour. Keep the boats down to that and you're trying to run them at landing speed, muffling the tubes, balling up their efficiency, creating a terrible waste of fuel, and inviting a crash which you're likely to get before you're through."

"Then it's high time we had Blieder-drive lifeboats on Blieder-drive ships."

"I agree, your excellency. But the smallest Blieder engine has an Earth mass of more than three hundred tons—far too much for little boats." Picking up the photographs, Grayder slid them into a drawer. "What we need is an ancient, propeller-driven airplane. They could do something we can't do—they could go slow."

"You might as well yearn for a bicycle," scoffed the ambassador, feeling thwarted.

"We have a bicycle," Grayder informed. "Tenth Engineer Harrison owns one."

"And he has brought it with him?"

"It goes everywhere with him. There is a rumor that he sleeps with it."

"A spaceman toting a bicycle!" The ambassador blew his nose with a loud honk. "I take it that he is thrilled by the sense of immense velocity it gives him, an ecstatic feeling of rushing headlong through space?"

"I wouldn't know, your excellency."

"Hmmm! Bring this Harrison in to me. We'll set a nut to catch a nut."

Grayder blinked, went to the caller board, and spoke over the ship's system. "Tenth Engineer Harrison wanted in the chartroom immediately."

Within ten minutes Harrison appeared. He had walked nearly threequarters of a mile from the Blieder room. He was thin and wiry, with dark, monkeylike eyes and a pair of ears that made pedaling unnecessary when the wind was behind him. The ambassador examined him curiously, much as a zoologist would inspect a pink giraffe.

"Mister, I understand that you possess a bicycle."

Becoming wary, Harrison said, "There's nothing against it in the regulations, sir, and therefore—"

"Darn the regulations!" The ambassador made an impatient gesture. "We're stalled in the middle of a crazy situation and we're turning to crazy methods to get moving."

"I see, sir."

"So I want you to do a job for me. Get out your bicycle, ride down to town, find the mayor, sheriff, grand panjandrum, supreme galootie, or whatever he's called, and tell him he's officially invited to evening dinner along with any other civic dignitaries he cares to bring and, of course, their wives."

"Very well, sir."

"Informal attire," added the ambassador.

Harrison jerked up one ear, drooped the other, and said, "Beg pardon, sir?"

"They can dress how they like."

40

"I get it. Do I go right now, sir?"

"At once. Return as quickly as you can and bring me the reply."

Saluting sloppily, Harrison went out. His Excellency found an easychair, reposed in it at full length and ignored the others' stares.

"As easy as that!" He pulled out a long cigar and carefully bit off its end. "If we can't touch their minds, we'll appeal to their bellies." He cocked a knowing eye at Grayder. "Captain, see that there is plenty to drink. Strong stuff. Venusian cognac or something equally potent. Give them an hour at a well-filled table and they'll talk plenty. We won't be able to shut them up all night." He lit the cigar and puffed luxuriously. "That is the tried and trusted technique of diplomacy—the insidious seduction of the distended gut. It always works —you'll see."

Pedaling briskly down the road, Tenth Engineer Harrison reached the first street on either side of which were small detached houses with neat gardens front and back. A plump, amiable-looking woman was clipping a hedge halfway along. He pulled up near to her, politely touching his cap.

" 'Scuse me, ma'am, I'm looking for the biggest man in town."

She half-turned, gave him no more than a casual glance, then pointed her clipping shears southward. "That'd be Jeff Baines. First on the right, second on the left. It's a small delicatessen."

"Thank you."

He moved on, hearing the *snip-snip* resume behind him. First on the right. He curved around a long, low, rubber-balled truck parked by the corner. Second on the left. Three children pointed at him and yelled shrill warnings that his back wheel was going round. He found the delicatessen, propped a pedal on the curb, gave his machine a reassuring pat before he went inside and had a look at Jeff.

There was plenty to see. Jeff had four chins, a twenty-two-inch neck, and a paunch that stuck out half a yard. An ordinary mortal could have got into either leg of his pants without taking off a diving suit. He weighed at least three hundred and undoubtedly *was* the biggest man in town.

"Wanting something?" inquired Jeff, lugging it up from far down.

"Not exactly." Tenth Engineer Harrison eyed the succulent food display and decided that anything unsold by nightfall was not given to the cats. "I'm looking for a certain person."

"Are you now? Usually I avoid that sort—but every man to his taste." He plucked at a fat lip while he mused a moment, then suggested, "Try Sid Wilcock over on Dane Avenue. He's the most certain man I know."

"I didn't mean it that way," said Harrison. "I meant I was searching for somebody particular."

"Then why the dub didn't you say so?" Jeff Baines worked over the new problem, finally offered, "Tod Green ought to fit that bill. You'll find him in the shoe-shop end of this road. He's particular enough for anyone. He's downright finicky."

"You misunderstand me," Harrison explained. "I'm hunting a bigwig so's I can invite him to a feed."

Resting himself on a high stool which he overlapped by a foot all round, Jeff Baines eyed him peculiarly and said, "There's something lopsided about this. In the first place, you're going to use up a considerable slice of your life finding a guy who wears a wig, especially if you insist on a big one. And where's the point of dumping an ob on him just because he uses a bean-blanket?"

"Huh?"

"It's plain common sense to plant an ob where it will cancel an old one out, isn't it?"

"Is it?" Harrison let his mouth hang open while his mind moiled around the strange problem of how to plant an ob.

"So you don't know?" Jeff Baines massaged a plump chop and sighed. He pointed at the other's middle. "Is that a uniform you're wearing?"

"Yes."

"A genuine, pukka, dyed-in-the-wool uniform?"

"Of course."

"Ah!" said Jeff. "That's where you've fooled me—coming in by yourself, on your ownsome. If there had been a gang of you dressed identically the same, I'd have known at once it was a uniform. That's what uniform means—all alike. Doesn't it?"

"I suppose so," agreed Harrison, who had never given it a thought.

"So you're off that ship. I ought to have guessed it in the first place. I must be slow on the uptake today. But I didn't expect to see one, just one, messing around on a pedal contraption. It goes to show, doesn't it?"

"Yes," said Harrison, glancing around to make sure that no confederate had swiped his bicycle while he was detained in conversation. The machine was still there. "It goes to show."

"All right, let's have it—what have you come here for?"

"I've been trying to tell you all along. I've been sent to—"

"Been sent?" Jeff's eyes widened a little. "Mean to say you actually let yourself be *sent*?"

Harrison gaped at him. "Of course. Why not?"

"Oh, I get it now," said Jeff Baines, his puzzled features suddenly clearing. "You confuse me with the

43

queer way you talk. You mean you planted an ob on someone?"

Desperately Harrison asked "What's an ob?"

"He doesn't know," commented Jeff Baines, looking prayerfully at the ceiling. "He doesn't even know that!" He gave out a resigned sigh. "You hungry by any chance?"

"Going on that way."

"O.K. I could tell you what an ob is, but I'll do something better—I'll show you." Heaving himself off the stool, he waddled to a door at back. "Don't know why I should bother to try and educate a uniform. It's just that I'm bored. C'mon, follow me."

Obediently, Harrison went behind the counter, paused to give his bicycle a reassuring nod, then trailed the other through a passage and into a yard.

Jeff Baines pointed to a stack of cases. "Canned goods." He indicated an adjacent store. "Bust 'em open and pile the stuff in there. Stack the empties outside. Please yourself whether you do it or not. That's freedom, isn't it?" He lumbered back into the shop.

Left by himself, Harrison scratched his ears and thought it over. Somewhere, he felt, there was an obscure sort of gag. A candidate named Harrison was being tempted to qualify for his sucker certificate. But if the play was beneficial to its organizer it might be worth learning because the trick could then be passed on. One must speculate in order to accumulate.

So he dealt with the cases as required. It took him twenty minutes of brisk work, after which he returned to the shop.

"Now," explained Baines, "you've done something for me. That means you've planted an ob on me. I don't thank you for what you've done. There's no need to. All I have to do is get rid of the ob."

"Ob?"

44

"Obligation. Why use a long word when a short one is good enough? An obligation is an ob. I shift it this way: Seth Warburton, next door but one, has got half a dozen of my obs saddled on him. So I get rid of mine to you and relieve him of one of his to me by sending you around for a meal." He scribbled briefly on a slip of paper. "Give him this."

Harrison stared at it. In casual scrawl, it read, "Feed this bum. Jeff Baines."

Slightly dazed, he wandered out, stood by the bicycle and again eyed the paper. Bum, it said. He could think of several on the ship who would have exploded with wrath over that. His attention drifted to the second shop farther along. It had a window crammed with comestibles and two big words on the sign-strip above: *Seth's Gulper*.

Coming to a decision which was encouraged by his innards, he went into Seth's still holding the paper as if it were a death warrant. Inside there was a long counter, some steam and a clatter of crockery. He chose a seat at a marble-topped table occupied by a gray-eyed brunette.

"Do you mind?" he inquired politely, as he lowered himself into a chair.

"Mind what?" She examined his ears as if they were curious phenomena. "Babies, dogs, aged relations or going out in the rain?"

"Do you mind me being here?"

"I can please myself whether or not I endure it. That's freedom, isn't it?"

"Yeah," said Harrison. "Sure it is." He fidgeted in his seat, feeling somehow that he'd made a move and promptly lost a pawn. He sought around for something else to say and at that point a thin-featured man in a white coat dumped before him a plate loaded with fried chicken and three kinds of unfamiliar vegetables.

The sight unnerved him. He couldn't remember how many years it was since he last saw fried chicken, nor how many months since he'd had vegetables in other than powder form.

"Well," said the waiter, mistaking his fascinated gaze upon the food. "Doesn't it suit you?"

"Yes." Harrison handed over the slip of paper. "You bet it does."

Glancing at the note, the other called to someone semivisible in the steam at one end of the counter, "You've killed another of Jeff's." He went away, tearing the slip into small pieces.

"That was a fast pass," commented the brunette, nodding at the loaded plate. "He dumps a feed-ob on you and you bounce it straight back, leaving all quits. I'll have to wash dishes to get rid of mine, or kill one Seth has got on somebody else."

"I stacked a load of canned stuff." Harrison picked up knife and fork, his mouth watering. There were no knives and forks on the ship. They weren't needed for powders and pills. "Don't give you any choice here, do they? You take what you get."

"Not if you've got an ob on Seth," she informed. "In that case, he's got to work it off the best way he can. You should have put that to him instead of waiting for fate and complaining afterward."

"I'm not complaining."

"It's your right. That's freedom, isn't it?" She mused a bit, then went on, "Isn't often I'm a plant ahead of Seth, but when I am I scream for iced pineapple and he comes running. When *he's* a plant ahead, *I* do the running." Her gray eyes narrowed in sudden suspicion, and she added, "You're listening like it's all new to you. Are you a stranger here?"

He nodded, his mouth full of chicken. A little later he managed, "I'm off that spaceship."

"Good grief!" She froze considerably. "An Antigand! I wouldn't have thought it. Why, you look almost human."

"I've long taken pride in that similarity." His wit was rising along with his belly. He chewed, swallowed, looked around. The white-coated man came up. "What's to drink?" Harrison asked.

"Dith, double-dith, shemak or coffee."

"Coffee. Big and black."

"Shemak is better," advised the brunette as the waiter went away. "But why should I tell you?"

The coffee came in a pint-sized mug. Dumping it, the waiter said, "It's your choice, seeing Seth's working one off. What'll you have for after—apple pie, yimpik delice, grated tarfelsoufers or canimelon in syrup?"

"Iced pineapple."

"Ugh!" The other blinked at Harrison, gave the brunette an accusing stare, went away and got it.

Harrison pushed it across. "Take the plunge and enjoy yourself."

"It's yours."

"Couldn't eat it if I tried." He dug up another load of chicken, stirred his coffee, and began to feel at peace with the world. "Got as much as I can manage right here." He made an inviting motion with his fork. "G'wan, be greedy and to heck with the waistline."

"No." Firmly she pushed the pineapple back at him. "If I got through that, I'd be loaded with an ob."

"So what?"

"I don't let strangers plant obs on me."

"Quite right, too. Very proper of you," approved Harrison. "Strangers often have strange notions."

"You've been around," she agreed. "Only I don't know what's strange about the notions."

"Dishwasher!"

"Eh?"

47

"Cynic," he translated. "One washes dishes in a cynic." The pineapple got another pass in her direction. "If you feel I'll be dumping an ob which you'll have to pay off, you can do it in seemly manner right here. All I want is some information. Just tell me where I can put my finger on the ripest cheese in the locality."

"That's an easy one. Go round to Alec Peters' place, middle of Tenth Street." With that, she dug into the dish.

"Thanks. I was beginning to think everyone was dumb or afflicted with the funnies."

He carried on with his own meal, finished it, and finally lay back expansively. Unaccustomed nourishment got his brain working a bit more dexterously, for after a minute an expression of deep suspicion clouded his face and he inquired, "Does this Peters run a cheese warehouse?"

"Of course." Emitting a sigh of pleasure, she put aside her empty dish.

He groaned low down, then informed, "I'm chasing the mayor."

"What is that?"

"Number one. The big boss. The sheriff, pohanko, or whatever you call him."

"I'm no wiser," she said, genuinely puzzled.

"The man who runs this town. The leading citizen."

"Make it a little clearer," she suggested, trying hard to help him. "Who or what should this citizen be leading?"

"You and Seth and everyone else." He waved a hand to encompass the entire burg.

Frowning, she said, "Leading us *where?*"

"Wherever you're going."

She gave up, beaten, and signed the white-coated waiter to come to her assistance.

"Matt, are we going any place?"

48

"How should I know?"

"Well, ask Seth then."

He went away and came back with, "Seth says he's going home at six o'clock and what's it to you?"

"Anyone leading him there?" she inquired.

"Don't be daft," Matt advised. "He knows his own way and he's cold sober."

Harrison chipped in with, "Look, I don't see why there should be so much difficulty about this. Just tell me where I can find an official, any official—the police chief, the city treasurer, the mortuary keeper or even a mere justice of the peace."

"What's an official?" asked Matt, openly puzzled.

"What's a justice of the peace?" added the brunette.

His mind side-slipped and did a couple of spins. It took him quite a while to reassemble his thoughts and try another tack.

"Supposing," he said to Matt, "this joint catches fire. What would you do?"

"Fan it to keep it going," responded Matt, fed up and making no effort to conceal the fact. He returned to the counter with the air of one who has no time to waste on half-wits.

"He'd put it out," informed the brunette. "What else would you expect him to do?"

"Supposing he couldn't?"

"He'd call in others to help him."

"And would they?"

"Of course," she assured, surveying him with pity. "They'd jump at the chance. They'd be planting a nice crop of strong obs, wouldn't they?"

"Yes, I guess so." He began to feel stalled, but made a last shot at the problem. "What if the fire were too big and fast for passers-by to tackle?"

"Seth would summon the fire squad."

Defeat receded. A touch of triumph replaced it.

"Ah, so there is a fire squad! That's what I meant by something official. That's what I've been after all along. Quick, tell me where I can find the depot."

"Bottom end of Twelfth. You can't miss it."

"Thanks." He got up in a hurry. "See you again sometime." Going out fast, he grabbed his bicycle and shoved off from the curb.

The fire depot was a big place holding four telescopic ladders, a spray tower and two multiple pumps, all motorized on the usual array of fat rubber balls. Inside, Harrison came face to face with a small man wearing immense plus-fours.

"Looking for someone?" asked the small man.

"The fire chief," said Harrison.

"Who's he?"

By this time prepared for that sort of thing, Harrison spoke as one would to a child. "See here, mister, this is a fire-fighting outfit. Somebody bosses it. Somebody organizes the shebang, fills forms, presses buttons, recommends promotions, kicks the shiftless, takes all the credit, transfers all the blame and generally lords it around. He's the most important guy in the bunch and everybody knows it." His forefinger tapped the other's chest. "And he's the fella I'm going to talk to if it's the last thing I do."

"Nobody's any more important than anybody else. How can they be? I think you're crazy."

"You're welcome to think what you like, but I'm telling you that—"

A shrill bell clamored, cutting off the sentence. Twenty men appeared as if by magic, boarded a ladder and a multi pump, and roared into the street.

Squat, basin-shaped helmets were the crews' only item of common attire. Apart from these, they plumbed the depths of sartorial iniquity. The man with the plus-fours, who had gained the pump in one bold leap, was whirled out standing between a fat firefighter wearing a rainbow-hued cummerbund and a thin one sporting a canary-yellow kilt. A latecomer decorated with earrings shaped like little bells hotly pursued the pump, snatched at its tailboard, missed, and disconsolately watched the outfit disappear from sight. He mooched back, swinging his helmet in one hand.

"Just my lousy luck," he informed the gaping Harrison. "The sweetest call of the year. A big brewery. The sooner they get there the bigger the obs they'll plant on it." He licked his lips at the thought, sitting on a coil of canvas hose. "Oh, well, maybe it's all for the good of my health."

"Tell me something," Harrison insisted. "How do you get a living?"

"There's a heck of a question. You can see for yourself. I'm on the fire squad."

"I know. What I mean is, who pays you?"

"Pays me?"

"Gives you money for all this."

"You talk kind of peculiar. What is money?"

Harrison rubbed his cranium to assist the circulation of blood through the brain. What is money? Yeouw. He tried another angle.

"Supposing your wife needs a new coat, how does she get it?"

"Goes to a store saddled with fire-obs, of course. She kills one or two for them."

"But what if no clothing store has had a fire?"

"You're pretty ignorant, brother. Where in this world do you come from?" His ear bells swung as he studied the other a moment, then went on, "Almost all stores have fire-obs. If they've any sense, they allocate so many per month by way of insurance. They look ahead, just in case, see? They plant obs on us, in a way, so that when we rush to the rescue we've got to kill off a dollop of theirs before we can plant any new ones of our own. That stops us overdoing it and making hogs of ourselves. Sort of cuts down the stores' liabilities. It makes sense, doesn't it?"

"Maybe, but—"

"I get it now," interrupted the other, narrowing his eyes. "You're from that spaceship. You're an Antigand."

"I'm a Terran," said Harrison with suitable dignity. "What's more, all the folk who originally settled this planet were Terrans."

"You trying to teach me history?" He gave a harsh laugh. "You're wrong. There was a five percent strain of Martian."

"Even the Martians are descended from Terran settlers," riposted Harrison.

"So what? That was a devil of a long time back. Things change, in case you haven't heard. We've no Terrans or Martians on this world—except for your crowd which has come in unasked. We're all Gands here. And you nosey pokes are Antigands."

"We aren't anti-anything that I know of. Where did you get that idea?"

"Myob!" said the other, suddenly determined to refuse further agreement. He tossed his helmet to one side and spat on the floor.

"Huh?"

"You heard me. Go trundle your scooter."

Harrison gave up and did just that. He pedaled gloomily back to the ship.

His Excellency pinned him with an authoritative optic. "So you're back at last, mister. How many are coming and at what time?"

"None, sir," said Harrison, feeling kind of feeble.

"None?" August eyebrows rose up. "Do you mean that they have refused my invitation?"

52

"No, sir."

The ambassador waited a moment, then said, "Come out with it, mister. Don't stand there gawping as if your push-and-puff contraption has just given birth to a roller skate. You say they haven't refused my invitation—but nobody is coming. What am I to make of that?"

"I didn't ask anyone."

"So you didn't ask!" Turning, he said to Grayder, Shelton and the others, "He didn't ask!" His attention came back to Harrison. "You forgot all about it, I presume? Intoxicated by liberty and the power of man over machine, you flashed around the town at nothing less than eighteen miles per hour, creating consternation among the citizenry, tossing their traffic laws into the ashcan, putting persons in peril of their lives, not even troubling to ring your bell or—"

"I haven't got a bell, sir," denied Harrison, inwardly resenting this list of enormities. "I have a whistle operated by rotation of the rear wheel."

"There!" said the ambassador, like one abandoning all hope. He sat down, smacking his forehead several times. "Somebody's going to get a bubble-pipe." He pointed a tragic finger. "And *he's* got a whistle."

"I designed it myself, sir," Harrison told him, very informatively.

"I'm sure you did. I can imagine it. I would expect it of you." The ambassador got a fresh grip on himself. "Look, mister, tell me something in strict confidence, just between you and me." He leaned forward and put the question in a whisper that ricocheted seven times around the room. "*Why* didn't you ask anyone?"

"Couldn't find anyone to ask, sir. I did my level best but they didn't seem to know what I was talking about. Or they pretended they didn't."

"Humph!" His Excellency glanced out of the nearest port, and consulted his wristwatch. "The light is fading already. Night will be upon us pretty soon. It's getting too late for further action." An annoyed grunt. "Another day gone to pot. Two days here and we're still fiddling around." His eye was jaundiced as it rested on Harrison. "All right, mister, we're wasting time anyway so we might as well hear your story in full. Tell us what happened in complete detail. That way, we may be able to dig some sense out of it."

Harrison told it, finishing, "It seemed to me, sir, that I could go on for weeks trying to argue it out with people whose brains are oriented east-west while mine points north-south. You can talk with them from now to doomsday, even get real friendly and enjoy the conversation—without either side knowing what the other is jawing about."

"So it seems, commented the ambassador, dryly. He turned to Captain Grayder. "You've been around a lot and seen many new worlds in your time. What do you make of all this twaddle, if anything?"

"A problem in semantics," said Grayder, who had been compelled by circumstances to study that subject. "One comes across it on almost every world that has been long out of touch, though usually it has not developed far enough to get really tough." He paused reminiscently. "First guy we met on Basileus said, cordially and in what he fondly imagined was perfect English, 'Joy you unboot now!' "

"Yeah? What did that mean?"

"Come inside, put on your slippers and be happy. In other words, welcome! It wasn't difficult to get, your excellency, especially when you expect that sort of thing." Grayder cast a thoughtful glance at Harrison and went on, "Here, things appear to have developed to a greater extreme. The language remains fluent, retains enough surface similarities to conceal deeper changes, but meanings have been altered, concepts discarded, new

54

ones substituted, thought-forms reangled—and, of course, there is the inevitable impact of locally developed slang."

"Such as 'myob,'" offered His Excellency. "Now there's a queer word without recognizable Earth root. I don't like the way they use it. Sounds downright insulting. Obviously it has some sort of connection with these obs they keep batting around. It means 'my obligation' or something like that, but the significance beats me."

"There is no connection, sir," Harrison contradicted. He hesitated, saw they were waiting for him, then plunged boldly on. "Coming back I met the lady who directed me to Baines' place. She asked whether I'd found him and I said yes, thank you. We chatted a bit. I asked her what 'myob' meant. She said it was initial-slang." He stopped at that point.

"Keep going," advised the ambassador. "After some of the sulphurous comments I've heard coming out the Blieder-room ventilation shaft, I can stomach anything. What does it mean?"

"M-y-o-b," informed Harrison, blinking. "Mind your own business."

"So!" His Excellency gained color. "So that's what they've been telling me all along?"

"I'm afraid so, sir."

"Evidently they've a lot to learn." His neck swelled with sudden undiplomatic fury as he smacked a large hand on the table and said, loudly, "And they are going to learn it!"

"Yes, sir," agreed Harrison, becoming more uneasy and wanting out. "May I go now and attend to my bicycle?"

"Get out of my sight!" shouted the ambassador. He made a couple of meaningless gestures and turned a florid face on Captain Grayder. "Bicycle! Does anyone on this vessel own a slingshot?"

"I doubt it, your excellency, but I will make inquiries, if you wish."

"Don't be an imbecile," ordered His Excellency. "We have our full quota of hollow-heads already."

Postponed until early morning, the next conference was relatively short and sweet. His Excellency took a seat, harumphed, straightened and frowned around the table.

"Let's have another look at what we've got. We know that this planet's mules call themselves Gands, don't take much interest in their Terran origin and insist on referring to us as Antigands. That implies an education and resultant outlook inimical to ourselves. They've been trained from childhood to take it for granted that whenever we appeared upon the scene we would prove to be against whatever they are for."

"And we haven't the remotest notion of what they're for," put in Colonel Shelton, quite unnecessarily. But it served to show that he was among those present and paying attention.

"I am grimly aware of our ignorance in that respect," endorsed the ambassador. "They are maintaining a conspiracy of silence about their prime motivation. We've got to break it somehow." He cleared his throat and continued: "They have a peculiar nonmonetary economic system which, in my opinion, manages to function only because of large surpluses. It won't stand a day when overpopulation brings serious shortages. This economic setup appears to be based on cooperative techniques, private enterprise, a kindergarten's honor system and plain unadorned gimme. That makes it a good deal crazier than that food-in-the-bank wackidoo they've got on the four outer planets of the Epsilon system."

"But it works," observed Grayder, pointedly.

"After a fashion. That flap-eared engineer's bicycle works—and so does he! A motorized job would save him a lot of sweat." Pleased with this analogy, the ambassador mused it a few seconds. "This local scheme of economics—if you can call it a scheme—almost certainly is the end result of the haphazard development of some hick eccentricity brought in by the original settlers. It is overdue for motorizing, so to speak. They know it but don't want it because mentally they're three hundred years behind the times. They're afraid of change, improvement, efficiency—like most backward peoples. Moreover, some of them have a vested interest in keeping things as they are." He sniffed loudly to express his contempt. "They are antagonistic toward us simply because they don't want to be disturbed."

His authoritative stare went round the table, daring one of them to remark that this might be as good a reason as any. They were too disciplined to fall into that trap. None offered comment, so he went on.

"In due time, after we've got a grip on affairs, we are going to have a long and tedious task on our hands. We'll have to overhaul their entire educational system with a view to eliminating anti-Terran prejudices and bringing them up to date on the facts of life. We've had to do that on several other planets, though not to anything like the same extent as will be necessary here."

"We'll cope," promised someone.

Ignoring him, the ambassador finished, "However, all of that is in the future. We've a problem to solve in the present. It's in our laps right now, namely, where are the reins of power and who's holding them? We've got to solve that before we can make progress. How're we going to do it?" He leaned back in his chair and added, "Get your wits working and let me have some bright suggestions."

Captain Grayder stood up, a big, leather-bound book

in his hands. "Your excellency, I don't think we need exercise our minds over new plans for making contact and gaining essential information. It looks as if the next move is going to be imposed upon us."

"How do you mean?"

"There are a good many old-timers in my crew. Space lawyers, every one of them." He tapped the book. "They know official space regulations as well as I do. Sometimes I think they know too much."

"And so . . . ?"

Grayder opened the book. "Regulation 127 says that on a hostile world a crew serves on a war footing until back in space. On a nonhostile world, they serve on a peace footing."

"What of it?"

"Regulation 131A says that on a peace footing, the crew—with the exception of a minimum number required to keep the vessel's essential services in trim—is entitled to land-leave immediately after unloading of cargo or within seventy-two Earth hours of arrival, whichever period is the shorter." He glanced up. "By midday the men will be all set for land-leave and itching to go. There will be ructions if they don't get it."

"Will there now?" said the ambassador, smiling lopsidedly. "What if I say this world is hostile? That'll pin their ears back, won't it?"

Impassively consulting his book, Grayder came back with, "Regulation 148 says that a hostile world is defined as any planet that systematically opposes Empire citizens by force." He turned the next page. "For the purpose of these regulations, force is defined as any course of action calculated to inflict physical injury, whether or not said action succeeds in its intent."

"I don't agree." The ambassador registered a deep frown. "A world can be psychologically hostile without

58

resorting to force. We've an example right here. It isn't a friendly world."

"There are no friendly worlds within the meaning of space regulations," Grayder informed. "Every planet falls into one of two classifications: hostile or nonhostile." He tapped the hard leather cover. "It's all in the book."

"We would be prize fools to let a mere book boss us around or allow the crew to boss us, either. Throw it out of the port. Stick it into the disintegrator. Get rid of it any way you like—and forget it."

"Begging your pardon, your excellency, but I can't do that." Grayder opened the tome at the beginning. "Basic regulations 1A, 1B and 1C include the following: whether in space or on land, a vessel's personnel remain under direct command of its captain or his nominee who will be guided entirely by space regulations and will be responsible only to the space committee situated upon Terra. The same applies to all troops, officials and civilian passengers aboard a space-traversing vessel, whether in flight or grounded—regardless of rank or authority they are subordinate to the captain or his nominee. A nominee is defined as a ship's officer performing the duties of an immediate superior when the latter is incapacitated or absent."

"All that means you are king of your castle," said the ambassador, none too pleased. "If we don't like it, we must get off the ship."

"With the greatest respect to yourself, I must agree that that is the position. I cannot help it—regulations are regulations. And the men know it!" Grayder dumped the book and poked it away from him. "Ten to one the men will wait to midday, pressing their pants, creaming their hair and so forth. They will then make approach to me in proper manner to which I cannot object. They will request the first mate to submit their leave-roster for my approval." He gave a deep sigh. "The worst I could

59

do would be to quibble about certain names on the roster and switch a few men around—but I couldn't refuse leave to a full quota."

"Liberty to paint the town red might be a good thing after all," suggested Colonel Shelton, not averse to doing some painting himself. "A dump likes this wakes up when the fleet's in port. We ought to get contacts by the dozens. That's what we want, isn't it?"

"We want to pin down this planet's leaders," the ambassador pointed out. "I can't see them powdering their faces, putting on their best hats and rushing out to invite the yoohoo from a bunch of hungry sailors." His plump features quirked. "We have got to find the needles in this haystack. That job won't be done by a gang of ratings on the rampage."

Grayder put in, "I'm inclined to agree with you, your excellency, but we'll have to take a chance on it. If the men want to go out, the circumstances deprive me of power to prevent them. Only one thing can give me the power."

"And what is that?"

"Evidence enabling me to define this world as hostile within the meaning of space regulations."

"Well, can't we arrange that somehow?" Without waiting for a reply, the ambassador continued, "Every crew has its incurable troublemaker. Find yours, give him a double shot of Venusian cognac, tell him he's being granted immediate leave—but you doubt whether he'll enjoy it because these Gands view us as reasons why people dig up the drains. Then push him out of the lock. When he comes back with a black eye and a boastful story about the other fellow's condition, declare this world hostile." He waved an expressive hand. "And there you are. Physical violence. All according to the book."

"Regulation 148A, emphasizing that opposition by

60

force must be systematic, warns that individual brawls may not be construed as evidence of hostility."

The ambassador turned an irate face upon the senior civil servant: "When you get back to Terra—if ever you do get back—you can tell the appropriate department how the space service is balled up, hamstrung, semiparalyzed and generally handicapped by bureaucrats who write books."

Before the other could think up a reply complimentary to his kind without contradicting the ambassador, a knock came at the door. First Mate Morgan entered, saluted smartly and offered Captain Grayder a sheet of paper.

"First liberty roll, sir. Do you approve it?"

Four hundred twenty men hit the town in the early afternoon. They advanced upon it in the usual manner of men overdue for the bright lights, that is to say eagerly, expectantly, in buddy-bunches of two, three, six or ten.

Gleed attached himself to Harrison. They were the two odd rankers, Gleed being the only sergeant on leave, Harrison the only tenth engineer. They were also the only two fish out of water since both were in civilian clothes and Gleed missed his uniform while Harrison felt naked without his bicycle. These trifling features gave them enough in common to justify at least one day's companionship.

"This one's a honey," declared Gleed with immense enthusiasm. "I've been on a good many liberty jaunts in my time but this one's a honey. On all other trips the boys ran up against the same problem—what to use for money. They had to go forth like a battalion of Santa Clauses, loaded up with anything that might serve for barter. Almost always nine-tenths of it wasn't of any use and had to be carted back again."

"On Persephone," informed Harrison, "a long-shanked Milik offered me a twenty-karat, blue-tinted first-water diamond for my bike."

"Jeepers, didn't you take it?"

"What was the good? I'd have had to go back sixteen light-years for another one."

"You could do without a bike for a bit."

"I can do without a diamond. I can't ride around on a diamond."

"Neither can you sell a bicycle for the price of a sportster moonboat."

"Yes I can. I just told you this Milik offered me a rock like an egg."

"It's a crying shame. You'd have got two hundred to two fifty thousand credits for that blinder, if it was flawless." Sergeant Gleed smacked his lips at the thought of so much moola stacked on the head of a barrel. "Credits and plenty of them—that's what I love. And that's what makes this trip a honey. Every other time we've gone out, Grayder has first lectured us about creating a favorable impression, behaving in a spacemanlike manner, and so forth. This time, he talks about credits."

"The ambassador put him up to that."

"I liked it, all the same," said Gleed. "Ten credits, a bottle of cognac and double liberty for every man who brings back to the ship an adult Gand, male or female, who is sociable and willing to talk."

"It won't be easily earned."

"One hundred credits to whoever gets the name and address of the town's chief civic dignitary. A thousand credits for the name and accurate location of the world's capitol city." He whistled happily and added, "Somebody's going to be in the dough and it won't be Bidworthy. He didn't come out of the hat. I know—I was holding it."

He ceased talking as he turned to watch a tall, lithe

blonde striding past. Harrison pulled at his arm.

"Here's Baines' place that I told you about. Let's go in."

"Oh, all right." Gleed followed with much reluctance, his gaze still down the street.

"Good afternoon," said Harrison brightly.

"It ain't," contradicted Jeff Baines. "Trade's bad. There's a semifinal being played and it's taken half the town away. They'll think about their bellies after I've closed. Probably make a rush on me tomorrow and I won't be able to serve them fast enough."

"How can trade be bad if you don't take money even when it's good?" inquired Gleed, reasonably applying what information Harrison had given him.

Jeff's big moon eyes went over him slowly, then turned to Harrison. "So he's another bum off your boat. What's he talking about?"

"Money," said Harrison. "It's stuff we use to simplify trade. It's printed stuff, like documentary obs of various sizes."

"That tells me a lot," Jeff Baines observed. "It tells me a crowd that has to make a printed record of every ob isn't to be trusted—because they don't even trust each other." Waddling to his high stool, he squatted on it. His breathing was labored and wheezy. "And that confirms what our schools have always taught—that an Antigand would swindle his widowed mother."

"Your schools have got it wrong," assured Harrison.

"Maybe they have." Jeff saw no need to argue the point. "But we'll play safe until we know different." He looked them over. "What do you two want, anyway?"

"Some advice," shoved in Gleed, quickly. "We're out on the spree. Where's the best places to go for food and fun?"

"How long you got?"

"Until nightfall tomorrow."

63

"No use." Jeff Baines shook his head sorrowfully. "It'd take you from now to then to plant enough obs to qualify for what's going. Besides, lots of folk wouldn't let any Antigand dump an ob on them. They're kind of particular, see?"

"Look," said Harrison. "Can't we get so much as a square meal?"

"Well, I dunno about that." Jeff thought it over, rubbing several chins. "You might manage so much—but I can't help you this time. There's nothing I want of you, so you can't use any obs I've got planted."

"Can you make any suggestions?"

"If you were local citizens, it'd be different. You could get all you want right now by taking on a load of obs to be killed sometime in the future as and when the chances come along. But I can't see anyone giving credit to Antigands who are here today and gone tomorrow."

"Not so much of the gone tomorrow talk," advised Gleed. "When an Imperial Ambassador is sent it means that Terrans will be here for keeps."

"Who says so?"

"The empire says so. You're part of it, aren't you?"

"Nope," said Jeff. "We weren't part of anything and don't want to be, either. What's more, nobody's going to make us part of anything."

Gleed leaned on the counter and gazed absently at a large can of pork. "Seeing I'm out of uniform and not on parade, I sympathize with you though I still shouldn't say it. I wouldn't care to be taken over body and soul by otherworld bureaucrats myself. But you folk are going to have a tough time beating us off. That's the way it is."

"Not with what we've got," Jeff opined. He seemed mighty self-confident.

"You ain't got so much," scoffed Gleed, more in

64

friendly criticism than open contempt. He turned to Harrison. "Have they?"

"It wouldn't appear so," ventured Harrison.

"Don't go by appearances," Jeff advised. "We've more than you'd care to guess at."

"Such as what?"

"Well, just for a start, we've got the mightiest weapon ever thought up by mind of man. We're Gands, see? So we don't need ships and guns and suchlike playthings. We've got something better. It's effective. There's no defense against it."

"I'd like to see it," Gleed challenged. Data on a new and exceptionally powerful weapon should be a good deal more valuable than the mayor's address. Grayder might be sufficiently overcome by the importance thereof to increase the take to five thousand credits. With a touch of sarcasm, he added, "But, of course, I can't expect you to give away secrets."

"There's nothing secret about it," said Jeff, very surprisingly. "You can have it for free any time you want. Any Gand would give it to you for the asking. Like to know why?"

"You bet."

"Because it works one way only. We can use it against you—but you can't use it against us."

"There's no such thing. There's no weapon inventable which the other guy can't employ once he gets his hands on it and knows how to operate it."

"You sure?"

"Positive," said Gleed, with no hesitation whatever. "I've been in the space-service troops for twenty years and you can't fiddle around that long without learning all about weapons from string bows to H-bombs. You're trying to kid me—and it won't work. A one-way weapon is impossible."

"Don't argue with him," Harrison suggested to Baines.

65

"He'll never be convinced until he's shown."

"I can see that." Jeff Baines' face creased in a slow grin. "I told you that you could have our wonder weapon for the asking. Why don't you ask?"

"All right, I'm asking." Gleed put it without much enthusiasm. A weapon that would be presented on request, without even the necessity of first planting a minor ob, couldn't be so mighty after all. His imaginary five thousand credits shrank to five thence to none. "Hand it over and let me try it."

Swiveling heavily on his stool, Jeff reached to the wall, removed a small, shiny plaque from its hook, and passed it across the counter.

"You may keep it," he informed. "And much good may it do you."

Gleed examined it, turning it over and over between his fingers. It was nothing more than an oblong strip of substance resembling ivory. One side was polished and bare. The other bore three letters deeply engraved in bold style:

F—I. W.

Glancing up, his features puzzled, he said, "Call this a weapon?"

"Certainly."

"Then I don't get it." He passed the plaque to Harrison. "Do you?"

"No," Harrison had a good look at it and spoke to Baines. "What does this F—I.W. mean?"

"Initial-slang," informed Baines. "Made correct by common usage. It has become a worldwide motto. You'll see it all over the place, if you haven't noticed it already."

"I have spotted it here and there but attached no importance to it and thought nothing of it. I remember now I've seen it inscribed in several places, including Seth's and the fire depot."

"It was on the sides of that bus we couldn't empty," added Gleed. "Didn't mean anything to me."

"It means plenty," said Jeff. *"Freedom—I Won't!"*

"That kills me," Gleed told him. "I'm stone dead already. I've dropped in my tracks." He watched Harrison thoughtfully pocketing the plaque. "A bit of abracadabra. What a weapon!"

"Ignorance is bliss," remarked Baines, strangely certain of himself. "Especially when you don't know that what you're playing with is the safety catch of something that goes bang."

"All right," challenged Gleed, taking him up on that. "Tell us how it works."

"I won't." The grin reappeared. Baines seemed highly satisfied about something.

"That's a fat lot of help." Gleed felt let down, especially over those momentarily hoped-for credits. "You boast about a one-way weapon, toss across a slip of stuff with three letters on it and then go dumb. Any guy can talk out the back of his neck. How about backing up your talk?"

"I won't," said Baines, his grin becoming broader than ever. He favored the onlooking Harrison with a fat, significant wink.

It made something spark vividly inside Harrison's mind. His jaw dropped and he took the plaque from his pocket, staring at it as if seeing it for the first time.

"Give it me back," requested Baines, watching him.

Replacing it in his pocket, Harrison said very firmly, "I won't."

Baines chuckled. "Some folk catch on quicker than others."

Resenting that remark, Gleed held his hand out to Harrison. "Let's have another look at that thing."

"I won't," said Harrison, meeting him eye for eye.

"Hey, that's not the way—" Gleed's protesting voice

67

died out. He stood there a moment, his optics slightly glassy while his brain performed several loops. Then, in hushed tones, he said, "Good grief!"

"Precisely," approved Baines. "Grief, and plenty of it. You were a bit slow on the uptake."

Overcome by the flood of insubordinate ideas now pouring upon him, Gleed said hoarsely to Harrison, "Come on, let's get out of here. I gotta think. I gotta think someplace quiet."

There was a tiny park with seats and lawns and flowers and a little fountain around which a small bunch of children were playing. Choosing a place facing a colorful carpet of exotic un-Terran blooms, they sat and brooded a while.

In due course, Gleed commented, "For one solitary guy it would be martyrdom, but for a whole world—" His voice drifted off, then came back. "I've been taking this about as far as I can make it go and the results give me the leaping fantods."

Harrison said nothing.

"F'rinstance," Gleed continued, "supposing when I go back to the ship that snorting rhinoceros Bidworthy gives me an order. I give him the frozen wolliker and say, 'I won't!' He either drops dead or throws me in the clink."

"That would do you a lot of good."

"Wait a bit—I ain't finished. I'm in the clink, but the job still needs doing. So Bidworthy picks on someone else. The victim, being a soul-mate of mine, also donates the icy optic and says, 'I won't!' In the clink he goes and I've got company. Bidworthy tries again. And again. There's more of us warming the jug. It'll only hold twenty. So they take over the engineer's mess."

"Leave our mess out of this," Harrison requested.

"They take the mess," Gleed insisted, thoroughly determined to penalize the engineers. "Pretty soon it's crammed to the roof with I-won'ters. Bidworthy's still raking 'em in as fast as he can go—if by that time he hasn't burst a dozen blood vessels. So they take over the Blieder dormitories."

"Why keep picking on my crowd?"

"And pile them with bodies ceiling-high," Greed said, getting sadistic pleasure out of the notion. "Until in the end Bidworthy has to get buckets and brushes and go down on his knees and do his own deck-scrubbing while Grayder, Shelton and the rest act as clink guards. By that time, His Loftiness the ambassador is in the galley busily cooking for you and me, assisted by a disconcerted bunch of yessing pen-pushers." He had another somewhat awed look at the picture and finished, "Holy smoke!"

A colored ball rolled his way. He stooped, picked it up and held on to it. Promptly a boy of about seven ran up, eyeing him gravely.

"Give me my ball, please."

"I won't," said Gleed, his fingers firmly around it.

There was no protest, no anger, no tears. The child merely registered disappointment and turned to go away.

"Here you are, sonny." He tossed the ball.

"Thanks." Grabbing it, the other ran off.

Harrison said, "What if every living being in the empire, all the way from Prometheus to Kaldor Four, across eighteen hundred light-years of space, gets an income-tax demand, tears it up and says, 'I won't!'? What happens then?"

"We'd need a second universe for a pen and a third one to provide the guards."

"There would be chaos," Harrison went on. He nodded toward the fountain and the children playing around it. "But it doesn't look like chaos here. Not to my eyes. So that means they don't overdo this blank refusal business. They apply it judiciously on some mutually recognized basis. What that basis might be beats me completely."

"Me, too."

An elderly man stopped near them, surveyed them hesitantly, then decided to pick on a passing youth.

"Can you tell me where I can find the roller for Martinstown?"

"Other end of Eighth," informed the youth. "One every hour. They'll fix your manacles before they start."

"Manacles?" The oldster raised white eyebrows. "Whatever for?"

"That route runs past the spaceship. The Antigands may try to drag you out."

"Oh, yes, of course." He ambled on, glanced again at Gleed and Harrison and remarked in passing, "These Antigands—such a nuisance."

"Definitely," endorsed Gleed. "We keep telling them to get out and they keep on saying, 'We won't.'"

The old gentleman missed a step, recovered, gave him a peculiar look, and continued on his way.

"One or two seem to cotton on to our accents," Harrison remarked. "Though nobody noticed mine when I was having that feed in Seth's."

Gleed perked up with sudden interest. "Where you've had one feed you can get another. C'mon, let's try. What have we got to lose?"

"Our patience," said Harrison. He stood up. "We'll pick on Seth. If he won't play, we'll have a try at someone else. And if nobody will play, we'll skin out fast before we starve to death."

"Which appears to be exactly what they want us to do," Gleed pointed out. He scowled to himself. "They'll get their way over my dead body."

"That's how," agreed Harrison. "Over your dead body."

70

Matt came up with a cloth over one arm. "I'm serving no Antigands."

"You served me last time," Harrison told him.

"That's as may be. I didn't know you were off that ship. But I know now!" He flicked the cloth across one corner of the table. "No Antigands served by me."

"Is there any other place where we might get a meal?"

"Not unless somebody will let you plant an ob on them. They won't do that if they're wise to you, but there's a chance they might make the same mistake I did." Another flick across the corner. "I don't make them twice."

"You're making another right now," said Gleed, his voice tough and authoritative. He nudged Harrison. "Watch this!" His hand came out of a side pocket holding a tiny blaster. Pointing it at Matt's middle, he continued, "Ordinarily, I could get into trouble for this, if those on the ship were in the mood to make trouble. But they aren't. They're soured up on you two-legged mules." He motioned the weapon. "Get walking and bring us two full plates."

"I won't," said Matt, firming his jaw and ignoring the gun.

Gleed thumbed the safety catch, which moved with an audible click. "It's touchy now. It'd go off at a sneeze. Start moving."

"I won't," insisted Matt.

Gleed disgustedly shoved the weapon back into his pocket. "I was only kidding you. It isn't energized."

"Wouldn't have made the slightest difference if it had been," Matt assured. "I serve no Antigands, and that's that!"

"Suppose I'd gone haywire and blown you in half?"

"How could I have served you then?" he inquired. "A dead person is of no use to anyone. Time you Antigands learned a little logic."

71

With that parting shot he went away.

"He's got something there," observed Harrison, patently depressed. "What can you do with a waxie one? Nothing whatever! You'd have put him clean out of your own power."

"Don't know so much. A couple of stiffs lying around might sharpen the others. They'd get really eager."

"You're thinking of them in Terran terms," Harrison said. "It's a mistake. They're not Terrans, no matter where they came from originally. They're Gands." He mused a moment. "I've no notion of just what Gands are supposed to be but I reckon they're some kind of fanatics. Terra exported one-track-minders by the millions around the time of the Great Explosion. Look at that crazy crowd they've got on Hygeia."

"I was there once and I tried hard not to look," confessed Gleed, reminiscently. "Then I couldn't stop looking. Not so much as a fig leaf between the lot. They insisted that we were obscene because we wore clothes. So eventually we had to take them off. Know what I was wearing at the time we left?"

"A dignified poise," Harrison suggested.

"That and an identity disk, cupro-silver, official issue, spacemen, for the use of," Gleed informed. "Plus three wipes of greasepaint on my left arm to show I was a sergeant. I looked every inch a sergeant—like heck I did!"

"I know. I had a week in that place."

"We'd a rear admiral on board," Gleed went on. "As a fine physical specimen he resembled a pair of badly worn suspenders. He couldn't overawe anyone while in his birthday suit. Those Hygeians cited his deflation as proof that they'd got real democracy, as distinct from our fake version." He clucked his tongue. "I'm not so sure they're wrong."

"The creation of the empire has created a queer

proposition," Harrison meditated. "Namely, that Terra is always right while sixteen hundred and forty-two planets are invariably wrong."

"You're getting kind of seditious, aren't you?"

Harrison said nothing. Gleed glanced at him, found his attention elsewhere, and followed his gaze to a brunette who had just entered.

"Nice," approved Gleed. "Not too young, not too old. Not too fat, not too thin. Just right."

"I know her." Harrison waved to attract her attention. She tripped lightly across the room and sat at their table. Harrison made the introduction.

"Friend of mine. Sergeant Gleed."

"Arthur," corrected Gleed, eating her.

"Mine's Elissa," she told him. "What's a sergeant supposed to be?"

"A sort of over-above underthing," Gleed informed. "I pass along the telling to the guys who do the doing."

Her eyes widened. "Do you mean that people really allow themselves to be told?"

"Of course. Why not?"

"It sounds crazy to me." Her gaze shifted to Harrison. "I'll be ignorant of *your* name forever, I suppose?"

He hastened to repair the omission, adding, "But I don't like James. I prefer Jim."

"Then we'll let it be Jim." She examined the place, looking over the counter, the other tables. "Has Matt been to you two?"

"Yes. He refuses to serve us."

She shrugged warm shoulders. "It's his right. Everyone has the right to refuse. That's freedom, isn't it?"

"We call it mutiny," said Gleed.

"Don't be so childish," she reproved. She stood up and moved away. "You wait here. I'll go see Seth."

"I don't get this," admitted Gleed, when she had passed out of earshot. "According to that fat fella in the delicatessen, their technique is to give us the cold shoulder until we run away in a huff. But this dame acts friendly. She's . . . she's—" He stopped while he sought for a suitable word, found it and said, "She's un-Gandian."

"Not so," Harrison contradicted. "They've the right to say, 'I won't.' She's practicing it."

"By gosh, yes! I hadn't thought of that. They can work it any way they like, and please themselves."

"Sure." He dropped his voice. "Here she comes."

Resuming her seat, she primped her hair and said, "Seth will serve us personally."

"Another traitor," remarked Gleed with a grin.

"On one condition," she went on. "You two must wait and have a talk with him before you leave."

"Cheap at the price," Harrison decided. A thought struck him and he asked, "Does this mean you'll have to kill several obs for all three of us?"

"Only one for myself."

"How come?"

"Seth's got ideas of his own. He doesn't feel happy about Antigands any more than does anyone else."

"And so?"

"But he's got the missionary instinct. He doesn't agree entirely with the idea of giving all Antigands the ghost-treatment. He thinks it should be reserved only for those too stubborn or stupid to be converted." She smiled at Gleed, making his top hairs quiver. "Seth thinks that any intelligent Antigand is a would-be Gand."

"What is a Gand, anyway?" asked Harrison.

"An inhabitant of this world, of course."

"I mean, where did they dig up the name?"

"From Gandhi," she said.

Harrison frowned in puzzlement. "Who the deuce was he?"

74

"An ancient Terran. The one who invented The Weapon."

"Never heard of him."

"That doesn't surprise me," she remarked.

"Doesn't it?" He felt a little irritated. "Let me tell you that these days we Terrans get as good an education as—"

"Calm down, Jim." She made it more soothing by pronouncing it "Jeem". "All I mean is that ten-to-one he's been blanked out of your history books. He might have given you unwanted ideas, see? You couldn't be expected to know what you've been deprived of the chance to learn."

"If you mean that Terran history is censored, I don't believe it," he asserted.

"It's your right to refuse to believe. That's freedom, isn't it?"

"Up to a point. A man has duties. He's no right to refuse those."

"No?" She raised tantalizing eyebrows, delicately curved. "Who defines those duties—himself, or somebody else?"

"His superiors, most times."

"No man is superior to another. No man has the right to define another man's duties." She paused, eyeing him speculatively. "If anyone on Terra exercises such idiotic power, it is only because idiots permit him. They fear freedom. They prefer to be told. They like being ordered around. What men!"

"I shouldn't listen to you," protested Gleed, chipping in. His leathery face was flushed. "You're as naughty as you're pretty."

"Afraid of your own thoughts?" she jibed, pointedly ignoring his compliment.

He went redder. "Not on your life. But I—" His voice trailed off as Seth arrived with three loaded plates and dumped them on the table.

"See you afterward," reminded Seth. He was medium-sized, with thin features and sharp, quick-moving eyes. "Got something to say to you."

Seth joined them shortly after the end of the meal. Taking a chair, he wiped condensed steam off his face and looked them over.

"How much do you two know?"

"Enough to argue about it," put in Elissa. "They are bothered about duties, who defines them, and who does them."

"With good reason," Harrison riposted. "You can't escape them yourselves."

"Meaning . . . ?" asked Seth.

"This world runs on some strange system of swapping obligations. How will any person kill an ob unless he recognizes his duty to do so?"

"Duty has nothing to do with it," said Seth. "And if it did happen to be a matter of duty, every man would recognize it for himself. It would be outrageous impertinence for anyone else to remind him, unthinkable to anyone to order him."

"Some guys must make an easy living," interjected Gleed. "There's nothing to stop them that I can see." He studied Seth briefly before he continued. "How can you cope with a citizen who has no conscience?"

"Easy as pie."

Elissa suggested, "Tell them the story of Idle Jack."

"It's a kid's yarn," explained Seth. "All children here know it by heart. It's a classic fable like . . . like—" He screwed up his face. "I've lost track of the Terran tales the firstcomers brought with them."

"Red Riding Hood," offered Harrison.

"Yes." Seth seized on it gratefully. "Something like that one. A nursery story." He licked his lips and began, "This Idle Jack came from Terra as a baby, grew up in

76

our new world, studied our economic system and thought he'd be mighty smart. He decided to become a scratcher."

"What's a scratcher?" inquired Gleed.

"One who lives by taking obs and does nothing about killing them or planting any of his own. One who accepts everything that's going and gives nothing in return."

"I get it. I've known one or two like that in my time."

"Up to age sixteen, Jack got away with it. He was a kid, see. All kids tend to scratch to a certain extent. We expect it and allow for it. After sixteen, he was soon in the soup."

"How?" urged Harrison, more interested than he was willing to show.

"He went around the town gathering obs by the armful. Meals, clothes and all sorts for the mere asking. It's not a big town. There are no big ones on this planet. They're just small enough for everyone to know everyone—and everyone does plenty of gabbing. Within three or four months the entire town knew Jack was a determined scratcher."

"Go on," said Harrison, getting impatient.

"Everything dried up," said Seth. "Wherever Jack went, people gave him the 'I won't'. That's freedom, isn't it? He got no meals, no clothes, no entertainment, no company, nothing! Soon he became terribly hungry, busted into someone's larder one night, gave himself the first square meal in a week."

"What did they do about that?"

"Nothing. Not a thing."

"That would encourage him some, wouldn't it?"

"How could it?" Seth asked, with a thin smile. "It did him no good. Next day his belly was empty again. He had to repeat the performance. And the next day. And the next. People became leery, locked up their stuff,

77

kept watch on it. It became harder and harder. It became so unbearably hard that it was soon a lot easier to leave the town and try another. So Idle Jack went away."

"To do the same again," Harrison suggested.

"With the same results for the same reasons," retorted Seth. "On he went to a third town, a fourth, a fifth, a twentieth. He was stubborn enough to be witless.

"He was getting by," Harrison observed. "Taking all at the mere cost of moving around."

"No he wasn't. Our towns are small, like I said. And folk do plenty of visiting from one to another. In town number two Jack had to risk being seen and talked about by someone from town number one. As he went on it got a whole lot worse. In the twentieth he had to take a chance on gabby visitors from any of the previous nineteen." Seth leaned forward and said with emphasis, "He never got to town number twenty-eight."

"No?"

"He lasted two weeks in number twenty-five, eight days in twenty-six, one day in twenty-seven. That was almost the end."

"What did he do then?"

"Took to the open country, tried to live on roots and wild berries. Then he disappeared—until one day some walkers found him swinging from a tree. The body was emaciated and clad in rags. Loneliness and self-neglect had killed him. That was Idle Jack, the scratcher. He wasn't twenty years old."

"On Terra," informed Gleed, "we don't hang people merely for being lazy."

"Neither do we," said Seth. "We leave them free to go hang themselves." He eyed them shrewdly and went on, "But don't let it worry you. Nobody has been driven to such drastic measures in my lifetime, leastways not that I've heard about. People honor their obs as a matter of economic necessity and not from any sense of duty. Nobody gives orders, nobody pushes anyone around, but there's a kind of compulsion built into the circumstances of this planet's way of living. People play square—or they suffer. Nobody enjoys suffering—not even a numbskull."

"Yes, I suppose you're right," put in Harrison, much exercised in mind.

"You bet I'm dead right!" Seth assured. "But what I wanted to talk to you two about is something more important. It's this: What's your real ambition in life?"

Without hesitation, Gleed said, "To ride the spaceways while remaining in one piece."

"Same here," Harrison contributed.

"I guessed that much. You'd not be in the space service if it wasn't your choice. But you can't remain in it forever. All good things come to an end. What then?"

Harrison fidgeted uneasily. "I don't care to think of it."

"Someday you'll have to," Seth pointed out. "How much longer have you got?"

"Four and a half Earth years."

Seth's gaze turned to Gleed.

"Three Earth years."

"Not long," Seth commented. "I didn't expect you would have much time left. It's a safe bet that any ship penetrating this deeply into space has a crew composed mostly of old-timers getting near the end of their terms. The practiced hands get picked for the awkward jobs. By the day your boat lands again on Terra it will be the end of the trail for many of them, won't it?"

"It will for me," Gleed admitted, none too happy at the thought.

"Time—the older you get the faster it goes. Yet when you leave the service you'll still be comparatively young." He registered a faint, taunting smile. "I suppose you'll then obtain a private space vessel and continue roaming the cosmos on your own?"

"Impossible," declared Gleed. "The best a rich man can afford is a moonboat. Puttering to and fro between a satellite and its primary is no fun when you're used to Blieder-zips across the galaxy. The smallest space-going craft is far beyond reach of the wealthiest. Only governments can afford them."

"By 'governments' you mean communities?"

"In a way."

"Well, then, what are you going to do when your space-roving days are over?"

"I'm not like Big Ears here." Gleed jerked an indicative thumb at Harrison. "I'm a trooper and not a technician. So my choice is limited by lack of qualifications." He rubbed his chin, looking wistful. "I was born and brought up on a farm. I still know a good deal about farming. So I'd like to get a small one of my own and settle down."

"Think you'll manage it?" asked Seth, watching him.

"On Falder or Hygeia or Norton's Pink Heaven or some other undeveloped planet. But not on Terra. My savings won't extend to that. I don't get half enough to meet Earth costs."

"Meaning you can't pile up enough obs?"

"I can't," agreed Gleed, lugubriously. "Not even if I saved until I'd got a white beard four feet long."

"So there's Terra's reward for a long spell of faithful service—forego your heart's desire or get out?"

"Shut up!"

"I won't," said Seth. He leaned nearer. "Why do you think two hundred thousand Gands came to this world, Doukhobors to Hygeia, Quakers to Centauri B., and all the others to their selected haunts? Because Terra's reward for good citizenship was the peremptory order to knuckle down or get out. So we got out."

"It was just as well, anyway," Elissa interjected. "According to our history books, Terra was badly overcrowded. We went away and relieved the pressure."

"That's beside the point," reproved Seth. He continued with Gleed. "You want a farm. It can't be on Terra much as you'd like it there. Terra says, 'No! Get out!' So it's got to be some place else." He waited for that to sink in, then, "Here, you can have one for the mere taking." He snapped his fingers. "Like that!"

"You can't kid me," said Gleed, wearing the expression of one eager to be kidded. "Where are the hidden strings?"

"On this planet, any plot of ground belongs to the person in possession, the one who is making use of it. Nobody disputes his claim so long as he continues to use it. All you need do is look around for a suitable piece of unused territory—of which there is plenty—and start using it. From that moment it's yours. Immediately you cease using it and walk out, it's anyone else's, for the taking."

"Zipping meteors!" Gleed was incredulous.

"Moreover, if you look around long enough and strike really lucky," Seth continued, "you might stake first claim to a farm someone else has abandoned because of death, illness, a desire to move elsewhere, a chance at something else he liked better, or any other excellent reason. In that case, you would walk into ground already part-prepared, with farmhouse, milking shed, barns and the rest. And it would be yours, all yours."

"What would I owe the previous occupant?" asked Gleed.

"Nothing. Not an ob. Why should you? If he isn't buried, he has got out for the sake of something else equally free. He can't have the benefit both ways, coming and going."

"It doesn't make sense to me. Somewhere there's a

81

snag. Somewhere I've got to pour out hard cash or pile up obs."

"Of course you have. You start a farm. A handful of local folk help you build a house. They dump heavy obs on you. The carpenter wants farm produce for his family for the next couple of years. You give it, thus killing that ob. You continue giving it for a couple of extra years, thus planting an ob on *him*. First time you want fences mending, or some other suitable task doing, along he comes to kill *that* ob. And so with all the rest, including the people who supply your raw materials, your seeds and machinery, or do your trucking for you."

"They won't all want milk and potatoes," Gleed pointed out.

"Don't know what you mean by potatoes. Never heard of them."

"How can I square up with someone who may be getting all the farm produce he wants from elsewhere?"

"Easy," said Seth. "A tinsmith supplies you with several churns. He doesn't want food. He's getting all he needs from another source. His wife and three daughters are overweight and dieting. The mere thought of a load from your farm gives them the horrors."

"Well?"

"But this tinsmith's tailor, or his cobbler, have got obs on him which he hasn't had the chance to kill. So he transfers them to you. As soon as you're able, you give the tailor or cobbler what they need to satisfy the obs, thus doing the tinsmith's killing along with your own." He gave his usual half-smile, added, "And everyone is happy."

Gleed stewed it over, frowning while he did it. "You're tempting me. You shouldn't ought to. It's a criminal offense to try divert a spaceman from his allegiance. It's sedition. Terra is tough with sedition."

"Tough my eye!" said Seth, sniffing contemptuously. "We've Gand laws here."

"All you have to do," suggested Elissa, sweetly persuasive, "is say to yourself that you've got to go back to the ship, that it's your duty to go back, that neither the ship nor Terra can get along without you." She tucked a curl away. "Then be a free individual and say, 'I won't!'"

"They'd skin me alive. Bidworthy would preside over the operation in person."

"I don't think so," Seth offered. "This Bidworthy—whom I presume to be anything but a jovial character—stands with you and the rest of your crew at the same junction. The road before him splits two ways. He's got to take one or the other and there's no third alternative. Sooner or later he'll be hell-bent for home, eating his top lip as he goes, or else he'll be running around in a truck delivering your milk—because, deep inside himself, that's what he's always wanted to do."

"You don't know him like I do," mourned Gleed. "He uses a lump of old iron for a soul."

"Funny," remarked Harrison, "I always thought of *you* that way—until today."

"I'm off duty," said Gleed, as though that explained everything. "I can relax and let the ego zoom around outside of business hours." He stood up and firmed his jaw. "But I'm going back on duty. Right now!"

"You're not due before sundown tomorrow," Harrison protested.

"Maybe I'm not. But I'm going back all the same."

Elissa opened her mouth, then closed it as Seth nudged her. They sat in silence and watched Gleed march determinedly out.

"It's a good sign," commented Seth, strangely self-assured. "He's been handed a wallop right where he's weakest." He chuckled low down and turned to Harri-

83

son. "What's *your* ultimate ambition?"

"Thanks for the meal. It was a good one and I needed it." Harrison stood up, manifestly embarrassed. He gestured toward the door. "I'm going to catch him up. If he's returning to the ship, I think I'll do likewise."

Again Seth nudged Elissa. They said nothing as Harrison made his way out, carefully closing the door behind him.

"Sheep," decided Elissa, disappointed for no obvious reason. "One follows another. Just like sheep."

"Not so," Seth contradicted. "They're humans animated by the same thoughts, the same emotions, as were our forefathers who had nothing sheeplike about them." Twisting round in his chair, he beckoned to Matt. "Bring us two shemaks." Then to Elissa. "My guess is that it won't pay that ship to hang around too long."

The battleship's caller system bawled imperatively, "Fanshaw, Folsom, Fuller, Garson, Gleed, Gregory, Haines, Harrison, Hope—" and down through the alphabet.

A trickle of men flowed along the passages, catwalks and alleyways toward the fore chartroom. They gathered outside it in small clusters, chattering in undertones and sending odd scraps of conversation echoing down the corridor.

"Wouldn't say anything to us but, 'Myob!' Got sick and tired of it after a while."

"You ought to have split up, like we did. That showplace on the outskirts didn't know what a Terran looks like. I just walked in and took a seat."

"Hear about Meakin? He mended a leaky roof, chose a bottle of double dith in payment and mopped the lot. He was dead flat when we found him. Had to be carried back."

"Some guys have all the luck. We got the brush-off

wherever we showed our faces. It gets you down."

"You should have separated, like I said."

"Half the mess must be still lying in the gutter. They haven't turned up yet."

"Grayder will be hopping mad. He'd have stopped this morning's second quota if he'd known in time."

Every now and again First Mate Morgan stuck his head out of the chartroom door and uttered a name already voiced on the caller. Frequently there was no response.

"Harrison!" he yelled.

With a puzzled expression, Harrison went inside. Captain Grayder was there, seated behind a desk and gazing moodily at a list lying before him. Colonel Shelton was stiff and erect to one side, with Major Hame slightly behind him. Both wore the pained expressions of those tolerating a bad smell while the plumber goes looking for the leak.

His Excellency was tramping steadily to and fro in front of the desk, muttering deep down in his chins. "Barely five days and already the rot has set in." He turned as Harrison entered and fired off sharply, "So it's you, mister. When did you return from leave?"

"The evening before last, sir."

"Ahead of time, eh? That's curious. Did you get a puncture or something?"

"No, sir. I didn't take my bicycle with me."

"Just as well," approved the ambassador. "If you had done so, you'd have been a thousand miles away by now and still pushing hard."

"Why, sir?"

"Why? He asks me why! That's precisely what I'd like to know—why?" He fumed a bit, then inquired, "Did you visit this town by yourself, or in company?"

"I went with Sergeant Gleed, sir."

85

"Call him," ordered the ambassador, looking at Morgan.

Opening the door, Morgan obediently shouted, "Gleed! Gleed!"

No answer.

He tried again, without result. They put it over the caller system again. Sergeant Gleed refused to be among those present.

"Has he booked in?"

Grayder consulted his list. "In early. Twenty-four hours ahead of time. He may have sneaked out again with the second liberty quota this morning and omitted to book it. That's a double crime."

"If he's not on the ship, he's off the ship, crime or no crime."

"Yes, your excellency." Captain Grayder registered slight weariness.

"GLEED!" howled Morgan, outside the door. A moment later he poked his head inside, said, "Your excellency, one of the men says Sergeant Gleed is not on board because he saw him in town quite recently."

"Send him in." The ambassador made an impatient gesture at Harrison. "Stay where you are and keep those confounded ears from flapping. I've not finished with you yet."

A long, gangling grease-monkey came in and blinked around, a little awed by high brass.

"What do you know about Sergeant Gleed?" demanded the ambassador.

The other licked his lips, seemingly sorry that he had mentioned the missing man. "It's like this, your honor, I—"

"Call me 'sir'."

"Yes, sir." More disconcerted blinking. "I went out with the second party early this morning, came back a couple of hours ago because my stomach was acting up.

On the way, I saw Sergeant Gleed and spoke to him."

"Where? When?"

"In town, sir. He was sitting in one of those big long-distance coaches. I thought it a bit queer."

"Get down to the roots, man! What did he tell you, if anything?"

"Not much, sir. He seemed pretty chipper about something. Mentioned a young widow struggling to look after two hundred acres. Someone had told him about her and he thought he'd take a peek." He hesitated and backed away a couple of paces, then added, "He also said I'd see him in irons or never."

"One of *your* men," said the ambassador to Colonel Shelton. "A trooper, allegedly well-disciplined. One with long service, three stripes, and a pension to lose." His attention returned to the informant. "Did he say exactly where he was going?"

"No, sir. I asked him, but he just grinned and said, 'Myob!' So I came back to the ship."

"All right. You may go." His Excellency watched the other depart, then continued with Harrison. "You were with that first quota."

"Yes, sir."

"Let me tell you something, mister. Four hundred twenty men went out. Only two hundred have returned. Forty of those were in various stages of alcoholic turpitude. Ten of them are in the clink yelling, 'I won't!' in steady chorus. Doubtless they'll go on yelling until they've sobered up."

He stared at Harrison as if that worthy were personally responsible, then went on, "There's something paradoxical about this. I can understand the drunks. There are always a few individuals who blow their tops first day on land. But of the two hundred who have condescended to come back, about half returned before time, the same as you did. Their reasons were identical

—the town was unfriendly, everyone treated them like ghosts until they'd had enough."

Harrison made no comment.

"So we have two diametrically opposed reactions," the ambassador complained. "One gang of men say the place stinks so much that they'd rather be back on the ship. Another gang finds it so hospitable that either they get filled to the gills on some stuff called double-dith, or they stay sober and desert the service. I want an explanation. There's got to be one somewhere. You've been twice in this town. What can you tell us?"

Carefully, Harrison said, "It all depends on whether or not you're spotted as a Terran. Also on whether you meet Gands who'd rather convert you than give you the brush-off." He pondered a moment, then finished, "Uniforms are a giveaway."

"You mean they're allergic to uniforms?"

"More or less, sir."

"Any idea why?"

"Couldn't say for certain, sir. I don't know enough about them yet. As a guess, I think they may have been taught to associate uniforms with the Terran regime from which their ancestors escaped."

"Escaped nothing!" scoffed the ambassador. "They grabbed the benefit of Terran inventions, Terran techniques and Terran manufacturing ability to go some place where they'd have more elbow room." He gave Harrison the sour eye. "Don't any of them wear uniforms?"

"Not that I could recognize as such. They seem to take pleasure in expressing their individual personalities by wearing anything they fancy, from pigtails to pink boots. Oddity in attire is the norm among the Gands. Uniformity is the real oddity—they think it's submissive and degrading."

"You refer to them as Gands. Where did they dig up that name?"

Harrison told him, thinking back to Elissa as she explained it. In his mind's eye he could see her now. And Seth's place with the tables set and steam rising behind the counter and mouth-watering smells oozing from the background. Now that he came to visualize the scene again, it appeared to embody an elusive but essential something that the ship had never possessed.

"And this person," he concluded, "invented what they call The Weapon."

"Hmmm! And they assert he was a Terran? What does he look like? Did you see a photograph or a statue?"

"They don't erect statues, sir. They say no person is more important than another."

"Bunkum!" snapped the ambassador, instinctively rejecting that viewpoint. "Did it occur to you to ask at what period in history this wonderful weapon was tried out?"

"No, sir," Harrison confessed. "I didn't think it important."

"You wouldn't. Some of you men are too slow to catch a Callistrian sloth wandering in its sleep. I don't criticize your abilities as spacemen, but as intelligence agents you're a dead loss."

"I'm sorry, sir," said Harrison.

Sorry? You louse! whispered something deep within his own mind. *Why should you be sorry? He's only a pompous fat man who couldn't kill an ob if he tried. He's no better than you. Those raw boys prancing around on Hygeia would maintain that he's not as good as you because he's got a pot belly. Yet you keep looking at his pot belly and saying, "Sir," and, "I'm sorry." If he tried to ride your bike, he'd fall off before he'd*

89

*gone ten yards. Go spit in his eye and say, "I won't."
You're not scared, are you?*

"No!" announced Harrison, loudly and firmly.

Captain Grayder glanced up. "If you're going to start answering questions before they've been asked, you'd better see the medic. Or have we a telepath on board?"

"I was thinking," Harrison explained.

"I approve of that," put in His Excellency. He lugged a couple of huge tomes out of the wall shelves and began to thumb rapidly through them. "Do plenty of thinking whenever you've the chance and it will become a habit. It will get easier and easier as time rolls on. In fact, a day may come when it can be done without pain."

He shoved the books back, pulled out two more, spoke to Major Hame who happened to be at his elbow. "Don't pose there glassy-eyed like a relic propped up in a military museum. Give me a hand with this mountain of knowledge. I want Gandhi, anywhere from three hundred to a thousand Earth years ago."

Hame came to life and started dragging out books. So did Colonel Shelton. Captain Grayder remained at his desk and continued to mourn the missing.

"Ah, here it is, four-seventy years back." His Excellency ran a plump finger along the printed lines. "Gandhi, sometimes called Bapu, or Father. Citizen of Hindi. Politico-philosopher. Opposed authority by means of an ingenious system called civil disobedience. Last remnants disappeared with the Great Explosion, but may still persist on some planet out of contact."

"Evidently it does," commented Grayder, his voice dry.

"Civil disobedience," repeated the ambassador, screwing up his eyes. He had the air of one trying to study something which was topsy-turvy. "They can't make *that* a social basis. It just won't work."

"It does work," asserted Harrison, forgetting to put in the "sir".

"Are you contradicting me, mister?"

"I'm stating a fact."

"Your excellency," Grayder began, "I suggest—"

"Leave this to me." His color deepening, the ambassador waved him off. His gaze remained angrily on Harrison. "You're very far from being an expert on socio-economic problems. Get that into your head, mister. Anyone of your caliber can be fooled by superficial appearances."

"It works," persisted Harrison, wondering where his own stubbornness was coming from.

"So does your tomfool bicycle. You've a bicycle mentality."

Something snapped, and a voice remarkably like his own said, "Nuts!" Astounded by this phenomenon, Harrison waggled his ears.

"What was that, mister?"

"Nuts!" he repeated, feeling that what has been done can't be undone.

Beating the purpling ambassador to the draw, Captain Grayder stood up and exercised his own authority.

"Regardless of further leave quotas, if any, you are confined to the ship until further notice. Now get out!"

He went out, his mind in a whirl but his soul strangely satisfied. Outside, First Mate Morgan glowered at him.

"How long d'you think it's going to take me to work through this list of names when guys like you squat in there for a week?" He grunted with ire, cupped hands round his mouth and bellowed, "Hope! Hope!"

No reply.

"Hope's been abandoned," remarked a wit.

"That's funny," sneered Morgan. "Look at me shaking all over." He cupped again and tried the next name. "Hyland! Hyland!"

No response.

Four more days, long, tedious, dragging ones. That made nine in all since the battleship formed the rut in which it was still sitting.

There was trouble on board. The third and fourth leave quotas, put off repeatedly, were becoming impatient, irritable.

"Morgan showed him the third roster again this morning. Same result. Grayder admitted this world can't be defined as hostile and that we're entitled to run free."

"Well, why the heck doesn't he keep to the book? The space commission could crucify him for disregarding it."

"Same excuse. He says he's not denying leave, he's merely postponing it. That's a crafty evasion, isn't it? He says he'll grant it immediately the missing men come back."

"That might be never. Darn him, he's using them as an excuse to gyp me out of my time."

It was a strong and legitimate complaint. Weeks, months, years of close confinement in a constantly trembling bottle, no matter how large, demands ultimate release if only for a comparatively brief period. Men need fresh air, the good earth, the broad, clear-cut horizon, bulk food, femininity, new faces.

"He *would* ram home the stopper just when we've learned the best way to get around. Civilian clothes and act like Gands, that's the secret. Even the first-quota boys are ready for another try."

"Grayder daren't risk it. He's lost too many already. One more quota cut in half and he won't have enough crew to take off and get back. We'd be stuck here for keeps. How'd you like that?"

"I wouldn't grieve."

"He could train the bureaucrats. Time those guys did some honest work."

"It'd take three years. That's how long it took to train you, wasn't it?"

Harrison came along holding a small envelope. Three of them picked on him at sight.

"Look who sassed Hizonner and got confined to ship —same as us!"

"That's what I like about it," Harrison observed. "Better to get fastened down for something than for nothing."

"It won't be long, you'll see! We're not going to hang around bellyaching for ever. Mighty soon we'll *do* something."

"Such as what?"

"We're thinking it over," evaded the other, not liking to be taken up so fast. He noticed the envelope. "What have you got there? The day's mail?"

"Exactly that," Harrison agreed.

"Have it your own way. I wasn't being nosey. I thought maybe you'd got some more snafu. You engineers usually pick up that paper stuff first."

"It *is* mail," said Harrison.

"G'wan, nobody has letters in this neck of the cosmos."

"I do."

"How did you get it?"

"Worrall brought it from town an hour back. Friend of mine gave him dinner, let him bring the letter to kill the ob." He pulled a large ear. "Influence, that's what you boys need."

Registering annoyance, one demanded, "What's Worrall doing off the boat? Is he privileged?"

"Sort of. He's married, with three kids."

"So what?"

"The ambassador figures that some people can be

trusted more than others. They're not so likely to disappear, having too much to lose. So a few have been sorted out and sent into town to seek information about the missing men."

"They found out anything?"

"Not much. Worrall says it's a waste of time. He found a few of our men here and there, tried to persuade them to return, but each said, 'I won't.' The Gands all said, 'Myob!' And that's that."

"There must be something in it," decided one of them, thoughtfully. "I'd like to go see for myself."

"That's what Grayder's afraid of."

"We'll give him more than that to worry about if he doesn't become reasonable soon. Our patience is evaporating."

"Mutinous talk," Harrison reproved. He shook his head, looking sad. "You shock me."

He continued along the corridor to his own cabin, eyeing the envelope. The writing inside might be feminine. He hoped so. He tore it open and had a look. It wasn't.

Signed by Gleed, the missive read, "Never mind where I am or what I'm doing—this might get into the wrong hands. All I'll tell you is that I'll be fixed up topnotch providing I wait a decent interval to improve acquaintance. The rest of this concerns *you*."

"Huh?" He leaned back on his bunk and held the letter nearer the light.

"I found a little fat guy running an empty shop. He just sits there, waiting. Next, I learn that he's established possession by occupation. He's doing it on behalf of a factory that makes two-ball rollers—those fan-driven cycles. They want someone to operate the place as a local roller sales and service depot. The little fat man has had four applications to date, but none with any engineering ability. The one who eventually gets this

94

place will plant a functional-ob on the town, whatever that means. Anyway, this joint is yours for the taking. Don't be stupid. Jump in—the water's fine."

"Zipping meteors!" said Harrison. His eyes traveled on to the bottom.

"P.S. Seth will give you the address. P.P.S. This burg is your brunette's home town and she's thinking of coming back. She wants to live near her sister—and so do I. Said sister is a honey!"

He stirred restlessly, read it through a second time, got up and paced around his tiny cabin. There were twelve hundred occupied worlds within the scope of the empire. He'd seen about one-tenth of them. No spaceman could live long enough to get a look at the lot. The service was divided into cosmic groups, each dealing with its own sector.

Except by hearsay, of which there was plenty and most of it highly colored, he would never know what heavens or pseudo-heavens existed in other sectors. In any case, it would be a blind gamble to pick an unfamiliar world for landbound life on someone else's recommendation. Not all think alike, or have the same tastes. One man's meat may be another man's poison.

The choice for retirement—which was the unlovely name for beginning another, different but vigorous life —was high-priced Terra or some more desirable planet in his own sector. There was the Epsilon group, fourteen of them, all attractive providing you could suffer the gravity and endure lumbering around like a tired elephant. There was Norton's Pink Heaven if, for the sake of getting by in peace, you could pander to Septimus Norton's rajah complex and put up with his delusions of grandeur.

Up on the edge of the Milky Way was a matriarchy run by blonde amazons, and a world of wizards, and a pentecostal planet, and a globe where semisentient vegetables cultivated themselves under the direction of human masters; all scattered across forty light-years of space but readily accessible by Blieder-drive.

There were more than a hundred known to him by personal experience, though merely a tithe of the whole. All offered life and that company which is the essence of life. But this world, Gand, had something the others lacked. It had the quality of being present. It was part of the existing environment from which he drew data on which to build his decisions. The others were not. They lost virtue by being absent and faraway.

Unobtrusively he made his way to the Blieder-room lockers and spent an hour cleaning and oiling his bicycle. Twilight was approaching when he returned. Taking a thin plaque from his pocket, he hung it on the wall, lay on his bunk and stared at it.

F—I.W.

The caller system clicked, cleared its throat, and announced, "All personnel will stand by for general instructions at eight hours tomorrow."

"I won't," said Harrison. He closed his eyes.

Seven-twenty in the morning, but nobody thought it early. There is little sense of earliness or lateness among space-roamers—to regain it they have to be landbound a month, watching a sun rise and set.

The chartroom was empty but there was much activity in the control cabin. Grayder was there with Shelton, Hame, Navigators Adamson, Werth and Yates and, of course, His Excellency.

"I never thought the day would come," groused the latter, frowning at the star map over which the navigators pored. "Less than a couple of weeks, and we get out, admitting defeat."

"With all respect, your excellency, it doesn't look that way to me," said Captain Grayder. "One can be defeated only by enemies. These people are not enemies. That's precisely where they've got us by the short hairs. They're not definable as hostile."

"That may be. I still say it's defeat. What else could you call it?"

"We've been outwitted by awkward relations. There's not much we can do about it. A man doesn't beat up his nieces and nephews merely because they won't speak to him."

"That's your viewpoint as a ship's commander. You're confronted by a situation that requires you to go back to base and report. It's routine. The whole service is hidebound with routine." The ambassador again eyed the star map as if he found it offensive. "My own status is different. If I get out, it's a diplomatic defeat, an insult to the dignity and prestige of Terra. I'm far from sure that I ought to go. It might be better if I stayed put—though that would give them the chance to offer further insults."

"I would not presume to advise you what to do for the best," Grayder said. "All I know is this: we carry troops and armaments for any policing or protective purposes that might be found necessary here. But I can't use them offensively against these Gands because they've provided no pretext and because, in any case, our full strength isn't enough to crush twelve millions of them. We need an armada for that. We'd be fighting at the extreme of our reach—and the reward of victory would be a useless world."

"Don't remind me. I've stewed it until I'm sick of it."

Grayder shrugged. He was a man of action so long as it was action in space. Planetary shenanigans were not properly his pigeon. Now that the decisive moment was drawing near, when he would be back in his own attenuated element, he was becoming phlegmatic. To him, Gand was a visit among a hundred such, with plenty more to come.

"Your excellency, if you're in serious doubt whether to remain or come with us, I'd be favored if you'd reach a decision fairly soon. Morgan has given me the tip that if I haven't approved the third leave quota by ten o'clock the men are going to take matters into their own hands and walk off."

"That would get them into trouble of a really hot kind, wouldn't it?"

"Some," agreed Captain Grayder, "but not so hot. They intend to turn my own quibbling against me. Since I have not officially forbidden leave, a walk-out won't be mutiny. I've merely been postponing leave. They could plead before the space commission that I've deliberately ignored regulations. They might get away with it if the members were in the mood to assert their authority."

"The commission ought to be taken on a few long flights," opined His Excellency. "They'd discover some things they'll never learn behind a desk." He eyed the other in mock hopefulness. "Any chance of accidentally dropping our cargo of bureaucrats overboard on the way back? A misfortune like that might benefit the spaceways, if not humanity."

"That idea strikes me as Gandish," observed Grayder.

"They wouldn't think of it. Their technique is to say no, no, a thousand times no. That's all—but judging by what has happened here, it is enough." The ambassador pondered his predicament and reached a decision. "I'm coming with you. It goes against the grain because it smacks of surrender. To stay would be a defiant gesture, but I've got to face the fact that it won't serve any useful purpose at the present stage."

"Very well, your excellency." Grayder went to a port and looked through it toward the town. "I'm down about four hundred men. Some of them have deserted, for keeps. The rest will come back if I wait long enough. They've struck lucky, got their legs under somebody's table and gone A.W.O.L. and they're likely to extend their time for as long as the fun lasts on the principle that they may as well be hung for sheep as lambs. I get that sort of trouble on every long trip. It's not so bad on short ones." A pause while moodily he surveyed a terrain bare of returning prodigals. "But we can't wait for them. Not here."

"No, I reckon not."

"If we hang around any longer, we're going to lose another hundred or two. There won't be enough skilled men to take the boat up. Only way I can beat them to the draw is to give the order to prepare for take-off. They all come under flight regulations from that moment." He registered a lopsided smile. "That will give the space lawyers something to think about!"

"As soon as you like," approved the ambassador. He joined the other at the port and studied the distant road, watching as three Gand coaches whirled along it without stopping. He frowned, still upset by the type of mind which insists on pretending that a mountain isn't there. His attention shifted sidewise, toward the tail-end. He stiffened and said, "What are those men doing outside?"

Shooting a swift glance in the same direction, Grayder grabbed the caller mike and rapped, "All personnel will prepare for take-off at once!" Juggling a couple of switches, he changed lines. "Who is that? Sergeant major Bidworthy? Look, sergeant major, there are half a dozen men beyond the midship lock. Get them in immediately—we're lifting as soon as everything's ready."

The fore and aft gangways had been rolled into their stowage spaces long before. Some fast-thinking quartermaster prevented further escapes by operating the midship ladder-wind, thus trapping Bidworthy along with more would-be sinners.

Finding himself stalled, Bidworthy stood in the rim of the lock and glared at those outside. His mustache not only bristled, but quivered. Five of the offenders had been members of the first leave quota. One of them was a trooper. That got his rag out, a trooper. The sixth was Harrison, complete with bicycle polished and shining.

Searing the lot of them, the trooper in particular, Bidworthy rasped, "Get back on board. No arguments. No funny business. We're taking off."

"Hear that?" asked one, nudging the nearest. "Get back on board. If you can't jump thirty feet, you'd better flap your arms and fly."

"No sauce from you," roared Bidworthy. "I've got my orders."

"He takes orders," remarked the trooper. "At his age."

"Can't understand it," commented another, shaking a sorrowful head.

Bidworthy scrabbled the lock's smooth rim in vain search of something to grasp. A ridge, a knob, a projection of some sort was needed to take the strain.

"I warn you men that if you try me too—"

"Save your breath, Biddy," interjected the trooper. "From now on, I'm a Gand." With that, he turned and walked rapidly toward the road, four following.

Getting astride his bike, Harrison put a foot on a pedal. His back tire promptly sank with a loud *wheeee*.

"Come back!" howled Bidworthy at the retreating five. He made extravagant motions, even tried to tear the ladder from its automatic grips. A siren keened thinly inside the vessel. That upped his agitation by several ergs.

"Hear that?" With vein-pulsing ire, he watched Harrison tighten the rear valve and apply his hand pump.

"We're about to lift. For the last time—"

Again the siren, this time in a quick series of shrill toots. Bidworthy jumped backward as the seal came down. The lock closed. Harrison again mounted his machine and settled a foot on a pedal but remained watching.

The metal monster shivered from nose to tail then rose slowly and in utter silence. There was stately magnificence in the ascent of such enormous bulk. It increased its rate of climb gradually, went faster, faster, became a toy, a dot and finally disappeared.

For just a moment, Harrison felt a touch of doubt, a hint of regret. It soon passed away. He glanced toward the road.

The five self-elected Gands had thumbed a coach which was picking them up. That was cooperation apparently precipitated by the ship's disappearance. Quick on the uptake, these people. He saw it move off on huge rubber balls, bearing the five with it. A fan-cycle raced in the opposite direction, humming into the distance.

"Your brunette," Gleed had described her. What gave him that idea? Had she made some remark which he'd construed as complimentary because it made no reference to outsize ears?

He had a last look around. The earth to his left bore a great curved rut one mile long by twelve feet deep. Two thousand Terrans had been there.

Then about eighteen hundred.

Then sixteen hundred.

Less five.

"One left—me!" he said to himself.

Giving a fatalistic shrug, he put the pressure on and rode to town.

And then there were none.

101

William Tenn does not exist; he is a penname, concealing the identity of a marvelously amusing college professor whose career includes demonstrating Christmas toys in a department store, doing comedy turns in the early days of television . . . and writing some of the brightest science-fiction humor around. If *The Liberation of Earth* strikes you as a pungent comment on some currently newsworthy bit of human folly—oh, say, at random, something going on in Indochina—reflect that it was written at a time when most Americans thought Viet Nam was a disaster belonging exclusively to the French. This proves something: either that science fiction does indeed deserve its reputation for predicting the future . . . or that human beings deserve their reputation for dumbness.

THE LIBERATION OF EARTH
by William Tenn

This, then, is the story of our liberation. Suck air and grab clusters. Heigh-ho, here is the tale.

August was the month, a Tuesday in August. These words are meaningless now, so far have we progressed; but many things known and discussed by our primitive ancestors, our unliberated, unreconstructed forefathers, are devoid of sense to our free minds. Still the tale must be told, with all of its incredible place names and vanished points of reference.

Why must it be told? Have any of you a *better* thing to do? We have had water and weeds and lie in a valley of gusts. So rest, relax and listen. And suck air, suck air.

On a Tuesday in August, the ship appeared in the sky over France in a part of the world then known as Europe. Five miles long the ship was, and word has come down to us that it looked like an enormous silver cigar.

The tale goes on to tell of the panic and consternation among our forefathers when the ship abruptly materialized in the summer-blue sky. How they ran, how they shouted, how they pointed!

How they excitedly notified the United Nations, one of their chiefest institutions, that a strange metal craft of incredible size had materialized over their land. How they sent an order *here* to cause military aircraft to surround it with loaded weapons, gave instructions *there* for hastily grouped scientists, with signaling apparatus, to approach it with friendly gestures. How, under the great ship, men with cameras took pictures of it; men with typewriters wrote stories about it; and men with concessions sold models of it.

All these things did our ancestors, enslaved and unknowing, do.

Then a tremendous slab snapped up in the middle of the ship and the first of the aliens stepped out in the complex tripodal gait that all humans were shortly to know and love so well. He wore a metallic garment to protect him from the effects of our atmospheric peculiarities, a garment of the opaque, loosely folded type that these, the first of our liberators, wore throughout their stay on Earth.

Speaking in a language none could understand, but booming deafeningly through a huge mouth about halfway up his twenty-five feet of height, the alien discoursed for exactly one hour, waited politely for a response when he had finished, and, receiving none, retired into the ship.

That night, the first of our liberation! Or the first of our first liberation, should I say? *That* night, anyhow! Visualize our ancestors scurrying about their primitive intricacies: playing ice hockey, televising, smashing atoms, red-baiting, conducting giveaway shows and signing affidavits—all the incredible minutiae that made the olden times such a frightful mass of cumulative detail in which to live—as compared with the breathless

103

and majestic simplicity of the present.

The big question, of course, was—what had the alien said? Had he called on the human race to surrender? Had he announced that he was on a mission of peaceful trade and, having made what he considered a reasonable offer—for, let us say, the north polar ice cap—politely withdrawn so that we could discuss his terms among ourselves in relative privacy? Or, possibly, had he merely announced that he was the newly appointed ambassador to Earth from a friendly and intelligent race —and would we please direct him to the proper authority so that he might submit his credentials?

Not to know was quite maddening.

Since decision rested with the diplomats, it was the last possibility which was held, very late that night, to be most likely; and early the next morning, accordingly, a delegation from the United Nations waited under the belly of the motionless starship. The delegation had been instructed to welcome the aliens to the outermost limits of its collective linguistic ability. As an additional earnest of mankind's friendly intentions, all military craft patrolling the air about the great ship were ordered to carry no more than one atom bomb in their racks, and to fly a small white flag—along with the U.N. banner and their own national emblem. Thus did our ancestors face this, the ultimate challenge of history.

When the alien came forth a few hours later, the delegation stepped up to him, bowed, and, in the three official languages of the United Nations—English, French and Russian—asked him to consider this planet his home. He listened to them gravely, and then launched into his talk of the day before—which was evidently as highly charged with emotion and significance to him as it was completely incomprehensible to the representatives of world government.

Fortunately, a cultivated young Indian member of

104

the secretariat detected a suspicious similarity between the speech of the alien and an obscure Bengali dialect whose anomalies he had once puzzled over. The reason, as we all know now, was that the last time Earth had been visited by aliens of this particular type, humanity's most advanced civilization lay in a moist valley in Bengal; extensive dictionaries of that language had been written, so that speech with the natives of Earth would present no problem to any subsequent exploring party.

However, I move ahead of my tale, as one who would munch on the succulent roots before the dryer stem. Let me rest and suck air for a moment. Heigh-ho, truly those were tremendous experiences for our kind.

You, sir, now you sit back and listen. You are not yet of an age to Tell the Tale. I remember, *well enough do I remember* how my father told it, and his father before him. You will wait your turn as I did; you will listen until too much high land between water holes blocks me off from life.

Then *you* may take your place in the juiciest weed patch and, reclining gracefully between sprints, recite the great epic of our liberation to the carelessly exercising young.

Pursuant to the young Hindu's suggestions, the one professor of comparative linguistics in the world capable of understanding and conversing in this peculiar version of the dead dialect was summoned from an academic convention in New York where he was reading a paper he had been working on for eighteen years: *An Initial Study of Apparent Relationships Between Several Past Participles in Ancient Sanscrit and an Equal Number of Noun Substantives in Modern Szechuanese.*

Yea, verily, all these things—and more, many more —did our ancestors in their besotted ignorance contrive to do. May we not count our freedoms indeed?

The disgruntled scholar, minus—as he kept insisting

bitterly—some of his most essential word lists, was flown by fastest jet to the area south of Nancy which, in those long-ago days, lay in the enormous black shadow of the alien spaceship.

Here he was acquainted with his task by the United Nations delegation, whose nervousness had not been allayed by a new and disconcerting development. Several more aliens had emerged from the ship carrying great quantities of immense, shimmering metal which they proceeded to assemble into something that was obviously a machine—though it was taller than any skyscraper man had ever built, and seemed to make noises to itself like a talkative and sentient creature. The first alien still stood courteously in the neighborhood of the profusely perspiring diplomats; ever and anon he would go through his little speech again, in a language that had been almost forgotten when the cornerstone of the library of Alexandria was laid. The men from the U.N. would reply, each one hoping desperately to make up for the alien's lack of familiarity with his own tongue by such devices as hand gestures and facial expressions. Much later, a commission of anthropologists and psychologists brilliantly pointed out the difficulties of such physical, gestural communication with creatures possessing—as these aliens did—five manual appendages and a single, unwinking compound eye of the type the insects rejoice in.

The problems and agonies of the professor as he was trundled about the world in the wake of the aliens, trying to amass a usable vocabulary in a language whose peculiarities he could only extrapolate from the limited samples supplied him by one who must inevitably speak it with the most outlandish of foreign accents—these vexations were minor indeed compared to the disquiet felt by the representatives of world government. They beheld the extraterrestrial visitors move every day to a new site on their planet and proceed to assemble there a titanic structure of flickering metal which muttered nostalgically to itself, as if to keep alive the memory of those faraway factories which had given it birth.

True, there was always the alien who would pause in his evidently supervisory labors to release the set little speech; but not even the excellent manners he displayed, in listening to upward of fifty-six replies in as many languages, helped dispel the panic caused whenever a human scientist, investigating the shimmering machines, touched a projecting edge and promptly shrank into a disappearing pinpoint. This, while not a frequent occurrence, happened often enough to cause chronic indigestion and insomnia among human administrators.

Finally, having used up most of his nervous system as fuel, the professor collated enough of the language to make conversation possible. He—and, through him, the world—was thereupon told the following:

The aliens were members of a highly advanced civilization which had spread its culture throughout the entire galaxy. Cognizant of the limitations of the as yet underdeveloped animals who had latterly become dominant upon Earth, they had placed us in a sort of benevolent ostracism. Until either we or our institutions had evolved to a level permitting, say, at least *associate* membership in the galactic federation (under the sponsoring tutelage, for the first few millennia, of one of the older, more widespread and more important species in that federation)—until that time, all invasions of our privacy and ignorance—except for a few scientific expeditions conducted under conditions of great secrecy —had been strictly forbidden by universal agreement.

Several individuals who had violated this ruling—at great cost to our racial sanity, and enormous profit to our reigning religions—had been so promptly and severely punished that no known infringements had occurred for some time. Our recent growth curve had been satisfactory enough to cause hopes that a bare thirty or forty centuries more would suffice to place us on applicant status with the federation.

Unfortunately, the peoples of this stellar community were many, and varied as greatly in their ethical outlook as their biological composition. Quite a few species lagged a considerable social distance behind the Dendi, as our visitors called themselves. One of these, a race of horrible, wormlike organisms known as the Troxxt —almost as advanced technologically as they were retarded in moral development—had suddenly volunteered for the position of sole and absolute ruler of the galaxy. They had seized control of several key suns, with their attendant planetary systems, and, after a calculated decimation of the races thus captured, had announced their intention of punishing with a merciless extinction all species unable to appreciate from these object lessons the value of unconditional surrender.

In despair, the galactic federation had turned to the Dendi, one of the oldest, most selfless, and yet most powerful of races in civilized space, and commissioned them, as the military arm of the federation, to hunt down the Troxxt, defeat them wherever they had gained illegal suzerainty, and destroy forever their power to wage war.

This order had come almost too late. Everywhere the Troxxt had gained so much the advantage of attack, that the Dendi were able to contain them only by enormous sacrifice. For centuries now, the conflict had careened across our vast island universe. In the course of it, densely populated planets had been disintegrated; suns had been blasted into novae; and whole groups of stars ground into swirling cosmic dust.

A temporary stalemate had been reached a short while

ago, and, reeling and breathless, both sides were using the lull to strengthen weak spots in their perimeter.

Thus, the Troxxt had finally moved into the till-then peaceful section of space that contained our solar system —among others. They were thoroughly uninterested in our tiny planet with its meager resources; nor did they care much for such celestial neighbors as Mars or Jupiter. They established their headquarters on a planet of Proxima Centaurus, the star nearest our own sun, and proceeded to consolidate their offensive-defensive network between Rigel and Aldebaran. At this point in their explanation, the Dendi pointed out, the exigencies of interstellar strategy tended to become too complicated for anything but three-dimensional maps; let us here accept the simple statement, they suggested, that it became immediately vital for them to strike rapidly, and make the Troxxt position on Proxima Centaurus untenable—to establish a base inside their lines of communication.

The most likely spot for a such a base was Earth.

The Dendi apologized profusely for intruding on our development, an intrusion which might cost us dear in our delicate developmental state. But, as they explained—in impeccable pre-Bengali—before their arrival we had, in effect, become (all unknowingly) a satrapy of the awful Troxxt. We could now consider ourselves liberated.

We thanked them much for that.

Besides, their leader pointed out proudly, the Dendi were engaged in a war for the sake of civilization itself, against an enemy so horrible, so obscene in its nature, and so utterly filthy in its practices, that it was unworthy of the label of intelligent life. They were fighting, not only for themselves, but for every loyal member of the galactic federation; for every small and helpless species; for every obscure race too weak to defend itself against a ravaging conqueror. Would humanity stand aloof from such a conflict?

There was just a slight bit of hesitation as the information was digested. Then: "*No!*" humanity roared back through such mass-communication media as television, newspapers, reverberating jungle drums, and mule-mounted backwoods messenger. "*We will not stand aloof! We will help you destroy this menace to the very fabric of civilization! Just tell us what you want us to do!*"

Well, nothing in particular, the aliens replied with some embarrassment. Possibly in a little while there might *be* something—*several* little things, in fact—which could be *quite* useful; but, for the moment, if we would concentrate on not getting in their way when they serviced their gunmounts, they would be very grateful, really. . . .

This reply tended to create a large amount of uncertainty among the two billion of Earth's human population. For several days afterward, there was a planetwide tendency—the legend has come down to us—of people failing to meet each other's eyes.

But then man rallied from this substantial blow to his pride. He would be useful, be it ever so humbly, to the race which had liberated him from potential subjugation by the ineffably ugly Troxxt. For this, let us remember well our ancestors! Let us hymn their sincere efforts amid their ignorance!

All standing armies, all air and sea fleets, were reorganized into guard patrols around the Dendi weapons: no human might approach within two miles of the murmuring machinery, without a pass countersigned by the Dendi. Since they were never known to sign such a pass during the entire period of their stay on this planet, however, this loophole provision was never exercised as far as is known; and the immediate neighborhood of the extraterrestrial weapons became and remained henceforth wholesomely free of two-legged creatures.

Cooperation with our liberators took precedence over all other human activities. The order of the day was a slogan first given voice by a Harvard professor of government in a querulous radio round table on "Man's Place in a Somewhat Overcivilized Universe."

"Let us forget our individual egos and collective conceits," the professor cried at one point. "Let us subordinate everything—to the end that the freedom of the solar system in general, and Earth in particular, must and shall be preserved!"

Despite its mouth-filling qualities, this slogan was repeated everywhere. Still, it was difficult sometimes to know exactly what the Dendi wanted—partly because of the limited number of interpreters available to the heads of the various sovereign states, and partly because of their leader's tendency to vanish into his ship after ambiguous and equivocal statements, such as the curt admonition to "Evacuate Washington!"

On that occasion, both the Secretary of State and the American President perspired fearfully through five hours of a July day in all the silk-hatted, stiff-collared, dark-suited diplomatic regalia that the barbaric past demanded of political leaders who would deal with the representatives of another people. They waited and wilted beneath the enormous ship—which no human had ever been invited to enter, despite the wistful hints constantly thrown out by university professors and aeronautical designers—they waited patiently and wetly for the Dendi leader to emerge and let them know whether he had meant the State of Washington or Washington, D.C.

The tale comes down to us at this point as a tale of glory. The capitol building taken apart in a few days, and set up almost intact in the foothills of the Rocky Mountains; the missing Archives, that were later to turn up in the children's room of a public library in Duluth, Iowa; the bottles of Potomac River water carefully borne westward and ceremoniously poured into the circular concrete ditch built around the President's mansion (from which unfortunately it was to evaporate within a week because of the relatively low humidity of the region)—all these are proud moments in the galactic history of our species, from which not even the later knowledge that the Dendi wished to build no gun site on the spot, nor even an ammunition dump, but merely a recreation hall for their troops, could remove any of the grandeur of our determined cooperation and most willing sacrifice.

There is no denying, however, that the ego of our race was greatly damaged by the discovery, in the course of a routine journalistic interview, that the aliens totaled no more powerful a group than a squad; and that their leader, instead of the great scientist and key military strategist that we might justifiably have expected the Galactic Federation to furnish for the protection of Terra, ranked as the interstellar equivalent of a buck sergeant.

That the President of the United States, the Commander-in-Chief of the Army and the Navy, had waited in such obeisant fashion upon a mere noncommissioned officer was hard for us to swallow; but that the impending Battle of Earth was to have a historical dignity only slightly higher than that of a patrol action was impossibly humiliating.

And then there was the matter of "lendi".

The aliens, while installing or servicing their planet-wide weapon system, would occasionally fling aside an evidently unusable fragment of the talking metal. Separated from the machine of which it had been a com-

112

ponent, the substance seemed to lose all those qualities which were deleterious to mankind and retain several which were quite useful indeed. For example, if a portion of the strange material was attached to any terrestial metal and insulated carefully from contact with other substances it would, in a few hours, itself become exactly the metal that it touched, whether that happened to be zinc, gold, or pure uranium.

This stuff—"lendi", men have heard the aliens call it—was shortly in frantic demand in an economy ruptured by constant and unexpected emptyings of its most important industrial centers.

Everywhere the aliens went, to and from their weapon sites, hordes of ragged humans stood chanting—well outside the two-mile limit—"Any lendi, Dendi?" All attempts by law enforcement agencies of the planet to put a stop to this shameless, wholesale begging were useless, especially since the Dendi themselves seemed to get some unexplainable pleasure out of scattering tiny pieces of lendi to the scrabbling multitude. When policemen and soldiery began to join the trampling, murderous dash to the corner of the meadows wherein had fallen the highly versatile and garrulous metal, governments gave up.

Mankind almost began to hope for the attack to come, so that it would be relieved of the festering consideration of its own patent inferiorities. A few of the more fanatically conservative among our ancestors probably even began to regret liberation.

They did, children; they did! Let us hope that these would-be troglodytes were among the very first to be dissolved and melted down by the red flameballs. One cannot, after all, turn one's back on progress!

Two days before the month of September was over, the aliens announced that they had detected activity upon one of the moons of Saturn. The Troxxt were

113

evidently threading their treacherous way inward through the solar system. Considering their vicious and deceitful propensities, the Dendi warned, an attack from these wormlike monstrosities might be expected at any moment.

Few humans went to sleep as the night rolled up to and past the meridian on which they dwelt. Almost all eyes were lifted to a sky carefully denuded of clouds by watchful Dendi. There was a brisk trade in cheap telescopes and bits of smoked glass in some sections of the planet; while other portions experienced a substantial boom in spells and charms of the all-inclusive, or omnibus, variety.

The Troxxt attacked in three cylindrical black ships simultaneously; one in the southern hemisphere, and two in the northern. Great gouts of green flame roared out of their tiny craft; and everything touched by this imploded into a translucent, glasslike sand. No Dendi was hurt by these, however, and from each of the now-writhing gunmounts there bubbled forth a series of scarlet clouds which pursued the Troxxt hungrily, until forced by a dwindling velocity to fall back upon Earth.

Here they had an unhappy aftereffect. Any populated area into which these pale pink cloudlets chanced to fall was rapidly transformed into a cemetery—a cemetery, if the truth be told as it has been handed down to us, that had more the odor of the kitchen than the grave. The inhabitants of these unfortunate localities were subjected to enormous increases of temperature. Their skin reddened, then blackened; their hair and nails shriveled; their very flesh turned into liquid and boiled off their bones. Altogether a disagreeable way for one-tenth of the human race to die.

The only consolation was the capture of a black cylinder by one of the red clouds. When, as a result of this, it had turned white-hot and poured its substance

114

down in the form of a metallic rainstorm, the two ships assaulting the northern hemisphere abruptly retreated to the asteroids into which the Dendi, because of severely limited numbers, steadfastly refused to pursue them.

In the next twenty-four hours the aliens—*resident* aliens, let us say—held conferences, made repairs to their weapons and commiserated with us. Humanity buried its dead. This last was a custom of our forefathers that was most worthy of note; and one that has not, of course, survived into modern times.

By the time the Troxxt returned, man was ready for them. He could not, unfortunately, stand to arms as he most ardently desired to do; but he could and did stand to optical instrument and conjurer's oration.

Once more the little red clouds burst joyfully into the upper reaches of the stratosphere; once more the green flames wailed and tore at the chattering spires of lendi; once more men died by the thousands in the boiling backwash of war. But this time, there was a slight difference: the green flames of the Troxxt abruptly changed color after the engagement had lasted three hours; they became darker, more bluish. And, as they did so, Dendi after Dendi collapsed at his station and died in convulsions.

The call for retreat was evidently sounded. The survivors fought their way to the tremendous ship in which they had come. With an explosion from her stern jets that blasted a red-hot furrow southward through France, and kicked Marseilles into the Mediterranean, the ship roared into space and fled home ignominiously.

Humanity steeled itself for the coming ordeal of horror under the Troxxt.

They were truly wormlike in form. As soon as the two night-black cylinders had landed, they strode from

115

their ships, their tiny segmented bodies held off the ground by a complex harness supported by long and slender metal crutches. They erected a domelike fort around each ship—one in Australia and one in the Ukraine—captured the few courageous individuals who had ventured close to their landing sites, and disappeared back into the dark craft with their squirming prizes.

While some men drilled about nervously in the ancient military patterns, others pored anxiously over scientific texts and records pertaining to the visit of the Dendi, in the desperate hope of finding a way of preserving terrestrial independence against this ravening conqueror of the star-spattered galaxy.

And yet all this time, the human captives inside the artificially darkened spaceships (the Troxxt, having no eyes, not only had little use for light but the more sedentary individuals among them actually found such radiation disagreeable to their sensitive, unpigmented skins) were not being tortured for information—nor vivisected in the earnest quest of knowledge on a slightly higher level—but educated.

Educated in the Troxxtian language, that is.

True it was that a large number found themselves utterly inadequate for the task which the Troxxt had set them, and temporarily became servants to the more successful students. And another, albeit smaller, group developed various forms of frustration hysteria—ranging from mild unhappiness to complete catatonic depression—over the difficulties presented by a language whose every verb was irregular, and whose myriads of prepositions were formed by noun-adjective combinations derived from the subject of the previous sentence. But, eventually, eleven human beings were released, to blink madly in the sunlight as certified interpreters of Troxxt.

These liberators, it seemed, had never visited Bengal

in the heyday of its millennia-past civilization.

Yes, these *liberators*. For the Troxxt had landed on the sixth day of the ancient, almost mythical month of October. And October the Sixth is, of course, the Holy Day of the Second Liberation. Let us remember, let us revere. (If only we could figure out which day it is on our calendar!)

The tale the interpreters told caused men to hang their heads in shame and gnash their teeth at the deception they had allowed the Dendi to practice upon them.

True, the Dendi had been commissioned by the Galactic Federation to hunt the Troxxt down and destroy them. This was largely because the Dendi *were* the Galactic Federation. One of the first intelligent arrivals on the interstellar scene, the huge creatures had organized a vast police force to protect them and their power against any contingency of revolt that might arise in the future. This police force was ostensibly a congress of all thinking life forms throughout the galaxy; actually, it was an efficient means of keeping them under rigid control.

Most species thus far discovered were docile and tractable, however; the Dendi had been ruling from time immemorial, said they—very well, then, let the Dendi continue to rule. Did it make that much difference?

But, throughout the centuries, opposition to the Dendi grew; and the nuclei of the opposition were the protoplasm-based creatures. What, in fact, had come to be known as the Protoplasmic League.

Though small in number, the creatures whose life cycles were derived from the chemical and physical properties of protoplasm varied greatly in size, structure, and specialization. A galactic community deriving the main wells of its power from them would be a dynamic instead of a static place, where extragalactic

117

travel would be encouraged, instead of being inhibited, as it was at present because of Dendi fears of meeting a superior civilization. It would be a true democracy of species—a real biological republic—where all creatures of adequate intelligence and cultural development would enjoy a control of their destinies at present experienced by the silicon-based Dendi alone.

To this end, the Troxxt, the only important race which had steadfastly refused the complete surrender of armaments demanded of all members of the Federation, had been implored by a minor member of the Protoplasmic League to rescue it from the devastation which the Dendi intended to visit upon it, as punishment for an unlawful exploratory excursion outside the boundaries of the galaxy.

Faced with the determination of the Troxxt to defend their cousins in organic chemistry, and the suddenly aroused hostility of at least two-thirds of the interstellar peoples, the Dendi had summoned a rump meeting of the Galactic Council; declared a state of revolt in being; and proceeded to cement their disintegrating rule with the blasted life forces of a hundred worlds. The Troxxt, hopelessly outnumbered and outequipped, had been able to continue the struggle only because of the great ingenuity and selflessness of other members of the Protoplasmic League, who had risked extinction to supply them with newly developed secret weapons.

Hadn't we guessed the nature of the beast from the enormous precautions it had taken to prevent the exposure of any part of its body to the intensely corrosive atmosphere of Earth? Surely the seamless, barely translucent suits which our recent visitors had worn for every moment of their stay on our world should have made us suspect a body chemistry developed from complex silicon compounds rather than those of carbon?

Humanity hung its collective head and admitted that

the suspicion had never occurred to it.

Well, the Troxxt admitted generously, we were extremely inexperienced and possibly a little too trusting. Put it down to that. Our naiveté, however costly to them, our liberators, would not be allowed to deprive us of that complete citizenship which the Troxxt were claiming as the birthright of all.

But as for our leaders, our probably corrupted, certainly irresponsible leaders. . . .

The first executions of U.N. officials, heads of states, and pre-Bengali interpreters as "Traitors to Protoplasm" —after some of the lengthiest and most nearly perfectly fair trials in the history of Earth—were held a week after G-J Day, the inspiring occasion on which, amidst gorgeous ceremonies, humanity was invited to join, first the Protoplasmic League and thence the New and Democratic Galactic Federation of All Species, All Races.

Nor was that all. Whereas the Dendi had contemptuously shoved us to one side as they went about their business of making our planet safe for tyranny, and had, in all probability, built special devices which made the very touch of their weapons fatal for us, the Troxxt —with the sincere friendliness which had made their name a byword for democracy and decency wherever living creatures came together among the stars—our Second Liberators, as we lovingly called them, actually *preferred* to have us help them with the intensive, accelerating labor of planetary defense.

So men's intestines dissolved under the invisible glare of the forces used to assemble the new, incredibly complex weapons; men sickened and died, in scrabbling hordes, inside the mines which the Troxxt had made deeper than any we had dug hitherto; men's bodies broke open and exploded in the undersea oil-drilling sites which the Troxxt had declared were essential.

119

Children's schooldays were requested, too, in such collecting drives as "Platinum Scrap for Procyon" and "Radioactive Debris for Deneb". Housewives also were implored to save on salt whenever possible—this substance being useful to the Troxxt in literally dozens of incomprehensible ways—and colorful posters reminded: *"Don't salinate—sugarfy!"*

And over all, courteously caring for us like an intelligent parent, were our mentors, taking their giant supervisory strides on metallic crutches, while their pale little bodies lay curled in the hammocks that swung from each paired length of shining leg.

Truly, even in the midst of a complete economic paralysis caused by the concentration of all major productive facilities on otherworldly armaments, and despite the anguished cries of those suffering from peculiar industrial injuries which our medical men were totally unequipped to handle, in the midst of all this mind-wracking disorganization, it was yet very exhilarating to realize that we had taken our lawful place in the future government of the galaxy and were even now helping to make the universe safe for democracy.

But the Dendi returned to smash this idyll. They came in their huge, silvery spaceships and the Troxxt, barely warned in time, just managed to rally under the blow and fight back in kind. Even so, the Troxxt ship in the Ukraine was almost immediately forced to flee to its base in the depths of space. After three days, the only Troxxt on Earth were the devoted members of a little band guarding the ship in Australia. They proved, in three or more months, to be as difficult to remove from the face of our planet as the continent itself; and since there was now a state of close and hostile siege, with the Dendi on one side of the globe, and the Troxxt on the other, the battle assumed frightful proportions.

Seas boiled; whole steppes burned away; the climate itself shifted and changed under the gruelling pressure of the cataclysm. By the time the Dendi solved the problem, the planet Venus had been blasted from the skies in the course of a complicated battle maneuver, and Earth had wobbled over as orbital substitute.

The solution was simple: since the Troxxt were too firmly based on the small continent to be driven away, the numerically superior Dendi brought up enough fire-power to disintegrate all Australia into an ash that muddied the Pacific. This occurred on the twenty-fourth of June, the Holy Day of First Reliberation. A day of reckoning for what remained of the human race, however.

How could we have been so naive, the Dendi wanted to know, as to be taken in by the chauvinistic pro-protoplasm propaganda? Surely, if physical characteristics were to be the criteria of our racial empathy, we would not orient ourselves on a narrow chemical basis! The Dendi life plasma was based on silicon instead of carbon, true, but did not vertebrates—*appendaged* vertebrates, at that, such as we and the Dendi—have infinitely more in common, in spite of a *minor* bio-chemical difference or two, than vertebrates and legless, armless, slime-crawling creatures who happened, quite accidentally, to possess an identical organic substance?

As for this fantastic picture of life in the galaxy . . . *well!* The Dendi shrugged their quintuple shoulders as they went about the intricate business of erecting their noisy weapons all over the rubble of our planet. Had we ever seen a representative of these protoplasmic races the Troxxt were supposedly protecting? No, nor would we. For as soon as a race—animal, vegetable or mineral—developed enough to constitute even a *potential* danger to the sinuous aggressors, its civilization was systematically dismantled by the watchful Troxxt. We were in so primitive a state that they had not considered it at all risky to allow us the outward seeming of full participation.

Could we say we had learned a single useful piece of information about Troxxt technology, for all of the work we had done on their machines, for all of the lives we had lost in the process? No, of course not! We had merely contributed our mite to the enslavement of far-off races who had done us no harm.

There was much that we had cause to feel guilty about, the Dendi told us gravely—once the few surviving interpreters of the pre-Bengali dialect had crawled out of hiding. But our collective onus was as nothing compared to that borne by "vermicular collaborationists"—those traitors who had supplanted our martyred former leaders. And then there were the unspeakable human interpreters who had had linguistic traffic with creatures destroying a two-million-year-old galactic peace! Why, killing was almost too good for them, the Dendi murmured as they killed them.

When the Troxxt ripped their way back into possession of Earth some eighteen months later, bringing us the sweet fruits of the Second Reliberation—as well as a complete and most convincing rebuttal of the Dendi—there were few humans found who were willing to accept with any real enthusiasm the responsibilities of newly opened and highly paid positions in language, science, and government.

Of course, since the Troxxt, in order to reliberate Earth, had found it necessary to blast a tremendous chunk out of the northern hemisphere, there were very few humans to be found in the first place. . . .

Even so, many of these committed suicide rather than assume the title of Secretary General of the United Nations when the Dendi came back for the glorious Re-

Reliberation, a short time after that. This was the liberation, by the way, which swept the deep collar of matter off our planet, and gave it what our forefathers came to call a pear-shaped look.

Possibly it was at this time—possibly a liberation or so later—that the Troxxt and the Dendi discovered the Earth had become far too eccentric in its orbit to possess the minimum safety conditions demanded of a combat zone. The battle, therefore, zigzagged coruscatingly and murderously away in the direction of Aldebaran.

That was nine generations ago, but the tale that has been handed down from parent to child, to child's child, has lost little in the telling. You hear it now from me almost exactly as *I* heard it. From my father I heard it as I ran with him from water puddle to distant water puddle, across the searing heat of yellow sand. From my mother I heard it as we sucked air and frantically grabbed at clusters of thick green weed, whenever the planet beneath us quivered in omen of a geological spasm that might bury us in its burned-out body, or a cosmic gyration threatened to fling us into empty space.

Yes, even as we do now did we do then, telling the same tale, running the same frantic race across miles of unendurable heat for food and water; fighting the same savage battles with the giant rabbits for each other's carrion—and always, ever and always, sucking desperately at the precious air, which leaves our world in greater quantities with every mad twist of its orbit.

Naked, hungry, and thirsty came we into the world, and naked, hungry, and thirsty do we scamper our lives out upon it, under the huge and never-changing sun.

The same tale it is, and the same traditional ending it has as that I had from my father and his father before him. Suck air, grab clusters, and hear the last holy observation of our history:

"*Looking about us, we can say with pardonable pride*

that we have been about as thoroughly liberated as it is possible for a race and a planet to be!"

Raymond Z. Gallun is a gentle and self-effacing man who for a good many decades wrote first-rate science fiction of all kinds. *Old Faithful* is perhaps his best-known story, and it is one that is a particular favorite of my own (the male half of the editorial collaboration speaking). I was well pleased when the female half of the collaboration enthusiastically voted to include this, because it gives me a chance to tell a story. Once upon a time I was Ray Gallun's literary agent. As such, I sold this story to a television program, and in due course it was scripted, produced and broadcast. The response was very good from all the viewers but one, and that one was the agent for one of the most famous writers in science fiction, who called up in blinding anger because he had seen the story on TV, and he knew that it was an indisputable plagiarism from one of his client's stories. I played it cool. Are you *sure* there's plagiarism? I asked. Bet your life, he said, there are simply too many features in common for anyone to have written either story without having read the other. Ah, I said, knowing the answer to the question before I asked it, and *when* did your writer's story appear? Because my writer's was first published in 1934, at which time your fellow, I happen to know, was like thirteen years old. . . .

OLD FAITHFUL
By Raymond Z. Gallun

If Number 774 had been a human being, he might have cursed bitterly or he might have wept. Certainly he had reason to do so. But Number 774 was not a human being. His fragile form bore not the slightest resemblance to that of a man; he knew nothing of smiles or frowns or tears, and whatever emotions passed within his cool, keen mind were hidden even to members of his own race.

The two messengers who had come to his workshop

that afternoon had not seen into his heart, and he received their message with the absolute outward calm that was characteristic of his kind—at the end of forty days Number 774 must die. He had lived the allotted span fixed by the Rulers.

With food and water as scarce as they were, no one had the right to live longer unless he had proved through the usefulness of his achievements that it was for the good of all that he be granted an extension. Otherwise the young and strong must always replace the old and weak.

In the opinion of the Rulers the work of Number 774 was not useful; it was without value and was even wasteful. An extension of life-span could not be considered; Number 774 must die.

Having imparted this information the messengers had crept into the streamlined hull of their ornithopter. Silvery wings had flapped, and the weird craft had lifted lightly, circled the great isolated workshop once in parting salute, and then had sped off into the west toward a distant city.

In obedience to some impulse Number 774 had ascended to a high-placed window in the towering wall of his domicile, to watch the ornithopter go. But long after the glinting metallic speck of its form had vanished into the sunset, Number 774 continued to stare out toward the west. Pools of purple shade swelled and broadened in the hollows between the dunes of the Martian desert that stretched in undulating flatness to the far horizon.

The sun sank out of sight, leaving only a faint reddish glow that quickly faded out at the rim of the world. The Martian sky, deep purple and shot with stars even during the day, became almost black, and the stars, veiled by an atmosphere only one-sixth as dense as that of Earth, gleamed with a steady and eerie brilliance that is never seen by terrestrial observers.

It was a strange, beautiful sight, and perhaps in other circumstances something fine and paradoxically human in Number 774's being might have appreciated its wild and lonely grandeur. But natural splendors could scarcely have interested him now, for his mind was too full of other things.

In the sky was a tiny gray-green streak which he knew marked the position of an approaching comet. For a long moment he stared at it; and then his gaze wandered up among the welter of stars and sought out a greenish silver speck far brighter than any of its fellows.

For many minutes his attention clung unwavering to that brilliant point of light. He knew more about that planet than any other inhabitant of Mars. He had never heard its name, nor in fact did he have a vocal name of his own for it. To him it was just the world which held the third orbital position in order from the sun. And yet, for him, there was concentrated in it all the hopes and all the fascination of a lifetime of painstaking work and effort.

Gradually, by patient, methodical observation, he had wrested a few of its secrets from it. He had learned the composition of its atmosphere; he could describe its climates accurately; he even knew something about its soil. But beyond such superficial information for a long time it seemed that he could never go.

And then one night when, with stoical resignation, he had all but laid aside his fondest dream, a sign had come. The third planet, Earth, was inhabited by thinking beings. It was not a spectacular sign; neither was his conclusion guesswork. Number 774's telescope had revealed, on the darkened side of Earth, between the limbs of its crescent, a barely discernible flicker of light flashes, evenly spaced, and repeated at perfectly regular intervals. Only a high order of intelligence could have produced such signals.

Dominated by a new zeal, Number 774 had constructed a gigantic apparatus and had duplicated the Earthian signals flash for flash. Immediately he had been answered. Then he had tried a new arrangement of flashes, and the unknown beings on Planet Three had seen, for they had repeated his signals perfectly.

For five Martian years, the equivalent of nearly ten passages of the Earth around the sun, he and the unimaginable entities on that other world, hardly ever less than thirty-five million miles away, had labored on the colossal problem of intelligent communication.

The results of their efforts had been small and discouraging; yet in ten or twenty years even that gigantic enigma might have yielded to persistence, ingenuity, and the indomitable will to do. But now no such thing could be. In forty days Number 774 would no longer exist. Nor would there be another to carry on his work.

Study of the third world could not produce more food or make water more plentiful. The Rulers would dismantle all the marvelous equipment that he had assembled to aid him in his quest for useless and impractical knowledge. The veil of mystery would remain drawn over Planet Three for many thousands of years, perhaps forever.

But it was the Rulers' privilege to command and to expect unquestioning obedience. Never once in a millennium had their authority been disputed; for the very existence of the dominant race of Mars, a world aged almost to the limit of its ability to support life, depended on absolute spartan loyalty and discipline. Revolt now was unheard of; it could not be.

Did Number 774 feel resentment over his fate? Or did he accept his sentence with the stoicism of a true child of Mars? There was no way of telling. His position was almost unduplicated in the annals of the Red Planet, and, in consequence, his reactions may have been out of the ordinary. Almost never before had a creature of his kind wandered so far along the road of impractical knowledge, or had received the notice of the termination of life-span so inopportunely.

And so Number 774 continued to gaze up at the green star that had been included in every dream and effort of his existence. Thoughts and feelings must have tumbled in riotous confusion inside his brain.

After a while Phobos, the nearer moon, mounted up over the western * horizon and began its rapid march among the stars. Its pallid radiance converted everything into a half-seen fairyland of tarnished silver and ebony, the dunes of the lonely desert extending mile on mile in every direction, the low, fortlike walls of Number 774's workshop, the great shining dome of metal that capped it. Nothing was clearly discernible, nothing seemed real.

The coming of Phobos aroused Number 774 from his lethargy. It may be that he realized that time was fleeting, and that an hour could ill be spared from the forty days of life that still remained to him. At a deft touch the crystal pane that glazed the window before him slipped aside, and a faint night breeze, arid and chilled far below zero, blew in upon him.

Edging his strange form forward, he leaned far out of the window and seemed intent upon creeping headlong down the rough stone wall. Long slender portions of his anatomy clutched the sill, and he hung inverted like

* Mars rotates on its axis in 24 hours, 37 minutes, 22.67 seconds. Phobos, the nearer Moon, which is only 3,700 miles distant from Mars, completes its orbit in only 7 hours, 39 minutes, thus circling its primary more than three times in every Martian day. Since Phobos follows its path in the same direction that the planet rotates, it is evident that to an observer on Mars, it would appear to rise in the west and set in the east.

a roosting bat of Earth. But otherwise there was not the remotest resemblance between Number 774 and a winged terrestrial mammal.

If, by means of some miraculous transition, an Earthman had suddenly found himself standing there on the desert and looking up at the wall of the workshop close above, he might not even have recognized Number 774 as a living creature in the shifting, uncertain moonlight. Amid the fantastic jumble of light and shade he would have seen only a blob of rusty brown color that might have been just the distorted shadow of one of the stone projections that jutted from the wall.

If he had looked closer he might have believed that the thing he saw was a small bundle of ancient and rotten rags dangling from the window ledge, with long, loose tatters stirring idly in the faint breeze. Still, the glint of bright metal from Number 774's equipment would have puzzled him, and perhaps his flesh would have tingled slightly at the suggestively gruesome aspect of this unknown and poorly illuminated object.

From his dangling position Number 774 sucked a great breath of cold air into his complex breathing organs. The frigid tang of the night refreshed him and seemed to endow him with new life. One last glance he cast toward the glory of the Martian heavens. At sight of Earth and the threadlike speck of the comet, his great eyes, dark and limpid and more nearly human than anything else about him, flashed briefly with a vague, slumberous suggestion of something pent up behind a barrier that was none too strong to hold it back. Then Number 774 drew himself up into the window.

Three jointed rods of metal unfolded themselves from the complicated arrangement of mechanisms that was fastened to his fragile body, and in a moment he was striding along on them like a man, down a green-lighted cylindrical passage that extended off into misty obscurity. A faint and regular clicking came from the device, but Number 774 did not hear it. He knew of sound only as a vibration detectable by his keen sense of touch, and as a phenomenon registered by his scientific instruments, for Number 774 had no organs of hearing.

His steps seemed hurried and feverish. Perhaps some un-Martian plan was already half formulated in his restless and troubled mind.

The tunnel debouched at last into a colossal chamber where gigantic flying buttresses swept up and up through a misty green glow to meet the sides of an enormous rotunda of white metal that roofed the room.

Enigmatic forms of weird apparatus crowded in bewildering complexity against the walls. Tipped at a steep angle at the center of the floor was a vast cylinder of webby girders. Piercing the dome, opposite the upper end of the cylinder, was a circular opening through which a portion of the starlit sky was visible; and at the base of the cylinder a great bowl rotated rapidly, like a huge wheel.

Here was the observatory of Number 774, housing his telescope, and here were the controlling mechanisms of his signaling apparatus. He hurried up a steep ramp, from the upper end of which he could look down into the interior of the great rotating bowl. His eyes glanced critically over the device, searching for any possible slight disorder in its function. But there was none.

To an Earthman acquainted with astronomical equipment, the purpose of the rotating bowl would have been at once apparent, and he would have marveled at the simple cleverness of this piece of Martian ingenuity.

The bowl contained mercury. As the container spun on its perfectly balanced axis, centrifugal force caused the mercury to spread in a thin, precisely distributed layer over the inside of the bowl, forming a convex surface that acted admirably as a mirror for Number 774's gigantic reflecting telescope. Its area, and its consequent light-collecting capacity, was many times greater than any rigid mirror that could have been constructed without flaws.

Satisfied with his inspection, Number 774 hoisted himself nimbly to a small platform, placed high among the spidery girders of the chamber. His movements were quick and catlike, yet coolly efficient, and he seemed bent upon making use of every moment of life that remained to him.

His eyes almost lambent with eagerness, he stared into the large crystal sphere which the platform supported. From a prismatic arrangement fixed to the telescope arrangement above, an invisible beam of light came down, impinging on the sphere and causing the picture which Number 774 was so intent upon to appear.

In the depths of the crystal was an image of the third world, Earth. Since it was to sunward and nearing inferior conjunction with Mars, most of its surface that was turned to the Red Planet was in shadow and could not be seen. Only a thin curve of light fringed one hemisphere.

Visible in the crescent were mottled areas of gray and green and brown, which Number 774 knew were oceans, continents, deserts, and verdant countryside. The shifting blurs of clouds, the winding rivers, and the snow-capped mountain chains, he could recognize and understand, too; but there was so much that distance and the distorting effects of two atmospheres left hidden and seemingly unattainable—things about which he had longed so passionately to see and to know.

A delicate bundle of pink filaments that terminated one of Number 774's stalklike limbs rested on a tiny lever before him. The threadlike tentacles, marvelously adapted and trained for the finest and most accurate sort of work, moved the lever slightly to the right.

Immediately there was responding movement in the heavy parts of the huge telescope, and the image of Planet Three in the crystal globe began to grow. Mountains loomed larger; seas and continents swelled until the whole of the image of the terrestrial sphere could not occupy the globe, and all that could be seen was a small part of the illuminated crescent.

For a while, as the increase in magnification went on, details on Planet Three were brought more clearly into view; but presently, as the picture grew larger and larger, it began to tremble and to undulate, as if it were seen through a million atmospheric heat waves.

As the power of the telescope was increased still further, the flickering, jumping, shifting luminescence that appeared in the vision globe became totally incoherent and meaningless and bore no slight relationship to an Earthly scene. Number 774's huge optical instrument was failing before one of the same obstacles to magnification that terrestrial observers have noted in their telescopes.

The gaseous envelopes of Earth and Mars, with their countless irregular air currents and varying indices of refraction due to differences in temperature and humidity, were distorting the image-bearing rays of light coming from Earth across fifty million miles of space and rendering magnification beyond a certain point useless. The telescope of Number 774 still had many Martian units of magnification in reserve, but for probing into the mysteries of Planet Three that reserve was of not the least value.

Still, Number 774 often gave his instrument full power in the vain hope, perhaps, that some day, by some trick of fate, the atmospheres of the two worlds would be quiet enough and clear enough to give him a momentary glimpse into the unknown. But the opportunity for such a glimpse had never come.

Cool and collected, Number 774 brought his telescope back to the limit of effective magnification. In response to the manipulation of some instrument, the image of Planet Three shifted so that no portion of the crescent was visible. The crystal globe was dark, but Number 774 knew that the third world was within the field of view.

Unerringly, guided by his instruments, he fixed his telescope on a certain spot on the dark side of Planet Three. He knew that shrouded in the shadows of the night hemisphere of that distant world there was a great continent extending broad and diversified, between two vast oceans. It had lofty ranges of snow-crowned mountains, extensive plains green with an unknown vegetation, great lakes, and winding rivers. In the southwestern portion of that continent was a desert, and near the edge of that desert was the Place of the Light—the light that was the voice of the friend he had never seen, and whose form was unimaginable to him, much though he might imagine and long to know.

The light was not there now; only the vague, white blurs of Earthly cities dotting the darkened continent, adding the mystery of their existence to the enigma of Planet Three. But Number 774 was not troubled by the absence of the light, for he had faith in it. When he had signaled, it had always appeared in answer; it would appear this time, too.

At his touch a vast mechanism in a room far beneath the chamber of the telescope began to function silently and efficiently, building up power. Feeble and delicate and hideous though Number 774 was by Earthly standards, at a mere gesture he could evoke forces that were worthy of the gods.

Number 774 watched a Martian version of a potentiometer. It was not like a terrestrial potentiometer. It had no graduated scale, no nervous pointer. It was just a globe of something that looked like frosted glass, from which a soft luminescence proceeded.

First, Number 774 saw in its depths a slumberous glow of a beautiful shade, quite unknown and unseeable to human eyes. It was what is called infrared on Earth. The color, being invisible to men, was of course quite indescribable, but to Number 774 it was as common as blue or yellow, for his eyes, like the eyes of some of the lower forms of Earth, were constructed to see it.

In addition, like all Martians, he was able to distinguish the slightest difference between one shade of color and another.

It is upon this fact that Martians depend for the accurate reading of instruments which, among men, would ordinarily have pointers and graduated scales. In any Martian meter, infrared, and of course the various shades of infrared, in their order of appearance in the spectrum, means a low reading. Red, and the shades of red, advancing toward orange, constitute somewhat higher readings. Orange, yellow, green, blue, and violet are progressively higher; while the shade at the extreme outer end of the ultraviolet band, which Martian eyes can also see, represents the highest reading.

In short, light of various wavelengths is used in practically all Martian meters to designate readings. Low readings are represented by long wavelengths near the infrared end of the spectrum; while high readings are designated by short wavelengths near the ultraviolet end of the spectrum.

Number 774 waited until the changing kaleidoscope of ordinary colors had passed and the delicate hue of ultraviolet had reached its maximum in the globe of the potentiometer before he made any further move. Then his tense body swayed forward, closing a complicated switch.

The result was instantaneous. Through the circular opening in the rotunda, at which the muzzle of the telescope was pointed, a dazzling blaze of incandescence was visible in a sudden tremendous flash. The detonation that accompanied it was of a magnitude which one would have scarcely believed the rarefied atmosphere of old Mars capable of transmitting. The whole building, solidly constructed though it was, trembled with the concussion.

For a moment the Martian night, within a radius of twenty miles or more of Number 774's workshop, became brighter than midday, as an enormous store of energy, released from the outer surface of the metal dome which capped the observatory, poured suddenly into the atmosphere, thus forming above the workshop a vast canopy of cold light, far more intense than any aurora borealis of Earth.

But the sudden flare died out as quickly as it had come; the echoes of the crash faded, and the calm of lonely desert and stars reasserted itself. Some eerie monster, which had unwittingly buried itself in the sand too close to the lair of Number 774, scrambled out of its warm sleeping place amid a cloud of dust and on gauzy wings sped hurriedly away from the zone of the thunder that had terrified it. As it flew, its fantastic shadow bobbed crazily over the moonlit sand.

But Number 774 was quite oblivious of any fears his experiments might arouse in the creatures of Mars. As far as his mind was concerned, for the time being things Martian had almost ceased to exist for him. Earth, Planet Three, claimed all his attention, and there was room for nothing else. He had given his sign; now he would wait for the answer that was sure to come.

It would take approximately nine minutes for Earth

to get signals back to him. For that was the time which light, traveling at a speed of 186,000 miles per second, required to bridge twice the fifty-million-mile void lying between the two planets.

Number 774's weird, fragile body hunched eagerly forward on the small mat on which he squatted. His great eyes burned with the same fire of fascination which they had held when, a little while ago, he had gazed up at Earth and the approaching comet from the window in the wall of his workshop. Unwaveringly they were fixed on the spot in the darkened vision globe where the light would appear.

Sometimes that light was too dim for his trained and sensitive eyes to see; but arranged and hooded on a carefully shaded portion of the vision globe was a Martian photoelectric cell which would pick up the faintest of light signals and convert them into electrical impulses which would be amplified and relayed to an instrument close beside Number 774.

This instrument would reproduce the signals just as they came from Earth, but bright enough to be easily watched. Another device would record each flash for later study.

II

The body of Number 774 tensed suddenly. There was the first signal, flickering faint and feeble across the millions of miles of space; yet on the desert of Earth it doubtless represented flashes almost comparable with those which Number 774's powerful sending equipment produced.

Number 774 could barely see them in his vision globe, but the little glass bulb of the reproducing apparatus flickered them out plain and clear—long flashes, short flashes, representing the dots and dashes of the Morse code of Earth.

Flash—flash—flash—flash——

"Hello, Mars! Hello, Mars! Hello, Mars! Earth calling. Earth calling. Earth calling," the message spelled, and Number 774 was grimly in the midst of the colossal task he had set for himself.

Lurking in the back of his mind was the realization that his death was decreed and that soon, unless something unprecedented happened, all this work of his, and of his friend of the light, must end, unfinished, before the intelligences of two worlds could really meet and exchange ideas freely. But it did not divert him or make his attention to the task in hand less keen. In fact it seemed to sharpen his wits and to add pressure to his determination.

Still, his mind seemed divided into two parts, one of which was cool and logical and scientific, the other in a turmoil, fighting with itself and its loyalty to time-honored traditions.

"Hello, Mars! Hello, Mars! Earth calling. Man of Mars is late—late—late—late—— One, two, three, four, five, six, seven, eight, nine, ten. Four and five are nine. Two times three is six. Man of Mars is late—late—late —late—"

How much of this queer jangle of light flashes, spelling out Earth words and numbers in the Morse code, did Number 774 understand? How much *could* he understand?

Intelligent comprehension of anything new is almost always based on an understanding of similar things previously in the experience of the individual in question. The mind of Number 774 was brilliantly clever and methodical, but what can an Earthman and a Martian have in common? Many points of contact exist, it is true, but for two entities so far removed from one another in physical form, senses, environment, and modes of living, with not the vaguest conception of what the other upon the distant world is like, such similarities of experience are extremely hard to find.

In the first place, the messages that were coming to Number 774 were the code representations of alphabetical letters standing for various sounds which, when taken in groups, made up words of vocal speech.

As previously stated, Number 774 had no idea of sound except as an interesting phenomenon recorded by his scientific instruments, and as a vibration detectable by his touch sense in the same way that human beings can feel sound vibrations in solid objects. He had no ears; neither did he have well-developed vocal organs.

Strange as it may seem to us, prior to his experience with the light, he had not the faintest idea of what a word was, either a vocal word or a written word, or a word represented in the form of a group of signals. Because Martian methods of communicating with one another, and of recording knowledge, are so different from ours that a word would have been as great a mystery to him as it would have been to a newborn kitten.

Describing sound to him, as we know it through our sense of hearing, would have been as hopeless a task as describing red to a man who has been stone-blind since birth. It simply could not be done. He might know that sound and vocal speech existed, but short of trading actual sensations with an Earthman, he could never fully comprehend. Neither could he have told us in any way how the color of ultraviolet or infrared looked, for such things are totally out of our experience.

In the face of these enormous handicaps, in spite of his intelligence and scientific knowledge, he had been like a little child, humbly and intensely eager to learn, yet bungling and quick to make mistakes which, from an Earthman's point of view, would often have seemed more than childish.

Once he had tried a method of his own of establishing communication. If Earth had been peopled by a race physically and psychologically similar to the Martians, quick success might have been expected; but his efforts had evoked only a, to him, meaningless jumble of flashes from the light. Realizing that his method was not suited to Earthmen, he had given up trying to be teacher and had assumed instead the rôle of conscientious pupil.

"Hello, Mars!" Those two groups of symbols had always been the beginning of every message flashed by the light; but except for seeing the unmistakable evidence of intelligence in the oft-repeated and unvarying signal, Number 774 had been quite unable at first to grasp in it any thread of meaning.

A greeting phrase was, if possible, even more incomprehensible to him than a word itself. Try as he might, he could not understand. On Mars, where speech is not the mode of communication, greeting phrases did not exist.

Then Earthly genius, doubtless assisted a great deal by chance, had come to his aid. Number 774 had no difficulty in separating the twenty-six alphabetical symbols of the Morse code. Nor when the Earth entities, controlling the flickerings of the light, had sent out code symbols for numerals in a sequence of 0, 1, 2, 3, 4, 5, and so on, did he have any trouble in recognizing and cataloguing each separate signal, though their meanings were still entirely unfathomable to him.

It was when the counting proceeded above nine, and numbers of more than one digit appeared, that Number 774, after a long period of association with the riddle, had received his first faint glimmer of understanding. No; it was not really understanding yet; just a vague, intuitive intimation that something concrete and graspable was not far off.

He had noted that there were but ten separate signals in this strange system, which was apparently quite distinct from that other mysterious system of twenty-six symbols, for the two had never yet been mixed in one signal group or word; and that, as the flashing of the signals proceeded, each symbol seemed to bear a definite relationship to the others.

They always were in fixed sequence. 1 was followed by 2, 2 by 3, and so on through a sequence of ten. The first symbol of a two-digit number was always repeated ten times as the counting went on, while the second symbol changed according to the fixed rule which he had already noted.

Perhaps Number 774 already had a dim notion of the terrestrial numeral system, when his friend of the light conceived the plan of sending simple problems of arithmetic. Obviously, one plus one of anything is two on the planet Mars just as certainly as it is on Earth.

There was the real beginning. Number 774 had studied carefully the simple equations that had come to him, and at length he had been able to grasp what was meant. In a message like "3 and 3 are 6" he was presently able to see the relationship between the numeral signals. The last in the group was the sum of the preceding two.

Finally he understood. Here was some quaint terrestrial method of expressing the unit quantity of anything. The first point of contact between Earth and Mars had been established.

Flushed with success, Number 774 had made rapid progress for a while after he had learned about the terrestrial decimal system. If 3 and 3 are 6, and 2 and 5 are 7, then 4 and 5 are 9. Reproducing faithfully, though without clear comprehension, the intermediate letter groups of the Earthly equation he had invented, "a-n-d" and "a-r-e", he had flashed the equation to his friend of the light: "4 and 5 are 9."

And the answering flicker of the light seemed to dance with an eager exultation: "4 and 5 are 9. 4 and 5 are 9. Yes, yes, yes. 5 and 5 are 10. 8 and 4 are 12. 9 and 7 are? 9 and 7 are?"

Keyed to a high pitch, Number 774 had sensed immediately what was required of him. Answers were wanted. Though two-digit numbers were still something of a mystery to him, making his reply partly guesswork, he lit upon the correct representation of the sum: "9 and 7 are 16."

Through the succeeding months, during which the positions of the two planets were favorable for astronomical observation of each other, the work had gone on, various methods being employed. Sometimes Number 774 presented his own problems of addition, giving the answers. If his answer was correct, the light invariably flashed "Yes, yes, yes," exultantly, and repeated the equation.

On those rare occasions when the problems became more complex, Number 774 made mistakes, the answering message was "No, no, no," and the correction was made.

Thus Number 774 had gained his first knowledge of words, as represented by the twenty-six letter code alphabet. "Yes, yes, yes," meant that he was right, and "no, no, no," meant that he was wrong. It trickled into his mind that each group of alphabetical symbols represented, in its crude way, some definite idea. "And" and "are" in a simple addition problem, showed certain relationships between the numbers; and those relationships were different from the ones expressed by other words.

A mistake he had once made had clearly demonstrated

this fact to him. It was in the transition from addition problems to problems of multiplication. 10 and 2 was different from 10 times 2. 10 and 2 made 12, while 10 times 2 made 20. "Times" represented a different relationship between numbers than "and." One indicated that the sum was to be taken, while the other indicated that the two were to be multiplied together.

In a similar way he found out what "divided by", "plus", "minus", and other words meant by noting the relationship of the numbers of the equation to the final answer.

Once understanding simple division as it is done on Earth, Number 774 quickly grasped the decimal-position system of representing fractions. In an equation like $36 \div 5$ equals 7.2, he could substitute Martian methods of representing values and division and correlate them with terrestrial methods. In the Martian way he knew what $36 \div 5$ was, and of course his answer thus obtained might just as well be represented by the Earthly 7.2, for they were the same.

Number 774 had found in the number 3.1416, part of which was a decimal fraction, the relationship of the circumference of a circle to its diameter, and so the oft-repeated message of the light, "Diameter times 3.1416 equals the circumference of a circle," had a certain vague meaning for him that was not by any means completely understandable at once.

"Earth, Planet 3, Mars, Planet 4," was a message he was able to guess the meaning of correctly because in the Martian system numbers were used to designate planets in their order from the sun. Aided by the message, "Earth Planet 3, has 1 moon. Mars, Planet 4, has 2 moons," he had been half able to clinch his guess.

Stumblingly, yet reproducing the Earth words with the faithfulness of a good mimic, he had flashed: "Planet 1 has 0 moon. Planet 2 has 0 moon. Earth,

Planet 3, has 1 moon. Mars, Planet 4, has 2—"

And an enthusiastic "yes, yes, yes" had come from the light, and the dim flickering glow had gone on to tell that: "Mercury, Planet 1, has no moon. Venus, Planet 2, has no moon. Jupiter, Planet 5, has 9 moons. Saturn, Planet 6, has 10 moons—" And so on out to Pluto, Planet Nine, beyond Neptune.

Thus Number 774 had learned the names of the planets and the meaning of the words "moon" and "planet". In the same way he received a dim idea of such simple verbs as "has."

And so the process of his Earthly education had gone on, slowly, depending to a large extent upon brilliant though not very certain guesswork, and demanding a degree of patience in instructor and pupil for which teaching a person to talk who has been deaf, blind, and dumb since birth is but a feeble and inadequate analogy.

Number 774 had certain knowledge of a few Earthly words and the privilege of guessing more or less accurately on a number of others. Words like "snow", "clouds", or "storm", he could perhaps gather the general sense of fairly well. For whenever a great atmospheric disturbance appeared over the continent of the light, disturbing observations, the light repeated these words over and over again.

He knew a little about the structure of the simplest of verbs and perhaps somewhat more about the forming of the plurals of nouns by the addition of an "s" symbol. "Hello!" in the phrase "Hello, Mars!" still was beyond him. He could answer it correctly with "Hello, Earth!" knowing that this was the Earthly way; but the human sentiment of the greeting eluded him completely. And of course he had no sound values to give to those Earthly words which he did understand.

Progress had been made, but the forms which the

143

intelligences of Planet Three inhabited, their manner of living, their machines and their accomplishments, were still as much of an enigma as ever. Consummation of the great dream of intelligent communication still belonged to the future, and now there would be no future—only death and a mighty prophecy unfulfilled.

That prophecy had been, and still was, the essence of Number 774's life. In the face of defeat he still worked on the fulfillment of it now, as though a thousand years of usefulness still lay ahead of him. It was habit, perhaps; and meanwhile his mind smoldered with thoughts which we of Earth can only guess at.

"You are late, Man of Mars. Late, late, late," the dim flicker in the vision globe, and the brighter light in the reproducer bulb beside him, spelled; and Number 774 bent to his task.

He understood sketchily most of the message. He knew that the light referred to him as "Man of Mars". He knew that "you are" should be followed by a group of signals describing him. Only "late", the essence of the sentence, the word which gave it sense, was new. What could "late" mean?

Intuition told him that some circumstances which existed only for the present had combined to make him "late", since he had never been called that before. What were those circumstances? He racked his brain over the question. Perhaps the light wished to indicate that he had been delayed in sending out his flash call-signal. But this was only a guess which could be right or wrong.

Still, perhaps it could be clinched. Some other day he might be purposely several minutes behind in sending out his call; then, by way of beginning he could admit that he was "late" and, if his surmise had been correct, the light would confirm it.

But the matter of this new combination of signals

could wait now. Number 774 must watch for other, possibly intelligible, things which the light might flash.

"Comet coming. Comet coming. Comet coming," the flicker in the reproducer bulb spelled. "Comet coming toward sun, Mars, and Earth. Comet coming. Comet coming. Comet coming."

If Number 774 had been a man, he might have given a sudden start. And it was not the message itself that would have been responsible, even though he caught some of its meaning. "Comet" was not a word that was new in his experience; for on several occasions when one of those long-tailed wanderers had come back into the solar system, after taking its long dive out toward interstellar space, the light had flashed the information: "Comet coming."

Number 774 knew what "comet" meant, and he could differentiate vaguely between "comet coming" and "comet going", for one indicated that the celestial visitor was entering the solar system, and the other that it was leaving. For several evenings the light had been telling him that a comet was arriving, and he had accepted the information as nothing particularly startling or new; he had been puzzled only at the significance of the other words of the message, "toward", for instance. So far he had not been quite able to grasp "toward".

No; it was not the message itself that was so startling to Number 774. Somehow, tonight, the flashing of the distant light on Earth, telling in its cryptic way of the arrival of the visitor, bridged a gap between two of Number 774's thoughts and furnished him with an inspiration—a colossal inspiration which only genius, backed up by a knowledge considerably in excess of that of mankind, and a wonder-deadening familiarity with marvelous scientific triumphs, would have dreamed possible of fulfillment.

In one timeless instant, all of Number 774's dreams

and hopes became linked together with the comet. Might he not still be guilty of revolt against the age-honored conventions of old Mars?

III

Something almost electrical seemed suddenly to take possession of Number 774. His cold eyes, fixed on the reproducer bulb, glittered with impatience. The flickering message, which a moment before would have held the complete attention of his every deductive faculty, had little interest for him now. He translated the signals perfunctorily, gathering what little meaning he could from them and not bothering to puzzle over what was new. He waited with tense eagerness for the moment when the light would go out, and it would be his turn to speak. There was something which he *must* tell his friend of Planet Three, and he *must* tell it so that it would be understood. But how? How could he direct those strange, clumsy signals, of which he knew so very little, so that the information he wished to convey would be received and properly understood?

There! The closing phrase of the message from Planet Three was coming: "Earth standing by for Mars. Earth standing by—" The scarcely noticeable speck of light in the vision globe of the telescope disappeared; the pulsating purple glow in the reproducer bulb faded out, and the darkness there seemed tense with expectancy and eager waiting. It seemed to fling an insurmountable challenge at the intellect and ingenuity of Number 774.

In their present relative positions, Earth and Mars were about fifty million miles, or four and a half light-minutes, apart. Thus any message depending on light would of course take four and a half minutes to travel from Earth to Mars, or vice versa.

To avoid confusion in exchanging their communications, Number 774 and his friend of Planet Three had worked out a system whereby each would send out his signals for two minutes, with an intervening pause of two minutes, during which the other could answer. This Earthly time interval Number 774 had learned to recognize and to interpret in terms of the Martian method of measuring time.

It was his turn now; and though he had something far more important to say than ever before, he hesitated, all his cleverness seemingly checkmated by the immensity of his problem. But the lagging, slipping moments lashed his mind, driving it by sheer tenseness of determination to a higher pitch of keenness, almost, than ever before. At least he could try. He could guess, and he could stumble, but he could try.

The little lever of the signaling mechanism trembled in his grasp, and in response to its feeble movements the signals thundered and flared from the outer surface of the dome overhead. For a full three minutes, violating the rule, Number 774 continued to send, repeating the same phrase over and over again, changing certain words each time, in the hope of hitting the right combination that would convey his meaning.

He did not wait for a reply. Earth had already sunk low in the west, and before a reply could come the flashes arriving from the feeble station on Earth would be rendered too dim and wavering and uncertain by the almost imperceptible haze of the Martian horizon to be properly recorded. Besides, he had so little time and so much to do.

Ponderously, under his guidance, the great telescope tube swung into line with the comet, which still rode high up in the west. The circular opening in the dome shifted automatically with the telescope, keeping opposite to its muzzle.

The huge form of the comet's head filled the vision

globe, spreading brilliant and silvery and tenuous around the more solid spot of the glowing central nucleus.

Delicate instruments came into play, recording and measuring speeds, distances, and densities. But this was no mere quest for abstract scientific knowledge. His eyes smoldered with a grimly definite purpose, in which the shadow of death was very near.

But toward death Number 774's reactions were hardly human. In the torrent of his thoughts one thing shone out clear—the comet would pass close to Mars, and it would also pass close to Earth. That fact offered a slender and stupendous possibility. But in ten days the comet would pass and his chance would be gone. Unless he could cram into that brief time more work than anything human or Martian had ever before been called upon to do, his opportunity would be gone forever.

He finished his measurements quickly and efficiently. Switches clicked, and great mechanisms, and incredibly delicate and sensitive instruments, ceased functioning. The circular opening in the rotunda closed, hiding the stars and the comet. The observatory was at rest, for its eerie, fragile master needed it no more.

Number 774 was hurrying down a passage, the stalky limbs of the machine that carried him making a regular, clicking sound.

He came to a great wall that tumbled away in a murky, green-lighted haze, far beneath. Without hesitation he leaped into it and, seemingly supported and retarded in his fall by the emerald substance of the glow from the metal walls, he floated downward as gently and securely as a feather in the heavy atmosphere of Earth.

At the bottom of the well another vast, low-ceiled chamber spread out, its remote walls lost in the luminescent emerald murk, through which the burnished forms of gigantic machines gleamed elfinly.

148

This was Number 774's workroom, and here, now, he set to work, laboring with cool, unhurried efficiency, so characteristic of the children of dying Mars.

Many times before he had struggled with the same problem which now held his attention, and he had learned much concerning it, yet the technical difficulties he had encountered had convinced him that the solution of that problem still lay many years in the future.

But now something had happened. An unforeseen chance had come—a chance which might or might not be possible. It was all a gamble.

There was no time for further experiments. Perhaps with this new opportunity there was no need for further experiments, for Number 774 grasped the underlying principles. He must plan and build; above all he must be quick and sure.

He was thinking of a certain barren valley far out in the desert. In a thousand years, perhaps, no one had visited it except him. Aircraft hardly ever flew over that waterless sand pocket set amid the arid hills of Mars. There would be the ideal spot for the completion of his task, for here in his workshop he knew that he dared not stay.

Delicate electrical impulses transmitted his commands, and in response five giant shapes, paradoxically human travesties wrought in shining metal, rose from their resting places to do his bidding. Under his guidance they made preparation for the exodus, gathering instruments, tools, and other paraphernalia, and packing them in metal cases; binding long arms of metal into great sheafs that would be easy to carry. Meanwhile Number 774 busied himself with a complicated Martian calculating machine.

Thus the night passed. In the almost momentary twilight that preceded the dawn, the strange caravan set out. Number 774 had changed his identity; instead of being only a fragile lump of living protoplasm, he was now a giant of metal, like the five automatons that served him, for the powerful machine he rode was so versatile, and so quick and accurate in its responses to his every guiding gesture, that it was to all intents and purposes his body.

A pair of wings of metal fabric disengaged themselves from the intricacies of his machine and began to flap ponderously. Number 774 soared upward on them, over his servitors that plodded along on the ground, bearing their heavy burdens. His gaze darted back briefly toward the silvery dome of his workshop and at its dusty walls, matching the slightly ocher-tinged dun color of the desert.

But the fact that he had lived in that structure most of his life, and that he was now leaving it forever, aroused no sentiment in his mind. He had no time for sentiment now, for time was precious. Besides, he was looking forward to the trials and dangers that were certain to come soon and to the triumphs that might come with them.

He swung and turned in the air, scanning the terrain with wary watchfulness, on guard for any possible approaching aircraft. It would not be well if he were seen, and if a flier should appear he must take cover. But there was really little danger to face as far as his own people were concerned.

Avoidance of the death sentence imposed by the Rulers was practically without precedent. For thousands of years Martians had obeyed their Rulers' commands so implicitly that now prisons for the detention of the condemned were unknown. When the order came, the people of Mars went to their deaths willingly and without a guard. And so it was unlikely that any one would suspect that Number 774 had intentions of escaping execution now.

It is hardly likely that Number 774 felt triumphant over his revolt against ancient law—possibly he even felt guilty—but his earnest eagerness to learn things that he did not know, and to give himself to the cause to which his life had been pledged, was an urge that surpassed and defied even age-old code and tradition.

The stars, and leisurely Deimos, the farther moon, shone on an ashen haze that obscured the horizon in every direction. A mounting breeze, keen and cutting for all its thinness, blew out of the west. When the sun rose, it changed the haze of the dust-laden air to a tumultuous, fiery murk that flung long, ominous streamers of orange and red across the sky. Number 774 knew what was coming and knew the hazards that it brought.

The wind became more and more violent, increasing by puffs and gusts, and at last settling down to a steady powerful blast of the proportions of a terrestrial hurricane. If human ears had been there to hear, they would have detected the mounting whisper and rustle of millions of flying sand particles, rubbing and sliding over each other, making a blurred and soothing purr of sound.

As the streaming, flame-hued trains of sand thickened and mounted higher in the atmosphere, the sun dimmed to a red bubble floating in the murk, and only a bloody reminder of its normal brilliance reached the ground.

Number 774 had descended to join his robots in their march on the ground. He had seen many of these fierce dust storms of Mars, and he accepted them as a matter of course, just as an experienced old mariner of Earth accepts tempests at sea. He himself was safely incased in an airtight glass cage atop the machine he rode; he was breathing pure filtered air.

The chief dangers were that the filtering equipment which fed oxygen to the engines of his automations would become clogged, or that he would accidentally be engulfed in some newly formed bed of quicksand, hidden beneath the clouds of dust that swirled about him. But these were unavoidable dangers which must be faced.

Under the pressure of necessity, Number 774 urged his robots to the fastest pace they could attain in the shifting desert soil. The metal giants' long, webby limbs swung on and on steadily, into the east, breasting sand and wind, and climbing several steep rocky ridges they encountered with agile ease, in spite of their great bulk and the weight of the burdens they carried.

Twice they crossed deep, twenty-mile-wide artificial gorges, which on Earth have earned the not entirely correct name of "canals". Now and then during each crossing, the dry and lifeless stalks of some weird Martian vegetation would loom dimly through the storm like grotesque totem poles. The canals were as desolate as the desert itself, for it was very early in the spring, and the water from the melting polar snowcaps had not yet come down through the network of conduits and perforated pipettes buried beneath the canal bed.

When the water did appear, vegetation would spring up in rapid growth along the bottoms of the hundreds of straight scars that had been dredged across the barren desert ages before. But as yet there was no sign of the great Martian planting machines, for it was still too early in the season even for them.

Number 774's wariness in crossing seemed completely unnecessary, for his eyes caught no sign of his own kind, or, in fact, of any living creature. He was as completely alone in the flat expanses of the canals as he was in the desert proper.

Late in the afternoon he arrived at his destination. By sunset the wind had subsided and the air was clearing. The work was already underway. Two of the robots, equipped now with great scooplike claws, had excavated a vast hole in the sand. Feverishly active, the other two were assisting Number 774 with other tasks. Rods were being arranged around the pit. Something of a strange, dark substance was taking form. A stream of molten metal was pouring from a broad, squat mechanism. A thin trickle of white vapor trailed up in the quiet air.

At dusk Number 774 paused to look up, over the rounded hills that ringed the valley, at Planet Three that hung in the western sky, gleaming regally amid its retinue of stars. The light on that distant world would flicker in vain tonight, calling eagerly to the Man of Mars. There would be no answer. Higher up, fainter and less conspicuous, was the silvery dart of the comet.

Perhaps Number 774 was trying to imagine what his unknown friend of the light would think when no replying flicker appeared on the disk of Mars. Perhaps he was trying to imagine, as he had done so often before, what his friend of the light was like. Maybe he was wondering whether he should soon know.

His pause was only momentary. There was much to do, for in effect he was racing with the comet. Martians need very little sleep, and it was certain that Number 774 would get no sleep this night, nor the next, nor the next.

IV

Young Jack Cantrill cast a brief glance at the big diesel engine he had been inspecting, and then, with an air of finality, wiped his grease-blackened hands on a fistful of cotton waste. The outfit was functioning perfectly. Ordinarily he might have paused for a moment to admire the easy strength and motion of the machinery to which he played nursemaid, but, lover of machines though he certainly was, he had no time now.

His eyes did not linger on the reflection of the glow-

153

ing electric lightbulbs mirrored on the polished circumference of the spinning flywheel, as they usually did; nor did his attention wander to the sparks that purred blue and steady on the brushes of the gigantic dynamo attached to the engnie.

He had something far more interesting to occupy his mind, and besides, a rather astounding idea had just occurred to him. Old Doc Waters and Yvonne might laugh at the notion; and then again they might be struck by it just as he had been. He'd have to try it out on them right away.

He tossed the handful of waste carelessly into a metal box, then made a perfunctory reading of the meters and instruments banked close and bewilderingly on the switchboard. He adjusted a small rheostat and jotted something down on a chart on the wall with a red crayon. Then, heedless of his light clothing and his perspiring condition, he hurried out into the frosty desert night.

The breeze, cold and untainted by the smell of burning fuel oil, chilled his damp body uncomfortably, but he did not heed it. The steady thud of the exhaust of the high-compression motor in the iron shack receded rapidly behind him as he ran up a path which led to the summit of a low hill.

On the crest of a neighboring knoll, a broad patch of dazzling light winked on and off regularly, where scores of huge searchlights poured their billions of candlepower toward the twinkling stars, in systematically arranged long and short spurts. Jack Cantrill's glance toward them was brief but intense. His lips moved as though he were counting to himself.

The door of the domed observatory building at the top of the hill opened at his touch. He passed through a small lean-to and entered the brick-lined circular chamber that housed the telescope. Here a single shaded lamp cast a subdued glow over a big desk on which various opened notebooks and papers were scattered. Amid the litter an astronomer's chronometer ticked loudly in shadowed stillness. The gloom was eerie and soft and strange.

Jack Cantrill made his way quietly to the low platform under the eyepiece of the telescope, where the other two occupants of the room stood.

The girl was pretty in a blond, elfin sort of way. She smiled briefly at Jack's approach.

"Any luck, folks?" he inquired.

He was trying to make his voice sound calm and casual, but a tense and excited huskiness crept into his words and spoiled his bluff.

Professor Waters looked up from the eyepiece of the big instrument. The glow coming from the nearby lamp accentuated the tired lines of his face, making him look almost haggard. He grinned wearily.

"Not yet, boy," he said. "It seems as though Old Faithful has deserted us completely. It's funny, too, when you remember that when conditions were at all favorable for observation, he hasn't failed me once in nine years. And yet this is the second night that he hasn't given us a sign. The shaded side of Mars hasn't shown a single flicker that you can see, and even the photoelectric cell doesn't detect anything."

The young man glanced uncertainly at the girl and then back at her father. The fingers of one of his hands crept slowly through his curly red hair. With the air of a small schoolboy about to make his first public address, he was fumbling with a soiled sheet of paper he had taken from his pocket. He felt rather sheepish about that idea he had thought of.

"Yvonne— Doc—" he said almost plaintively, in an awkward attempt to get their undivided attention centered on what he was going to say. "I'm not much of a scientist, and maybe I'm a darned fool; but—well, this message—the final one we received the night before

155

last—we thought it was just a jumble but, when you read it, it almost has meaning. Here, listen to it once."

Clearing his throat he proceeded to read from the sheet of paper: "Comet coming. Yes. Comet coming. Yes. Comet coming of Man of Mars. Comet Man of Mars coming toward Earth. Comet coming Man of Mars. Man of Mars. Comet. Man of Mars. Comet. Man of Mars. Comet. Yes, yes, yes. Man of Earth. Yes, yes, yes. Signing off. Signing off."

Jack Cantrill's thin cheeks were flushed when he stopped reading.

"Get it?" he asked in a husky whisper. "Get any sense out of that?"

Yvonne Waters' pretty face had paled slightly. "You mean, Jack—you mean that he wanted to say that he was coming *here*, across fifty million miles of emptiness? He can't do that! He can't! It's too far and too impossible!"

Her concerned manner bolstertd up the youth's confidence in his idea. "You caught on to exactly what I thought of," he said.

Professor Waters did not betray any outward excitement. His manner was musing, and he rubbed his cheek reflectively. "I thought of that, too," he admitted after a moment. "But it seemed too wild for serious consideration. Still there's a chance—that you are right."

The thought put into words seemed suddenly to startle the old man. "Gad, boy!" he exploded suddenly. "Supposing it *is* the truth! Old Faithful signaled about the comet. If there's anything to this at all, the comet must be tied up with his coming. And for all we know the comet might help. It passes close to both Earth and Mars. If in some way he could fall into its gravitation field, it would drag him almost all the way. That's it! It would save an enormous energy. It would put his trip, otherwise still impossible, into the realm of possibility!"

"You get me at last, doc," Jack said quickly. "And

when you say, 'Supposing it's the truth,' think of what it means! The navigation of interplanetary space, maybe! Commerce between Earth and Mars! A new and wonderful era, with the minds of one world exchanging ideas with the minds of another."

Unconsciously Jack Cantrill had taken Yvonne Waters' hand. Her eyes were starry.

"If it did happen we'd all be heroes, Jack," she said. "Dad and you and I. We'd be the ones to get the credit."

"We would, Yvonne," Jack admitted with a chuckle.

It was the professor's turn to smile. "You two have got the whole business nicely ready-made, haven't you?" he chided. Then his face sobered as he went on: "The gap is pretty wide between Earthman and Martian; and in consequence yours may be very far off, even if that guess of ours about the message is right.

"We don't know that Martians are human beings. The chances are a million to one that they aren't. It is very unlikely that evolution, operating on so different a planet, could produce a being even remotely resembling a man. We don't even know that the people of Mars use speech as we use it. Old Faithful certainly is very intelligent, yet the way he has fumbled blunderingly with our code seems to indicate that even a faint conception of vocal speech is something new and strange to him.

"Those are some of the gaps, but there may be sinister similarities between Earthmen and Martians.

"Who knows but that something darker lies behind what we think is friendly interest in us? Sometimes conquest is more satisfying than commerce. We can't tell." Professor Waters paused.

"Making it extra strong, aren't you, doc?" Jack put in.

"I guess I am, and now I think I'll do a little newsspreading." The professor strode to the desk.

"Human or not, I hope the Martians are handsome," Yvonne confided impishly to Jack.

"And I hope they're not, darling," he replied, putting his arm affectionately about her waist. He was about to add something more when what the girl's father was saying into the telephone riveted their attention.

"Long distance? I'm calling Washington. I want to speak directly to Mr. Grayson, the Secretary of War. Strange call? Perhaps. But put it through."

Before dawn all the observatories of Earth had begun their watch.

v

Far away on the Red Planet, the work of Number 774 went steadily forward. Then came the night when all was ready except for one thing. A powerful urge, the roots of which are deeply implanted in the dominant forms of life on both Earth and Mars, and perhaps the whole universe, was calling him to a city at the joining place of four canals, far to the east. In that urge there was a pathetic something, perfectly understandable by human standards.

The bright stars reeled dizzily before Number 774 as he swooped out over the desert on the wings of the ornithopter that bore him and sped eastward. He must be cautious, but above all he must hurry.

An hour or so slipped by. The Martian's big eyes, keen and catlike, picked out in the broad cleft of a canal a gigantic angular shape, looming dim and uncertain in the gloom. Inconspicuous as a drifting shadow, he settled toward it. The talons of his automaton found a metal panel that slipped aside at a touch. The green glow of the immense well thus revealed dropped away into deserted obscurity. In a moment he was floating down it, past myriads of openings, from which radiated the labyrinthine tunnels of the buried Martian city.

He entered one of these passages and followed it for perhaps a mile, until he came to a vast chamber, pervaded by a moist, humid heat. The floor was covered with thousands of boxes of clear crystal; and in each box was a purple gob of something feeble and jellylike and alive.

Aided perhaps by some Martian numeral system, Number 774 found his way to the box he sought. At his touch the lid opened. He had dismounted from his automaton, and now, creeping forward, he thrust a slender appendage into the crystal case.

A score of nerve filaments, fine, almost, as human hair, darted out from the chitinous shell that protected them and roved caressingly over the lump of protoplasm. Immediately it responded to the gentle touch of the strange creature that had sired it. Its delicate integument quivered, and a thin pseudopod oozed up from its jellylike form and enveloped the nerve filaments of Number 774. For minutes the two remained thus, perfectly motionless.

It was a bizarre travesty of a touching and perfectly human situation; yet its utter strangeness by Earthly standards robbed it of some of its pathos. No words were spoken, no sign of affection that a terrestrial being could interpret was given; and yet perhaps the exchange of feeling and thought and emotion between parent and offspring was far more complete than anything of the kind possible on Earth.

Number 774 did not forget caution. Perhaps it was intuition that informed him that someone was coming. Quickly, yet without haste, he regained his automaton, replaced the lid on the crystal box, and slipped quietly away into the luminescent obscurity of the tunnel. In a few minutes he had safely reached the open of the canal bed. Broad wings flapped, and the starlit night swallowed him up.

As he hurried back toward his hidden valley, he saw the silvery green speck of Earth dip beneath the western horizon. The sight of it must have aroused a turmoil of forebodings within him; for absently, as if he were already facing unknown horrors in mortal combat, he moved a small switch, and in response a jagged flash of flame leaped from an apparatus carried on a long arm of his flying automaton. Where the bolt struck, the desert sand turned molten.

Above, the comet glowed, pallid and frosty and swollen. It was very near to Mars now.

Having reached his valley, Number 774 descended into the pit. A silvery thing that was illy defined in the uncertain light loomed over him. A door opened and closed, and Number 774 was alone and busy amid a bewildering array of machinery.

There came a blinding flash of incandescence, and a roar that sounded like the collision of two worlds; then a shrill, tortured, crackling whistle. The pit glowed white-hot, and the silvery thing was gone. Above the pit, towering many miles into the sky, was an immense jetted plume of vapor, shining rosy with heat. It would be many minutes before that huge gaseous cloud would cool sufficiently to be invisible.

The body of Number 774 was battered and torn and broken; the terrific acceleration was crushing him; consciousness was slipping, even though he was exerting a tremendous effort of will to cling to it. In a few minutes it would not matter if he did go out, but now there were controls to watch and to handle. If they were not manipulated properly everything he had done was for naught.

But the blackness of oblivion was closing in. He struggled valiantly to master himself and to fight through the gathering gloom that was misting his vision and clouding his mind. Though his whole being cried out for a cessation of torturing effort, still he kept fiercely at his task. There was too much at stake. That little globe there—it was glowing red when it should glow violet. It must be attended to. The craft was wobbling, and it must not wobble. A trifling adjustment of delicate stabilizers would fix that, if he could only somehow make the adjustment.

A dribble of sticky, oozy fluid welled from a wound in Number 774's side. His limbs, some of them broken, fumbled awkwardly and inefficiently with the complicated controls. He was gasping, and all the while his glazing eyes remained fixed grimly on the form of the comet, toward which he and the strange craft he had built were hurtling. Could he reach it? He must!

VI

On Earth, Professor Waters, his daughter, and his young engineer, watched and waited. It was a tense, grueling task, heavy-laden with monotony, a thousand weird imaginings, and a horde of questions, none of which could be answered with any certainty.

They were uncertain whether to be fearful of the unknown thing whose approach they sensed, or to be exultant. They did not even know whether their vigil was just a huge nerve-racking practical joke which their fancies had played upon them.

Time dragged with torturing slowness. Tardy seconds became minutes, tedious minutes were built up into hours, and hours became days that seemed like centuries. And over the rest of the world, the vigil was much the same.

On the ninth day after the last flickering message had come from Mars, Professor Waters had seen through his telescope, on the surface of the Red Planet, a fine dot of white light that, after its sudden appearance, faded quickly to red, and then, after a few minutes, disappeared altogether. A few hours later he thought he detected a slight and momentary ripple in the gaseous substance of the comet's head, which then had just passed Mars on its sunward journey.

Newspaper reporters who had come many miles to this lonely spot in the desert were constantly seeking interviews. The three watchers supplied them with all the information they knew; and at last, tiring of the additional strain of being constantly hounded by these persistent seekers after sensational news, they refused even to grant them admittance into the barbed-wire stockade of the camp.

At last the comet reached its point of closest approach to the Earth. Faint and ashy though it was, low down in the sunlit afternoon heavens, still it was an awesome, impressive object, with its colossal, fan-shaped head and the vast curved sweep of its gigantic ghost-silver tail.

When the desert dusk settled, the visiting wanderer increased a score of times in brilliance and glory. It had now passed the line and was hurtling away. And as yet nothing that would satisfy the eager hopes and fears of the watchers had happened.

The three were standing on the veranda of the little adobe house they inhabited. All of a sudden Doctor Waters' haggard face relaxed. He sighed heavily.

"I guess that it has been proved that we are all of us fools," he said wearily. "There hasn't been much of anything to reward us for our pains." His glance toward Jack Cantrill was slightly apologetic. "I think I'll go to bed," he added abruptly.

Jack's rather good-looking face twisted into a rueful smile. "Bed isn't at all a bad idea," he admitted. "I feel as though I could snooze a week straight without waking up. Well, anyway, if we're fools, I'm the biggest one, because I started all this." He looked at the old man and then at the girl. "Forgive me, Yvonne?" he queried good-humoredly.

"No," she replied with mock seriousness. "Making me lose so much of my beauty sleep like this! You ought to be ashamed of yourself." Her little speech was terminated by a faintly amused chuckle, and she pinched his cheek impishly.

It was some hours after they had retired that a faint soughing noise began from somewhere, apparently at a great distance. It was like the sound of a suddenly stiffening night breeze, sweeping through a grove of pine trees. Something that glowed rosy with the heat of atmospheric friction swept in hurtling flight across the sky. A mile or so beyond the camp, broad thin flanges of metal shot out from it, and it made a feeble attempt to steady itself and check its almost meteoric speed. It wobbled, then fluttered down weakly. A cloud of dust and sand rose where it smashed into the ground. But there was no human eye to see. For an hour or more it gave no further sign of life or motion.

Yvonne Waters was a light sleeper. Unusual night noises ordinarily aroused her. The momentary soughing rustle caused her to stir, but she did not awaken. Then, toward four in the morning, another disturbance came. It was a faint stretching, creaking, straining sound, that nevertheless held a suggestion of powerful forces acting stealthily.

Instantly Yvonne was wide awake. She sat up in bed, listening. What she heard produced quick and accurate associations in her nimble and cool young mind. A barbed-wire fence would make a creaking, straining noise like that, if something big and powerful were seeking tentatively to force an entrance. The stockade!

Yes; she was right. Presently there came the sharp snap and snarl that told of the sudden parting of a taut wire. Four times the sound was repeated.

Yvonne Waters had bounded out of her bunk and had rushed to a window. It was still very dark, but outlined against the stars she saw a vague shape that swayed and moved. The girl's hand groped quickly into the drawer of a small stand beside her and drew out a heavy automatic pistol. Then she hurried to the door and across the hallway.

"Dad! Jack!" she called in a husky whisper. "I've seen something big. It's coming toward the house!"

The young man responded quickly, his unshod feet thudding across the floor. His eyes narrowed when he leaned out of the window. There the thing stood, statuesquely now, not fifty paces away. It was not clearly defined in the darkness, but Jack Cantrill knew at once that it was something completely out of his experience. It seemed to have an upright, cylindrical body that rose perhaps fifteen feet above the ground. Leverlike limbs projected grotesquely from the upper end of this torso, and at the lower end there were shadowy suggestions of other limbs, long and spidery. An angular object surmounted the cylinder, and in its present position it was an outlandish travesty of the head of a man, cocked to one side, listening.

A minute passed. Obeying what must have been an automatic impulse, Yvonne Waters drew on her boots. About the camp she always dressed like the men, and during the last few nights, anticipating sudden developments, they had all slept in their clothing.

Jack Cantrill, crouching by the window, felt the short hairs at the nape of his neck stiffen. Doctor Waters' hand was on the young man's shoulder. The fingers were trembling slightly.

It was Jack who first put into words what they were all sure was the truth: "Old Faithful, I think," he whispered, without any apparent excitement.

He paused for a moment, during which neither of his companions made any comment, for even a slight sound, as far as they knew, might be heard, with disastrous consequences.

The young man was thinking fast. Something had to be done and done quickly, and it was perhaps very easy to do the wrong thing.

"Flashlight!" he whispered presently, taking command of the situation, and the girl, responding quickly to his leadership, slipped her big electric torch into his hand.

"Now out into the open—all of us," he ordered. "Armed?"

Each carried a pistol. They slipped around to the side of the house, with Cantrill in the lead. The weird giant stood as before, rigid and perfectly still.

Jack raised the flashlight. Working the flash button with his thumb, he proceeded to signal out in the Morse code, a familiar message: "Hello, Man of Mars! Hello, Man of Mars! Hello, Man of Mars!"

And the answer came immediately, flickering from a small spot of green light on the angular "head" of the automaton: "Hello, Man of Earth! Hello, Man of Earth! Comet. Comet. Comet. Comet." The message was clear enough, but there was an unusual halting, stumbling hesitancy in the way it was given. Old Faithful had always been precise and quick in the messages he had flashed from Mars.

As the three watchers stood spellbound, the great quasi-human machine started forward toward the house. Its movements were powerful, but drunken and unsteady. It seemed to be little more than an insensate mechanism running amuk. The intelligence that was guiding it was losing its hold. Nothing could avert an accident.

The robot struck the side of the house with a heavy thud, lurched forward, stumbled, and fell with a clatter and clang of metal across the low roof that collapsed under its weight and the force of its overthrow. Prostrate though it was, its lower limbs continued to simulate the movements of walking.

Its arms sprawled wide, and from a metal knob at the tip of one a torrent of blue sparks began to pour into the earth, causing the patch of sand it struck to turn molten and boil away in a cloud of incandescent vapor. A minute must have passed before the sparks burned out and the appendages of the machine ceased their ponderous thrashing.

Meanwhile the three watchers had been staring at the weird and inspiring sight, not knowing just what to do. But now, when quiet was restored, they edged cautiously toward the fallen machine. Jack Cantrill's flashlight beam played over the wreckage and halted upon the flattened "head" of the robot. It was pyramidal in form and had been supported by a flexible pillar of pointed metal. There was an opening in one side, and from it something had tumbled. A shadow veiled it, so that the watchers could not immediately see what it was. Then Jack leaped to a different position and poured the beam of the flashlight full upon it.

The effect of its strangeness did not come upon them right away, for they did not at once realize its true nature. It seemed at first only a sprawling mass of drab gray, as large, perhaps, as the open top of an ordinary umbrella. It might have been nothing more than a large lump of wet mud, flattened out by being dropped.

Then, after a moment, the three took note of the ragged tendrils that radiated out from the oblate form somewhat in the manner of the arms of a starfish. The ends of some of those tendrils were slender and stalklike and were terminated by incredibly fine filaments of coral pink. Those filaments were twitching convulsively.

166

Yvonne Waters was the first to find her voice. It was choking and tremulous: "The thing's alive!" she cried. "Dad! Jack! It's alive!"

Obscure primal instincts had taken possession of them. Like wary alley curs they inched their way forward, craning their necks to look closer at the creature, in which, for them, both fascination and fear were combined.

It was then they saw that the central lump of the thing was contracting in painful, jerky spasms. It was breathing, or gasping, rather. Feathery pink palps around a cone-shaped orifice that resembled the inside of a funnel coiled in agony. They could hear the monster's breath whistle through the opening in long, rasping sighs.

But the creature's eyes, fixed to the ends of two tentacular appendages that protruded from beneath the outer folds of its flattened body, regarded them with what seemed to be an interest which could not be dimmed by physical pain and suffering. They were very large eyes, three inches across, and there was in their alien, brooding intensity, slightly veiled now by the film of approaching death, a suggestion of an intelligence in this monstrous, inhuman body that was more than human.

Yvonne Waters had taken note of these things almost in the space of a moment. She saw the hideous festering gashes of wounds that must have been several days old on the body of the visiting being, and she saw that several of its limbs were shattered. Some of them seemed to be partly knit, but others were evidently recent injuries. From the fresh wounds bright red blood oozed, giving evidence of a very high hemoglobin content, which would be necessary for a creature accustomed to breathing an atmosphere much more rarefied than that of Earth.

Maybe it was because Yvonne Waters was a woman

that she bridged the gap between Earthman and Martian more quickly than her companions.

"He's hurt!" she gasped suddenly. "We've got to help him some way! We ought to—ought to—get a doctor." She halted a little in expressing this last idea. It seemed so totally wild and fantastic.

"A doctor for that horror?" Jack Cantrill asked, a trifle dazed.

"Yes! Well, maybe no," the girl amended. "But still we must do something. We've got to! He's human, Jack— human in everything but form. He has brains; he can feel pain like any human being. Besides, he has courage of the same kind that we all worship. Think of the pluck it took to make the first plunge across fifty million miles of cold, airless void! That's something to bow down to, isn't it? And, besides, this is our friend, Old Faithful!"

"By the gods, Yvonne, you're right!" the young man exploded with sudden realization. "And here I am, wasting time like a dumb fool!"

He dropped to his knees beside the injured Martian, and his big hands poised, ready and willing, but still uncertain how to help this bizarre entity of another world.

Doctor Waters had by this time shaken the fog of sleep from his older and less agile faculties, and he was now able to grasp the situation. With a brief and crisp, "I'll get the first-aid kit!" he hurried into the partially wrecked house, across the roof of which sprawled Old Faithful's automaton.

Conquering her natural revulsion, Yvonne brought herself to touch the dry, cold flesh of the Martian, and to try as best she might to ease its suffering. Presently the three of them were working over their weird patient, disinfecting and bandaging its wounds. But there was small hope that their efforts would be of any avail.

As their first touch, Old Faithful had started convulsively, as though in fear and repugnance of these, to him, horrid monsters; and a low, thick cry came from the opening in his body. But he must have realized that their intentions were harmless, for he had relaxed immediately. His breath, however, was rapidly growing weaker and more convulsive, and his eyes were glazing.

"We're dumb!" Jack stated with sudden vehemence. "He's badly hurt, but that's not all. This atmosphere is six times too dense for him. He's smothering in it—drowning! We've got to get him somewhere where the pressure won't be crushing him!"

"We'll rig up a vacuum tank down in the engine shed," said Doctor Waters. "It won't take but a minute."

It was done. However, when they were lifting Old Faithful onto the litter they had improvised, his body stiffened, shuddered, and grew suddenly limp. They knew that Old Faithful—Number 774—was gone. Still, to aid the remote possibility that he would revive, they placed him in the vacuum tank and exhausted most of the air so that the pressure inside duplicated that of the rarefield Martian atmosphere. Fresh air was admitted slowly through the pet cock. But within an hour Old Faithful's flesh had become stiff with *rigor mortis*. He was dead.

Much must have passed through the devious channels of his Martian mind during those brief hours on Planet Three. He must have felt satisfied that his eagerness to penetrate the unknown was partly rewarded, his ambition partly fulfilled. He had learned what lay back of, and what had guided, the flickerings of the light. He had seen the people of Planet Three. Perhaps, at the last, he had thought of Mars, his home, and the sorry plight of his race.

Maybe he thought of his growing offspring in that buried nursery chamber, fifty million miles away. Maybe the possibilities of Earth, as a means of aiding dying Mars, occurred to him, if it had not come into his mind before, and it is quite likely that his ideas in that direction were not altogether altruistic toward mankind.

Certainly he hoped that his friends of the light would find his space car and what it contained, out there in the desert, and that they would study and understand.

Dawn came, with the eastern sky sprinkled with a few pink feathery clouds that the bright sun would soon dissipate.

In one of the various corrugated iron sheds of the camp, Yvonne, Jack, and the doctor were bending over the body of Old Faithful, which lay stiff and lifeless on a long table.

"Kind of heartless to be preparing this intelligent being for immersion in a preservative spirit bath so that a lot of curious museum-goers can have a thrill, don't you think, folks?" Jack was complaining with make-believe gruffness. "How would you like it if the situation was reversed—if we were stiffs with the curious of Mars looking at us?"

"I wouldn't mind if I was dead." The girl laughed. "It would be an honor. Oh, look, Jack—the funny little mark an Old Faithful's skin—it's tattooed with red ink. What do you suppose it means?"

Jack had already seen the mark. It was a circle with a bar through the center and was, as the girl had said, an artificial decoration or symbol. Jack shrugged. "Search me, honey!" He chuckled. "Say, doc, do you suppose that space car is around here somewhere?"

The doctor nodded. "It must be."

"Well, come on! Let's look for it, then! This can wait."

After a very hasty and sketchy breakfast, they made their way on horseback out into the desert, following the tracks the Martian robot had made.

At the summit of a rocky ridge they found what they sought—a long cylinder of metal deeply imbedded in sand that seemed literally to have splashed like soft mud around it. The long fins of the space car were crumpled and broken and covered with the blue-gray ash of oxidation. Here and there a fragment had peeled away, revealing bright metal beneath.

The nose of the shell has become unscrewed, exposing burnished threads that glistened in the sun. Into the shadowed interior they made their way, rummagingly gingerly among the bewildering maze of Martian instruments. The place reeked with a scorched, pungent odor.

At the rear of the cylindrical compartment they found a great round drum of metal, fitting snugly into the interior of the shell. Sleepily they wondered what was in it and made several weary attempts to move it. At nine o'clock the police guard that Doctor Waters had sent for arrived.

"Tell those damned reporters who are trying to crash in on us to go to hell," Jack Cantrill told the lieutenant in charge, as he and his two companions were starting wearily back toward camp. "We've got to snooze."

Several weeks had passed. In a hotel room in Phoenix, Arizona, Doctor Waters was speaking to Mr. and Mrs. Cantrill, who had just arrived.

"I'm turning the camp and the signaling apparatus over to Radeau and his associates," he was saying. "No more signals from Mars, somehow, and I don't feel very much like continuing there anyway. There are a lot more interesting things on the horizon.

"That drum which Old Faithful brought us—it contained models and many charts and sheets of parchment with drawings on them. I'm beginning to see light through the mystery at last. There are suggestions there for constructing a spaceship. I'm going to work on that problem as long as I live.

"Maybe I'll succeed with the help of Old Faithful. Human ingenuity will have to be called on, too, of course. I

171

don't think that the Martians have the problem completely solved themselves. Old Faithful used the comet, you know."

The doctor's smile broadened as he went on: "Children, how would you like to go to Mars with me some day?"

"Don't ask silly questions, dad," said Yvonne. "We'd go in a minute!"

The young man nodded seriously. "What a honeymoon that would make, if we could have it now!" he enthused.

"A million times better than going to Seattle," the girl agreed.

The doctor grinned faintly. "Even if you were treated like poor Old Faithful—pickled and put in a museum?"

"Even if!"

Jack Cantrill's eyes narrowed and seemed to stare far away into nothing. His lips and his gaunt sunburned cheeks were stern. Perhaps he was looking into the future toward adventures that might or might not come.

Something of the same rugged spirit seemed suddenly to have infused itself into the strong, bronzed beauty of the girl at his side. They both loved adventure; they both knew life in the rough.

At the door Yvonne kissed her father good-bye. "Just a little run up to Seattle, dad," she explained cheerily, "two or three weeks, maybe. Then both of us back with you—to work."

When Lester del Rey and I (this is the male member of the editorial collaboration speaking) came back from the World Science Fiction Convention of 1947, we found we had had so much fun that we wanted it to keep on happening, and so we organized a New York City club of science-fiction writers and general hangers-on called The Hydra Club. We did it just in time, because it had only been going a few months when a visiting sf writer, on the point of

172

moving away from New York because he hadn't made many friends there, discovered its existence, came to a meeting and immediately became one of us. His name was Fredric Brown. In his life he wrote a stack of excellent mystery novels, a few (but also excellent) science-fiction books, and dozens of short, bright zany stories . . . rather like this one, most of them. Fred Brown died a few months ago as this is written; and the world is a poorer place.

PLACET IS A CRAZY PLACE
By Fredric Brown

Even when you're used to it, it gets you down sometimes. Like that morning—if you can call it a morning. Really, it was night. But we go by Earth time on Placet because Placet time would be as screwy as everything else on that goofy planet. I mean, you'd have a six-hour day and then a two-hour night and then a fifteen-hour day and a one-hour night and—well, you just couldn't keep time on a planet that does a figure-eight orbit around two dissimilar suns, going like a bat out of hell around and between them, and the suns going around each other so fast and so comparatively close that Earth astronomers thought it was only one sun until the Blakeslee expedition landed here twenty years ago.

You see, the rotation of Placet isn't any even fraction of the period of its orbit and there's the Blakeslee Field in the middle between the suns—a field in which light rays slow down to a crawl and get left behind and—well. . . .

If you've not read the Blakeslee reports on Placet, hold on to something, while I tell you this:

Placet is the only known planet that can eclipse itself twice at the same time, run headlong into itself every forty hours, and then chase itself out of sight.

I don't blame you.

173

I didn't believe it either, and it scared me stiff the first time I stood on Placet and saw Placet coming head-on to run into us. And yet I'd read the Blakeslee reports and knew what was really happening, and why. It's rather like those early movies when the camera was set up in front of a train and the audience saw the locomotive heading right toward them and would feel an impulse to run even though they knew the locomotive wasn't really there.

But I started to say, like that morning. I was sitting at my desk, the top of which was covered with grass. My feet were—or seemed to be—resting on a sheet of rippling water. But it wasn't wet.

On top of the grass of my desk lay a pink flowerpot, into which, nose first, stuck a bright green Saturnian lizard. That—reason and not my eyesight told me—was my pen and inkwell. Also an embroidered sampler that said "God Bless Our Home" in neat cross-stitching. It actually was a message from Earth Center which had just come in on the radiotype. I didn't know what it said because I'd come into my office after the B. F. effect had started. I didn't think it really said "God Bless Our Home" because it seemed to. And just then I was mad, I was fed up, and I didn't care a holler what it actually did say.

You see—maybe I'd better explain—the Blakeslee Field effect occurs when Placet is in midposition between Argyle I and Argyle II, the two suns it figure-eights around. There's a scientific explanation of it, but it must be expressed in formulas, not in words. It boils down to this: Argyle I is terrene matter and Argyle II is contraterrene, or negative matter. Halfway between them—over a considerable stretch of territory—is a field in which light rays are slowed down, way down. They move at about the speed of sound. The result is that if something is moving faster than sound—as Placet itself

174

does—you can still see it coming after it's passed you. It takes the visual image of Placet twenty-six hours to get through the field. By that time, Placet has rounded one of its suns and meets its own image on the way back. In midfield, there's an image coming and an image going, and it eclipses itself twice, occulting both suns at the same time. A little farther on, it runs into itself coming from the opposite direction—and scares you stiff if you're watching, even if you know it's not really happening.

Let me explain it this way before you get dizzy. Say an old-fashioned locomotive is coming toward you, only at a speed much faster than sound. A mile away, it whistles. It passes you and *then* you hear the whistle, coming from the point a mile back where the locomotive isn't any more. That's the auditory effect of an object traveling faster than sound; what I've just described is the visual effect of an object traveling—in a figure-eight orbit—faster than its own visual image.

That isn't the worst of it; you can stay indoors and avoid the eclipsing and the head-on collisions, but you can't avoid the physio-psychological effect of the Blakeslee Field.

And that, the physio-psychological effect, is something else again. The field does something to the optic nerve centers, or to the part of the brain to which the optic nerves connect, something similar to the effect of certain drugs. You have . . . you can't exactly call them hallucinations, because you don't ordinarily see things that aren't there, but you get an illusory picture of what *is* there.

I knew perfectly well that I was sitting at a desk the top of which was glass, and not grass; that the floor under my feet was ordinary plastiplate and not a sheet of rippling water; that the objects on my desk were not a pink flowerpot with a Saturnian lizard sticking in

it, but an antique twentieth century inkwell and pen—
and that the "God Bless Our Home" sampler was a radiotype message on ordinary radiotype paper. I could verify
any of those things by my sense of touch, which the
Blakeslee Field doesn't affect.

You *can* close your eyes, of course, but you don't—
because even at the height of the effect, your eyesight
gives you the relative size and distance of things and if
you stay in familiar territory your memory and your
reason tell you what they are.

So when the door opened and a two-headed monster
walked in, I knew it was Reagan. Reagan isn't a two-
headed monster, but I could recognize the sound of his
walk.

I said, "Yes, Reagan?"

The two-headed monster said, "Chief, the machine
shop is wobbling. We may have to break the rule not to
do any work in midperiods."

"Birds?" I asked.

Both of his heads nodded. "The underground part of
those walls must be like sieves from the birds flying
through 'em, and we'd better pour concrete quick. Do
you think those new alloy reinforcing bars the *Ark*'ll
bring will stop them?"

"Sure," I lied. Forgetting the field, I turned to look
at the clock, but there was a funeral wreath of white
lilies on the wall where the clock should have been. You
can't tell time from a funeral wreath. I said, "I was
hoping we wouldn't have to reinforce those walls till we
had the bars to sink in them. The *Ark*'s about due;
they're probably hovering outside right now waiting for
us to come out of the field. You think we could wait
till—"

There was a crash.

"Yeah, we can wait," Reagan said. "There went the
machine shop, so there's no hurry at all."

"Nobody was in there?"

"Nope, but I'll make sure." He ran out.

That's what life on Placet is like. I've had enough of it: I'd had too much of it. I made up my mind while Reagan was gone.

When he came back, he was a bright blue articulated skeleton.

He said, "O.K., chief. Nobody was inside."

"Any of the machines badly smashed?"

He laughed. "Can you look at a rubber beach horse with purple polka dots and tell whether it's an intact lathe or a busted one? Say, chief, you know what you look like?"

I said, "If you tell me, you're fired."

I don't know whether I was kidding or not; I was plenty on edge. I opened the drawer of my desk and put the "God Bless Our Home" sampler in it and slammed the drawer shut. I was fed up. Placet is a crazy place and if you stay there long enough you go crazy yourself. One out of ten of Earth Center's Placet employees has to go back to Earth for psychopathic treatment after a year or two on Placet. And I'd been there three years, almost. My contract was up. I made my mind up, too.

"Reagan," I said.

He'd been heading for the door. He turned. "Yeah, chief?"

I said, "I want you to send a message on the radiotype to Earth Center. And get it straight, two words: *I quit.*"

He said, "O.K., chief." He went on out and closed the door.

I sat back and closed my eyes to think. I'd done it now. Unless I ran after Reagan and told him not to send the message, it was done and over and irrevocable. Earth

Center's funny that way; the board is plenty generous in some directions, but once you resign they never let you change your mind. It's practically an iron-clad rule and ninety-nine times out of a hundred it's justified on interplanetary and intragalactic projects. A man must be a hundred percent enthusiastic about his job to make a go of it, and once he's turned against it, he's lost the keen edge.

I knew the midperiod was about over, but I sat there with my eyes closed just the same. I didn't want to open them to look at the clock until I could see the clock *as* a clock and not as whatever it might be this time. I sat there and thought.

I felt a bit hurt about Reagan's casualness in accepting the message. He'd been a good friend of mine for ten years; he could at least have said he was sorry I was going to leave. Of course, there was a fair chance that he might get the promotion, but even if he was thinking about that, he could have been diplomatic about it. At least, he could have—

Oh, quit feeling sorry for yourself, I told myself. *You're through with Placet and you're through with Earth Center, and you're going back to Earth pretty soon now, as soon as they relieve you, and you can get another job there, probably teaching again.*

But darn Reagan, just the same. He'd been my student at Earth City Poly, and I'd got him this Placet job and it was a good one for a youngster his age, assistant administrator of a planet with nearly a thousand population. For that matter, my job was a good one for a man *my* age—I'm only thirty-one myself. An excellent job, except that you couldn't put up a building that wouldn't fall down again and . . . *Quit crabbing*, I told myself; *you're through with it now. Back to Earth and a teaching job again. Forget it.*

I was tired. I put my head on my arms on top of the

178

desk, and I must have dozed off for a minute.

I looked up at the sound of footsteps coming through the doorway; they weren't Reagan's footsteps. The illusions were getting better now, I saw. It was—or appeared to be—a gorgeous redhead. It couldn't be, of course. There are a few women on Placet, mostly wives of technicians, but—

She said, "Don't you remember me, Mr. Rand?" It was a woman; her voice was a woman's voice, and a beautiful voice. Sounded vaguely familiar, too.

"Don't be silly," I said. "How can I recognize you at midper—" My eyes suddenly caught a glimpse of the clock past her shoulder, and it *was* a clock and not a funeral wreath or a cuckoo's nest, and I realized suddenly that everything else in the room was back to normal. And that meant midperiod was over, and I wasn't seeing things.

My eyes went back to the redhead. She must be real, I realized. And suddenly I knew her, although she'd changed, changed plenty. All changes were improvements, although Michaelina Witt had been a very pretty girl when she'd been in my Extraterrestrial Botany III class at Earth City Polytech four . . . no, five years ago.

She'd been pretty, then. Now she was beautiful. She was stunning. How had the teletalkies missed her? Or had they? What was she doing *here*? She must have just got off the *Ark*, but— I realized I was still gawking at her. I stood up so fast I almost fell across the desk.

"Of course I remember you, Miss Witt," I stammered. "Won't you sit down? How did you come here? Have they relaxed the no visitors rule?"

She shook her head, smiling. "I'm not a visitor, Mr. Rand. Center advertised for a technician-secretary for you, and I tried for the job and got it, subject to your approval, of course. I'm on probation for a month, that is."

"Wonderful," I said. It was a masterpiece of understatement. I started to elaborate on it: "Marvelous—"

There was the sound of someone clearing his throat. I looked around; Reagan was in the doorway. This time not as a blue skeleton or a two-headed monster. Just plain Reagan.

He said, "Answer to your radiotype just came." He crossed over and dropped it on my desk. I looked at it. "O.K. August 19th," it read. My momentary wild hope that they'd failed to accept my resignation went down among the widgie birds. They'd been as brief about it as I'd been.

August 19th—the next arrival of the *Ark*. They certainly weren't wasting any time—mine or theirs. Four days!

Reagan said, "I thought you'd want to know right away, Phil."

"Yeah," I told him. I glared at him. "Thanks." With a touch of spite—or maybe more than a touch—I thought, *well, my bucko, you don't get the job, or that message would have said so; they're sending a replacement on the next shuttle of the* Ark.

But I didn't say that; the veneer of civilization was too thick. I said, "Miss Witt, I'd like you to meet—" They looked at each other and started to laugh, and I remembered. Of course, Reagan and Michaelina had both been in my botany class, as had Michaelina's twin brother, Ichabod. Only, of course, no one ever called the redheaded twins Michaelina and Ichabod. It was Mike and Ike, once you knew them.

Reagan said, "I met Mike getting off the *Ark*. I told her how to find your office since you weren't there to do the honors."

"Thanks," I said. "Did the reinforcing bars come?"

"Guess so. They unloaded some crates. They were in a hurry to pull out again. They've gone."

I grunted.

Reagan said, "Well, I'll check the ladings. Just came to give you the radiotype; thought you'd want the good news right away."

He went out, and I glared after him. The louse. The—

Michaelina said, "Am I to start to work right away, Mr. Rand?"

I straightened out my face and managed a smile. "Of course not," I told her. "You'll want to look around the place, first. See the scenery and get acclimated. Want to stroll into the village for a drink?"

"Of course."

We strolled down the path toward the little cluster of buildings, all small, one-story, one square.

She said, "It's . . . it's nice. Feels like I'm walking on air, I'm so light. Exactly what is the gravity?"

"Point seven four," I said. "If you weigh . . . umm, a hundred twenty pounds on Earth, you weigh about eighty-nine pounds here. And on you, it looks good."

She laughed. "Thank you, professor—oh, that's right; you're not a professor now. You're now my boss, and I must call you Mr. Rand."

"Unless you're willing to make it Phil, Michaelina."

"If you'd call me Mike; I detest Michaelina, almost as much as Ike hates Ichabod."

"How is Ike?"

"Fine. Has a student instructor job at Poly, but he doesn't like it much." She looked ahead at the village. "Why so many small buildings instead of a few bigger ones?"

"Because the average life of a structure of any kind on Placet is about three weeks. And you never know when one is going to fall down—with someone inside. It's our biggest problem. All we can do is make them small and light, except the foundations, which we make as strong as possible. Thus far, nobody has been hurt

181

seriously in the collapse of a building, for that reason, but . . . Did you feel that?"

"The vibration? What was it, an earthquake?"

"No," I said. "It was a flight of birds."

"What?"

I had to laugh at the expression on her face. I said, "Placet is a crazy place. A minute ago, you said you felt as though you were walking on air. Well, in a way, you are doing just exactly that. Placet is one of the rare objects in the universe that is composed of both ordinary and *heavy* matter. Matter with a collapsed molecular structure, so heavy you couldn't lift a pebble of it. Placet has a core of that stuff; that's why this tiny planet, which has an area about twice the size of Manhattan Island, has a gravity three-quarters that of Earth. There is life—animal life, not intelligent—living on the core. There are birds, whose molecular structure is like that of the planet's core, so dense that ordinary matter is as tenuous to them as air is to us. They actually *fly* through it, as birds on Earth fly through the air. From their standpoint, we're walking on top of Placet's atmosphere."

"And the vibration of their flight under the surface makes the houses collapse?"

"Yes, and worse—they fly right through the foundations, no matter what we make them of. Any matter we can work with is just so much gas to them. They fly through iron or steel as easily as through sand or loam. I've just got a shipment of some specially tough stuff from Earth—the special alloy steel you heard me ask Reagan about—but I haven't much hope of it doing any good."

"But aren't those birds dangerous? I mean, aside from making the buildings fall down. Couldn't one get up enough momentum flying to carry it out of the ground and into the air a little way? And wouldn't it go right through anyone who happened to be there?"

"It would," I said, "but it doesn't. I mean, they never fly closer to the surface than a few feet. Some sense seems to tell them when they're nearing the top of their 'atmosphere'. Something analogous to the supersonics a bat uses. You know, of course, how a bat can fly in utter darkness and never fly into a solid object."

"Like radar, yes."

"Like radar, yes, except a bat uses sound waves instead of radio waves. And the widgie birds must use something that works on the same principle, in reverse; turns them back a few feet before they approach what to them would be the equivalent of a vacuum. Being heavy matter, they could no more exist or fly in air than a bird could exist or fly in a vacuum."

While we were having a cocktail apiece in the village, Michaelina mentioned her brother again. She said "Ike doesn't like teaching at all Phil. Is there any chance at all that you could get him a job here on Placet?"

I said, "I've been badgering Earth Center for another administrative assistant. The work is increasing plenty since we've got more of the surface under cultivation. Reagan really needs help. I'll—"

Her whole face was alight with eagerness. And I remembered. I was through. I'd resigned, and Earth Center would pay as much attention to any recommendation of mine as though I were a widgie bird. I finished weakly, "I'll . . . I'll see if I can do anything about it."

She said, "Thanks—Phil." My hand was on the table beside my glass, and for a second she put hers over it. All right, it's a hackneyed metaphor to say it felt as though a high-voltage current went through me. But it did, and it was a mental shock as well as a physical one, because I realized then and there that I was head over heels. I'd fallen harder than any of Placet's buildings ever had. The thump left me breathless. I wasn't watching

Michaelina's face, but from the way she pressed her hand harder against mine for a millisecond and then jerked it away as though from a flame, she must have felt a little of that current, too.

I stood up a little shakily and suggested that we walk back to headquarters.

Because the situation was completely impossible, now. Now that Center had accepted my resignation and I was without visible or invisible means of support. In a psychotic moment, I'd cooked my own goose. I wasn't even sure I could get a teaching job. Earth Center is the most powerful organization in the universe and has a finger in every pie. If they blacklisted me—

Walking back, I let Michaelina do most of the talking; I had some heavy thinking to do. I wanted to tell her the truth—and I didn't want to.

Between monosyllabic answers, I fought it out with myself. And, finally, lost. Or won. I'd not tell her—until just before the next coming of the *Ark*. I'd pretend everything was O.K. and normal for that long, give myself that much chance to see if Michaelina would fall for me. That much of a break I'd give myself. A chance, for four days.

And then—well, if by then she'd come to feel about me the way I did about her, I'd tell her what a fool I'd been and tell her I'd like to . . . No, I wouldn't let her return to Earth with me, even if she wanted to, until I saw light ahead through a foggy future. All I could tell her was that if and when I had a chance of working my way up again to a decent job—and after all I was still only thirty-one and might be able to. . . .

That sort of thing.

Reagan was waiting in my office, looking as mad as a wet hornet. He said, "Those saps at Earth Center shipping department gummed things again. Those crates of special steel—aren't."

"Aren't what?"

"Aren't anything. They're empty crates. Something went wrong with the crating machine and they never knew it."

"Are you sure that's what those crates were supposed to contain?"

"Sure I'm sure. Everything else on the order came, and the ladings specified the steel for those particular crates." He ran a hand through his tousled hair. It made him look more like an airedale than he usually does.

I grinned at him. "Maybe it's invisible steel."

"Invisible, weightless and intangible. Can *I* word the message to Center telling them about it?"

"Go as far as you like," I told him. "Wait here a minute, though. I'll show Mike where her quarters are and then I want to talk to you a minute."

I took Michaelina to the best available sleeping cabin of the cluster around headquarters. She thanked me again for trying to get Ike a job here, and I felt lower than a widgie bird's grave when I went back to my office.

"Yeah, chief?" Reagan said.

"About that message to Earth," I told him. "I mean the one I sent this morning. I don't want you to say anything about it to Michaelina."

He chuckled. "Want to tell her yourself, huh? O.K., I'll keep my yap shut."

I said, a bit wryly, "Maybe I was foolish sending it."

"Huh?" he said. "I'm sure glad you did. Swell idea."

He went out, and I managed not to throw anything at him.

The next day was a Tuesday, if that matters. I remember it as the day I solved one of Placet's two major problems. An ironic time to do it, maybe.

I was dictating some notes on greenwort culture— Placet's importance to Earth is, of course, the fact that certain plants native to the place and which won't grow

185

anywhere else yield derivatives that have become important to the pharmacopoeia. I was having heavy sledding because I was watching Michaelina take the notes; she'd insisted on starting work her second day on Placet.

And suddenly, out of a clear sky and out of a muggy mind, came an idea. I stopped dictating and rang for Reagan. He came in.

"Reagan," I said, "order five thousand ampoules of J-17 Conditioner. Tell 'em to rush it."

"Chief, don't you remember? We tried the stuff. Thought it might condition us to see normally in midperiod, but it didn't affect the optic nerves. We still saw screwy. It's great for conditioning people to high or low temperatures or—"

"Or long or short waking-sleeping periods," I interrupted him. "That's what I'm talking about, Reagan. Look, revolving around two suns, Placet has such short and irregular periods of light and dark that we never took them seriously. Right?"

"Sure, but—"

"But since there's no logical Placet day and night we could use, we made ourselves slaves to a sun so far away we can't see it. We use a twenty-four hour day. But midperiod occurs every twenty hours, regularly. We can use conditioner to adapt ourselves to a *twenty*-hour day—six hours sleep, twelve awake—with everybody blissfully sleeping through the period when their eyes play tricks on them. And in a darkened sleeping room so you couldn't see anything, even if you woke up. More and shorter days per year—and nobody goes psychopathic on us. Tell me what's wrong with it."

His eyes went bleak and blank and he hit his forehead a resounding whack with the palm of his hand.

He said, "Too simple, that's what's wrong with it. So darned simple only a genius could see it. For two years I've been going slowly nuts and the answer so easy nobody could see it. I'll put the order in right away."

He started out and then turned back. "Now how do we keep the buildings up? Quick, while you're fey or whatever you are."

I laughed. I said, "Why not try that invisible steel of yours in the empty crates?"

He said, "Nuts," and closed the door.

And the next day was a Wednesday and I knocked off work and took Michaelina on a walking tour around Placet. Once around is just a nice day's hike. But with Michaelina Witt, any day's hike would be a nice day's hike. Except, of course, that I knew I had only one more full day to spend with her. The world would end on Friday.

Tomorrow the *Ark* would leave Earth, with the shipment of conditioner that would solve one of our problems—and with whomever Earth Center was sending to take my place. It would warp through space to a point a safe distance outside the Argyle I-II system and come in on rocket power from there. It would be here Friday, and I'd go back with it. But I tried not to think about that.

I pretty well managed to forget it until we got back to headquarters and Reagan met me with a grin that split his homely mug into horizontal halves. He said, "Chief, you did it."

"Swell," I said. "I did what?"

"Gave me the answer what to use for reinforcing foundations. You solved the problem."

"Yeah?" I said.

"Yeah. Didn't he, Mike?"

Michaelina looked as puzzled as I must have. She said, "He was kidding. He said to use the stuff in the empty crates, didn't he?"

Reagan grinned again. "He just thought he was kidding. That's what we're going to use from now on.

187

Nothing. Look, chief, it's like the conditioner—so simple we never thought of it. Until you told me to use what was in the empty crates, and I got to thinking it over."

I stood thinking a moment myself, and then I did what Reagan had done the day before—hit myself a whack on the forehead with the heel of my palm.

Michaelina still looked puzzled.

"Hollow foundations," I told her. "What's the one thing widgie birds won't fly through? *Air*. We can make buildings as big as we need them, now. For foundations, we sink double walls with a wide air space between. We can—"

I stopped, because it wasn't "we" any more. *They* could do it after I was back on Earth looking for a job.

And Thursday went and Friday came.

I was working, up till the last minute, because it was the easiest thing to do. With Reagan and Michaelina helping me, I was making out material lists for our new construction projects. First, a three-story building of about forty rooms for a headquarters building.

We were working fast, because it would be midperiod shortly, and you can't do paper work when you can't read and can write only by feel.

But my mind was on the *Ark*. I picked up the phone and called the radiotype shack to ask about it.

"Just got a call from them," said the operator. "They've warped in, but not close enough to land before midperiod. They'll land right after."

"O.K.," I said, abandoning the hope that they'd be a day late.

I got up and walked to the window. We were nearing midposition, all right. Up in the sky to the north I could see Placet coming toward us.

"Mike," I said. "Come here."

She joined me at the window and we stood there,

watching. My arm was around her. I don't remember putting it there, but I didn't take it away, and she didn't move.

Behind us, Reagan cleared his throat. He said, "I'll give this much of the list to the operator. He can get it on the ether right after midperiod." He went out and shut the door behind him.

Michaelina seemed to move a little closer. We were both looking out the window at Placet rushing toward us. She said, "Beautiful, isn't it, Phil?"

"Yes," I said. But I turned, and I was looking at her face as I said it. Then—I hadn't meant to—I kissed her.

I went back, and sat down at my desk. She said, "Phil, what's the matter? You haven't got a wife and six kids hidden away somewhere, or something, have you? You were single when I had a crush on you at Earth Polytech—and I waited five years to get over it and didn't, and finally wangled a job on Placet just to . . . Do I have to do the proposing?"

I groaned. I didn't look at her. I said, "Mike, I'm nuts about you. But—just before you came, I sent a two-word radiotype to Earth. It said, 'I quit.' So I've got to leave Placet on this shuttle of the *Ark*, and I doubt if I can even get a teaching job, now that I've got Earth Center down on me, and—"

She said, "But, Phil!" and took a step toward me.

There was a knock on the door, Reagan's knock. I was glad, for once, of the interruption. I called out for him to come in, and he opened the door.

He said, "You told Mike yet, chief?"

I nodded, glumly.

Reagan grinned. "Good," he said; "I've been busting to tell her. It'll be swell to see Ike again."

"Huh?" I said. "Ike who?"

Reagan's grin faded. He said, "Phil, are you slipping or something? Don't you remember giving me the answer to that Earth Center radiotype four days ago, just before Mike got here?"

I stared at him with my mouth open. I hadn't even read that radiotype, let alone answer it. Had Reagan gone psychopathic, or had I? I remembered shoving it in the drawer of my desk. I jerked open the drawer and pulled it out. My hand shook a little as I read it.

REQUEST FOR ADDITIONAL ASSISTANT GRANTED. WHOM DO YOU WANT FOR THE JOB?

I looked up at Reagan again. I said, "You're trying to tell me I sent an answer to this?"

He looked as dumfounded as I felt.

"You told me to," he said.

"What did I tell you to send?"

"Ike Witt." He stared at me. "Chief, are you feeling all right?"

I felt so all right something seemed to explode in my head. I stood up and started for Michaelina. I said, "Mike, will you marry me?" I got my arms around her, just in time, before midperiod closed down on us, so I couldn't see what she looked like, and vice versa. But over her shoulder, I could see what must be Reagan. I said, "Get out of here, you ape," and I spoke quite literally because that's exactly what he appeared to be. A bright yellow ape.

The floor was shaking under my feet, but other things were happening to me, too, and I didn't realize what the shaking meant until the ape turned back and yelled, "A flight of birds going under us, chief! Get out quick, before—"

But that was as far as he got before the house fell down around us and the tin roof hit my head and knocked me out. Placet is a crazy place. I like it.

"James MacCreigh" (this is the female member of the

190

team speaking) is not who you think he is, he is my husband, and his name is Frederik Pohl. He bashfully allowed when we first began doing this book that he, too, had been writing quite a lot of copy in the Great Years of Science Fiction, and so maybe we ought to include one of his stories. So he gave me some; I read them; I hated them; I said so as tactfully as I could, along the general lines of, "Well, Fred, you've written a lot of really fine stuff, but this early work isn't it" . . . and so we began putting together the book without any of his dozen or so early pseudonyms represented in it. Then, almost at the last minute, he diffidently said, "Well, you might as well take a look at this one." And no one was more surprised than I when I liked it! It's adventure science fiction, and not much like *The Space Merchants* or *Day Million* or *The Gold at the Starbow's End* . . . but I enjoyed it a lot when I read it, and we're both hoping you will too.

WINGS OF THE LIGHTNING LAND
By James MacCreigh

I
Moon Madness

Thorssen and I had the same type of job. We worked together on one of the most important industries there was. We were mooncattle hunters in a period when the *acret* for which the mooncattle were sought was the only thing that saved the life and intelligence of billions of the world's population.

I'd volunteered for mooncattle herding on an emotional impulse. There was a certain poetic justice to it that fascinated me, for I had been born a cretin, too, like nearly a tenth of humanity. A deficiency in the thyroid glands of my father or mother had made me an idiot child, helpless and useless. The gland extract, given early and regularly, returned me to normalcy.

There was no shame attached to being a cretin in this

sad year of 2240, for there were too many such persons. But I had the feeling of being inferior, set apart, an intelligent human only by virtue of regular doses of *acret*, the anti-cretinism extract made from the thyroid glands of the mooncattle.

I didn't make friends very well, probably for that reason. It just wasn't possible for me to make a friend unless the other party went nearly twice halfway. And since Thorssen, though not a cretin, was much the same type of moody individual that I was, I never got to be on really good terms with him.

The plague of cretinism, they tell me, was incomprehensible, even to the best scientists of all the world. The graph showing incidence of this dreadful sickness had been taking a gradual, steady upturn for scores of years in the past, and nobody knew the reason why. It was beginning to be a rarity for any family to be without at least one person who, without his *acret*, would soon have lapsed to mumbling, drooling idiocy.

We were herding the mooncattle in the Flatside area when we came across it. Thorssen and myself saw it—a squarish, angular framework of metal bars.

I guess we both saw it at the same time. We weren't walking very close together, since we'd had a little disagreement that morning before we started out, so we couldn't nudge each other and point it out. And of course we couldn't speak about it. Radios were strictly not to be used. The mooncattle might pick up the vibrations and be frightened off. Also, we naturally couldn't take our helmets off and yell through the atmospheric vacuum to each other.

Without paying much attention to each other, we drew near and looked it over. I've described it to various people who know things. Most of them say what I'm talking about is a tesseract—a four-dimensional cube. They also say a tesseract cannot exist in a three-dimensional space, like ours. Then they explain away the contradiction. They claim I saw a three-dimensional representation of a four-dimensional object, like a photograph is a two-dimensional representation of a three-dimensional object.

All of that doesn't make a lot of sense to me, but I don't generally argue about it very much. To me, the angular thing Thorssen and I saw looked like a series of six cubes, jointed to each other rather oddly so that each seemed to be within the other. No one of them seemed to enclose any other, though.

The cubes themselves were only there in outline. Draw rods of a curious pink metal—not coppery, but more pink—formed the corners of the cubes. That was all that was to be seen.

Thorssen, in the excitement of discovering the strange object, tabled our little feud for the time being. His eyes narrowed with lively interest. He kept shifting his glance from our "discovery" to me, wondering if I were as curious as he. He lifted his hand, beckoning me to his side. It was a sudden gesture and a thrill of wonder ran through me. Taciturn Thorssen looked excited and strangely tense!

I hopped over—we were in light gravity, and there was no such thing as a walk. I peered into the mazy interior, where he pointed—and got the shock of my life.

On the moon we are accustomed to blackness, the absence of light and color. There's no air to shatter the rays of light and let them filter into corners not directly illuminated.

But even the black of a moonshadow, which ought to be the blackest thing imaginable, was a pale, luminous thing compared with the mad, ebony zero of light I saw. I should have been able to see right through the spaces between the bars. There was nothing solid about the framework. But I couldn't. This blackness got in the way.

It wasn't even a mere absence of light that got me. There was a frightening, bending sensation about looking into it. A dizzying knowledge of instability came to me as I peered into it. I couldn't look any more. I backed away and glanced at Thorssen, wondering at his reaction. I had a lot of respect for that guy. But this time he too was up against a tough one. The question in my eyes was answered with a shrug. Thorssen didn't know any more about it than I did.

We were saved from wasting a lot of time just standing there and speculating by a sudden crackle of static in our headphones. We couldn't use them for communication, but the receivers had been left on to tell us when the herders started milling the mooncattle around. They frightened them with bursts of static and chased them toward us for the kill.

Thorssen seemed reluctant to take cover. But he moved his big body fast enough at the second spurt of static. We scrambled to our positions and got out our electron rifles.

The mooncattle are curious, great things, larger than any earth land animal. They reach forty feet in length, at times, and are supernaturally vicious.

Their body chemistry is of a strange type. Living as they do, without air, they depend on water to furnish them with oxygen. Water they find in tiny crevices and subterranean ice wells, for which they excavate with almost human patience and skill. The water is broken down inside their bodies by a process resembling electrolysis. Like the electric eel on Earth, they generate electricity. Besides breaking down the water, they use it for communication in the form of radio.

The mooncattle can be said to smoulder where terrestrial animals burn. Instead of a direct oxidation and reduction series of reactions to furnish power to move their huge bodies, they ferment their food. There are certain micro-organisms on Earth operating on the same principle. It has long been thought that such a process couldn't supply any creature large enough to be visible with enough power to live by—but the mooncattle proved differently.

The high, whining crackle of the mooncalves resounded in our earphones. On they came at us, great, ungainly things, speeding over the jetty crags of the moon's surface on their long, fast-moving legs.

Thorssen raised his gun to fire. I did the same. I saw the soundless flare of his electron rifle once; then I was too absorbed in the kill. It's hard to shoot a mooncow where it hurts; they're too decentralized. Hunting them requires a good aim and a knowledge of their peculiar anatomy. With Thorssen it was almost instinct.

All of a sudden the assault was over. I hadn't done too badly, and I scrambled from my position feeling pretty cocky. All that cockiness was driven from me in the next moment. My stomach muscles tightened.

Thorssen had not been content with just inspecting the machine I had almost forgotten. With his hands grasping the metal bars, he was leaning over that unspeakable blackness!

Your reflexes get kind of mixed up when you can't talk or yell. I hurled my rifle in his direction and started running towards him, hoping to distract him from that magnetic blackness.

Suddenly my knees gave way with panic. Like the light from a snuffed-out candle, Thorssen disappeared from sight!

I was too horrified and numbed to have much intelligent thinking. I could have saved my own skin if I had. Hypnotized by the unholy machine, I scrambled up to it and clung to the bars even as Thorssen had.

Whatever made me think I could succeed where Thorssen's steel muscles had failed, I don't know. I peered into that blackness, thinking insanely I could discover some trace of him.

The blackness was impenetrable, and that feeling of instability stole over me again, only doubly strong this time. I felt my grip on the bars melting, a horrible dizziness set in. . . .

Then, like Thorssen, I was sucked into those awful depths!

There was a pain such as I had never known. There was a crushing, rending stress on my body that was sheer hell. Stars reeled around me overhead—actually reeled, danced and swung to new positions in the sky. It was not an illusion.

Then the pain was over and I was falling.

My fall was stopped with a shattering jolt. I was lying, after a seeming century of agony, flat on my back on some sticky, ridged growths I took to be bushes. A cliff wall towered beside me. There was a sky above me, with hideous-hued clouds floating in it.

The lunar landscape was completely gone. The vacuum of space no longer sucked at my exposed skin. The fiercely bright sun was gone.

I was on a planet!

II
Claws of Death

I don't think I can tell you what my emotions were—it was all so sudden. I remember being in a stuporlike daze through which facts slowly filtered, each a slap in the face of my reason. It was all so incredible, so unreal. That was the gist of my feeling. . . .

It was daylight, but not the kind of daylight we have on Earth. A tiny sun, the size of Jupiter as seen from

Earth, hung high in the heavens. The stars were clearly visible, though slightly dimmed. There was a twilight feeling about the place, the eeriness of between darkness and dawn. The landscape was lighted, perhaps a little better than the full moon lights Earth. Colors were visible. The motif of this world was red—hot red of a single, bloodlike hue!

The wall which towered above me was fifty feet of unscalable red rock. The bushes on which I lay were red, with slight yellow and brown variations in their thistly "flowers." The ground from which they grew was blank red sand, stretching off into the horizon, with only clumps of these weird growths to relieve its monotony. Over to my right was what seemed to be a range of distant, low-lying hills.

I don't know how long it was before I became a thinking, conscious human again. A grim resignation had set in when I discovered Thorssen. He was lying ten or twenty feet from me, unmoving. He had been rendered insensible by his own amazing fall.

I rose to go to him and discovered why the fall hadn't killed us both. The act of rising tossed me several feet into the air. Gravity here was low, almost as low as on the moon itself.

I recovered myself and stepped gingerly over to Thorssen. I hadn't been right about him and I should have guessed as much. There were no shock-absorbing bushes where he lay, only hard-packed sand with a crumbly red shale, but he wasn't unconscious—just dazed and thoroughly shaken up. In addition to everything else, he had the constitution of an ox.

He was coming out of his daze. I watched his steel-colored eyes narrow speculatively as he sat up. An ironical smile twisted up the corners of his mouth. It was almost a statement: "Well, what do you know!"

He waved away my offered hand and got lightly to

his feet. Recovering from the leap he took involuntarily, he stood, arms akimbo, surveying the horizon.

After a long second of thought, he looked at me and shrugged. I did the same, cursing the lack of radio facilities which prevented conversation. Not that I thought he knew any more about our predicament than I.

But he had an idea. He motioned me to come closer and touch helmets. In that way the vibrations would be transmitted directly from helmet to helmet. If we shouted we could hear each other and compare notes.

I was a little too hasty in complying. That was a mistake I almost paid for dearly. I moved towards him thoughtlessly, forgetting the small gravity. My helmet struck his with a deep bell note. He jerked back, startled. I smiled at his expression of alarm.

But my smile was quickly erased. I became conscious of something our unexpected transition had kept from me before. It was a thin, faint, but heart-stopping hiss —the hiss of air leaking from my helmet!

I hope never again to repeat my state of mind as I fumbled agonizingly around the base of my helmet. I searched with my fingers for the tiny pinpoint of a hole I couldn't hope to see. It was impossible to find it and doubly impossible to do anything about stopping the leak.

But with the unexpectedness of every good miracle, the hissing trailed off into a soft, panting sound, then halted completely. And I was still breathing!

How could that be, I wondered. Then I realized with a swift flash of insight that we were on a planet now. Planets generally had some sort of atmosphere, even low-gravity ones.

Again, if I had stopped to think, I wouldn't have been as hasty as I then was. It had been proven that the planet had air. But how much, and of what kind— that was still undiscovered. It could have been deadly methane or ammonia. It's no wonder Thorssen considered me seven kinds of a numbskull.

I didn't think of that till after I'd ripped my helmet off entirely, glad to be out of it. And by that time I had already survived for several seconds in air that was thin, strangely tangy—but obviously breathable.

Thorssen, regarding me with a frown my foolhardiness had earned, removed his helmet too. In the dead silence, his short, bitter laugh sounded unreal.

"I wonder how you've managed to stay alive this long," he said acidly. "You have a positive genius for blundering stupidity."

I felt the roof of my mouth go dry with humiliation. The old shame of inferiority swept over me. Could I never forget the brand that had plagued me from birth? I was a cretin, wasn't I? Without those precious doses of *acret* I would be the most pitiable and despicable form of humanity.

I was supersensitive on the subject. I imagined condemnation in every act of Thorssen's. I almost hated him for his perfectly functioning thyroid, his perfection in all things. With that a new dread numbed me. Was there pity in the glance Thorssen shot me as he stooped to the sand? Did he realize, as suddenly as I, that I had not long to last without *acret*?

Dazedly I watched him putter around silently. I watched him scoop up some of the pebbly sand and crumble it between his fingers.

"Fertile ground," he said more to himself than me. "I wonder why nothing but these infernal bushes grow here. . . ."

I hated him for his callousness. How could he ignore my terror? I was a human, wasn't I? I was entitled to a little comfort, a little comradeship with a fate as appalling as mine confronting me. Hating him took the edge off my despair. If we could get back. . . .

199

"It needs irrigation, of course," Thorssen went on, straightening. "It's drier than yesterday's toast."

"Your interest may be agricultural," I said scathingly, "but I want to get back. Let's take a look around, see what we can do about it."

Thorssen narrowed his eyes at me in amused curiosity. "Take a look around what?" he asked with strained good humor. "Where do *you* suggest we start?"

The question was a poser, all right. Standing with our backs to the cliff we could see clear to the sharp horizon in the inadequate light of the little sun. But there was nothing to see but the scarlet sands, with occasional clumps of the gum bushes. The slight hills were still to our right.

As for the cliff—we regarded it carefully. Fifty feet high it was, fifty feet with no jut or hollow for fingers to grip. In a wavering line, but always with its vertical sheerness intact, it meandered to the horizon.

Even in this weak gravity we couldn't hope to reach its top. A leap might carry us twenty to thirty feet in the air, but that left an impregnable twenty feet more.

It was probably simultaneously that we both spotted the curious red glow beyond the foothills. It could have been a city, though it scarcely resembled artificial light. It might have been the sun, if the sun hadn't been overhead. It was like the flaming color of an Earth sunset, or a small dose of the aurora borealis.

Thorssen looked at me and hesitated for a moment. "It's worth investigating," he suggested.

I said nothing, thinking that above us lay our only avenue of escape—that there must be some way of utilizing it before it was too late, before my loathesome birthright claimed me.

Thorssen was strangely human for a change. "There is nothing we can do here," he said quietly. "If that is a city, there must be intelligence behind it. With help we can probably get back. Without it—"

He looked at me pityingly. There was more concern for me than for his own fate in that glance. I was almost grateful for his thoughtfulness.

I had too much respect for him to contest his reasoning. If there was any way of saving both of us, and me especially, it was through following his advice.

"Let's go then," I said quickly. "How long do you think it will take?"

Thorssen smiled at my impetuousness.

"I haven't the faintest idea," he told me, "but we'll know soon enough."

So we stepped awkwardly toward the hills with the light behind them. At first we rose into the air with every step, and came down sprawling. But our moon-trained muscles soon enabled us to walk more efficiently.

When I felt the first draught of the breeze in my face, I thought it was only because of our movement. I accepted it and was glad for it. This planet, despite the insignificance of its primary, was hot. And our exercise made us hotter.

But suddenly the wind shifted abruptly, fanning our backs. Its velocity mounted until it became a gale, blowing along as we were going, in the direction of the red glow. In a few seconds the desert was responding to the caress of the wind. Whirls of sand formed and leaped about. Stinging particles of grit commenced to strike against our unprotected necks and backs.

The wind now made a loud, howling sound, uncomfortable to hear even though it broke the eerie silence that had before reigned over this apparently dead planet. Over the wind's noise, I heard Thorssen shouting to me.

"Your helmet, stupid!" he yelled impatiently. "Put it on—don't close it. Just cover your head with it. Protect your eyes!"

I complied, and we stopped for a second to sneeze

the grit out of our noses before proceeding.

But the gale continued to mount in intensity. We decided to wait it out. We huddled as close to the cliff as we could, sealed our helmets, and sat with our backs against it.

Before us was a pageant well worth watching.

Great spouts of sand were being formed all over the terrain. They rose, genii-like, in twisting columns. The noise, even filtered through our lucose helmets, was awe-inspiring. The bushes that I'd encountered before were everywhere being flung about violently in the grip of the tornados. They were tenacious, those bushes. I saw none of them dislodged from their clutch on the sands, however forcefully the wind tore at them.

But I was safe enough and comfortable enough. I had the stored air of my pressure helmet, which no sandstorm could penetrate. My body was well protected by the hunting garb I wore. And the curves of the cliff saved us from the worst buffetings of the wind. I began even to feel drowsy.

Everything had happened too quickly before that for me to devote any concentration on where we were and how we'd got there. Now my fatigued brain wasn't able to cope with the problem, and dismissed it entirely after a while. I was thinking with great detachment of food and the joys of eating when I amazed myself mildly by falling asleep while the wind still raged. Not even the terror of my personal problem could prevent that. Maybe it was Thorssen. He stared into that wild spectacle of wind-torn sand fearlessly. I couldn't help feeling glad that he was there.

When I woke it was a starless black night and something was pressing on my chest. I moved and found the answer. I was completely buried in sand. That accounted for the complete blackness. I struggled to a sitting position and found Thorssen's hand ready to pull me to my feet.

The windstorm over, the scene had the same depressing monotony as when we'd first seen it—identically the same. It occurred to me that it shouldn't be so. The sun shouldn't still be directly overhead. It indicated either a very short day, which I had slept through completely, and the coincidence of awaking at the exact same time. Or it indicated an impossibly long day— almost no day at all, for I'd surely slept for hours without any visible motion of that hot, small sun.

"You all right?" Thorssen demanded, and a little finger of fear crept into my brain. There was no determining time on this planet. Was my sluggish thyroid showing so soon?

"Sure," I said unsteadily. "A little groggy from sleep."

"You'll get over that," he assured me pleasantly. "Right now," he went on cheerfully, "we've got something interesting. Look over there."

Near the cliff some of the bushes, more protected than their brethren in the open desert, had grown much larger and had assumed vinelike characteristics. They clambered up the wall, very nearly to the top.

"I'm going to try climbing that," Thorssen told me. "There's a good chance of succeeding. The stuff is tough."

The grogginess disappeared completely as I watched him. He was climbing the vine as gently as possible, trying hard not to dislodge it from its precarious grip on microscopic faults in the smooth cliffside. If he could make it, I could certainly. I was much lighter than Thorssen.

I shook myself and unscrewed my helmet again. I squinted up at the sun and then over to the lights beyond. They were still there—not bright, but visible.

203

I inhaled the thin air, though my deepest breath still left me unsatisfied.

However thin, the air appeared to be all we'd get for breakfast. I inspected a clump of the gum bushes—not very hopefully. They were obviously inedible. One quality they had, which I thought might come in handy some time and tabulated away in my mind. They were amazingly strong. They were limber, like eel grass back on Earth, but could not be broken, no matter how hard I pulled. I managed, with my teeth, to break the surface of one of them. The sticky, fluid sap beaded out. I tasted it cautiously. It was almost as tasteless as flat water. But it could, conceivably, support life for a while if water in any other form were not forthcoming.

I heard a cry from Thorssen and wheeled in time to see him tumbling down. He'd reached the top of the vine, found it wasn't high enough and tried to retrace his steps. But the descent was harder. He'd pulled some of the growth from the wall, falling with it. The fall was thoroughly cushioned and only a matter of about fifteen feet; he was safe enough and unhurt.

He got to his feet lithely, ran his fingers through a shock of thick black hair and grinned ruefully. "There wasn't any harm in trying!" he laughed. He had a funny sense of humor. Adversity always seemed to amuse him.

I was grateful for that laugh. It took away some of the grimness. We started walking again in the direction of that unchanged red glow.

"Maybe we'll have better luck along a little farther."

I nodded and we continued to walk along in silence.

"Got any idea where we might be?" I asked abruptly.

He shrugged without replying immediately, stooped for a handful of sand and fingered it thoughtfully.

Then he looked at me, sardonic humor in his face.

"A planet, I guess," he said taciturnly.

"I figured as much," I said patiently. "But what planet?"

The smile faded from his wide mouth. He squinted at the sky.

"Pluto, maybe," he said softly. "Not Mars, or anything nearer the sun. Probably not Pluto either. The sun's too small."

"One of the moons of Jupiter or Saturn?" I suggested, conscious that we had exchanged more words in one day than we had in six months!

"Maybe," he agreed, and was silent for a moment. "And maybe not," he said suddenly. "Maybe another star. That one isn't the right color. No yellow—sol's trademark is yellow."

"Another star! How could we be in another system?"

"How could we be on Pluto?" he muttered ironically. "One's as inconceivable as the other!"

That was true enough, I thought, as I abstractly repeated his process of scooping up sand and fingering it. It was friable, as crumbly as cheesecake, fresh and light.

"Well, how do *you* think we got here?" I asked.

"You idiot," he stormed, "if I knew that, I'd know pretty damn near everything!"

It was the first time he'd really lost his temper. Cowed, I walked beside him silently.

We walked on in those low-gravity, flat, sailing strides for what ought to have been a couple of hours. The sun didn't change position then any more than it had while we were asleep.

Used to the long silences that accompanied hunting the mooncattle, we were occupied with our own thoughts when our walk was suddenly interrupted.

It was just after I had had a brain wave. If we could climb to the top of the cliff, we might be able to see something, either on the cliff or on the desert, from its vantage point. If we could dig footholds into the cliff. . . .

I was about to communicate this sudden rush of brains to the head to Thorssen, when the only cry of pure astonishment I'd ever heard from him stopped me in my tracks. It reminded me, a little too late, that we hadn't had any evidence that this world really was sterile. It might still harbor animal life. Maybe inimical animal life.

Well, it did!

Thorssen's eyes were wide with shock as he stared up into the sky. I looked.

Above us, soaring and wheeling, looking down on us, was a living creature. At least a thousand feet in the air it was, but it was huge—greater than the pterodactyl of Earth's youth. It was like a bird, but its wings were unlike anything avian—more like the longitudinal fins of an eel, the ribbon fins that extend in an unbroken line from gills to tail. Its eyes must have been wonderfully sharp, for it saw us looking up at it, and abruptly came plummeting down toward us!

"Duck!" I screamed. "Down on the ground! If that thing grabs you . . . !"

But it was too late. There was no place to hide. No shelter for as much as a cricket.

The thing, its featherless wings screaming through the thin air, came sweeping down in a power dive faster than any plane of Earth. The wonder of the thing gripped me even as I dropped to earth. This thin air— how could anything fly in it?

I found out. The thing dropped with a shrill sound of displaced atmosphere till it was almost on us. Then its ribbon wings rippled and humped as it slowed and straightened out. It swooped down and clutched at Thorssen with bristling claws. I could feel those claws, almost, in my own flesh. . . .

And it caught him. I saw him wince as the needle-sharp talons pierced skin and flesh, and grab despairingly at the sand as though he expected the thing to carry him off into the sky.

But the creature was not built to lift loads like Thorssen. It was not strong enough to withstand a sharp blow such as the inertia an Earth-heavy man's body gave it.

When it gripped Thorssen's wide shoulder, its claws sank in and held—held too well, held while the forearm of the creature snapped off and the bird, with a thin, piglike squeal of agony, plummeted into the sand, thrown off balance by the unexpected shock.

It must have died immediately. It was dead, anyhow, by the time we got around to examining it.

The immediate concern was Thorssen's shoulder. It took all my strength to pull the rigid claws apart and out of his flesh. You'd think it was my shoulder, the way my face screwed up. But those claws were devilish instruments. They were compound, with little retractable barbs set in the claw itself. I had to pull those barbs out through Thorssen's flesh.

He turned pale and a little bit grimmer. "Go on," he said quietly, "*get them out!*"

If you think it was an easy or a pleasant job, try looking at a fishhook sometime and imagining how you would like eight of them dragged through your skin!

We finally got through with that ordeal though, and Thorssen himself bandaged the bleeding, dirty mass of cuts with his undershirt. There was no water to wash it, no iodine to sterilize it. We had to trust to nature.

Thorssen tied the last bandage and smiled wryly. "What rotten luck," he grunted, and appeared to dismiss it that lightly. He moved over to examine the carcass.

It was a fantastic thing. Thorssen lifted it easily with his one good hand. Huge as it was, it could not have weighed more than a hundred pounds even on Earth. It came to a quarter of that on this planet of slight pull.

We dissected it as best we could. The best we could

do, lacking all the things we lacked, was to pull it apart with our fingers and brute force. My primary interest in the bird-thing vanished as soon as I touched it, for it was obviously totally inedible. Its flesh was so dry as to be almost powdery.

The fall had smashed its backbone and it had died instantly. Its body was hot to the touch. No trace of blood could be found. Certain parts of its body were soggy with the sticky fluid we'd found in the bushes before—or with something like it. Its skeleton, though as fragile as calcined bone, was very like that of terrestrial bird.

The most mysterious thing about it, though, I found, was a bulge in the breast of the thing, just below where its neckless head sat directly on its "shoulders". I prodded it, and finally tore it out completely. It proved to be a solid, polyhedral lump. Polyhedral, I say—it was perfectly regular, and of an odd consistency. It was partly transparent, prismatic.

The transparency was only on the surface. Held up to the sun, it was clear at the very edge. Then it began to deepen rapidly into color, passing through yellows, oranges and deep reds to utter blackness a fraction of an inch below the surface.

And it was hot—hotter than the bird's body, which was almost too warm to be comfortable. Nor did it lose its heat as long as we had it. It weighed a little more than a quarter of a pound.

"It's a curious thing," Thorssen said quietly, inspecting it. "It looks machine-made."

He turned it in the broad palm of his hand thoughtfully and then stuffed it into his sweater, the arms of which he had looped about his neck. I don't know whether he had any rational purpose in keeping it. I didn't want to leave it there myself, but I was happy to let him carry the thing. Later, it became very important to us.

We set off again down the line of the wall, Thorssen stoic about his wound. I should have known better than to assume, because he made no fuss about it, that it was trivial.

III
City of Emptiness

Half an hour later we came across steps!

"These were never made for a human foot," Thorssen volunteered, after a cursory look. There was wonder in his voice. "They're too small, in the first place, and they aren't shaped right."

They certainly weren't natural. They were merely flat pieces of woody substance projecting across cup-shaped, hewn depressions in the rock. The woody substance puzzled me. I tried my belt buckle on it, the nearest thing I had to a cutting edge. I found I could shave off long splinters with ease. But it was impossible to cut against the grain, and surprisingly hard to break.

I tested the strength of the highest one I could reach, hanging from it. It held firm.

"This is it," I said happily. "We can pull ourselves up, hand over hand. It's a way out."

I dropped off and let Thorssen test them himself. He was so much heavier than I, and it had to be good for both of us. Without a word he chinned himself once for luck, and began to climb. As soon as his swinging feet cleared the level of my head, I followed.

The climb was hot work, though brief. Sweat trickled down my face in rivulets, quickly evaporating in the rarefied air. How Thorssen, with that wound in his shoulder, managed, I'll never know.

I heard a smothered exclamation above me and quickly

lifted myself the rest of the way.

The top of the cliff was something I hadn't at all expected. I stared with wide eyes for a moment.

"It's like a wall," I said. "A wall that keeps nothing out of nowhere!"

Thorssen nodded silently. His brows drew together, though. It was becoming increasingly clear that there was some manner of intelligent life on this planet. First the apparently manufactured steps, then this obviously artificial wall. But where was this life?

"If intelligence constructed this wall," Thorssen speculated, "it was obviously to keep out enemies, enemies such as the vicious creature that attacked us—"

A far-fetched comparison came to me of the Earth eagle stealing glittering objects. Could this bird-thing have stolen the object Thorssen carried in his sweater? It was almost evidence of civilization.

I mentioned as much to him and he shrugged. "I am almost certain the bird had an intelligence of its own. If it stole the polyhedral object it was for a purpose."

It was interesting to speculate, but it got us nowhere. We gazed down the narrow, perfectly flat, perfectly even ribbon of rock. It stretched into infinity in either direction. The other side of the wall was just like the side we had come from—sand and bushes.

"Well, what now?" My voice must have sounded very tired. I felt that way. There seemed nothing to hope for—no way of returning, ever, to Earth, with its beautiful, rich, thick air, with its gravity that held you snugly to the ground. With, most especially, its millions and billions of people, and cities and animals and trees, and *acretin*. . . .

"We'll keep on," Thorssen decided, and I heard his words through a miasma of despair. "It will be easier walking up here. It's a flat, solid surface."

Thirst was becoming a problem with me. It became

harder to breathe, with my throat clogging up stickily. I began to remember with longing the nice, cold, viscid sap from those gum bushes. I decided to put the problem to Thorssen.

"Thorssen—"

He looked around at me. I saw his face relax as from a strain.

"What?"

"I'm thirsty."

There was sour amusement in his voice. "So am I."

"I'm hungry too," I went on determinedly. "Do you have any ideas?"

He shrugged and looked ahead once more. He picked his steps with care. We were now in a narrower spot.

"No," he replied thoughtfully. "I've been thinking about it. We'll have to keep going—"

"There was a sort of sap in those weeds," I said. "Not very good maybe, but it must have had water in it."

"Forget it. I tried it. It burned my mouth off."

I loosened my collar and rubbed the back of my neck. It was stinging, hot to the touch—why?

Thorssen's neck supplied the answer. I saw him rub it as I had rubbed mine. It was red and beginning to blister —sunburn!

I told him.

"From what?" he said, staring without troubling to narrow his eyes at the tiny luminary above.

"It must be," I said. "There is no other sun."

"It's impossible," Thorssen snapped, and I watched his eyes narrow on that red glow in the distance. All the same, maybe because he had come to a conclusion about that glow, he protected his neck from the sun with his sweater. He put the polyhedral object in his helmet and slung it from his waist.

We continued for about ten miles over the wall. The territory was unchanged on either side of us—only ahead of us the little range of hills drew imperceptibly nearer. The mystery of the ruddy glow behind them remained unsolved.

The hunger and thirst I felt had grown and grown until now it was all of my existence. I would have given my soul for food, but I would have given my chances of ever eating again for a small whisky glass of water.

I was almost dead on my feet. I didn't have a thought to spare for anything else.

I was so absorbed in myself and my thirst, it was only when I caught myself actually lifting my foot to step over his prostrate body that I really noticed Thorssen. He had been walking about twenty feet ahead of me and had, without warning, fallen to the ground, where he lay unmoving.

I sank to my knees beside him, shaking myself out of my stupor. The wound was horribly inflamed. He was alive, but his pulse was faint, his breathing heavy. In his sleep he winced as I touched the bandages. I had an idea then of what he must have gone through, and a surge of wild admiration for him went through me.

Waking him would have done no good—rest was the only curative I had to offer. So I sat down beside him and abruptly dropped off myself into a horrid black sleep.

When I awoke I looked around twice to make sure. But my first impression was right—Thorssen had utterly disappeared! Nothing but Thorssen had disappeared. The sweater I had loosened from him was still where I'd dropped it. His helmet with the polyhedral object still lay on the red stone of the wall-top.

It was as if he had risen deliriously and staggered off in a semicoma. I looked over the sides of the wall— both sides. He hadn't fallen. In either direction along the wall itself there was no sign of him. I was alone, totally alone.

Lack of water and food had cost too much for sleep to restore. Mental and physical agony descended with equal force, and in a daze, clutching Thorssen's helmet and sweater, I continued in the same direction we had been traveling. Without the strength of dauntless Thorssen to buoy me up, the horror of what had befallen us doubled in intensity.

I walked for several hours. The little hills were close, when finally I decided I could walk no longer. I tottered to the edge of the wall and peered weakly over. The enticing red gum bushes held out their promises of the cooling, drinkable sap they contained. I might have disregarded Thorssen's warning about them, had it not been for something new.

In the utter silence, now that my scuffling footfalls on smooth rock had ceased, were only two sounds. One, irregular and recognizable, was the soft whispering of the wind on the red sands.

The other was a low murmuring that I had heard before. It had been occurring all along. I remembered now that I had heard it every time I consciously devoted my mind to listening. I had dismissed it each time; it was that faint. Even on a planet where absolute silence was the norm, and any variation was worthy of immediate and complete attention, this sound had been faint enough to be dismissed.

Now it was louder, appreciably louder, and it sounded to my willing ears like *running water!*

It didn't occur to me that my sensory equipment would have been willing to interpret anything as what it wanted most of all to hear. But it did occur to me that there was an odd note to that murmur. It could be running water, but there was something—something wrong.

I began moving again, faster this time, with a purpose.

And I thought I saw the place the sound was coming from. Up ahead, where the wall broadened more than ever before, it rose to a slight crater.

It wasn't very hard for me to convince myself that that crater was a well.

Maybe it was. But when I got to it, not even my willing brain could convince me that the liquid flowing below was water.

There was some sort of liquid torrenting along in the depths of the crater. I could hear it perfectly. Though it was utterly dark down there, I could see the glint of the dim sun reflected from it. But the sound was more of a sustained metallic clinking than that of tinkling, bubbling fountains.

And an acrid, chemical aroma came from that hellish river or whatever it was.

My first thought had been to dive right into the water. Now I became more prudent. I loosened my helmet, retaining Thorssen's and the polyhedron, and dropped it.

The liquid was about a hundred feet below. And the splash made by the falling helmet was not that of water.

But still I did not want to give up. Nor did I have to. A search soon showed me another of the ladderlike affairs cut directly into the wall of the well. Without pausing to ask why or wherefore, I eased myself down onto the first rung and swung down.

The river was definitely not water. It was molten metal—a metal I didn't recognize. Though molten, it was cool enough for me to touch without discomfort.

I know of a couple of metals that act like that—with fusing points low enough to be tolerable to humans. There's woodsmetal for one, and there's potassium. But this didn't seem to be either of them. I had no idea what it might be. And I didn't care much. I wasn't physically able to care much about anything.

There was a faint exhalation given off by that stream, a thin chemical reek that added to my killing thirst. My throat was drier than the flesh of that bird-thing Thorssen and I had killed. Thorssen—he was a shadowy outline in my privation-maddened thoughts. With him there had been some sense of security. . . .

It was darker than the holes of hell in that little pit with the noisy river running close beside. But I could see faintly the mark of a small hewn pathway beside the stream. Tottering groggily, I stepped out along it, determined to follow it wherever it led.

After I don't know how many hours and miles, there was an abrupt turning in the river's course. I found hot, white light shining ahead. I called on a reserve of strength that surely couldn't have belonged to me, and hastened to see what caused the light. I reached the end of the tunnel, where the accompanying river splashed metallically down a brief falls, and stood petrified in sheer astonishment.

Before me was a huge lake of the metallic liquid, surrounded by a profusion of splashing fountains, not metal, this time, but real *water!* There were trees and plants of a hundred ornamental shapes. It was not only beautifully landscaped, but well kept.

On the other side of the dozen-acre lake was a city, a city unlike anything on Earth, reminiscent, somehow, of ancient New York and other cities of the past whose towers clutched at the sky. The mountainous moon's horizon would have showed the same tracery of elevations and depressions that this city's skyline revealed. But where the moon's markings were the result of cataclysmic chance, this city's jaggedness was planned.

Behind me were the mountains. I'd passed under them while following the stream. And ahead, beyond the city, that same red light shone with multiplied brilliance.

I had enough sense not to drink the water that was in those delightful fountains with too great haste. I took it in sips, slow deep sips. And I rested by the side of the fountains. Before I got up I had drunk enough water to hold me for another day at least.

That light puzzled me, now that I was in condition to be puzzled again. It could not be the lights of the city, as Thorssen and I had believed. Here was the city, and the light came from still farther away, from behind the city and with an intensity that was inconceivable.

I stretched out by the side of the fountains and planned a campaign. There were three things I had to do—find food, find Thorssen, find a way to get home.

Food I might likely find growing from one of the bushes or trees. Thorssen and the way home were more difficult. But a city meant people—well, intelligent creatures at least. Within the city I might find help.

After a few minutes of this thought, I slept again. For how many hours, I cannot tell. The tiny sun was still motionless overhead. Time had almost stood still. Time that was so precious for me. No, I had not forgotten that—the curse that dogged me and so many of my fellow humans.

A sickeningly sweet nut was all I could find that seemed edible. I swallowed a dozen or so of them with their paper-thin shells. They were four or five inches long and half as broad. I tucked as many as would fit in Thorssen's helmet, along with the polyhedral thing, and made off toward the city.

The astounding thing about the city, I found, once inside it, was its emptiness—that and the fact that it seemed unfinished, incomplete.

The buildings, some of which must have been close to a thousand feet in height above the depressed floor of the valley, were constructed in varicolored rocks. Not one of them contained a single window. Some were incomplete, showing how they had been built. It seemed that a synthetic substance had been poured into flat vertical molds and cast on the spot. Within these partly completed buildings, one of which I was able to enter through a gap in the side, there seemed to be no interior walls.

The building was a jagged shell, stretching emptily to the sky. This incomplete one was roofless.

The completed buildings had doors, rather large doors. But they were securely locked by some means I could not determine.

I wandered along streets paved with shifting colors. I would be standing on a section of purest blue. I would walk and within a dozen yards the blue would imperceptibly have become purple. A bit farther on the purple would fade into red, and the red into orange.

It was a gorgeous view but not inspiring. For it robbed me, through its emptiness, of my hope for friendly aid.

The buildings seemed to be higher in the center of the city. I walked that way, my footfalls sounding awesomely loud in the utter silence of these great cathedrals of emptiness.

IV
The Lightning Strikes

Like all persons suffering from a physical defect, I knew everything there was to know on the subject of cretinism. In front of one of those magnificent shells, I felt the dizzying impact of head-splitting ache, and my blood turned to water. I recognized the mark. *It was the beginning of atavism.*

Never was I so totally alone, so completely struck by the hopelessness of my position. Thorssen, marooned on this alien world, could reconcile himself to the prospect of living on it forever. It would not have been the ideal existence, but it would have been life. For me there was nothing like that. Either I got back to Earth soon—or I descended to the level of a moron.

Death was preferable. Over and over again I cursed the horror that plagued so many men and women of Earth. Ours was a horrible existence. For all our seeming normalcy, there were so many strictures. We were deplored and pitied. We were shipped away from home to far-off places in ever increasing numbers. We were discouraged from marriage and forbidden children. We were shunned and feared. . . .

Yes, death was preferable. It came to me with cold clearness that I would have to decide soon. How many hours or days had I before I became a cretin? I felt well enough, of course. There was no perceptible dimming of my intellectual faculties. It seemed to me that I could reason as well as ever, that I was still human and a bit above the average. But it would seem that way. I would never be able to mark the transition.

Was I already on the way to drooling, horrid idiocy? Was my sense of well-being the mark of a mind that had abandoned reason?

Not likely. Facts bore me out. With close figuring I reckoned I had about three days to go before I began to revert. Three days! Perhaps I could do it. Perhaps I could find how I had got here, and how I could reverse the process and get home again in three days. If I couldn't, I would kill myself.

I started to walk again, immersed in this morbidity. Suddenly my feet slid from under me, slipped on something, and I fell to the ground. On arising, I discovered a dark red, damp smear on my hand. *It was blood!*

And I discovered a trail of blood, a few drops at spaces of three or four yards, leading away before me.

It was human blood, red and rich. Thorssen! My head cleared for the first time in hours. There was hope. With him there was always hope.

There seemed to be a clear deduction. Thorssen had come along here and suddenly begun to bleed. Perhaps he had been engaged in violent physical struggle with an unknown adversary who was also now gone. Or perhaps the old wound had opened. In any case, I followed the blood drops with new courage. My hatred for him, a protective feeling because I feared him so greatly, melted. Thorssen! But where was he and how would I find him?

I followed the trail, all right. But while I didn't find him, I did find something interesting—an open door.

The door was in a small but somewhat imposing, squat building, set a bit apart from the others, in the middle of a stretch of pure white paving.

I entered and found myself in a huge, low-ceilinged hall. A chill breeze followed me through the door. I drew my clothing tighter about me and gazed around.

Nothing of much interest was visible. It was a bare hall without ornamentation or furniture. Only at one side there was a ramp, climbing through a gap in the ceiling to a higher floor.

The trail of blood went that way. So did I.

The second floor of this building was also the top floor. The walls here were set with floor-to-ceiling slabs of transparent substance. It was an observatory of sorts.

In the center of the room was a pyramidal bank of studs, levers, pointers, and other less easily identifiable things. Clearly this must have been a control room of sorts.

I approached the controls and circled them speculatively. The whole affair looked like some modernistic form of a Christmas tree, of which the gadgets were the ornaments. It was about that shape and a little taller than me. The purpose of the controls, if they were controls, was, of course, beyond me.

It was distinctly cold in the room. I began to realize that, ever since I'd left the direct light of the small but potent sun, I had felt chill.

A low benchlike affair ran the periphery of the room. I seated myself on it and considered the situation. One amazing thing that escaped my notice before now came to me. There was no conceivable way out but the way I'd come in. Nor could I have been following a double trail, for I'd watched for that. Thorssen had come into this room and never gone out of it. If my sense of humor had been operating, I would have been tired of the way he had of disappearing into thin air every so often.

Except for the pyramidal array of gadgets, the room was stark bare. If Thorssen were still in this room, there was only one place he could be. That was in the pyramid.

I examined it more carefully. It seemed to be all of one piece, but there was a curious handle-shaped affair down at the bottom that seemed to have no relation to the rest of the controls. I yanked on it boldly and a panel slid open.

Yes, Thorssen was there. But he was a sick man, conscious enough to recognize me, but drawn and haggard. His principal need, it was evident, was air. He came out of that small, wire-crammed closet gasping. It was all I could do to support him to the bench. But I did more than my best. The condition of his makeshift bandage convinced me he had been through hell.

He rallied swiftly and smiled at the expression of concern on my face. It was almost impertinent that I should be supporting him, ministering to his needs. I felt that old wave of inferiority sweep over me. I edged farther off so that he would not feel the need to thank me too profusely.

He watched though, curiously perturbed. It must have embarrassed him to have me so humble. It may have been what he disliked so about me, my cringing deference.

"Don't do that!" he said sharply, and I flushed stupidly.

I covered my confusion with words. I wanted to know what had happened, but he wouldn't say until I had told him my story.

The wound of the bird-thing had given him more pain by far than I'd realized, he said. But there was nothing to be gained by complaining. We were working against time.

He had endured that for my sake!

He'd awakened while I slept on the red, rock wall. Half-crazy with agony, lack of food and water, he'd walked away. It was a delirium. He remembered nothing of his walk. He came back to consciousness to find himself sprawled on the brink of one of the fountains which surrounded the lake. Apparently he had followed the same route I had.

He drank and ate just as I had, then entered the city.

"Then I got into a little trouble," he said. "I found a door that would open, and I went into one of the buildings. It was pretty much like this one inside, with very little furniture. But it seemed a kind of barracks. There were cotlike affairs, hundreds of them, scattered all over the upper floors. And one of the cots was in use."

"The thing that was sleeping in it didn't look even vaguely human. It had arms and legs, but it needed a head to be complete. It had none. As far as I can tell, it's deaf, blind and only God knows how it eats. It had a couple of rows of short diagonal slits in its sides which opened and closed regularly as it lay there. I guess it breathed through them."

I leaned forward, fascinated. "Was it a living organism, or a machine?"

Thorssen smiled grimly. "It's hard to say. They have intelligence all right, but nothing that could have constructed this city. Will you let me get on?"

I shut up meekly.

Thorssen took a breath. "Well, I woke it up. Not intentionally, mind you. I got too close to it. Somehow, it sensed someone was there. And it woke up mad.

"This wasn't any fragile creature, either," he went on. "It wasn't like the monster who gave me this souvenir." He patted his healing shoulder. "It was as dense and as strong as we. Probably a lot stronger.

"Anyway, it grabbed at me with powerful-looking bony claws. But I dodged back in time and it missed. Then I ran—fast.

"It followed me, and that thing could run! But with pretty constant dodging, and taking advantage of the fact that it could neither see nor hear, I managed to keep out of its reach. How the devil it kept on my trail, I don't know. Maybe it was sensitive to the heat of my body—or maybe it smelled me.

"Well, it finally caught up with me. We had a big tussle, and that scratch on my shoulder opened up again. It didn't get its claws into my flesh. Strangely, it didn't seem to want to hurt me, just capture me. But I was in no mood for guessing games. So when it got its claw hooked in a piece of my bandage, I let it rip and ran like hell! I covered a good eighth of a mile before I even stopped and looked around. It had discarded the piece of bandage and was nosing around, trying to figure where I'd gone. Then I heard a deep noise, like a factory whistle. A couple of seconds later another one just like it came racing along the sidestreets. It turned into the street I was on not more than a dozen feet from me. I don't know whether it didn't know I was there, or just hadn't been told to look for me yet. A couple of others came loping along from other directions. Then the whole gang of them started coming after me!

"They were moving a little slower this time. I guess they were following the blood I was dripping. I didn't wait to find out. Then I found this place and ran in. The door was standing open to this pyramid affair and it was as good a cubbyhole as any. I got in and pulled it shut.

"But I found I couldn't open it from the inside either. I was good and stuck! The door was so perfectly fitted that I was just out of luck as far as air was concerned—none came in."

"And then," I said huskily, "I stumbled along."

"And saved my life. I can't say thanks."

He put out his hand and I felt it close over mine with a grip that made me wince.

"Here's your sweater, Thorssen," I said. "You can use it."

I turned away and looked again into the little cubbyhole where Thorssen had so long been secreted. There was barely space for him, with his broad, powerful body, to crouch. Certainly he could neither stand nor lie down. I admired, no I nearly worshipped, his stamina and resilience.

The headless things Thorssen had described had gone away long before I came. Where they'd gone we didn't know. We didn't stop to enquire. Thorssen had a hunch that they were directed by a greater intelligence. And we were in search of that intelligence.

But we should have exercised greater caution. We'd gone only a short distance when I heard that deep-throated hoot Thorssen had described. We whirled and saw, close behind us, one of the creatures.

It was coming at us cautiously, evidently waiting for reinforcements. It was a tall thing—Thorssen hadn't mentioned that, but he should have, for the creature was huge. It was a deep gold in color, almost bronze, with the lips of the openings in its side a contrasting livid green. It was horribly beautiful, but I had no eye for its beauty. Together Thorssen and I swiveled around again and ran for our lives.

You can really run in a low gravity, once you get the hang of it, and Thorssen and I had the knack of it down pat. Thorssen's wound seemed to be bothering him again, or maybe it was just consideration that kept his speed down to mine. In spite of it we must have made better than thirty miles an hour.

The group of things behind us—there must have been a dozen of them by now—paced us evenly. They seemed to have reserve power in their long, sailing strides, but they didn't make use of it. Could it be they were merely waiting to tire us out, so we would be easier prey?

I thought so. But I didn't know what we could do about it. And so we continued to run with the things pursuing us.

Thorssen, beside me, suddenly grabbed my arm. "We'd better face it," he said hoarsely. "We'll never out-distance those creatures! We've still got some strength left and it's better than collapsing in their path."

We both halted and faced the oncoming monstrosities.

Thorssen's grip on my arm tightened, but the expected battle never materialized. The monstrosities halted too and stood in silent conference for a moment. Then they moved forward. As we tensed for the struggle, their ranks divided. They split into two groups and encircled us.

We stood that way for several moments without saying a word and without a motion or sound from the headless ones. Then we heard a stir of motion behind us, and saw that those who had passed us were closing in on us. We backed away from them.

It was incredible! The whole circle moved too, at a slow walk. Still encircling us, keeping the circle perfect, they walked on. We walked too, inside the circle, back the way we had come. Thorssen and I stared into each other's eyes for a long second. Then Thorssen shrugged and his steel-colored glance seemed vaguely amused. It was incomprehensible to both of us—and funny. We continued our walk without words.

The headless ones herded us back to their little squat building and up the ramp to the second floor. They would not follow up, but ranged themselves around the lower hall in attitudes which seemed curiously expectant. There were a dozen additions to the group and more came in as we watched from above.

Thorssen studied them, an odd, speculative light in his eyes.

"They're waiting for us to do something!" he said softly. "Heaven knows what it is, but they'll stay there until we do it."

The silence drew in on me and I shivered with cold. Thorssen, naked to the waist, the sweater wound over the shred of his bandage, didn't seem to feel the cold. It puzzled me. I was freezing and couldn't ignore it so easily.

Or *was* it cold?

My hand trembled as it rose to my scalp. I hardly dared touch my hair, I feared there would be full confirmation there. . . .

And there was!

My blood congealed with terror. I had miscalculated. My hair was coarse and dry; the hairline had crept lower, almost to the brows and well past the ears. It

225

had been difficult for me to speak, I remembered. I had attributed it to thirst, but it wasn't thirst.

My skin was cold. My hair was thick and brittle. My tongue was numbing; it had swollen and become ridged. I ground my teeth in helpless, angry horror, and the horror was increased as I felt how loose they were in my gums.

Every symptom was beginning to be present. My *acret* treatment long overdue, I was becoming a *cretin!* And Thorssen had known, had seen! Yet he was silent, keeping me in ignorance. What was there to do? I couldn't hate him. I only wished to die.

Was there any hope for me? In this new and virulent form of the sickness that was as old as humanity, the physical changes preceeded the intellectual by a few hours, no more. I had perhaps half a day left of adult ability. At the end of that time I would be worthless to anyone. I would be a ghastly, crawling, stupid horror.

Would Thorssen help, could his stomach stand the sight of me until we had found the way out of this mess we were in? I looked at him in helpless wonder. He probably would. There was a lot I had learned about Thorssen—a lot. But even if he found a way out, would it be such that he could take me with him?

Wasn't it better to die before that happened? To be left like an ape on this arid, terrible planet was a far worse fate.

The numerical value of pi is 3.14159, I told myself silently. *Light travels at the speed of* 186,000 *miles per second. A logarithm is that power of a number which gives ten as a result. You know these things now. As long as you remember and understand them you are all right. When it becomes hard to remember them, you are going. Then you have to kill yourself. But until you begin to forget, you still have a chance.*

"I've got it!" Thorssen interrupted me with suppressed excitement. "The difference between them and us—there's something we can do that they can't do. What is it?"

I braced myself and dismissed my plan for suicide for the time being. Thorssen must never suspect the promise I had made myself. He would never allow it. I had to act.

"I don't know," I said. "What?"

"We can see," he said patiently. "They can't! Therefore, they want us to do something that requires vision. It's up to us to find out what that something is."

"More likely they want us to stay where we are until they get around to us," I objected. "How do you know we're not being kept for sacrifice, or for eating? How do you know that they're not intelligent?"

"I don't know anything about them specifically," Thorssen said swiftly. "All I know is that intelligence is responsible for this high form of civilization, that intelligence guided them in the ingenious way they brought us here. Whether that intelligence is within them or comes from another source, I cannot say."

There was logic in that. "Well what do they want?" I cried irritably.

"Whatever they want," he said, his gray eyes fixed speculatively on the control board, "It's up here. And the only thing up here is that pyramidal control board. Suppose we see if we can make it tick?"

The dials and levers and pointers meant no more to Thorssen, superficially, than they did to me. It's not possible to take one look at a completely unknown piece of machinery and say what it is and how to work it.

But Thorssen is an electrician by hobby and managed to solve a few problems of the control board. "I've located the power leads," he said. "I don't know what they're hooked up to, but there's juice in them. There's a pattern all set up on the control board. I don't know what would be happening if it were functioning, but I know that it's supposed to be functioning now. Only there's a fault somewhere keeping it from delivering. It seems to me we're expected to find that fault and fix it!"

He dove back into the closet in which he had spent stifling hours.

After a while he announced, "Looks like this rod isn't making contact."

The people who'd built this control board used inflexible rods instead of wires. Just as efficient, of course, and more durable, providing you belonged to a race of supermechanics who knew just exactly what connection they wanted to make where, long before they made it. Thorssen puttered a while longer, as I sat repeating my formula to myself. Yes, I was still of normal intellect. My memory hadn't gone yet.

Thorssen came out of the closet groaning, "If I had some tools, I might know what I'm doing. I might even be able to do what I'm supposed to be doing."

"How does it look?" I asked, conscious of the thickening in my speech. It was like waiting for a poison to take effect.

He considered. "Not too bad," he said finally. "But that power rod is sprung. Lord knows what happened to it, but it's bent a little and doesn't make contact at the end. If you lean on the middle of it and straighten it out, it works—I guess."

"Why don't you try it?" I asked impatiently. How many hours of sanity could I have left?

He shrugged. "Because I'd have to leave the master switch on. And this board is rigged oddly. I don't mean only that it's totally different from anything I ever dreamed of in my whole life. But even for a board out of a nightmare, there are some funny bugs in this one. That switch"— he pointed to a silvery medallion, ridged

so that a nearly human hand could grasp and turn it
—"is the master switch, the one that activates the whole
board. At least, it's cut in on every power lead I've been
able to trace."

"Then turn it on and fix up the bar," I suggested,
probably apathetically. I was more interested in the
recurrence of that splitting headache which came and
went in tides of nausea. I tried to remember back to my
infancy. Was that a part of cretinism? If it was, I
wanted to die, for I couldn't bear the mere idea of
enduring that pain for long.

Thorssen was saying something. He was shaping
words with his firm, wide lips. "I can't do that. I tried it,
and it won't work. I think the only chance for us to
hold down the rod is for one of us to hold it down
while the other works the switch. If you turn on the
switch while a part of the board isn't functioning, it
seems to have no effect. A sort of automatic cut-off."

That was all I heard. Then the sickness of my headache came rushing in on me, with a high keening sound
that I could hear in my ears. The pain was blinding. I
stood perfectly still, waiting for it to subside. *The
numerical value of pi is three point one four one nine
fi—no! Five nine. Be careful! Light travels at the speed
of. . . .*

My vision began to clear again and I could see Thorssen. He seemed to be angry with me. He wanted me to
come over to him. I walked carefully to his side and
stood peering up into his face. Thorssen was tall and
wide and strong. I hated him to see me this way. I
wanted to cover my face with my hands. I wanted to
die. I was horrible.

Thorssen was angry with me. He put my hand on
the little bright thing and turned it. I understood immediately what he wanted me to do, and I also turned
it. Maybe I turned it too hard. It came off in my hand.

I thought that would make Thorssen angry with me, but it didn't. He started to shout, but he stopped and stood looking at the silver thing and at me, a little puzzled, a little angry. Then he put the silver thing back where it had been. There was a nice hole under where the silver thing had been, a hole that looked like that thing we had found would fit in it—that thing we had gotten from the bird that attacked us. I would have tried to fit it in but Thorssen had already put the silvery thing back on.

Thorssen made me get down on my hands and knees and go into the little closet where he had hidden. He put a helmet in my hands and pushed them against the rod. The helmet kept my hand from touching the rod, but it was my hand pushing it just the same.

Suddenly, the pain pushed back into my head, clearing it slightly. *Have I gone yet?* I wondered. *Am I a cretin? The numerical value of pi is three point one eighty six thousand miles per logarithm. Is the power of ten which makes. . . .*

That was wrong, I knew. As soon as I started forgetting, I had to do something—kill myself.

I had to kill myself. How?

I was still holding the helmet against the rod. I had to. The helmet protected me, insulated me from a shock.

The shock would kill me.

Thorssen wanted me to keep pressing the rod. I did not want to disappoint Thorssen. I carefully pressed on the rod all the time. My left hand was on the helmet. My right hand reached up and touched the charged rod. A jolt of livid green flame lighted my way to darkness.

I was in a rocket plane where the pilot was doing stunts. *Zipp* would go the rocket jets and we would zoom up. Then we would straighten out, glide down, and *zipp* would go the jets again.

I opened my eyes. Thorssen was carrying me, striding

dexterously along that incredible wall that had marked the beginning of our adventures here. Leaping agilely ahead of us was one of the headless ones.

I shut my eyes tightly, remembering. Despite everything, Thorssen had kept faith with me. He had saved me, wretched wreck of humanity that I was . . . but was I?

My mind was clear, clearer than it had been since I could remember. The splitting ache was completely gone. My body was strangely relaxed, vital. I felt wonderful. *I wasn't a cretin!* But why not?

In fact, why wasn't I dead? I had committed suicide, hadn't I?

I opened my eyes wide and stared at Thorssen.

I moved a little and he stopped instantly, smiling down at me. There was something about his smile that dazed me.

"Martha," he said gently, "there's nothing to be afraid of—not now, with what you have ahead of you."

But I was frightened now. There was something to be frightened about, something changed. He was not looking at me as if I were a pitiable creature of a shunned race. I saw myself as a woman in his eyes, the woman I had never been for him before.

I struggled to be put down. The instant I touched the red rock wall, I felt the difference. I was changed! I was longlimbed and slim with a new grace. Shakily, I touched my hair. It was luxuriant and silken. My skin was clear and smooth. Wordlessly he handed me a highly polished bit of metal he used for shaving.

The face was almost a mockery, it was so different. All my features were refined to the point of sheer exquisiteness. My eyes were wide, clear and a frightened green. My hair, dull before and lank, was a glory of shimmering gold-red. The trembling lips reflected were red and soft—vibrantly young. I was beautiful, more beautiful than any woman I had ever seen and envied.

The mirror fell with a clatter from my nerveless hand. I stared at Thorssen. He lifted my face with his hand.

"Do you believe me now?" he said softly. "You have the universe in the palm of your hand!"

"But how did it happen?" I cried.

He tucked my hand under his arm. "I'll tell you as we go along. We have to hurry. We have a time limit. But we're going home."

The tesseract we came to was like the one we had seen on the moon.

"But why wasn't it visible before?" I demanded.

"It was operating from the moon to this planet then. It is only visible when it's operating at the source for exit. That's why there's a time limit on us. Only so much atmosphere can be allowed to blow through. We were sucked from the moon," he went on smilingly. "We are going to get blown back."

It was beginning to be clear in my head now.

"Will you tell me what happened—back there?" I begged.

Thorssen's eyes glistened. "The oddest things," he said at last. "I don't rightly know how to tell you about them. The polyhedron we got from the bird's body turned out to be important. It was the key, you might say, to the whole thing.

"Anyway, someone else entered the room when the juice was turned on—someone who had come from a great distance, someone who was grateful that I had made it possible for him to come. He was invisible, but talked to me by telepathy.

"This planet was his original home—his and his race's. They had to flee because of something frightful that evolved here, some new animal enemy, in league with creatures like the bird-thing we killed, who had intelligence of a sort. They left their servants here—the headless things—but they were almost powerless when the bird-things stole the last of the communicators—the polyhedron."

We ranged ourselves before the tesseract. "We wait for it to be reversed," Thorssen said. "It will be in a few minutes."

The headless one, having guided us this far, turned suddenly and leaped away.

"You see," Thorssen explained again, "this tesseract exists in two places at once by virtue of its fourth-dimensional construction. It's here, on a planet of a star in what I strongly suspect is a different universe. It's a transportation device, part of a cosmos-wide chain that once existed. From this planet the race that built that tesseract sent out colonies to a thousand other worlds by means of the tesseracts. One of the worlds so colonized was the moon—back when even it had a breathable atmosphere.

"The tesseracts transmit matter from one of the places in which each of them is located to the other. This one is sent for transmission from the moon to here. I have an idea that that is one reason why the moon has no air today. It has all been sucked out by the tesseract.

"Anyway, when they ran away from the mother world they couldn't get back again, and we made it possible for them, with dumb luck. I was instructed in how to set the control panel to reopen the tesseract gateway between here and the planet where they are now. He made me leave before they began coming back. I still don't know what his race looks like."

"You can tell me now," I said slowly, "why—why I'm alive. I tried to kill myself when I found I was becoming a cretin. How did I fail? And why am I not a cretin right now? And this miraculous change—"

He took my hand in his and held it tight. "That

wasn't electricity, Martha. I don't know what it was, but it seems to have been a sort of basic life force. As a favor, my visitor gave me a slight dose of it—look!" He bared his shoulder. It was healed entirely. "Your cretinism was cured at the same time. Your thyroid has been regenerated. You'll never need treatments again. In fact, with a dose of the force you had, I doubt you'll ever need treatments for anything."

He paused and stared anxiously at the tesseract, which showed no signs of change.

"And another thing," he went on in an altered tone. "Another very important thing. I don't think there'll be any more cretinism—at least not of the new type—among Earth's people. My visitor found that in my mind, and seemed to sense guilt and sorrow. I got the impression there was some radiation which came from the tesseract on the moon which caused the atrophy of the thyroid. They're going to withdraw the tesseract as soon as we get through."

Thorssen fitted my helmet over my head and helped me seal it. I watched him fit his own and then snap to attention. He grasped my hand in his. It tightened as we watched the tesseract shifting its color. Its ruddy gold was deepening and changing to a cobalt blue. Simultaneously I became aware of rushing atmosphere, Thorssen's hand gripping mine. . . .

Together Thorssen and I leaped into the tesseract and, mounted on a jet of air, were borne back whence we had come.

Cyril Kornbluth was a close friend and collaborator of mine (male member speaking) until his untimely death in the late fifties. We worked together on seven or eight books and several dozen shorter pieces that appeared under joint by-lines, such as *The Space Merchants*, *Gladiator-at-Law* and so on. But we also worked with each other in some ways on stories that were not exactly collaborations. In between the collaborating we would discuss our individual writing projects; sometimes we would contribute. *The Little Black Bag* represented a case in point. I didn't really contribute a thing—except the whole story. Cyril, years before the story was written, had told me he was thinking of a story about a case of medical instruments from the future somehow finding their way to the present. Good idea, I said, and put it out of my mind as one does with other people's good ideas, until he dropped in one day in 1949, allowed that he would like to write a science-fiction story that week but couldn't think of an idea for one and did I have anything to suggest? Why don't you write the medical-instrument-from-the-future story you were talking about ten years ago? I asked. He looked thunderstruck. Because I forgot I ever had the idea, he said, but now I remember, and I'll go home and write it. And he did; and this is it.

THE LITTLE BLACK BAG
By C. M. Kornbluth

Old Dr. Full felt the winter in his bones as he limped down the alley. It was the alley and the back door he had chosen rather than the sidewalk and the front door because of the brown paper bag under his arm. He knew perfectly well that the flat-faced stringy-haired women of his street and their gap-toothed, sour-smelling husbands did not notice if he brought a bottle of cheap wine to his room. They all but lived on the stuff themselves, varied by whiskey when paychecks were boosted by overtime. But Dr. Full, unlike them, was ashamed.

A complicated disaster occurred as he limped down the littered alley. One of the neighborhood dogs—a mean little black one he knew and hated with its teeth always bared and always snarling with menace—hurled at his legs through a hole in the board fence that lined his path. Dr. Full flinched, then swung his leg in what was to have been a satisfying kick to the animal's gaunt ribs. But the winter in his bones weighed down the leg. His foot failed to clear a half-buried brick, and he sat down abruptly, cursing. When he smelled unbottled wine and realized his brown paper package had slipped from under his arm and smashed, his curses died on his lips. The snarling black dog was circling him at a yard's distance, tensely stalking, but he ignored it in the greater disaster.

With stiff fingers as he sat in the filth of the alley, Dr. Full unfolded the brown paper bag's top, which had been crimped over, grocer-wise. The early autumnal dusk had come; he could not see plainly what was left. He lifted out the jug-handled top of his half gallon, and some fragments, and then the bottom of the bottle. Dr. Full was far too occupied to exult as he noted that there was a good pint left. He had a problem, and emotions could be deferred until the fitting time.

The dog closed in, its snarl rising in pitch. He set down the bottom of the bottle and pelted the dog with the curved triangular glass fragments of its top. One of them connected, and the dog ducked back through the fence, howling. Dr. Full then placed a razorlike edge of the half-gallon bottle's foundation to his lips and drank from it as though it were a giant's cup. Twice he had to put it down to rest his arms, but in one minute he had swallowed the pint of wine.

He thought of rising to his feet and walking through the alley to his room, but a flood of well-being drowned the notion. It was, after all, inexpressibly pleasant to sit there and feel the frost-hardened mud of the alley turn soft, or seem to, and to feel the winter evaporating from his bones under a warmth which spread from his stomach through his limbs.

A three-year-old girl in a cut-down winter coat squeezed through the same hole in the board fence from which the black dog had sprung its ambush. Gravely she toddled up to Dr. Full and inspected him, with her dirty forefinger in her mouth. Dr. Full's happiness had been

236

providentially made complete; he had been supplied with an audience.

"Ah, my dear," he said hoarsely. And then: "Preposserous accuzation. 'If that's what you call evidence,' I should have told them, 'you better stick to your doctoring.' I should have told them: 'I was here before your County Medical Society. And the License Commissioner never proved a thing on me. So, gennulmen, doesn't it stand to reason? I appeal to you as fellow memmers of a great profession—' "

The little girl, bored, moved away, picking up one of the triangular pieces of glass to play with as she left. Dr. Full forgot her immediately, and continued to himself earnestly: "But so help me, they *couldn't* prove a thing. Hasn't a man got any *rights?*" He brooded over the question, of whose answer he was so sure, but on which the Committee on Ethics of the County Medical Society had been equally certain. The winter was creeping into his bones again, and he had no money and no more wine.

Dr. Full pretended to himself that there was a bottle of whiskey somewhere in the fearful litter of his room. It was an old and cruel trick he played on himself when he simply had to be galvanized into getting up and going home. He might freeze there in the alley. In his room he would be bitten by bugs and would cough at the moldy reek from his sink, but he would not freeze and be cheated of the hundreds of bottles of wine that he still might drink, the thousands of hours of glowing content he still might feel. He thought about that bottle of whiskey—was it back of a mounded heap of medical journals? No; he had looked there last time. Was it under the sink, shoved well to the rear, behind the rusty drain? The cruel trick began to play itself out again. Yes, he told himself with mounting excitement, yes, it might be! Your memory isn't so good nowadays, he told himself with rueful good-fellowship. You know perfectly well you might have bought a bottle of whiskey and shoved it behind the sink drain for a moment just like this.

The amber bottle, the crisp snap of the sealing as he cut it, the pleasurable exertion of starting the screw cap on its threads, and then the refreshing tangs in his throat, the warmth in his stomach, the dark, dull happy oblivion of drunkenness—they became real to him. You *could* have, you know! You *could* have! he told himself. With the blessed conviction growing in his mind—it *could* have happened, you know! It *could* have!—he struggled to his right knee. As he did, he heard a yelp behind him, and curiously craned his neck around while resting. It was the little girl, who had cut her hand quite badly on her toy, the piece of glass. Dr. Full could see the rilling bright blood down her coat, pooling at her feet.

He almost felt inclined to defer the image of the amber bottle for her, but not seriously. He knew that it was there, shoved well to the rear under the sink, behind the rusty drain where he had hidden it. He would have a drink and then magnanimously return to help the child. Dr. Full got to his other knee and then his feet, and proceeded at a rapid totter down the littered alley toward his room, where he would hunt with calm optimism at first for the bottle that was not there, then with anxiety, and then with frantic violence. He would hurl books and dishes about before he was done looking for the amber bottle of whiskey, and finally would beat his swollen knuckles against the brick wall until old scars on them opened and his thick old blood oozed over his hands. Last of all, he would sit down somewhere on the floor, whimpering, and would plunge into the abyss of purgulent nightmare that was his sleep.

After twenty generations of shilly-shallying and "we'll

cross that bridge when we come to it," *genus homo* had bred himself into an impasse. Dogged biometricians had pointed out with irrefutable logic that mental subnormals were outbreeding mental normals and supernormals, and that the process was occurring on an exponential curve. Every fact that could be mustered in the argument proved the biometricians' case, and led inevitably to the conclusion that *genus homo* was going to wind up in a preposterous jam quite soon. If you think that had any effect on breeding practices, you do not know *genus homo*.

There was, of course, a sort of masking effect produced by that other exponential function, the accumulation of technological devices. A moron trained to punch an adding machine seems to be a more skillful computer than a medieval mathematician trained to count on his fingers. A moron trained to operate the twenty-first century equivalent of a linotype seems to be a better typographer than a Renaissance printer limited to a few fonts of movable type. This is also true of medical practice.

It was a complicated affair of many factors. The supernormals "improved the product" at greater speed than the subnormals degraded it, but in smaller quantity because elaborate training of their children was practiced on a custom-made basis. The fetish of higher education had some weird avatars by the twentieth generation: "colleges" where not a member of the student body could read words of three syllables; "universities" where such degrees as "Bachelor of Typewriting," "Master of Shorthand" and "Doctor of Philosophy (Card Filing)" were conferred, with the traditional pomp. The handful of supernormals used such devices in order that the vast majority might keep some semblance of a social order going.

Some day the supernormals would mercilessly cross

the bridge; at the twentieth generation they were standing irresolutely at its approaches wondering what had hit them. And the ghosts of twenty generations of biometricians chuckled malignantly.

It is a certain Doctor of Medicine of this twentieth generation that we are concerned with. His name was Hemingway—John Hemingway, B. Sc., M. D. He was a general practitioner, and did not hold with running to specialists with every trifling ailment. He often said as much, in approximately these words: "Now, uh, what I mean is you got a good old G.P. See what I mean? Well, uh, now a good old G.P. don't claim he knows all about lungs and glands and them things, get me? But you got a G.P., you got, uh, you got a, well, you got a . . . *all-around man!* That's what you got when you got a G.P.—you got a all-around man."

But from this, do not imagine that Dr. Hemingway was a poor doctor. He could remove tonsils or appendixes, assist at practically any confinement and deliver a living, uninjured infant, correctly diagnose hundreds of ailments and prescribe and administer the correct medication or treatment for each. There was, in fact, only one thing he could not do in the medical line, and that was violate the ancient canons of medical ethics. And Dr. Hemingway knew better than to try.

Dr. Hemingway and a few friends were chatting one evening when the event occurred that precipitates him into our story. He had been through a hard day at the clinic, and he wished his physicist friend Walter Gillis, B. Sc., M. Sc., Ph. D., would shut up so he could tell everybody about it. But Gillis kept rambling on, in his stilted fashion: "You got to hand it to old Mike; he don't have what we call the scientific method, but you got to hand it to him. There this poor little dope is, puttering around with some glassware and I come up and I ask him, kidding of course, 'How's about a time-travel machine, Mike?' "

Dr. Gillis was not aware of it, but "Mike" had an I.Q. six times his own, and was—to be blunt—his keeper. "Mike" rode herd on the pseudo-physicists in the pseudo-laboratory, in the guise of a bottle washer. It was a social waste—but as has been mentioned before, the supernormals were still standing at the approaches to a bridge. Their irresolution led to many such preposterous situations. And it happens that "Mike," having grown frantically bored with his task, was malevolent enough to . . . but let Dr. Gillis tell it:

"So he gives me these here tube numbers and says, 'Series circuit. Now stop bothering me. Build your time machine, sit down at it and turn on the switch. That's all I ask, Dr. Gillis—that's all I ask.' "

"Say," marveled a brittle and lovely blonde guest, "you remember real good, don't you, doc?" She gave him a melting smile.

"Heck," said Gillis modestly, "I always remember good. It's what you call an inherent facility. And besides I told it quick to my secretary, so she wrote it down. I don't read so good, but I sure remember good, all right. Now, where was I?"

Everybody thought hard, and there were various suggestions:

"Something about bottles, doc?"

"You was starting a fight. You said, 'Time somebody was traveling.' "

"Yeah—you called somebody a swish. Who did you call a swish?"

"Not swish—*switch*."

Dr. Gillis' noble brow grooved with thought, and he declared: "Switch is right. It was about time travel. What we call travel through time. So I took the tube number he gave me and I put them into the circuit builder, I

241

set it for 'series' and there it is—my time-traveling machine. It travels things through time real good." He displayed a box.

"What's in the box?" asked the lovely blonde.

Dr. Hemingway told her: "Time travel. It travels things through time."

"Look," said Gillis, the physicist. He took Dr. Hemingway's little black bag and put it on the box. He turned on the switch and the little black bag vanished.

"Say," said Dr. Hemingway, "that was, uh, swell. Now bring it back."

"Huh?"

"Bring back my little black bag."

"Well," said Dr. Gillis, "they don't come back. I tried it backwards and they don't come back. I guess maybe that dummy Mike give me a bum steer."

There was wholesale condemnation of "Mike" but Dr. Hemingway took no part in it. He was nagged by a vague feeling that there was something he would have to do. He reasoned: "I am a doctor, and a doctor has got to have a little black bag. I ain't got a little black bag—so ain't I a doctor no more?" He decided that this was absurd. He *knew* he was a doctor. So it must be the bag's fault for not being there. It was no good, and he would get another one tomorrow from that dummy Al, at the clinic. Al could find things good, but he was a dummy—never liked to talk sociable to you.

So the next day Dr. Hemingway remembered to get another little black bag from his keeper—another little black bag with which he could perform tonsilectomies, appendectomies and the most difficult confinements, and with which he could diagnose and cure his kind until the day when the supernormals could bring themselves to cross that bridge. Al was kinda nasty about the missing little black bag, but Dr. Hemingway didn't exactly

242

remember what had happened, so no tracer was sent out, so. . . .

Old Dr. Full awoke from the horrors of the night to the horrors of the day. His gummy eyelashes pulled apart convulsively. He was propped against a corner of his room, and something was making a little drumming noise. He felt very cold and cramped. As his eyes focused on his lower body, he croaked out a laugh. The drumming noise was being made by his left heel, agitated by fine tremors against the bare floor. It was going to be the D.T.'s again, he decided dispassionately. He wiped his mouth with his bloody knuckles, and the fine tremor coarsened; the snare-drum beat became louder and slower. He was getting a break this fine morning, he decided sardonically. You didn't get the horrors until you had been tightened like a violin string, just to the breaking point. He had a reprieve, if a reprieve into his old body with the blazing, endless headache just back of his eyes and the screaming stiffness in the joints were anything to be thankful for.

There was something or other about a kid, he thought vaguely. He was going to doctor some kid. His eyes rested on a little black bag in the center of the room, and he forgot about the kid. "I could have sworn," said Dr. Full, "I hocked that two years ago!" He hitched over and reached the bag, and then realized it was some stranger's kit, arriving here he did not know how. He tentatively touched the lock and it snapped open and lay flat, rows and rows of instruments and medications tucked into loops in its four walls. It seemed vastly larger open than closed. He didn't see how it could possibly fold up into that compact size again, but decided it was some stunt of the instrument makers. Since his time—that made it worth more at the hock shop, he thought with satisfaction.

Just for old times' sake, he let his eyes and fingers rove over the instruments before he snapped the bag shut and headed for Uncle's. More than a few were a little hard to recognize—exactly that. You could see the things with blades for cutting, the forceps for holding and pulling, the retractors for holding fast, the needles and gut for suturing, the hypos—a fleeting thought crossed his mind that he could peddle the hypos separately to drug addicts.

Let's go, he decided, and tried to fold up the case. It didn't fold until he happened to touch the lock, and then it folded all at once into a little black bag. Sure have forged ahead, he thought, almost able to forget that what he was primarily interested in was its pawn value.

With a definite objective, it was not too hard for him to get to his feet. He decided to go down the front steps, out the front door and down the sidewalk. But first. . . .

He snapped the bag open again on his kitchen table, and pored through the medication tubes. "Anything to sock the autonomic nervous system good and hard," he mumbled. The tubes were numbered, and there was a plastic card which seemed to list them. The left margin of the card was a rundown of the systems—vascular, muscular, nervous. He followed the last entry across to the right. There were columns for "stimulant", "depressant", and so on. Under "nervous system" and "depressant" he found the number 17, and shakily located the little glass tube which bore it. It was full of pretty blue pills and he took one.

It was like being struck by a thunderbolt.

Dr. Full had so long lacked any sense of well-being except the brief glow of alcohol that he had forgotten its very nature. He was panic-stricken for a long moment at the sensation that spread through him slowly, finally tingling in his fingertips. He straightened up, his pains gone and his leg tremor stilled.

That was great, he thought. He'd be able to *run* to the hock shop, pawn the little black bag and get some booze. He started down the stairs. Not even the street, bright with midmorning sun, into which he emerged made him quail. The little black bag in his left hand had a satisfying, authoritative weight. He was walking erect, he noted, and not in the somewhat furtive crouch that had grown on him in recent years. A little self-respect, he told himself, that's what I need. Just because a man's down doesn't mean—

"Docta, please-a come wit'!" somebody yelled at him, tugging his arm. "Da litt-la girl, she's-a burn' up!" It was one of the slum's innumerable flat-faced, stringy-haired women, in a slovenly wrapper.

"Ah, I happen to be retired from practice—" he began hoarsely, but she would not be put off.

"In by here, docta!" she urged, tugging him to a doorway. "You come look-a da litt-la girl. I got two dolla, you come look!" That put a different complexion on the matter. He allowed himself to be towed through the doorway into a mussy, cabbage-smelling flat. He knew the woman now, or rather knew who she must be—a new arrival who had moved in the other night. These people moved at night, in motorcades of battered cars supplied by friends and relations, with furniture lashed to the tops, swearing and drinking until the small hours. It explained why she had stopped him: she did not yet know he was old Dr. Full, a drunken reprobate whom nobody would trust. The little black bag had been his guarantee, outweighing his whiskery face and stained black suit.

He was looking down on a three-year-old girl who had, he rather suspected, just been placed in the mathematical center of a freshly changed double bed. God

245

knew what sour and dirty mattress she usually slept on. He seemed to recognize her as he noted a crusted bandage on her right hand. Two dollars, he thought. . . . An ugly flush had spread up her pipestem arm. He poked a finger into the socket of her elbow, and felt little spheres like marbles under the skin and ligaments roll apart. The child began to squall thinly; beside him, the woman gasped and began to weep herself.

"Out," he gestured briskly at her, and she thudded away, still sobbing.

Two dollars, he thought—give her some mumbo jumbo, take the money and tell her to go to a clinic. Strep, I guess, from that stinking alley. It's a wonder any of them grow up. He put down the little black bag and forgetfully fumbled for his key, then remembered and touched the lock. It flew open, and he selected a bandage shears, with a blunt wafer for the lower jaw. He fitted the lower jaw under the bandage, trying not to hurt the kid by its pressure on the infection, and began to cut. It was amazing how easily and swiftly the shining shears snipped through the crusty rag around the wound. He hardly seemed to be driving the shears with fingers at all. It almost seemed as though the shears were driving his fingers instead as they scissored a clean, light line through the bandage.

Certainly have forged ahead since my time, he thought —sharper than a microtome knife. He replaced the shears in their loop on the extraordinarily big board that the little black bag turned into when it unfolded, and leaned over the wound. He whistled at the ugly gash, and the violent infection which had taken immediate root in the sickly child's thin body. Now what can you do with a thing like that? He pawed over the contents of the little black bag, nervously. If he lanced it and let some of the pus out, the old woman would think he'd done something for her and he'd get the two dollars.

246

But at the clinic they'd want to know who did it and if they got sore enough they might send a cop around. Maybe there was something in the kit. . . .

He ran down the left edge of the card to "lymphatic" and read across to the column under "infection". It didn't sound right at all to him; he checked again, but it still said that. In the square to which the line and column led were the symbols: "IV-g-3cc". He couldn't find any bottles marked with Roman numerals, and then noticed that that was how the hypodermic needles were designated. He lifted number IV from its loop, noting that it was fitted with a needle already and even seemed to be charged. What a way to carry those things around! So—three c.c.'s of whatever was in hypo number IV ought to do something or other about infections settled in the lymphatic system—which, God knows, this one was. What did the lowercase "g" mean, though? He studied the glass hypo and saw letters engraved on what looked like a rotating disk at the top of the barrel. They ran from "a" to "i", and there was an index line engraved on the barrel on the opposite side from the calibrations.

Shrugging, old Dr. Full turned the disk until "g" coincided with the index line, and lifted the hypo to eye level. As he pressed in the plunger he did not see the tiny thread of fluid squirt from the tip of the needle. There was a sort of dark mist for a moment about the tip. A closer inspection showed that the needle was not even pierced at the tip. It had the usual slanting cut across the bias of the shaft, but the cut did not expose and oval hole. Baffled, he tried pressing the plunger again. Again *something* appeared around the tip and vanished. "We'll settle this," said the doctor. He slipped the needle into the skin of his forearm. He thought at first that he had missed—that the point had glided over the top of his skin instead of catching and slipping under it. But he saw a tiny blood spot and realized that somehow he just hadn't felt the puncture. Whatever was in the barrel, he decided, couldn't do him any harm if it lived up to his billing—and if it could come out through a needle that had no hole. He gave himself three c.c. and twitched the needle out. There was the swelling—painless, but otherwise typical.

Dr. Full decided it was his eyes or something, and gave three c.c. of "g" from hypodermic IV to the feverish child. There was no interruption to her wailing as the needle went in and the swelling rose. But a long instant later, she gave a final gasp and was silent.

Well, he told himself, cold with horror, you did it that time. You killed her with that stuff.

Then the child sat up and said: "Where's my mommy?"

Incredulously, the doctor seized her arm and palpated the elbow. The gland infection was zero, and the temperature seemed normal. The blood-congested tissues surrounding the wound were subsiding as he watched. The child's pulse was stronger and no faster than a child's should be. In the sudden silence of the room he could hear the little girl's mother sobbing in her kitchen, outside. And he also heard a girl's insinuating voice:

"She gonna be O.K., doc?"

He turned and saw a gaunt-faced, dirty-blonde sloven of perhaps eighteen leaning in the doorway and eyeing him with amused contempt. She continued: "I heard about you, *Doc-tor* Full. So don't go try and put the bite on the old lady. You couldn't doctor up a sick cat."

"Indeed?" he rumbled. This young person was going to get a lesson she richly deserved. "Perhaps you would care to look at my patient?"

"Where's my mommy?" insisted the little girl, and the blonde's jaw fell. She went to the bed and cautiously asked: "You O.K. now, Teresa? You all fixed up?"

"Where's my mommy?" demanded Teresa. Then,

accusingly, she gestured with her wounded hand at the doctor. "You *poke* me!" she complained, and giggled pointlessly.

"Well—" said the blonde girl, "I guess I got to hand it to you, doc. These loudmouth women around here said you didn't know your . . . I mean, didn't know how to cure people. They said you ain't a real doctor."

"I *have* retired from practice," he said. "But I happened to be taking this case to a colleague as a favor, your good mother noticed me, and—" a deprecating smile. He touched the lock of the case and it folded up into the little black bag again.

"You stole it," the girl said flatly.

He sputtered.

"Nobody'd trust you with a thing like that. It must be worth plenty. You stole that case. I was going to stop you when I come in and saw you working over Teresa, but it looked like you wasn't doing her any harm. But when you give me that line about taking that case to a colleague I know you stole it. You gimme a cut or I go to the cops. A thing like that must be worth twenty-thirty dollars."

The mother came timidly in, her eyes red. But she let out a whoop of joy when she saw the little girl sitting up and babbling to herself, embraced her madly, fell on her knees for a quick prayer, hopped up to kiss the doctor's hand, and then dragged him into the kitchen, all the while rattling in her native language while the blonde girl let her eyes go cold with disgust. Dr. Full allowed himself to be towed into the kitchen, but flatly declined a cup of coffee and a plate of anise cakes and St. John's Bread.

"Try him on some wine, ma," said the girl sardonically.

"Hyass! Hyass!" breathed the woman delightedly. "You like-a wine, docta?" She had a carafe of purplish liquid before him in an instant, and the blonde girl snickered as the doctor's hand twitched out at it. He drew his hand back, while there grew in his head the old image of how it would smell and then taste and then warm his stomach and limbs. He made the kind of calculation at which he was practiced; the delighted woman would not notice as he downed two tumblers, and he could overawe her through two tumblers more with his tale of Teresa's narrow brush with the Destroying Angel, and then—why, then it would not matter. He would be drunk.

But for the first time in years, there was a sort of counter-image: a blend of the rage he felt at the blonde girl to whom he was so transparent, and of pride at the cure he had just effected. Much to his own surprise, he drew back his hand from the carafe and said, luxuriating in the words: "No, thank you. I don't believe I'd care for any so early in the day." He covertly watched the blonde girl's face, and was gratified at her surprise. Then the mother was shyly handing him two bills and saying: "Is no much-a money, docta—but you come again, see Teresa?"

"I shall be glad to follow the case through," he said. "But now excuse me—I really must be running along." He grasped the little black bag firmly and got up; he wanted very much to get away from the wine and the older girl.

"Wait up, doc," she said, "I'm going your way." She followed him out and down the street. He ignored her until he felt her hand on the black bag. Then old Dr. Full stopped and tried to reason with her:

"Look, my dear. Perhaps you're right. I might have stolen it. To be perfectly frank, I don't remember how I got it. But you're young and you can earn your own money—"

"Fifty-fifty," she said, "or I go to the cops. And if I get

another word outta you, it's sixty-forty. And you know who gets the short end, don't you, doc?"

Defeated, he marched to the pawnshop, her impudent hand still on the handle with his, and her heels beating out a tattoo against his stately tread.

In the pawnshop, they both got a shock.

"It ain't stendard," said Uncle, unimpressed by the ingenious lock. "I ain't nevva seen one like it. Some cheap Jap stuff, maybe? Try down the street. This I nevva could sell."

Down the street they got an offer of one dollar. The same complaint was made: "I ain't a collecta, mista—I buy stuff that got resale value. Who could I sell this to, a Chinaman who don't know medical instruments? Every one of them looks funny. You sure you didn't make these yourself?" They didn't take the one-dollar offer.

The girl was baffled and angry; the doctor was baffled too, but triumphant. He had two dollars, and the girl had a half-interest in something nobody wanted. But he suddenly marveled, the thing had been all right to cure the kid, hadn't it?

"Well," he asked her, "do you give up? As you see, the kit is practically valueless."

She was thinking hard. "Don't fly off the handle, doc. I don't get this but something's going on all right . . . would those guys know good stuff if they saw it?"

"They would. They make a living from it. Wherever this kit came from—"

She seized on that, with a devilish faculty she seemed to have of eliciting answers without asking questions. "I thought so. You don't know either, huh? Well, maybe I can find out for you. C'mon in here. I ain't letting go of that thing. There's money in it—some way, I don't know how, there's money in it." He followed her into a cafeteria and to an almost empty corner. She was ob-

251

livious to stares and snickers from the other customers as she opened the little black bag—it almost covered a cafeteria table—and ferreted through it. She picked out a retractor from a loop, scrutinized it, contemptuously threw it down, picked out a speculum, threw it down, picked out the lower half of an O.B. forceps, turned it over, close to her sharp young eyes—and saw what the doctor's dim old ones could not have seen.

All old Dr. Full knew was that she was peering at the neck of the forceps and then turned white. Very carefully, she placed the half of the forceps back in its loop of cloth and then replaced the retractor and the speculum. "Well?" he asked. "What did you see?"

" 'Made in U.S.A.,' " she quoted hoarsely. " 'Patent Applied for July 2450.' "

He wanted to tell her she must have misread the inscription, that it must be a practical joke, that. . . .

But he knew she had read correctly. Those bandage shears: they *had* driven his fingers, rather than his fingers driving them. The hypo needle that had no hole. The pretty blue pill that had struck him like a thunderbolt.

"You know what I'm going to do?" asked the girl, with sudden animation. "I'm going to go to charm school. You'll like that, won't ya, doc? Because we're sure going to be seeing a lot of each other."

Old Dr. Full didn't answer. His hands had been playing idly with that plastic card from the kit on which had been printed the rows and columns that had guided him twice before. The card had a slight convexity; you could snap the convexity back and forth from one side to the other. He noted, in a daze, that with each snap a different text appeared on the cards. *Snap.* "The knife with the blue dot in the handle is for tumors only. Diagnose tumors with your Instrument Seven, the Swelling Tester. Place the Swelling Tester—" *Snap.* "An overdose of the pink pills in Bottle 3 can be fixed with one

252

white pill from Bottle—" *Snap*. "Hold the suture needle by the end without the hole in it. Touch it to one end of the wound you want to close and let go. After it has made the knot, touch it—" *Snap*. "Place the top half of the O.B. Forceps near the opening. Let go. After it has entered and conformed to the shape of—" *Snap*.

The slot man saw "FLANNERY 1—MEDICAL" in the upper left corner of the hunk of copy. He automatically scribbled "trim to .75" on it and skimmed it across the horseshoe-shaped copy desk to Piper, who had been handling Edna Flannery's quack exposé series. She was a nice youngster, he thought, but like all youngsters she overwrote. Hence, the "*trim*".

Piper dealt back a city hall story to the slot, pinned down Flannery's feature with one hand and began to tap his pencil across it, one tap to a word, at the same steady beat as a teletype carriage traveling across the roller. He wasn't exactly reading it this first time. He was just looking at the letters and words to find out whether, as letters and words, they conformed to *Herald* style. The steady tap of his pencil ceased at intervals as it drew a black line ending with a stylized letter "d" through the word "breast" and scribbled in "chest" instead, or knocked down the capital "E" in "East" to lowercase with a diagonal, or closed up a split word—in whose middle Flannery had bumped the space bar of her typewriter—with two curved lines like parentheses rotated through ninety degrees. The thick black pencil zipped a ring around the "30" which, like all youngsters, she put at the end of her stories. He turned back to the first page for the second reading. This time, the pencil drew lines with the stylized "d's" at the end of them through adjectives and whole phrases, printed big "L's" to mark paragraphs, hooked some of Flannery's own paragraphs together with swooping recurved lines.

At the bottom of "FLANNERY ADD 2—MEDICAL" the pencil slowed down and stopped. The slot man, sensitive to the rhythm of his beloved copy desk, looked up almost at once. He saw Piper squinting at the story, at a loss. Without wasting words, the copy reader skimmed it back across the masonite horseshoe to the chief, caught a police story in return and buckled down, his pencil tapping. The slot man read as far as the fourth add, barked at Howard, on the rim: "Sit in for me," and stumped through the clattering city room toward the alcove where the managing editor presided over his own bedlam.

The copy chief waited his turn while the make-up editor, the pressroom foreman and the chief photographer had words with the M. E. When his turn came, he dropped Flannery's copy on his desk and said: "She says this one isn't a quack."

The M. E. read:

"FLANNERY 1—MEDICAL, by Edna Flannery, *Herald* Staff Writer.

"The sordid tale of medical quackery which the *Herald* has exposed in this series of articles undergoes a change of pace today which the reporter found a welcome surprise. Her quest for the facts in the case of today's subject started just the same way that her exposure of one dozen shyster M.D.'s and faith-healing phonies did. But she can report for a change that Dr. Bayard Kendrick Full is, despite unorthodox practices which have drawn the suspicion of the rightly hypersensitive medical associations, a true healer living up to the highest ideals of his profession.

"Dr. Full's name was given to the *Herald's* reporter by the ethical committee of a county medical association, which reported that he had been expelled from the association on July 18, 1941 for allegedly 'milking' several patients suffering from trivial complaints. According to

254

sworn statements in the committee's files, Dr. Full had told them they suffered from cancer, and that he had a treatment which would prolong their lives. After his expulsion from the association, Dr. Full dropped out of their sight—until he opened a midtown 'sanitarium' in a brownstone front which had for years served as a rooming house.

"The *Herald's* reporter went to that sanitarium, on East 89th Street, with the full expectation of having numerous imaginary ailments diagnosed and of being promised a sure cure for a flat sum of money. She expected to find unkempt quarters, dirty instruments and the mumbo-jumbo paraphernalia of the shyster M. D. which she had seen a dozen times before.

"She was wrong.

"Dr. Full's sanitarium is spotlessly clean, from its tastefully furnished entrance hall to its shining, white treatment rooms. The attractive blonde receptionist who greeted the reporter was soft-spoken and correct, asking only the reporter's name, address and the general nature of her complaint. This was given, as usual, as 'nagging backache'. The receptionist asked the *Herald's* reporter to be seated, and a short while later conducted her to a second-floor treatment room and introduced her to Dr. Full.

"Dr. Full's alleged past, as described by the medical society spokesman, is hard to reconcile with his present appearance. He is a clear-eyed, white-haired man in his sixties, to judge by his appearance—a little above middle height and apparently in good physical condition. His voice was firm and friendly, untainted by the ingratiating whine of the shyster M. D. which the reporter has come to know too well.

"The receptionist did not leave the room as he began his examination after a few questions as to the nature and location of the pain. As the reporter lay face down on a treatment table the doctor pressed some instrument to the small of her back. In about one minute he made this astounding statement: 'Young woman, there is no reason for you to have any pain where you say you do. I understand they're saying nowadays that emotional upsets cause pains like that. You'd better go to a psychologist or psychiatrist if the pain keeps up. There is no physical cause for it, so I can do nothing for you.'

"His frankness took the reporter's breath away. Had he guessed she was, so to speak, a spy in his camp? She tried again: 'Well, doctor, perhaps you'd give me a physical checkup. I feel run-down all the time, besides the pains. Maybe I need a tonic.' This is never-failing bait to shyster M. D.'s—an invitation for them to find all sorts of mysterious conditions wrong with a patient, each of which 'requires' an expensive treatment. As explained in the first article of this series, of course, the reporter underwent a thorough physical checkup before she embarked on her quack hunt, and was found to be in one hundred percent perfect condition, with the exception of a 'scarred' area at the bottom tip of her left lung resulting from a childhood attack of tuberculosis and a tendency toward 'hyperthyroidism'—overactivity of the thyroid gland which makes it difficult to put on weight and sometimes causes a slight shortness of breath.

"Dr. Full consented to perform the examination, and took a number of shining, spotlessly clean instruments from loops in a large board literally covered with instruments—most of them unfamiliar to the reporter. The instrument with which he approached first was a tube with a curved dial in its surface and two wires that ended on flat disks growing from its ends. He placed one of the disks on the back of the reporter's right hand and the other on the back of her left. 'Reading the meter', he called out some number which the attentive receptionist took down on a ruled form. The same procedure was repeated several times, thoroughly covering the reporter's anatomy and thoroughly convincing her that the doctor was a complete quack. The reporter had never seen any such diagnostic procedure practiced during the weeks she put in preparing for this series.

"The doctor then took the ruled sheet from the receptionist, conferred with her in low tones and said: 'You have a slightly overactive thyroid, young woman. And there's something wrong with your left lung—not seriously, but I'd like to take a closer look.'

"He selected an instrument from the board which, the reporter knew, is called a 'speculum'—a scissorlike device which spreads apart body openings such as the orifice of the ear, the nostril and so on, so that a doctor can look in during an examination. The instrument was, however, too large to be an aural or nasal speculum but too small to be anything else. As the *Herald's* reporter was about to ask further questions, the attending receptionist told her: 'It's customary for us to blindfold our patients during lung examinations—do you mind?' The reporter, bewildered, allowed her to tie a spotlessly clean bandage over her eyes, and waited nervously for what would come next.

"She still cannot say exactly what happened while she was blindfolded—but X-rays confirm her suspicions. She felt a cold sensation at her ribs on the left side—a cold that seemed to enter inside her body. Then there was a snapping feeling, and the cold sensation was gone. She heard Dr. Full say in a matter-of-fact voice: 'You have an old tubercular scar down there. It isn't doing any particular harm, but an active person like you needs all the oxygen she can get. Lie still and I'll fix it for you.'

"Then there was a repetition of the cold sensation, lasting for a longer time. 'Another batch of alveoli and some more vascular glue,' the *Herald's* reporter heard

Dr. Full say, and the receptionist's crisp response to the order. Then the strange sensation departed and the eye bandage was removed. The reporter saw no scar on her ribs, and yet the doctor assured her: 'That did it. We took out the fibrosis—and a good fibrosis it was, too; it walled off the infection so you're still alive to tell the tale. Then we planted a few clumps of alveoli—they're the little gadgets that get the oxygen from the air you breathe into your blood. I won't monkey with your thyroxin supply. You've got used to being the kind of person you are, and if you suddenly found yourself easygoing and all the rest of it, chances are you'd only be upset. About the backache: just check with the county medical society for the name of a good psychologist or psychiatrist. And look out for quacks; the woods are full of them.'

"The doctor's self-assurance took the reporter's breath away. She asked what the charge would be, and was told to pay the receptionist fifty dollars. As usual, the reporter delayed paying until she got a receipt signed by the doctor himself, detailing the services for which it paid. Unlike most, the doctor cheerfully wrote: 'For removal of fibrosis from left lung and restoration of alveoli,' and signed it.

"The reporter's first move when she left the sanitarium was to head for the chest specialist who had examined her in preparation for this series. A comparison of X-rays taken on the day of the 'operation' and those taken previously would, the *Herald's* reporter then thought, expose Dr. Full as a prince of shyster M. D.'s and quacks.

"The chest specialist made time on his crowded schedule for the reporter, in whose series he has shown a lively interest from the planning stage on. He laughed uproariously in his staid Park Avenue examining room as she described the weird procedure to which she had

258

been subjected. But he did not laugh when he took a chest X-ray of the reporter, developed it, dried it and compared it with the ones he had taken earlier. The chest specialist took six more X-rays that afternoon, but finally admitted that they all told the same story. The *Herald's* reporter has it on his authority that the scar she had eighteen days ago from her tuberculosis is now gone and has been replaced by healthy lung tissue. He declares that this is a happening unparalleled in medical history. He does not go along with the reporter in her firm conviction that Dr. Full is responsible for the change.

"The *Herald's* reporter, however, sees no two ways about it. She concludes that Dr. Bayard Kendrick Full —whatever his alleged past may have been—is now an unorthodox but highly successful practitioner of medicine, to whose hands the reporter would trust herself in any emergency.

"Not so is the case of 'Rev.' Annie Dimsworth—a female harpy who, under the guise of 'faith' preys on the ignorant and suffering who come to her sordid 'healing parlor' for help and remain to feed 'Rev.' Annie's bank account, which now totals up to $53,283.64. Tomorrow's article will show, with photostats of bank statements and sworn testimony, that—"

The managing editor turned down "FLANNERY LAST ADD—MEDICAL" and tapped his front teeth with a pencil, trying to think straight. He finally told the copy chief: "Kill the story. Run the teaser as a box." He tore off the last paragraph—the "teaser" about "Rev." Annie—and handed it to the desk man, who stumped back to his masonite horseshoe.

The make-up editor was back, dancing with impatience as he tried to catch the M. E.'s eye. The interphone buzzed with the red light which indicated that the editor and publisher wanted to talk to him. The M. E.

thought briefly of a special series on this Dr. Full, decided nobody would believe it and that he probably was a phony anyway. He spiked the story on the "dead" hook and answered his interphone.

Dr. Full had become almost fond of Angie. As his practice had grown to engross the neighborhood illnesses, and then to a corner suite in an uptown taxpayer building, and finally to the sanitarium, she seemed to have grown with it. Oh, he thought, we have our little disputes. . . .

The girl, for instance, was too much interested in money. She had wanted to specialize in cosmetic surgery —removing wrinkles from wealthy old women and whatnot. She didn't realize, at first, that a thing like this was in their trust, that they were the stewards and not the owners of the little black bag and its fabulous contents.

He had tried, ever so cautiously, to analyze them, but without success. All the instruments were slightly radioactive, for instance, but not quite so. They would make a Geiger-Mueller counter indicate, but they would not collapse the leaves of an electroscope. He didn't pretend to be up on the latest developments, but as he understood it, that was just plain *wrong*. Under the highest magnification, there were lines on the instruments' superfinished surfaces: incredibly fine lines, engraved in random hatchments which made no particular sense. Their magnetic properties were preposterous. Sometimes the instruments were strongly attracted to magnets, sometimes less so, and sometimes not at all.

Dr. Full had taken X-rays in fear and trembling lest he disrupt whatever delicate machinery worked in them. He was *sure* they were not solid, that the handles and perhaps the blades must be mere shells filled with busy little watchworks—but the X-rays showed nothing of the sort. Oh, yes—and they were always sterile, and they wouldn't rust. Dust *fell* off them if you shook them: now, that was something he understood. They ionized the dust, or were ionized themselves, or something of the sort. At any rate, he had read of something similar that had to do with phonograph records.

She wouldn't know about that, he proudly thought. She kept the books well enough, and perhaps she gave him a useful prod now and then when he was inclined to settle down. The move from the neighborhood slum to the uptown quarters had been her idea, and so had the sanitarium. Good; good; it enlarged his sphere of usefulness. Let the child have her mink coats and her convertible, as they seemed to be calling roadsters nowadays. He himself was too busy and too old. He had so much to make up for.

Dr. Full thought happily of his master plan. She would not like it much, but she would have to see the logic of it. This marvelous thing that had happened to them must be handed on. She was herself no doctor; even though the instruments practically ran themselves, there was more to doctoring than skill. There were the ancient canons of the healing art. And so, having seen the logic of it, Angie would yield; she would assent to his turning over the little black bag to all humanity.

He would probably present it to the College of Surgeons, with as little fuss as possible—well, perhaps a *small* ceremony, and he would like a souvenir of the occasion, a cup or a framed testimonial. It would be a relief to have the thing out of his hands, in a way; let the giants of the healing art decide who was to have its benefits. No; Angie would understand. She was a good-hearted girl.

It was nice that she had been showing so much interest in the surgical side lately—asking about the instruments, reading the instruction card for hours, even practicing on guinea pigs. If something of his love for humanity

261

had been communicated to her, old Dr. Full sentimentally thought, his life would not have been in vain. Surely she would realize that a greater good would be served by surrendering the instruments to wiser hands than theirs, and by throwing aside the cloak of secrecy necessary to work on their small scale.

Dr. Full was in the treatment room that had been the brownstone's front parlor; through the window he saw Angie's yellow convertible roll to a stop before the stoop. He liked the way she looked as she climbed the stairs; neat, not flashy, he thought. A sensible girl like her, she'd understand. There was somebody with her— a fat woman, puffing up the steps, overdressed and petulant. Now, what could she want?

Angie let herself in and went into the treatment room, followed by the fat woman. "Doctor," said the blonde girl gravely, "may I present Mrs. Coleman?" Charm school had not taught her everything, but Mrs. Coleman, evidently *noveau riche* thought the doctor, did not notice the blunder.

"Miss Aquella told me *so* much about you, doctor, and your remarkable system!" she gushed.

Before he could answer, Angie smoothly interposed: "Would you excuse us for just a moment, Mrs. Coleman?"

She took the doctor's arm and led him into the reception hall. "Listen," she said swiftly, "I know this goes against your grain, but I couldn't pass it up. I met this old thing in the exercise class at Elizabeth Barton's. Nobody else'll talk to her there. She's a widow, I guess her husband was a black marketeer or something, and she has a pile of dough. I gave her a line about how you had a system of massaging wrinkles out. My idea is, you blindfold her, cut her neck open with the Cutaneous Series knife, shoot some Firmol into the muscles, spoon out some of that blubber with an Adipose Series curette and spray it all with Skintite. When you take the blind-fold off she's got rid of a wrinkle and doesn't know what happened. She'll pay five hundred dollars. Now, don't say 'no', doc. Just this once, let's do it my way, can't you? I've been working on this deal all along too, haven't I?"

"Oh," said the doctor, "very well." He was going to have to tell her about the master plan before long any-way. He would let her have it her way this time.

Back in the treatment room, Mrs. Coleman had been thinking things over. She told the doctor sternly as he entered: "Of course, your system is permanent, isn't it?"

"It is, madam," he said shortly. "Would you please lie down there? Miss Aquella, get a sterile three-inch bandage for Mrs. Coleman's eyes." He turned his back on the fat woman to avoid conversation, and pretended to be adjusting the lights. Angie blindfolded the woman, and the doctor selected the instruments he would need. He handed the blonde girl a pair of retractors, and told her: "Just slip the corners of the blades in as I cut—" She gave him an alarmed look, and gestured at the re-clining woman. He lowered his voice: "Very well. Slip in the corners and rock them along the incision. I'll tell you when to pull them out."

Dr. Full held the Cutaneous Series knife to his eyes as he adjusted the little slide for 3 cm. depth. He sighed a little as he recalled that its last use had been in the extirpation of an "inoperable" tumor of the throat.

"Very well," he said, bending over the woman. He tried a tentative pass through her tissues. The blade dipped in and flowed through them, like a finger through quicksilver, with no wound left in the wake. Only the retractors could hold the edges of the incision apart.

Mrs. Coleman stirred and jabbered: "Doctor, that felt

so peculiar! Are you sure you're rubbing the right way?"

"Quite sure, madam," said the doctor wearily. "Would you please try not to talk during the massage?"

He nodded at Angie, who stood ready with the retractors. The blade sank in to its three centimeters, miraculously cutting only the dead horny tissues of the epidermis and the live tissue of the dermis, pushing aside mysteriously all major and minor blood vessels and muscular tissue, declining to affect any system or organ except the one it was—tuned to, could you say? The doctor didn't know the answer, but he felt tired and bitter at this prostitution. Angie slipped in the retractor blades and rocked them as he withdrew the knife, then pulled to separate the lips of the incision. It bloodlessly exposed an unhealthy string of muscle, sagging in a dead-looking loop from blue-gray ligaments. The doctor took a hypo, Number IX, preset to "g" and raised it to his eye level. The mist came and went; there probably was no possibility of an embolus with one of these gadgets, but why take chances? He shot one c.c. of "g" —identified as "Firmol" by the card—into the muscle. He and Angie watched as it tightened up against the pharynx.

He took the Adipose Series curette, a small one, and spooned out yellowish tissue, dropping it into the incinerator box, and then nodded to Angie. She eased out the retractors and the gaping incision slipped together into unbroken skin, sagging now. The doctor had the atomizer—dialed to "Skintite"—ready. He sprayed, and the skin shrank up into the new firm throat line.

As he replaced the instruments, Angie removed Mrs. Coleman's bandage and gayly announced: "We're finished! And there's a mirror in the reception hall—"

Mrs. Coleman didn't need to be invited twice. With incredulous fingers she felt her chin, and then dashed for the hall. The doctor grimaced as he heard her yelp of delight, and Angie turned to him with a tight smile. "I'll get the money and get her out," she said. "You won't have to be bothered with her any more."

He was grateful for that much.

She followed Mrs. Coleman into the reception hall, and the doctor dreamed over the case of instruments. A ceremony, certainly—he was *entitled* to one. Not everybody, he thought, would turn such a sure source of money over to the good of humanity. But you reached an age when money mattered less, and when you thought of these things you had done that *might* be open to misunderstanding if, just if, there chanced to be any of that, well, that judgment business. The doctor wasn't a religious man, but you certainly found yourself thinking hard about some things when your time drew near. . . .

Angie was back, with a bit of paper in her hands. "Five hundred dollars," she said matter-of-factly. "And you realize, don't you, that we could go over her an inch at a time—at five hundred dollars an inch?"

"I've been meaning to talk to you about that," he said.

There was bright fear in her eyes, he thought—but why?

"Angie, you've been a good girl and an understanding girl, but we can't keep this up forever, you know."

"Let's talk about it some other time," she said flatly. "I'm tired now."

"No—I really feel we've gone far enough on our own. The instruments—"

"Don't say it, doc!" she hissed. "Don't say it, or you'll be sorry!" In her face there was a look that reminded him of the hollow-eyed, gaunt-faced, dirty-blonde creature she had been. From under the charm-school finish there burned the guttersnipe whose infancy had been spent on a sour and filthy mattress, whose childhood had

265

been play in the littered alley and whose adolescence had been the sweatshops and the aimless gatherings at night under the glaring streetlamps.

He shook his head to dispel the puzzling notion. "It's this way," he patiently began. "I told you about the family that invented the O.B. forceps and kept them a secret for so many generations, how they could have given them to the world but didn't?"

"They knew what they were doing," said the guttersnipe flatly.

"Well, that's neither here nor there," said the doctor, irritated. "My mind is made up about it. I'm going to turn the instruments over to the College of Surgeons. We have enough money to be comfortable. You can even have the house. I've been thinking of going to a warmer climate, myself." He felt peeved with her for making the unpleasant scene. He was unprepared for what happened next.

Angie snatched the little black bag and dashed for the door, with panic in her eyes. He scrambled after her, catching her arm, twisting it in a sudden rage. She clawed at his face with her free hand, babbling curses. Somehow, somebody's finger touched the little black bag, and it opened grotesquely into that enormous board, covered with shining instruments, large and small. Half a dozen of them joggled loose and fell to the floor.

"*Now* see what you've done!" roared the doctor, unreasonably. Her hand was still viselike on the handle, but she was standing still, trembling with choked-up rage. The doctor bent stiffly to pick up the fallen instruments. Unreasonable girl! he thought bitterly. Making a scene. . . .

Pain drove in between his shoulderblades and he fell facedown. The light ebbed. "Unreasonable girl!" he tried to croak. And then: "They'll know I tried, anyway—"

Angie looked down on his prone body, with the handle of the Number Six Cautery Series knife protruding from it. ". . . will cut through all tissues. Use for amputations before you spread on the Re-Gro. Extreme caution should be used in the vicinity of vital organs and major blood vessels or nerve trunks—"

"I didn't mean to do that," said Angie, dully, cold with horror. Now the detective would come, the implacable detective who would reconstruct the crime from the dust in the room. She would run and turn and twist, but the detective would find her out and she would be tried in a courtroom before a judge and jury; the lawyer would make speeches, but the jury would convict her anyway, and the headlines would scream: "BLONDE KILLER GUILTY!" and she'd maybe get the chair, walking down a plain corridor where a beam of sunlight struck through the dusty air, with an iron door at the end of it. Her mink, her convertible, her dresses, the handsome man she was going to meet and marry. . . .

The mist of cinematic clichés cleared, and she knew what she would do next. Quite steadily, she picked the incinerator box from its loop in the board—a metal cube with a different-textured spot on one side. ". . . to dispose of fibroses or other unwanted matter, simply touch the disk—" You dropped something in and touched the disk. There was a sort of soundless whistle, very powerful and unpleasant if you were too close, and a sort of lightless flash. When you opened the box again, the contents were gone. Angie took another of the Cautery Series knives and went grimly to work. Good thing there wasn't any blood to speak of. . . . She finished the awful task in three hours.

She slept heavily that night, totally exhausted by the wringing emotional demands of the slaying and the subsequent horror. But in the morning, it was as though the doctor had never been there. She ate breakfast, dressed with unusual care—and then undid the unusual care. Nothing out of the ordinary, she told herself. Don't do one thing different from the way you would have done it before. After a day or two, you can phone the cops. Say he walked out spoiling for a drunk, and you're worried. But don't rush it, baby—*don't rush it.*

Mrs. Coleman was due at 10:00 A.M. Angie had counted on being able to talk the doctor into at least one more five-hundred-dollar session. She'd have to do it herself now—but she'd have to start sooner or later.

The woman arrived early. Angie explained smoothly: "The doctor asked me to take care of the massage today. Now that he has the tissue-firming process beginning, it only requires somebody trained in his methods—" As she spoke, her eyes swiveled to the instrument case— open! She cursed herself for the single flaw as the woman followed her gaze and recoiled.

"What are those things?" she demanded. "Are you going to cut me with them? I *thought* there was something fishy—"

"Please, Mrs. Coleman," said Angie, "please, *dear* Mrs. Coleman—you don't understand about the . . . the massage instruments!"

"Massage instruments, my foot!" squabbled the woman shrilly. "That doctor *operated* on me. Why, he might have killed me!"

Angie wordlessly took one of the smaller Cutaneous Series knives and passed it through her forearm. The blade flowed like a finger through quicksilver, leaving no wound in its wake. *That* should convince the old cow!

It didn't convince her, but it did startle her. "What did you do with it? The blade folds up into the handle —that's it!"

"Now look closely, Mrs. Coleman," said Angie, thinking desperately of the five hundred dollars. "Look very closely and you'll see that the, uh, the subskin massager simply slips beneath the tissues without doing any harm, tightening and firming the muscles themselves instead of having to work through layers of skin and adipose tissue. It's the secret of the doctor's method. Now, how can outside massage have the effect that we got last night?"

Mrs. Coleman was beginning to calm down. "It *did* work, all right," she admitted, stroking the new line of her neck. "But your arm's one thing and my neck's another! Let me see you do that with your neck!"

Angie smiled. . . .

Al returned to the clinic after an excellent lunch that had almost reconciled him to three more months he would have to spend on duty. And then, he thought, and then a blessed year at the blessedly supernormal South Pole working on his specialty—which happened to be telekinesis exercises for ages three to six. Meanwhile, of course, the world had to go on and of course he had to shoulder his share in the running of it.

Before settling down to deskwork he gave a routine glance at the bag board. What he saw made him stiffen with shocked surprise. A red light was on next to one of the numbers—the first since he couldn't think when. He read off the number and murmured: "O.K., 674,101. That fixes *you*." He put the number on a card sorter and in a moment the record was in his hand. Oh, yes—Hemingway's bag. The big dummy didn't remember how or where he had lost it; none of them ever did. There were hundreds of them floating around.

Al's policy in such cases was to leave the bag turned on. The things practically ran themselves—it was practically impossible to do harm with them—so whoever found a lost one might as well be allowed to use it. You turn it off, you have a social loss—you leave it on, it may do some good. As he understood it, and not very well at that, the stuff wasn't "used up". A temporalist had tried to explain it to him with little success that the prototypes in the transmitter *had been transducted* through a series of point events of transfinite cardinality. Al had innocently asked whether that meant prototypes had been stretched, so to speak, through all time, and the temporalist had thought he was joking and left in a huff.

"Like to see him do this," thought Al darkly, as he telekinized himself to the combox, after a cautious look to see that there were no medics around. To the box he said: "Police chief," and then to the police chief: "There's been a homicide committed with Medical Instrument Kit 674,101. It was lost some months ago by one of my people, Dr. John Hemingway. He didn't have a clear account of the circumstances."

The police chief groaned and said: "I'll call him in and question him." He was to be astonished by the answers, and was to learn that the homicide was well out of his jurisdiction.

Al stood for a moment at the bag board by the glowing red light that had been sparked into life by a departing vital force giving, as its last act, the warning that Kit 674,101 was in homicidal hands. With a sigh, Al pulled the plug and the light went out.

"Yah," jeered the woman. "You'd fool around with my neck, but you wouldn't risk your own with that thing!"

Angie smiled with serene confidence, a smile that was to shock hardened morgue attendants. She set the Cutaneous Series knife to 3 centimeters before drawing it across her neck. Smiling, knowing the blade would cut only the dead horny tissue of the epidermis and the live tissue of the dermis, mysteriously push aside all major and minor blood vessels and muscular tissue. . . .

Smiling, the knife plunging in and its microtome-sharp

270

metal shearing through major and minor blood vessels and muscular tissue and pharynx, Angie cut her throat.

In the few minutes it took the police, summoned by the shrieking Mrs. Coleman, to arrive, the instruments had become crusted with rust, and the flasks which had held vascular glue and clumps of pink, rubbery alveoli and spare gray cells and coils of receptor nerves held only black slime, and from them when opened gushed the foul gases of decomposition.

When we collaborators on this volume were struggling young marrieds with a small baby and limited mobility, there was one night a week when we could Get Out of the House together with very little strain. Friday night was poker night at Horace Gold's apartment, and a merciful providence had so arranged things that it was an easy walk, even pushing a baby carriage, from our apartment to his. So it happened that little Karen Pohl spent hours every week playing with poker chips and being patted and dandled by people like John Cage, the avant-gardest composer alive, a few psychologists whose names are forgotten, an occasional editor and an awful lot of science-fiction writers (including a couple represented in this volume). But Horace Gold was not merely the proprietor of a gaming establishment, he spent his days brilliantly editing *Galaxy Magazine*, and his evenings and weekends brilliantly writing stories. This is one of them. For twenty years now Hollywood producers have been stumbling over it, thinking of making a movie out of it and then, for one reason or another, letting the idea fade and the options lapse. So you can't see it on the screen ... but you can read it, and now please do!

A MATTER OF FORM
By Horace L. Gold

Gilroy's telephone bell jangled into his slumber. With his eyes grimly shut, the reporter flopped over on his side, ground his ear into the pillow and pulled the cover over his head. But the bell jarred on.

When he blinked his eyes open and saw rain streaking the windows, he gritted his teeth against the insistent clangor and yanked off the receiver. He swore into the transmitter—not a trite blasphemy, but a poetic opinion of the sort of man who woke tired reporters at four in the morning.

"Don't blame me," his editor replied after a bitter silence. "It was your idea. You wanted the case. They found another whatsit."

Gilroy instantly snapped awake. "They found another catatonic!"

"Over on York Avenue near Ninety-first Street, about an hour ago. He's down in the observation ward at Memorial." The voice suddenly became low and confiding. "Want to know what I think, Gilroy?"

"What?" Gilroy asked in an expectant whisper.

"I think you're nuts. These catatonics are nothing but tramps. They probably drank themselves into catatonia, whatever that is. After all, be reasonable, Gilroy; they're only worth a four-line clip."

Gilroy was out of bed and getting dressed with one hand. "Not this time, chief," he said confidently. "Sure, they're only tramps, but that's part of the story. Look . . . hey! You should have been off a couple of hours ago. What's holding you up?"

The editor sounded disgruntled. "Old Man Talbot. He's seventy-six tomorrow. Had to pad out a blurb on his life."

"What! Wasting time whitewashing that murderer, racketeer—"

"Take it easy, Gilroy," the editor cautioned. "He's got a half interest in the paper. He doesn't bother us often."

"O.K. But he's still the city's one-man crime wave. Well, he'll kick off soon. Can you meet me at Memorial when you quit work?"

"In this weather?" The editor considered. "I don't

272

know. Your news instinct is tops, and if you think this is big—oh, hell . . . yes!"

Gilroy's triumphant grin soured when he ripped his foot through a sock. He hung up and explored empty drawers for another pair.

The street was cold and miserably deserted. The black snow was melting to grimy slush. Gilroy hunched into his coat and sloshed in the dirty sludge toward Greenwich Avenue. He was very tall and incredibly thin. With his head down into the driving swirl of rain, his coat flapping around his skinny shanks, his hands deep in his pockets, and his sharp elbows sticking away from his rangy body, he resembled an unhappy stork peering around for a fish.

But he was far from being unhappy. He was happy, in fact, as only a man with a pet theory can be when facts begin to fight on his side.

Splashing through the slush, he shivered when he thought of the catatonic who must have been lying in it for hours, unable to rise, until he was found and carried to the hospital. Poor devil! The first had been mistaken for a drunk, until the cop saw the bandage on his neck.

"Escaped post-brain-operatives," the hospital had reported. It sounded reasonable, except for one thing—catatonics don't walk, crawl, feed themselves or perform *any* voluntary muscular action. Thus Gilroy had not been particularly surprised when no hospital or private surgeon claimed the escaped post-operatives.

A taxi driver hopefully sighted his agitated figure through the rain. Gilroy restrained an urge to hug the hackie for rescuing him from the bitter wind. He clambered in hastily.

"Nice night for a murder," the driver observed conversationally.

"Are you hinting that business is bad?"

"I mean the weather's lousy."

"Well, damned if it isn't!" Gilroy exclaimed sarcastically. "Don't let it slow you down, though. I'm in a hurry. Memorial Hospital, quick!"

The driver looked concerned. He whipped the car out into the middle of the street and scooted through a light that was just an instant too slow.

Three catatonics in a month! Gilroy shook his head. It was a real puzzler. They couldn't have escaped. In the first place, if they had, they would have been claimed; and in the second place, it was physically impossible. And how did they acquire those neat surgical wounds on the backs of their necks, closed with two professional stitches and covered with a professional bandage? New wounds, too!

Gilroy attached special significance to the fact that they were very poorly dressed and suffered from slight malnutrition. But what was the significance? He shrugged. It was an instinctive hunch.

The taxi suddenly swerved to the curb and screeched to a stop. He thrust a bill through the window and got out. The night burst abruptly. Rain smashed against him in a roaring tide. He battered upwind to the hospital entrance.

He was soaked, breathless, half-repentant for his whim in attaching importance to three impoverished catatonics. He gingerly put his hand in his clammy coat and brought out a sodden identification card.

The girl at the reception desk glanced at it. "Oh, a newspaperman! Did a big story come in tonight?"

"Nothing much," he said casually. "Some poor tramp found on York and Ninety-first. Is he up in the screwball ward?"

She scanned the register and nodded. "Is he a friend of yours?"

"My grandson." As he moved off, both flinched at the

sound of water squishing in his shoes at each step. "I must have stepped in a puddle."

When he turned around in the elevator, she was shaking her head and pursing her lips maternally. Then the ground floor dropped away.

He went through the white corridor unhesitantly. Low, horrible moans came from the main ward. He heard them with academic detachment. Near the examination room, the sound of the rising elevator stopped him. He paused, turning to see who it was.

The editor stepped out, chilled, wet and disgusted. Gilroy reached down and caught the smaller man's arm, guiding him silently through the door and into the examination room. The editor sighed resignedly.

The resident physician glanced up briefly when they unobtrusively took places in the ring of interns about the bed. Without effort, Gilroy peered over the heads before him, inspecting the catatonic with clinical absorption.

The catatonic had been stripped of his wet clothing, toweled, and rubbed with alcohol. Passive, every muscle absolutely relaxed, his eyes were loosely closed, and his mouth hung open in idiotic slackness. The dark line of removed surgical plaster showed on his neck. Gilroy strained to one side. The hair had been clipped. He saw part of a stitch.

"Catatonia, doc?" he asked quietly.

"Who are you?" the physician snapped.

"Gilroy . . . *Morning Post*."

The doctor gazed back at the man on the bed. "It's catatonia, all right. No trace of alcohol or inhibiting drugs. Slight malnutrition."

Gilroy elbowed politely through the ring of interns. "Insulin shock doesn't work, eh? No reason why it should."

"Why shouldn't it?" the doctor demanded, startled.

275

"It always works in catatonia . . . at least, temporarily."

"But it didn't in this case, did it?" Gilroy insisted brusquely.

The doctor lowered his voice defeatedly. "No."

"What's this all about?" the editor asked in irritation. "What's catatonia, anyhow? Paralysis, or what?"

"It's the last stage of schizophrenia, or what used to be called dementia praecox," the physician said. "The mind revolts against responsibility and searches for a period in its existence when it was not troubled. It goes back to childhood and finds that there are childish cares; goes further and comes up against infantile worries; and finally ends up in a prenatal mental state."

"But it's a gradual degeneration," Gilroy stated. "Long before the complete mental decay, the victim is detected and put in an asylum. He goes through imbecility, idiocy, and after years of slow degeneration, winds up refusing to use his muscles or brain."

The editor looked baffled. "Why should insulin shock pull him out?"

"It shouldn't!" Gilroy rapped out.

"It should!" the physician replied angrily. "Catatonia is negative revolt. Insulin drops the sugar content of the blood to the point of shock. The sudden hunger jolts the catatonic out of his passivity."

"That's right," Gilroy said incisively. "But this isn't catatonia! It's mighty close to it, but you never heard of a catatonic who didn't refuse to carry on voluntary muscular action. There's no salivary retention! My guess is that it's paralysis."

"Caused by what?" the doctor asked bitingly.

"That's for you to say. I'm not a physician. How about the wound at the base of the skull?"

"Nonsense! It doesn't come within a quarter inch of the motor nerve. It's *cerias flexibilitas* . . . waxy flexibility." He raised the victim's arm and let go. It sagged slowly. "If it were general paralysis, it would have affected the brain. He'd have been dead."

Gilroy lifted his bony shoulders and lowered them. "You're on the wrong track, doc," he said quietly. "The wound has a lot to do with his condition, and catatonia can't be duplicated by surgery. Lesions can cause it, but the degeneration would still be gradual. And catatonics can't walk or crawl away. He was deliberately abandoned, same as the others."

"Looks like you're right, Gilroy," the editor conceded. "There's something fishy here. All three of them had the same wounds?"

"In exactly the same place, at the base of the skull and to the left of the spinal column. Did you ever see anything so helpless? Imagine him escaping from a hospital, or even a private surgeon!"

The physician dismissed the interns and gathered up his instruments preparatory to harried flight. "I don't see the motive. All three of them were undernourished, poorly clad; they must have been living in substandard conditions. Who would want to harm them?"

Gilroy bounded in front of the doctor, barring his way. "But it doesn't have to be revenge! It could be experimentation!"

"To prove what?"

Gilroy looked at him quizzically. "You don't know?"

"How should I?"

The reporter clapped his drenched hat on backward and darted to the door. "Come on, chief. We'll ask Moss for a theory."

"You won't find Dr. Moss here," the physician said. "He's off at night, and tomorrow, I think, he's leaving the hospital."

Gilroy stopped abruptly. "Moss . . . leaving the hospital!" he repeated in astonishment. "Did you hear that, chief? He's a dictator, a slave driver and a louse. But he's probably the greatest surgeon in America. Look at that. Stories breaking all around you, and you're white-washing Old Man Talbot's murderous life!" His coat bellied out in the wash of his swift, gaunt stride. "Three catatonics found lying on the street in a month. That never happened before. They can't walk or crawl, and they have mysterious wounds at the base of their skulls. Now the greatest surgeon in the country gets kicked out of the hospital he built up to first place. And what do you do? You sit in the office and write stories about what a swell guy Talbot is underneath his slimy exterior!"

The resident physician was relieved to hear the last of that relentlessly incisive, logical voice trail down the corridor. But he gazed down at the catatonic before leaving the room.

He felt less certain that it was catatonia. He found himself quoting the editor's remark—there definitely *was* something fishy there!

But what was the motive in operating on three obviously destitute men and abandoning them; and how had the operation caused a state resembling catatonia?

In a sense, he felt sorry that Dr. Moss was going to be discharged. The cold, slave-driving dictator might have given a good theory. That was the physician's scientific conscience speaking. Inside, he really felt that anything was worth getting away from that silkily mocking voice and the delicately sneering mouth.

At Fifty-fifth Street, Wood came to the last Sixth Avenue employment office. With very little hope, he read the crudely chalked signs. It was an industrial employment agency. Wood had never been inside a factory. The only job he could fill was that of apprentice upholsterer, ten dollars a week; but he was thirty-two years old and the agency would require five dollars immediate payment.

He turned away dejectedly, fingering the three dimes in his pocket. Three dimes—the smallest, thinnest American coins. . . .

"Anything up there, Mac?"

"Not for me," Wood replied wearily. He scarcely glanced at the man.

He took a last glance at his newspaper before dropping it to the sidewalk. That was the last paper he'd buy, he resolved; with his miserable appearance he couldn't answer advertisements. But his mind clung obstinately to Gilroy's article. Gilroy had described the horror of catatonia. A notion born of defeat made it strangely attractive to Wood. At least, the catatonics were fed and housed. He wondered if catatonia could be simulated. . . .

But the other had been scrutinizing Wood. "College man, ain't you?" he asked as Wood trudged away from the employment office.

Wood paused and ran his hand over his stubbled face. Dirty cuffs stood away from his fringing sleeves. He knew that his hair curled long behind his ears. "Does it still show?" he asked bitterly.

"You bet. You can spot a college man a mile away."

Wood's mouth twisted. "Glad to hear that. It must be an inner light shining through the rags."

"You're a sucker coming down here with an education. Down here they want poor slobs who don't know any better . . . guys like me, with big muscles and small brains."

Wood looked up at him sharply. He was too well-dressed and alert to have prowled the agencies for any length of time. He might have just lost his job; perhaps he was looking for company. But Wood had met his kind before. He had the hard eyes of the wolf who preyed on the jobless.

"Listen," Wood said coldly, "I haven't a thing you'd want. I'm down to thirty cents. Excuse me while I sneak my books and toothbrush out of my room before the super snatches them."

The other did not recoil or protest virtuously. "I ain't blind," he said quietly. "I can see you're down and out."

"Then what do you want?" Wood snapped ill-temperedly. "Don't tell me you want a threadbare but filthy college man for company—"

His unwelcome friend made a gesture of annoyance. "Cut out the mad-dog act. I was turned down on a job today because I ain't a college man. Seventy-five a month, room and board doctor's assistant. But I got the air because I ain't a grad."

"You've got my sympathy," Wood said, turning away.

The other caught up with him. "You're a college grad. Do you want the job? It'll cost you your first week's pay . . . my cut, see?"

"I don't know anything about medicine. I was a code expert in a stockbroker's office before people stopped having enough money for investments. Want any codes deciphered? That's the best I can do."

He grew irritated when the stranger stubbornly matched his dejected shuffle.

"You don't have to know anything about medicine. Long as you got a degree, a few muscles and a brain, that's all the doc wants."

Wood stopped short and wheeled.

"Is that on the level?"

"Sure. But I don't want to take a deadhead up there and get turned down. I got to ask you the questions they asked me."

In face of a prospective job Wood's caution ebbed away. He felt the three dimes in his pocket. They were exceedingly slim and unprotective. They meant two hamburgers and two cups of coffee, or a bed in some filthy hotel dormitory. Two thin meals and sleeping in the wet March air; or shelter for a night and no food. . . .

"Shoot!" he said deliberately.

"Any relatives?"

"Some fifth cousins in Maine."

"Friends?"

"None who would recognize me now." He searched the stranger's face. "What's this all about? What have my friends or relatives got to do—"

"Nothing," the other said hastily. "Only you'll have to travel a little. The doc wouldn't want a wife dragging along, or have you break up your work by writing letters. See?"

Wood didn't see. It was a singularly lame explanation; but he was concentrating on the seventy-five a month, room and *board*—food.

"Who's the doctor?" he asked.

"I ain't dumb." The other smiled humorlessly. "You'll go there with me and get the doc to hand over my cut."

Wood crossed to Eighth Avenue with the stranger. Sitting in the subway, he kept his eyes from meeting casual, disinterested glances. He pulled his feet out of the aisle, against the base of the seat, to hide the loose, flapping right sole. His hands were cracked and scaly, with tenacious dirt deeply embedded. Bitter, defeated, with the appearance of a mature waif. What a chance there was of being hired! But at least the stranger had risked a nickel on his fare.

Wood followed him out at 103rd Street and Central Park West; they climbed the hill to Manhattan Avenue and headed several blocks downtown. The other ran briskly up the stoop of an old house. Wood climbed the steps more slowly. He checked an urge to run away, but he experienced in advance the sinking feeling of being turned away from a job. If he could only have his hair cut, his suit pressed, his shoes mended! But what was the use of thinking about that? It would cost a couple of dollars. And nothing could be done about his ragged hems.

281

"Come on!" the stranger called.

Wood tensed his back and stood looking at the house while the other brusquely rang the doorbell. There were three floors and no card above the bell, no doctor's white glass sign in the darkly curtained windows. From the outside it could have been a neglected boardinghouse.

The door opened. A man of his own age, about middle height, but considerably overweight, blocked the entrance. He wore a white laboratory apron. Incongruous in his pale, soft face, his nimble eyes were harsh.

"Back again?" he asked impatiently.

"It's not for me this time," Wood's persistent friend said. "I got a college grad."

Wood drew back in humiliation when the fat man's keen glance passed over his wrinkled, frayed suit and stopped distastefully at the long hair blowing wildly around his hungry, unshaven face. There—he could see it coming: "Can't use him."

But the fat man pushed back a beautiful collie with his leg and held the door wide. Astounded, Wood followed his acquaintance into the narrow hall. To give an impression of friendliness, he stooped and ruffled the dog's ears. The fat man led them into a bare front room.

"What's your name?" he asked indifferently.

Wood's answer stuck in his throat. He coughed to clear it. "Wood," he replied.

"Any relatives?" Wood shook his head.

"Friends?"

"Not any more."

"What kind of degree?"

"Science, Columbia, 1925."

The fat man's expression did not change. He reached into his left pocket and brought out a wallet. "What arrangement did you make with this man?"

"He's to get my first week's salary." Silently, Wood observed the transfer of several green bills; he looked at them hungrily, pathetically. "May I wash up and shave, doctor?" he asked.

"I'm not the doctor," the fat man answered. "My name is Clarence, without a mister in front of it." He turned swiftly to the sharp stranger. "What are you hanging around for?"

Wood's friend backed to the door. "Well, so long," he said. "Good break for both of us, eh, Wood?"

Wood smiled and nodded happily. The trace of irony in the stranger's hard voice escaped him entirely.

"I'll take you upstairs to your room," Clarence said when Wood's business partner had left. "I think there's a razor there."

They went out into the dark hall, the collie close behind them. An unshaded lightbulb hung on a single wire above a gate-leg table. On the wall behind the table an oval, gilt mirror gave back Wood's hairy, unkempt image. A worn carpet covered the floor to a door cutting off the rear of the house, and narrow stairs climbed in a swift spiral to the next story. It was cheerless and neglected, but Wood's conception of luxury had become less exacting.

"Wait here while I make a telephone call," Clarence said.

He closed the door behind him in a room opposite the stairs. Wood fondled the friendly collie. Through the panel he heard Clarence's voice, natural and unlowered.

"Hello, Moss? . . . Pinero brought back a man. All his answers are all right. . . . Columbia, 1925. . . . Not a cent, judging from his appearance. . . . Call Talbot? For when? . . . O.K. . . . You'll get back as soon as you get through with the board? . . . O.K. . . . Well, what's the difference? You got all you wanted from them, anyhow."

Wood heard the receiver's click as it was replaced and taken off again. Moss? That was the head of Memorial

Hospital—the great surgeon. But the article about the catatonics hinted something about his removal from the hospital.

"Hello, Talbot?" Clarence was saying. "Come around at noon tomorrow. Moss says everything'll be ready then. . . . O.K., don't get excited. This is positively the last one! . . . Don't worry. Nothing can go wrong."

Talbot's name sounded familiar to Wood. It might have been the Talbot that the *Morning Post* had written about —the seventy-six-year-old philanthropist. He probably wanted Moss to operate on him. Well, it was none of his business.

When Clarence joined him in the dark hall, Wood thought only of his seventy-five a month, room and board; but more than that, he had a job! A few weeks of decent food and a chance to get some new clothes, and he would soon get rid of his defeatism.

He even forgot his wonder at the lack of shingles and waiting-room signs that a doctor's house usually had. He could only think of his neat room on the third floor, over-looking a bright back yard. And a shave. . . .

Dr. Moss replaced the telephone with calm delibera-tion. Striding through the white hospital corridor to the elevator, he was conscious of curious stares. His pink, scrupulously shaven, clean-scrubbed face gave no an-swer to their questioning eyes. In the elevator he stood with his hands thrust casually into his pockets. The op-erator did not dare to look at him or speak.

Moss gathered his hat and coat. The space around the reception desk seemed more crowded than usual, with men who had the penetrating look of reporters. He walked swiftly past.

A tall, astoundingly thin man, his stare fixed preda-torily on Moss, headed the wedge of reporters that swarmed after Moss.

"You can't leave without a statement to the press, doc!" he said.

"I find it very easy to do," Moss taunted without stopping.

He stood on the curb with his back turned coldly on the reporters and unhurriedly flagged a taxi.

"Well, at least you can tell us whether you're still director of the hospital," the tall reporter said.

"Ask the board of trustees."

"Then how about a theory on the catatonics?"

"Ask the catatonics." The cab pulled up opposite Moss. Deliberately he opened the door and stepped in. As he rode away, he heard the thin man exclaim: "What a cold, clammy reptile!"

He did not look back to enjoy their discomfiture. In spite of his calm demeanor, he did not feel too easy himself. The man on the *Morning Post*, Gilroy or whatever his name was, had written a sensational article on the abandoned catatonics, and even went so far as to claim they were not catatonics. He had had all he could do to keep from being involved in the conflicting riot of theory. Talbot owned a large interest in the paper. He must be told to strangle the articles, although by now all the papers were taking up the cry.

It was a clever piece of work, detecting the fact that the victims weren't suffering from catatonia at all. But the *Morning Post* reporter had cut himself a man-size job in trying to understand how three men with general paralysis could be abandoned without a trace of where they had come from, and what connection the incisions had on their condition. Only recently had Moss himself solved it.

The cab crossed to Seventh Avenue and headed uptown.

The trace of his parting smile of mockery vanished. His mobile mouth whitened, tight-lipped and grim.

Where was he to get money from now? He had milked the hospital funds to a frightening debt, and it had not been enough. Like a bottomless maw, his researches could drain a dozen funds.

If he could convince Talbot, prove to him that his failures had not really been failures, that this time he would not slip up. . . .

But Talbot was a tough nut to crack. Not a cent was coming out of his miserly pocket until Moss completely convinced him that he was past the experimental stage. This time there would be no failure!

At Moss's street, the cab stopped and the surgeon sprang out lightly. He ran up the steps confidently, looking neither to the left nor to the right, though it was a fine day with a warm yellow sun, and between the two lines of old houses Central Park could be seen budding greenly.

He opened the door and strode almost impatiently into the narrow, dark hall, ignoring the friendly collie that bounded out to greet him.

"Clarence!" he called out. "Get your new assistant down. I'm not even going to wait for a meal." He threw off his hat, coat and jacket, hanging them up carelessly on a hook near the mirror.

"Hey, Wood!" Clarence shouted up the stairs. "Are you finished?"

They heard a light, eager step race down from the third floor.

"Clarence, my boy," Moss said in a low, impetuous voice, "I know what the trouble was. We didn't really fail at all. I'll show you . . . we'll follow exactly the same technique!"

"Then why didn't it seem to work before?"

Wood's feet came into view between the rails on the second floor. "You'll understand as soon as it's finished," Moss whispered hastily, and then Wood joined them.

Even the short time that Wood had been employed was enough to transform him. He had lost the defeatist feeling of being useless human flotsam. He was shaved and washed, but that did not account for his kindled eyes.

"Wood . . . Dr. Moss," Clarence said perfunctorily.

Wood choked out an incoherent speech that was meant to inform them that he was happy, though he didn't know anything about medicine.

"You don't have to," Moss replied silkily. "We'll teach you more about medicine than most surgeons learn in a lifetime."

It could have meant anything or nothing. Wood made no attempt to understand the meaning of the words. It was the hint of withdrawn savagery in the low voice that puzzled him. It seemed a very peculiar way of talking to a man who had been hired to move apparatus and do nothing but the most ordinary routine work.

He followed them silently into a shining, tiled operating room. He felt less comfortable than he had in his room; but when he dismissed Moss's tones as a characteristically sarcastic manner of speech, hinting more than it contained in reality, his eagerness returned. While Moss scrubbed his hands and arms in a deep basin, Wood gazed around.

In the center of the room an operating table stood, with a clean sheet clamped unwrinkled over it. Above the table five shadowless light globes branched. It was a compact room. Even Wood saw how close everything lay to the doctor's hand—trays of tampons, swabs and clamps, and a sterilizing instrument chest that gave off puffs of steam.

"We do a lot of surgical experimenting," Moss said. "Most of your work'll be handling the anesthetic. Show him how to do it, Clarence."

Wood observed intently. It appeared simple—cut-ins

287

and shut-offs for cyclopropane, helium and oxygen; watch the dials for overrich mixture; keep your eye on the bellows and water filter. . . .

Trained anesthetists, he knew, tested their mixture by taking a few sniffs. At Clarence's suggestion he sniffed briefly at the whispering cone. He didn't know cyclopropane—so lightning-fast that experienced anesthetists are sometimes caught by it. . . .

Wood lay on the floor with his arms and legs sticking up into the air. When he tried to straighten them, he rolled over on his side. Still they projected stiffly. He was dizzy with the anesthetic. Something that felt like surgical plaster pulled on a sensitive spot on the back of his neck.

The room was dark, its green shades pulled down against the outer day. Somewhere above him and toward the end of the room, he heard painful breathing. Before he could raise himself to investigate, he caught the multiple tread of steps ascending and approaching the door. He drew back defensively.

The door flung open. Light flared up in the room. Wood sprang to his feet—and found he could not stand erect. He dropped back to a crawling position, facing the men who watched him with cold interest.

"He tried to stand up," the old one stated.

"What'd you think I'd do?" Wood snapped. His voice was a confused, snarling growl without words. Baffled and raging, he glared up at them.

"Cover him, Clarence," Moss said. "I'll look at the other one."

Wood turned his head from the threatening muzzle of the gun aimed at him, and saw the doctor lift the man on the bed. Clarence backed to the window and raised the shade. Strong noonlight roused the man. His profile was turned to Wood. His eyes fastened blankly on Moss's scrubbed pink face, never leaving it. Behind his ears curled long, wild hair.

"There you are, Talbot," Moss said to the old man. "He's sound."

"Take him out of bed and let's see him act like you said he would." The old man jittered anxiously on his cane.

Moss pulled the man's legs to the edge of the bed and raised him heavily to his feet. For a short time he stood without aid; then all at once he collapsed to his hands and knees. He stared full at Wood.

It took Wood a minute of startled bewilderment to recognize the face. He had seen it every day of his life, but never so detachedly. The eyes were blank and round, the facial muscles relaxed, idiotic.

But it was his own face. . . .

Panic exploded in him. He gaped down at as much of himself as he could see. Two hairy legs stemmed from his shoulders, and a dog's forepaws rested firmly on the floor.

He stumbled uncertainly toward Moss. "What did you do to me?" he shouted. It came out in an animal howl. The doctor motioned the others to the door and backed away warily.

Wood felt his lips draw back tightly over his fangs. Clarence and Talbot were in the hall. Moss stood alertly in the doorway, his hand on the knob. He watched Wood closely, his eyes glacial and unmoved. When Wood sprang, he slammed the door, and Wood's shoulder crashed against it.

"He knows what happened," Moss's voice came through the panel.

It was not entirely true. Wood knew something had happened. But he refused to believe that the face of the crawling man gazing stupidly at him was his own. It was, though. And Wood himself stood on the four legs of a dog, with a surgical plaster covering a burning wound in the back of his neck.

It was crushing, numbing, too fantastic to believe. He thought wildly of hypnosis. But just by turning his head, he could look directly at what had been his own body, braced on hands and knees as if it could not stand erect.

He was outside his own body. He could not deny that. Somehow he had been removed from it; by drugs or hypnosis, Moss had put him in the body of a dog. He had to get back into his own body again.

But how do you get back into your own body?

His mind struck blindly in all directions. He scarcely heard the three men move away from the door and enter the next room. But his mind suddenly froze with fear. His human body was complete and impenetrable, closed hermetically against his now-foreign identity.

Through his congealed terror, his animal ears brought the creak of furniture. Talbot's cane stopped its nervous, insistent tapping.

"That should have convinced even you, Talbot," he heard Moss say. "Their identities are exchanged without the slightest loss of mentality."

Wood started. It meant—no, it was absurd! But it did account for the fact that his body crawled on hands and knees, unable to stand on its feet. It meant that the collie's identity was in Wood's body!

"That's O.K.," he heard Talbot say. "How about the operation part? Isn't it painful, putting their brains into different skulls?"

"You can't put them into different skulls," Moss answered with a touch of annoyance. "They don't fit. Besides, there's no need to exchange the whole brain. How do you account for the fact that people have retained their identities with parts of their brains removed?"

There was a pause. "I don't know," Talbot said doubtfully.

"Sometimes the parts of the brain that were removed contained nerve centers, and paralysis set in. But the identity was still there. Then what part of the brain contained the identity?"

Wood ignored the old man's questioning murmur. He listened intently, all his fears submerged in the straining of his sharp ears, in the overwhelming need to know what Moss had done to him.

"Figure it out," the surgeon said. "The identity must have been in some part of the brain that wasn't removed, that couldn't be touched without death. That's where it was. At the absolute base of the brain, where a scalpel couldn't get at it without having to cut through the skull, the three medullae, and the entire depth of the brain itself. There's a mysterious little body hidden away safely down there—less than a quarter of an inch in diameter—called the pineal gland. In some way it controls the identity. Once it was a third eye."

"A third eye, and now it controls the identity?" Talbot exclaimed.

"Why not? The gills of our fish ancestors became the Eustachian canal that controls the sense of balance.

"Until I developed a new technique in removing the gland—by excising from beneath the brain instead of through it—nothing at all was known about it. In the first place, trying to get at it would kill the patient; and oral or intravenous injections have no effect. But when I exchanged the pineals of a rabbit and a rat, the rabbit acted like a rat, and the rat like a rabbit—within their limitations, of course. It's empiricism—it works, but I don't know why."

"Then why did the first three act like . . . what's the word?"

"Catatonics. Well, the exchanges were really successful, Talbot; but I repeated the same mistake three times, until I figured it out. And by the way, get that reporter on

291

something a little less dangerous. He's getting pretty warm. Excepting the salivary retention, the victims acted almost like catatonics, and for nearly the same reason. I exchanged the pineals of rats for the men's. Well, you can imagine how a rat would act with the relatively huge body of a man to control. It's beyond him. He simply gives up, goes into a passive revolt. But the difference between a dog's body and a man's isn't so great. The dog is puzzled, but at any rate he makes an attempt to control his new body."

"Is the operation painful?" Talbot asked anxiously.

"There isn't a bit of pain. The incision is very small, and heals in a short time. And as for recovery—you can see for yourself how swift it is. I operated on Wood and the dog last night."

Wood's dog's brain stampeded, refusing to function intelligently. If he had been hypnotized or drugged, there might have been a chance of his eventual return. But his identity had been violently and permanently ripped from his body and forced into that of a dog. He was absolutely helpless, completely dependent on Moss to return him to his body.

"How much do you want?" Talbot was asking craftily.

"Five million!"

The old man cackled in a high, cracked voice. "I'll give you fifty thousand, cash," he offered.

"To exchange your dying body for a young, strong, healthy one?" Moss asked, emphasizing each adjective with special significance. "The price is five million."

"I'll give you seventy-five thousand," Talbot said with finality. "Raising five million is out of the question. It can't be done. All my money is tied up in my . . . uh . . . syndicates. I have to turn most of the income back into merchandise, wages, overhead and equipment. How do you expect me to have five million in cash?"

"I don't," Moss replied with faint mockery.

Talbot lost his temper. "Then what are you getting at?"

"The interest on five million is exactly half your income. Briefly, to use your business terminology, I'm muscling into your rackets."

Wood heard the old man gasp indignantly. "Not a chance!" he rasped. "I'll give you eighty thousand. That's all the cash I can raise."

"Don't be a fool, Talbot," Moss said with deadly calm. "I don't want money for the sake of feeling it. I need an assured income, and plenty of it; enough to carry on my experiments without having to bleed hospitals dry and still not have enough. If this experiment didn't interest me, I wouldn't do it even for five million, much as I need it."

"Eighty thousand!" Talbot repeated.

"Hang onto your money until you rot! Let's see, with your advanced angina pectoris, that should be about six months from now, shouldn't it?"

Wood heard the old man's cane shudder nervelessly over the floor.

"You win, you cold-blooded blackmailer," the old man surrendered.

Moss laughed. Wood heard the furniture creak as they rose and set off toward the stairs.

"Do you want to see Wood and the dog again, Talbot?"

"No. I'm convinced."

"Get rid of them, Clarence. No more abandoning them in the street for Talbot's clever reporters to theorize over. Put a silencer on your gun. You'll find it downstairs. Then leave them in the acid vat."

Wood's eyes flashed around the room in terror. He and his body had to escape. For him to escape alone would mean the end of returning to his own body. Separation would make the task of forcing Moss to give him back his body impossible.

But they were on the second floor, at the rear of the house. Even if there had been a fire escape, he could not have opened the window. The only way out was through the door.

Somehow he had to turn the knob, chance meeting Clarence or Moss on the stairs or in the narrow hall, and open the heavy front door—guiding and defending himself and his body!

The collie in his body whimpered baffledly. Wood fought off the instinctive fear that froze his dog's brain. He had to be cool.

Below, he heard Clarence's ponderous steps as he went through the rooms looking for a silencer to muffle his gun.

Gilroy closed the door of the telephone booth and fished in his pocket for a coin. Of all of mankind's scientific gadgets, the telephone booth most clearly demonstrates that this is a world of five feet nine. When Gilroy pulled a coin out of his pocket, his elbow banged against the shut door; and as he dialed his number and stooped over the mouthpiece, he was forced to bend himself into the shape of a cane. But he had conditioned his lanky body to adjust itself to things scaled below its need. He did not mind the lack of room.

But he shoved his shapeless felt hat on the back of his head and whistled softly in a discouraged manner.

"Let me talk to the chief," he said. The receiver rasped in his ear. The editor greeted him abstractedly; Gilroy knew he had just come on and was scattering papers over his desk, looking at the latest. "Gilroy, chief," the reporter said.

"What've you got on the catatonics?"

Gilroy's sharply planed face wrinkled in earnest defeat. "Not a thing, chief," he replied hollowly.

"Where were you?"

"I was in Memorial all day, looking at the catatonics and waiting for an idea."

The editor became sympathetic. "How'd you make out?" he asked.

"Not a thing. They're absolutely dumb and motionless, and nobody around here has anything to say worth listening to. How'd you make out on the police and hospital reports?"

"I was looking at them just before you called." There was a pause. Gilroy heard the crackle of papers being shoved around. "Here they are—the fingerprint bureau has no records of them. No police department in any village, town or city recognizes their pictures."

"How about the hospitals outside New York?" Gilroy asked hopefully.

"No missing patients."

Gilroy sighed and shrugged his thin shoulders eloquently. "Well, all we have is a negative angle. They must have been picked damned carefully. All the papers around the country printed their pictures, and they don't seem to have any friends, relatives or police records."

"How about a human-interest story," the editor encouraged; "what they eat, how helpless they are, their torn, old clothes? Pad out a story about their probable lives, judging from their features and hands. How's that? Not bad, eh?"

"Aw, chief," Gilroy moaned, "I'm licked. That padding stuff isn't my line. I'm not a sob sister. We haven't a thing to work on. These tramps had absolutely no connection with life. We can't find out who they were, where they came from, or what happened to them."

The editor's voice went sharp and incisive. "Listen to me, Gilroy!" he rapped out. "You stop that whining, do you hear me? I'm running this paper, and as long as you don't see fit to quit, I'll send you out after birth lists if I want to.

"You thought this was a good story and you convinced me that it was. Well, I'm still convinced! I want these catatonics tracked down. I want to know all about them, and how they wound up behind the eight ball. So does the public. I'm not stopping until I *do* know. Get me?

"You get to work on this story and hang onto it. Don't let it throw you! And just to show you how I'm standing behind you . . . I'm giving you a blank expense account and your own discretion. Now track these catatonics down in any way you can figure out!"

Gilroy was stunned for an instant. "Well, gosh," he stammered, confused, "I'll do my best, chief. I didn't know you felt that way."

"The two of us'll crack this story wide open, Gilroy. But just come around to me with another whine about being licked, and you can start in as copy boy for some other sheet. Do you get me? That's final!"

Gilroy pulled his hat down firmly. "I get you, chief," he declared manfully. "You can count on me right up to the hilt."

He slammed the receiver on its hook, yanked the door open, and strode out with a new determination. He felt like the power of the press, and the feeling was not unjustified. The might and cunning of a whole vast metropolitan newspaper was ranged solidly behind him. Few secrets could hide from its searching probe.

All he needed was patience and shrewd observation. Finding the first clue would be hardest; after that the story would unwind by itself. He marched toward the hospital exit.

He heard steps hastening behind him and felt a light, detaining touch on his arm. He wheeled and looked down at the resident physician, dressed in streetclothes and coming on duty.

"You're Gilroy, aren't you?" the doctor asked. "Well, I was thinking about the incisions on the cataonics' necks—"

"What about them?" Gilroy demanded alertly, pulling out a pad.

"Quitting again?" the editor asked ten minutes later.

"Not me, chief!" Gilroy propped his stenographic pad on top of the telephone. "I'm hot on the trail. Listen to this. The resident physician over here at Memorial tipped me off to a real clue. He figured out that the incisions on the cataonics' necks aimed at some part of their brains. The incisions penetrate at a tangent a quarter of an inch off the vertebrae, so it couldn't have been to tamper with the spinal cord. You can't reach the posterior part of the brain from that angle, he says, and working from the back of the neck wouldn't bring you to any important part of the neck that can't be reached better from the front or through the mouth.

"If you don't cut the spinal cord with that incision, you can't account for general paralysis; and the cords definitely weren't cut.

"So he thinks the incisions were aimed at some part of the base of the brain that can't be reached from above. He doesn't know what part or how the operation would cause general paralysis.

"Got that? O.K. Well, here's the payoff:

"To reach the exact spot of the brain you want, you ordinarily take off a good chunk of skull, somewhere around that spot. But these incisions were predetermined to the last centimeter. And he doesn't know how. The surgeon worked entirely by measurements—like blind flying. He says only three or four surgeons in the country could've done it."

"Who are they, you cluck? Did you get their names?"

Gilroy became offended. "Of course. Moss in New York; Faber in Chicago; Crowninshield in Portland; maybe Johnson in Detroit."

"Well, what're you waiting for?" the editor shouted. "Get Moss!"

"Can't locate him. He moved from his Riverside Drive apartment and left no forwarding address. He was peeved. The board asked for his resignation and he left with a pretty bad name for mismanagement."

The editor sprang into action. "That leaves us four men to track down. Find Moss. I'll call up the other boys you named. It looks like a good tip."

Gilroy hung up. With half a dozen vast strides, he had covered the distance to the hospital exit, moving with ungainly, predatory swiftness.

Wood was in a mind-freezing panic. He knew it hindered him, prevented him from plotting his escape, but he was powerless to control the fearful darting of his dog's brain.

It would take Clarence only a short time to find the silencer and climb the stairs to kill him and his body. Before Clarence could find the silencer, Wood and his body had to escape.

Wood lifted himself clumsily, unsteadily, to his hind legs and took the doorknob between his paws. They refused to grip. He heard Clarence stop, and the sound of scraping drawers came to his sharp ears.

He was terrified. He bit furiously at the knob. It slipped between his teeth. He bit harder. Pain stabbed his sensitive gums, but the bitter brass dented. Hanging to the knob, he lowered himself to the floor, bending his neck sharply to turn it. The tongue clicked out of the lock. He threw himself to one side, flipping back the door as he fell. It opened a crack. He thrust his snout in the opening and forced it wide.

From below, he heard the ponderous footfalls moving again. Wood stalked noiselessly into the hall and peered down the well of the stairs. Clarence was out of sight.

He drew back into the room and pulled at his body's clothing, backing out into the hall again until the dog crawled voluntarily. It crept after him and down the stairs.

All at once Clarence came out of a room and made for the stairs. Wood crouched, trembling at the sound of metallic clicking that he knew was a silencer being fitted to a gun. He barred his body. It halted, its idiot face hanging down over the step, silent and without protest.

Clarence reached the stairs and climbed confidently. Wood tensed, waiting for Clarence to turn the spiral and come into view.

Clarence sighted them and froze rigid. His mouth opened blankly, startled. The gun trembled impotently at his side, and he stared up at them with his fat, white neck exposed and inviting. Then his chest heaved and his larynx tightened for a yell.

But Wood's long teeth cleared. He lunged high, directly at Clarence, and his fangs snapped together in midair.

Soft flesh ripped in his teeth. He knocked Clarence over; they fell down the stairs and crashed to the floor. Clarence thrashed around, gurgling. Wood smelled a sudden rush of blood that excited an alien lust in him. He flung himself clear and landed on his feet.

His body clumped after him, pausing to sniff at Clarence. He pulled it away and darted to the front door.

From the back of the house he heard Moss running to investigate. He bit savagely at the doorknob, jerking it back awkwardly, terrified that Moss might reach him before the door opened.

But the lock clicked, and he thrust the door wide with his body. His human body flopped after him on hands and knees to the stoop. He hauled it down the steps to the sidewalk and herded it anxiously toward Central Park West, out of Moss's range.

Wood glanced back over his shoulder, saw the doctor glaring at them through the curtain on the door, and, in terror, he dragged his body in a clumsy gallop to the corner where he would be protected by traffic.

He had escaped death, and he and his body were still together; but his panic grew stronger. How could he feed it, shelter it, defend it against Moss and Talbot's gangsters? And how could he force Moss to give him back his body?

But he saw that first he would have to shield his body from observation. It was hungry, and it prowled around on hands and knees, searching for food. The sight of a crawling, sniffing human body attracted disgusted attention; before long they were almost surrounded.

Wood was badly scared. With his teeth, he dragged his body into the street and guided its slow crawl to the other side, where Central Park could hide them with its trees and bushes.

Moss had been more alert. A black car sped through a red light and crowded down on them. From the other side a police car shot in and out of traffic, its siren screaming, and braked dead beside Wood and his body.

The black car checked its headlong rush.

Wood crouched defensively over his body, glowering at the two cops who charged out at them. One shoved Wood away with his foot; the other raised his body by the armpits and tried to stand it erect.

"A nut—he thinks he's a dog," he said interestedly. "The screwball ward for him, eh?"

The other nodded. Wood lost his reason. He attacked, snapping viciously. His body took up the attack, snarling horribly and biting on all sides. It was insane, hopeless; but he had no way of communicating, and he had to do something to prevent being separated from his body. The police kicked him off.

Suddenly he realized that if they had not been burdened with his body, they would have shot him. He darted wildly into traffic before they sat his body in the car.

"Want to get out and plug him before he bites somebody?" he heard.

"This nut'll take a hunk out of you," the other replied. "We'll send out an alarm from the hospital."

It drove off downtown. Wood scrambled after it. His legs pumped furiously; but it pulled away from him, and other cars came between. He lost it after a few blocks.

Then he saw the black car make a reckless turn through traffic and roar after him. It was too intently bearing down on him to have been anything but Talbot's gangsters.

His eyes and muscles coordinated with animal precision. He ran in the swift traffic, avoiding being struck, and at the same time kept watch for a footpath leading into the park.

When he found one, he sprinted into the opposite lane of traffic. Brakes screeched; a man cursed him in a loud voice. But he scurried in front of the car, gained the sidewalk, and dashed along the cement path until he came to a miniature forest of bushes.

Without hesitation, he left the path and ran through the woods. It was not a dense growth, but it covered him from sight. He scampered deep into the park.

His frightened eyes watched the carload of gangsters scour the trees on both sides of the path. Hugging the ground, he inched away from them. They beat the bushes a safe distance away from him.

While he circled behind them, creeping from cover to cover, there was small danger of being caught. But he was appalled by the loss of his body. Being near it had given him a sort of courage, even though he did not know how he was going to force Moss to give it back to him. Now, besides making the doctor operate, he had to find a way of getting near it again.

But his empty stomach was knotted with hunger. Before he could make plans he had to eat.

He crept furtively out of his shelter. The gangsters were far out of sight. Then, with infinite patience, he sneaked up on a squirrel. The alert little animal was observant and wary. It took an exhaustingly long time before he ambushed it and snapped its spine. The thought of eating an uncooked rodent revolted him.

He dug back into his cache of bushes with his prey. When he tried to plot a line of action, his dog's brain balked. It was terrified and maddened with helplessness.

There was good reason for its fear—Moss had Talbot's gangsters out gunning for him, and by this time the police were probably searching for him as a vicious dog.

In all his nightmares he had never imagined any so horrible. He was utterly impotent to help himself. The forces of law and crime were ranged against him; he had no way of communicating the fact that he was a man to those who could possibly help him; he was completely inarticulate; and besides, *who* could help him, except Moss? Suppose he *did* manage to evade the police, the gangsters, and sneaked past a hospital's vigilant staff, and somehow succeeded in communicating. . . .

Even so, only Moss could perform the operation!

He had to rule out doctors and hospitals; they were too routinized to have much imagination. But, more important than that, they could not influence Moss to operate.

He scrambled to his feet and trotted cautiously through the clumps of brush in the direction of Columbus Circle. First, he had to be alert for police and gangsters. He had to find a method of communicating —but to somebody who could understand him and exert tremendous pressure on Moss.

The city's smells came to his sensitive nostrils. Like a vast blanket, covering most of them, was a sweet odor that he identified as gasoline vapor. Above it hovered the scent of vegetation, hot and moist; and below it, the musk of mankind.

To his dog's perspective, it was a different world, with a broad, distant, terrifying horizon. Smells and sounds formed scenes in his animal mind. Yet it was interesting. The pad of his paws against the soft, cushioned ground gave him an instinctive pleasure; all the clothes he needed, he carried on him; and food was not hard to find.

While he shielded himself from the police and Talbot's gangsters, he even enjoyed a sort of freedom— but it was a cowardly freedom that he did not want, that was not worth the price. As a man, he had suffered hunger, cold, lack of shelter and security, indifference. In spite of all that, his dog's body harbored a human intelligence; he belonged on his hind legs, standing erect, living the life, good or bad, of a man.

In some way he must get back to that world, out of the solitary anarchy of animaldom. Moss alone could return him. He must be forced to do it! He must be compelled to return the body he had robbed!

But how could Wood communicate, and who could help him?

Near the end of Central Park, he exposed himself to overwhelming danger.

He was padding along a path that skirted the broad road. A cruising black car accelerated with deadly, predatory swiftness and sped abreast of him. He heard a muffled *pop*. A bullet hissed an inch over his head.

He ducked low and scurried back into the concealing bushes. He snaked nimbly from tree to tree, keeping obstacles between him and the line of fire.

The gangsters were out of the car. He heard them beating the brush for him. Their progress was slow, while his fleet legs pumped three hundred yards of safety away from them.

He burst out of the park and scampered across Columbus Circle, reckless of traffic. On Broadway he felt more secure, hugging the buildings with dense crowds between him and the street.

When he felt certain that he had lost the gangsters, he turned west through one-way streets, alert for signs of danger.

In coping with physical danger, he discovered that his animal mind reacted instinctively and always more cunningly than a human brain.

Impulsively, he cowered behind stoops, in doorways, behind any sort of shelter, when the traffic moved. When it stopped, packed tightly, for the light, he ran at topnotch speed. Cars skidded across his path, and several times he was almost hit; but he did not slow to a trot until he had zigzagged downtown, going steadily away from the center of the city, and reached West Street, along North River.

He felt reasonably safe from Talbot's gangsters. But a police car approached slowly under the express highway. He crouched behind an overflowing garbage can outside a filthy restaurant. Long after it was gone, he cowered there.

The shrill wind blowing over the river and across the covered docks picked a newspaper off the pile of garbage and flattened it against the restaurant window.

Through his animal mind, frozen into numbing fear, he remembered the afternoon before—standing in front of the employment agency, talking to one of Talbot's gangsters.

A thought had come to him then: that it would be pleasant to be a catatonic instead of having to starve. He knew better now. But. . . .

He reared to his hind legs and overturned the garbage can. It fell with a loud crash, rolling down toward the gutter, spilling refuse all over the sidewalk. Before a restaurant worker came out, roaring abuse, he pawed through the mess and seized a twisted newspaper in his mouth. It smelled of sour, rotting food, but he caught it up and ran.

Blocks away from the restaurant, he ran across a wide, torn lot, to cover behind a crumbling building. Sheltered from the river wind, he straightened out the paper and scanned the front page.

It was a day old, the same newspaper that he had thrown away before the employment agency. On the left column he found the catatonic story. It was signed by a reporter named Gilroy.

Then he took the edge of the sheet between his teeth and backed away with it until the newspaper opened clumsily, wrinkled, at the next page. He was disgusted by the fetid smell of putrifying food that clung to it; but he swallowed his gorge and kept turning the huge, stiff, unwieldy sheets with his inept teeth. He came to the editorial page and paused there, studying intently the copyright box.

He set off at a fast trot, wary against danger, staying close to walls of buildings, watching for cars that might contain either gangsters or policemen, darting across streets to shelter—trotting on. . . .

The air was growing darker, and the express highway

cast a long shadow. Before the sun went down, he covered almost three miles along West Street, and stopped not far from the Battery.

He gaped up at the towering *Morning Post* Building. It looked impregnable, its heavy doors shut against the wind.

He stood at the main entrance, waiting for somebody to hold a door open long enough for him to lunge through it. Hopefully, he kept his eyes on an old man. When he opened the door, Wood was at his heels. But the old man shoved him back with gentle firmness.

Wood bared his fangs. It was his only answer. The man hastily pulled the door shut.

Wood tried another approach. He attached himself to a tall, gangling man who appeared rather kindly in spite of his intent face. Wood gazed up, wagging his tail awkwardly in friendly greeting. The tall man stooped and scratched Wood's ears, but he refused to take him inside. Before the door closed, Wood launched himself savagely at the thin man and almost knocked him down.

In the lobby, Wood darted through the legs surrounding him. The tall man was close behind, roaring angrily. A frightened stampede of thick-soled shoes threatened to crush Wood; but he twisted in and out between the surging feet and gained the stairs.

He scrambled up them swiftly. The second-floor entrance had plateglass doors. It contained the executive offices.

He turned the corner and climbed up speedily. The stairs narrowed, artifically illuminated. The third and fourth floors were printing-plant rooms; he ran past; clambered by the business offices, classified advertising. . . .

At the editorial department he panted before the heavy fire door, waiting until he regained his breath. Then he gripped the knob between his teeth and pulled it around. The door swung inward.

Thick, bitter smoke clawed his sensitive nostrils; his ears flinched at the clattering, shouting bedlam.

Between rows of littered desks, he inched and gazed around hopefully. He saw abstracted faces, intent on typewriters that rattled out stories; young men racing around to gather batches of papers; men and women swarming in and out of the elevators. Shrewd faces, intelligent and alert. . . .

A few had turned for an instant to look at him as he passed, then turned back to their work, almost without having seen him.

He trembled with elation. These were the men who had the power to influence Moss, and the acuteness to understand him! He squatted and put his paw on the leg of a typing reporter, staring up expectantly. The reporter stared, looked down agitatedly, and shoved him away.

"Go on, beat it!" he said angrily. "Go home!"

Wood shrank back. He did not sense danger. Worse than that, he had failed. His mind worked rapidly: suppose he *had* attracted interest, how would he have communicated his story intelligibly? How could he explain in the equivalent of words?

All at once the idea exploded in his mind. He had been a code translator in a stockbroker's office. . . .

He sat back on his haunches and barked, loud, broken, long and short yelps. A girl screamed. Reporters jumped up defensively, surged away in a tightening ring. Wood barked out his message in Morse, painful, slow, straining a larynx that was foreign to him. He looked around optimistically for someone who might have understood.

Instead, he met hostile, annoyed stares—and no comprehension.

"That's the hound that attacked me!" the tall, thin man said.

"Not for food, I hope," a reporter answered.

Wood was not entirely defeated. He began to bark his message again; but a man hurried out of the glass-enclosed editor's office.

"What's all the commotion here?" he demanded. He sighted Wood among the ring of withdrawing reporters. "Get that damned dog out of here!"

"Come on—get him out of here!" the thin man shouted.

"He's a nice, friendly dog. Give him the hypnotic eye, Gilroy."

Wood stared pleadingly at Gilroy. He had not been understood, but he had found the reporter who had written the catatonic articles! Gilroy approached cautiously, repeating phrases calculated to sooth a savage dog.

Wood darted away through the rows of desks. He was so near to success—he only needed to find a way of communicating before they caught him and put him out!

He lunged to the top of a desk and crashed a bottle of ink to the floor. It splashed into a dark puddle. Swiftly, quiveringly, he seized a piece of white paper, dipped his paw into the splotch of ink, and made a hasty attempt to write.

His surge of hope died quickly. The wrist of his forepaw was not the universal joint of a human being; it had a single upward articulation! When he brought his paw down on the paper, it flattened uselessly, and his claws worked in a unit. He could not draw back three to write with one. Instead, he made a streaked pad print.

Dejectedly, rather than antagonize Gilroy, Wood permitted himself to be driven back into an elevator. He wagged his tail clumsily. It was a difficult feat, calling into use alien muscles that he employed with intellectual deliberation. He sat down and assumed a grin that would have been friendly on a human face; but, even so, it reassured Gilroy. The tall reporter patted his head. Nevertheless, he put him out firmly.

But Wood had reason to feel encouraged. He had managed to get inside the building and had attracted attention. He knew that a newspaper was the only force powerful enough to influence Moss, but there was still the problem of communication. How could he solve it? His paw was worthless for writing, with its single articulation; and nobody in the office could understand Morse code.

He crouched against the white cement wall, his harried mind darting wildly in all directions for a solution. Without a voice or prehensile fingers, his only method of communication seemed to be barking in code. In all that throng, he was certain there would be one to interpret it.

Glances *did* turn to him. At least, he had no difficulty in arousing interest. But they were uncomprehending looks.

For some moments he lost his reason. He ran in and out of the deep, hurrying crowd, barking his message furiously, jumping up at men who appeared more intelligent then the others, following them short distances until it was overwhelmingly apparent that they did not understand, then turning to other men, raising an ear-shattering din of appeal.

He met nothing but a timid pat or frightened rebuffs. He stopped his deafening yelps and cowered back against the wall, defeated. No one would attempt to interpret the barking of a dog in terms of code. When he was a man, he would probably have responded in the same way. The most intelligible message he could hope to convey by his barking was simply the fact that he was trying to attract interest. Nobody would search for any deeper meaning in a dog's barking.

He joined the traffic hastening toward the subway. He trotted along the curb, watchful for slowing cars, but more intent on the strewing of rubbish in the gutter. He was murderously envious of the human feet around him that walked swiftly and confidently to a known destination; smug, selfish feet, undeviating from their homeward path to help him. Their owners could convey the finest shadings and variations in emotion, commands, abstract thought, by speech, writing, print, through telephone, radio, books, newspapers. . . .

But his voice was only a piercing, inarticulate yelp that infuriated human beings; his paws were good for nothing but running; his pointed face transmitted no emotions.

He trotted along the curbs of three blocks in the business district before he found a pencil stump. He picked it up in his teeth and ran to the docks on West Street, though he had only the vague outline of a last experiment in communication.

There was plenty of paper blowing around in the river wind, some of it even clean. To the stevedores, waiting at the dock for the payoff, he appeared to be frisking. A few of them whistled at him. In reality, he chased the flying paper with deadly earnestness.

When he captured a piece, he held it firmly between his forepaws. The stub of pencil was gripped in the even space separating his sharp canine fangs.

He moved the pencil in his mouth over the sheet of paper. It was clumsy and uncertain, but he produced long, wavering block letters. He wrote: "I AM A MAN." The short message covered the whole page, leaving no space for further information.

He dropped the pencil, caught up the paper in his

teeth, and ran back to the newspaper building. For the first time since he had escaped from Moss, he felt assured. His attempt at writing was crude and unformed, but the message was unmistakably clear.

He joined a group of tired young legmen coming back from assignments. He stood passively until the door was opened, then lunged confidently through the little procession of cub reporters. They scattered back cautiously, permitting him to enter without a struggle.

Again he raced up the stairs to the editorial department, put the sheet of paper down on the floor, and clutched the doorknob between his powerful teeth.

He hesitated for only an instant, to find the cadaverous reporter. Gilroy was seated at a desk, typing out his article. Carrying his message in his mouth, Wood trotted directly to Gilroy. He put his paw on the reporter's sharp knee.

"What the hell!" Gilroy gasped. He pulled his leg away startledly and shoved Wood away.

But Wood came back insistently, holding his paper stretched out to Gilroy as far as possible. He trembled hopefully until the reporter snatched the message out of his mouth. Then his muscles froze, and he stared up expectantly at the angular face, scanning it for signs of growing comprehension.

Gilroy kept his eyes on the straggling letters. His face darkened angrily.

"Who's being a wise guy here?" he shouted suddenly. Most of the staff ignored him. "Who let this mutt in and gave him a crank note to bring to me? Come on—who's the genius?"

Wood jumped around him, barking hysterically, trying to explain.

"Oh, shut up!" Gilroy rapped out. "Hey, copy! Take this dog down and see that he doesn't get back in! He won't bite you."

Again Wood had failed. But he did not feel defeated. When his hysterical dread of frustration ebbed, leaving his mind clear and analytical, he realized that his failure was only one of degree. Actually, he had communicated, but lack of space had prevented him from detailed clarity. The method was correct. He only needed to augment it.

Before the copy boy cornered him, Wood swooped up at a pencil on an empty desk.

"Should I let him keep the pencil, Mr. Gilroy?" the boy asked.

"I'll lend you mine, unless you want your arm snapped off," Gilroy snorted, turning back to his typewriter.

Wood sat back and waited beside the copy boy for the elevator to pick them up. He clenched the pencil possessively between his teeth. He was impatient to get out of the building and back to the lot on West Street, where he could plan a system of writing a more explicit message. His block letters were unmanageably huge and shaky; but, with the same logical detachment he used to employ when he was a code translator, he attacked the problem fearlessly.

He knew that he could not use the printed or written alphabet. He would have to find a substitute that his clumsy teeth could manage, and that could be compressed into less space.

Gilroy was annoyed by the collie's insistent returning. He crumpled the enigmatic, unintelligible note and tossed it in the wastebasket, but beyond considering it as a practical joke, he gave it no further thought.

His long, large-jointed fingers swiftly tapped out the last page of his story. He ended it with a short line of zeros and dashes, gathered a sheaf of papers, and brought it to the editor.

312

The editor studied the lead paragraph intently and skimmed hastily through the rest of the story. He appeared uncomfortable.

"Not bad, eh?" Gilroy exulted.

"Uh—what?" The editor jerked his head up blankly. "Oh. No, it's pretty good. Very good, in fact."

"I've got to hand it to you," Gilroy continued admiringly. "I'd have given up. You know—nothing to work on, just a bunch of fantastic events with no beginning and no end. Now, all of a sudden, the cops pick up a nut who acts like a dog and has an incision like the catatonics. Maybe it isn't any clearer, but at least we've got something actually happening. I don't know—I feel pretty good. We'll get to the bottom—"

The editor listened abstractedly, growing more uneasy from sentence to sentence. "Did you see the latest case?" he interrupted.

"Sure. I'm in soft with the resident physician. If I hadn't been following this story right from the start, I'd have said the one they just hauled in was a genuine screwball. He goes bounding around on the floor, sniffs at things, and makes a pathetic attempt to bark. But he has an incision on the back of his neck. It's just like the others—even has two professional stitches, and it's the same number of millimeters away from the spine. He's a catatonic, or whatever we'll have to call it now—"

"Well, the story's shaping up faster than I thought it would," the editor said, evening the edges of Gilroy's article with ponderous care. "But—" His voice dropped huskily. "Well, I don't know how to tell you this, Gilroy."

The reporter drew his brows together and looked at him obliquely. "What's the hard word this time?" he asked, mystified.

"Oh, the usual thing. You know. I've got to take you off this story. It's too bad, because it was just getting

313

hot. I hated to tell you, Gilroy; but, after all, what the hell. That's part of the game."

"It is, huh?" Gilroy flattened his hands on the desk and leaned over them resentfully. "Whose toes did we step on this time? Nobody's. The hospital has no kick coming. I couldn't mention names because I didn't know any to mention. Well, then, what's the angle?"

The editor shrugged. "I can't argue. It's a front-office order. But I've got a good lead for you to follow to-morrow—"

Savagely, Gilroy strode to the window and glared out at the darkening street. The business department wasn't behind the order, he reasoned angrily; they weren't getting ads from the hospital. And as for the big boss— Talbot never interfered with policy, except when he had to squash a revealing crime story. By eliminating the editors, who yielded an inch when public opinion demanded a mile, the business department, who fought only when advertising was at stake, Gilroy could blame no one but Talbot.

Gilroy rapped his bony knuckles impatiently against the window casement. What was the point of Talbot's order? Perhaps he had a new way of paying off traitors. Gilroy dismissed the idea immediately; he knew Talbot wouldn't go to that expense and risk possible leakage when the old way of sealing a body in a cement block and dumping it in the river was still effective and cheap.

"I give up," Gilroy said without turning around. "I can't figure out Talbot's angle."

"Neither can I," the editor admitted.

At that confession, Gilroy wheeled. "Then you *know* it's Talbot!"

"Of course. Who else could it be? But don't let it throw you, pal." He glanced around cautiously as he spoke. "Let this catatonic yarn take a rest. Tomorrow you can find out what's behind this bulletin that Johnson phoned in from City Hall."

Gilroy absently scanned the scribbled note. His scowl wrinkled into puzzlement.

"What the hell is this? All I can make out of it is the A.S.P.C.A. and dog lovers are protesting to the mayor against organized murder of brown-and-white collies."

"That's just what it is."

"And you think Talbot's gang is behind it, naturally." When the editor nodded, Gilroy threw up his hands in despair. "This gang stuff is getting too deep for me, chief. I used to be able to call their shots. I knew why a torpedo was bumped off, or a crime was pulled; but I don't mind telling you that I can't see why a gang boss wants a catatonic yarn hushed up, or sends his mob around plugging innocent collies. I'm going home . . . get drunk—"

He stormed out of the office. Before the editor had time to shrug his shoulders, Gilroy was back again, his deep eyes blazing furiously.

"What a pair of prize dopes we are, chief!" he shouted. "Remember that collie—the one that came in with a hunk of paper in his mouth? We threw him out, remember? Well, *that's the hound Talbot's gang is out gunning for! He's trying to carry messages to us!*"

"Hey, you're right!" The editor heaved out of the chair and stood uncertainly. "Where is he?"

Gilroy waved his long arms expressively.

"Then come on! To hell with hats and coats!"

They dashed into the staff room. The skeleton night crew loafed around, reading papers before moping out to follow up undeveloped loads.

"Put those papers down!" the editor shouted. "Come on with me—every one of you."

He herded them, baffled and annoyed, into the elevator. At the entrance to the building, he searched up and down the street.

"He's not around, Gilroy. All right, you deadbeats, divide up and chase around the streets, whistling. When you see a brown-and-white collie, whistle to him. He'll come to you. Now beat it and do as I say."

They moved off slowly. "Whistle?" one called back anxiously.

"Yes, whistle!" Gilroy declared. "Forget your dignity. Whistle!"

They scattered, whistling piercingly the signals that are supposed to attract dogs. The few people around the business district that late were highly interested and curious, but Gilroy left the editor whistling at the newspaper building, while he whistled toward West Street. He left the shrill calls blowing away from the river, and searched along the wide highway in the growing dark.

For an hour he pried into dark spaces between the docks, patiently covering his ground. He found nothing but occasional longshoremen unloading trucks and a light uptown traffic. There were only homeless, prowling mongrels and starving drifters: no brown-and-white collie.

He gave up when he began to feel hungry. He returned to the building hoping the others had more luck, and angry with himself for not having followed the dog when he had the chance.

The editor was still there, whistling more frantically than ever. He had gathered a little band of inquisitive onlookers, who waited hopefully for something to happen. The reporters were also returning.

"Find anything?" the editor paused to ask.

"Nope. He didn't show up here?"

"Not yet. Oh, he'll be back, all right. I'm not afraid of that." And he went back to his persistent whistling, disregarding stares and rude remarks. He was a man with an iron will. He sneered openly at the defeated reporters when they slunk past him into the building.

In the comparative quiet of the city, above the editor's shrills, Gilroy heard swiftly pounding feet. He gazed over the heads of the pack that had gathered around the editor.

A reporter burst into view, running at top speed and doing his best to whistle attractively through dry lips at a dog streaking away from him.

"Here he comes!" Gilroy shouted. He broke through the crowd and his long legs flashed over the distance to the collie. In his excitement, empty, toneless wind blew between his teeth; but the dog shot straight for him just the same. Gilroy snatched a dirty piece of paper out of his mouth. Then the dog was gone, toward the docks; and a black car rode ominously down the street.

Gilroy half started in pursuit, paused, and stared at the slip of paper in his hand. For a moment he blamed the insufficient light, but when the editor came up to him, yelling blasphemy for letting the dog escape, Gilroy handed him the unbelievable note.

"That dog can take care of himself," Gilroy said. "Read this."

The editor drew his brows together over the message. It read:

;;;,.;;   ;,,..;,".:..,.:.   ;;.   ..";,.   .;;:...:..;,,"..;.;   ..:;".";,..   "..;   ".".;.
::;..;".,."""   ";.;;   .:.";,..:.;;..   ;;.   ".:.";;   ..";.;;

"Well, I'll be damned!" the editor exclaimed. "Is it a gag?"

"Gag, my eye!"

"Well, I can't make head or tail of it!" the editor protested.

Gilroy looked around undeterminedly, as if for someone to help them. "You're not supposed to. It's a code message." He swung around, stabbing an enormously long, knobbed finger at the editor. "Know anyone who

317

can translate code—cryptograms?"

"Uh—let's see. How about the police, or the G-men—"

Gilroy snorted. "Give it to the bulls before we know what's in it!" He carefully tucked the crudely penciled note into his breast pocket and buttoned his coat. "You stick around outside here, chief. I'll be back with the translation. Keep an eye out for the pooch."

He loped off before the editor could more than open his mouth.

In the index room of the Forty-second Street Library, Gilroy crowded into the telephone booth and dialed a number. His eyes ached and he had a dizzy headache. Close reasoning always scrambled his wits. His mind was intuitive rather than ploddingly analytical.

"Executive office, please," he told the night operator. "There must be somebody there. I don't care if it's the business manager himself. I want to speak to somebody in the executive office. I'll wait." He lolled, bent into a convenient shape, against the wall. "Hello. Who's this? . . . Oh, good. Listen, Rothbart, this is Gilroy. Do me a favor, huh? You're nearest the front entrance. You'll find the chief outside the door. Send him into the telephone, and take his place until he gets through. While you're out there, watch for a brown-and-white collie. Nab him if he shows up and bring him inside. . . . Will you? . . . Thanks!"

Gilroy held the receiver to his ear, defeatedly amusing himself by identifying the sounds coming over the wire. He was no longer in a hurry, and when he had to pay another nickel before the editor finally came to the telephone, he did not mind.

"What's up, Gilroy?" the editor asked hopefully.

"Nothing, chief. That's why I called up. I went through a military code book, some kids' stuff, and a history of cryptography through the ages. I found some good codes, but nobody seems to've thought of this punctuation code. Ever see the Confederate cipher? Boy, it's a real dazzler—wasn't cracked until after the Civil War was over! The old Greeks wound strips of paper around identical sticks. When they were unrolled, the strips were gibberish; around the sticks, the words fell right into order."

"Cut it out," the editor snapped. "Did you find anything useful?"

"Sure. Everybody says the big clue is the table of frequency—the letters used more often than others. But, on the other hand, they say that in short messages, like ours, important clues like the single words 'a' and 'I', bigrams like 'am', 'as', and even trigrams like 'the' or 'but', are ofetn omitted entirely."

"Well, that's fine. What're you going to do now?"

"I don't know. Try the cops after all, I guess."

"Nothing doing," the editor said firmly. "Ask a librarian to help."

Gilroy seized the inspiration. He slammed down the receiver and strode to the reference desk.

"Where can I get hold of somebody who knows cryptograms?" he rasped.

The attendant politely consulted his colleagues. "The guard of the manuscript room is pretty good," he said, returning. "Down the hall—"

Gilroy shouted his thanks and broke into an ungainly run, ignoring the attendant's order to walk. At the manuscript room he clattered the gate until the keeper appeared and let him in.

"Take a look at this," he commanded, flinging the message on a table.

The keeper glanced curiously at it. "Oh, cryptogram, eh?"

"Yeah. Can you make anything out of it?"

"Well, it looks like a good one," the guard replied

cautiously, "but I've been cracking them all for the last twenty years." They sat down at the table in the empty room. For some time the guard stared fixedly at the scrawled note. "Five symbols," he said finally. "S colon, period, comma, colon, quotation marks. Thirteen word units, each with an even number of symbols. They must be used in combinations of two."

"I figured that out already," Gilroy rapped out. "What's it *say?*"

The guard lifted his head, offended. "Give me a chance. Bacon's code wasn't solved for three centuries."

Gilroy groaned. He did not have so much time on his hands.

"There're only thirteen word units here," the guard went on, undaunted by the Bacon example. "Can't use frequency, bigrams or trigrams."

"I know that already," Gilroy said hoarsely.

"Then why'd you come to me if you're so smart?"

Gilroy hitched his chair away. "O. K., I won't bother you."

"Five symbols to represent twenty-six letters. Can't be. Must be something like the Russian nihilist code. They can represent only twenty-five letters. The missing one is either 'q' or 'j', most likely, because they're not used much. Well, I'll tell you what I think."

"What's that?" Gilroy demanded, all alert.

"You'll have to reason *a priori*, or whatever it is."

"Any way you want," Gilroy sighed. "Just get on with it."

"The square root of twenty-five is five. Whoever wrote this note must've made a square of letters, five wide and five deep. That sounds right." The guard smiled and nodded cheerfully. "Possible combinations in a square of twenty-five letters is . . . uh . . . 625. The double symbols must identify the lines down and across. Possible combinations, twenty-five. Combinations all told . . . hmmm . . . 15,625. Not so good. If there's a key word, we'll have to search the dictionary until we find it. Possible combinations, 15,625 multiplied by the English vocabulary—that is, if the key word *is* English."

Gilroy raised himself to his feet. "I can't stand it," he moaned. "I'll be back in an hour."

"No, don't go," the guard said. "You've been helping me a lot. I don't think we'll have to go through more than 625 combinations at the most. That'll take no time at all."

He spoke, of course, in relative terms. Bacon code, three centuries; Confederate code, fifteen years; wartime Russian code, unsolved. Cryptographers must look forward to eternity.

Gilroy seated himself, while the guard plotted a square:

	"	,	.	:	;
a	b	c	d	e	"
f	g	h	i	j	,
k	l	m	n	o	.
p	r	s	t	u	:
v	w	x	y	z	

The first symbol combination, two semicolons, translated to "a", by reading down the first line, from the top semicolon, and across from the side semicolon. The next, a semicolon and a comma, read "l". He went on in this fashion until he screwed up his face and pushed the half-completed translation to Gilroy. It read:

"akdd kyoiztou kp tbo eztztkprepd"

"Does it make sense to you?" he asked anxiously.

Gilroy strangled, unable to reply.

"It could be Polish," the guard explained, "or Japanese."

The harassed reporter fled.

When he returned an hour later, after having eaten and tramped across town, nervously chewing cigarettes, he found the guard defended from him by a breastwork of heaped papers.

"Does it look any better?" Gilroy asked hoarsely.

The guard was too absorbed to look up or answer. By peering over his shoulder, Gilroy saw that he had plotted another square. The papers on the table were covered with discarded letter keys; at a rough guess, Gilroy estimated that the keeper had made over a hundred of them.

The one he was working with had been formed as the result of methodical elimination. His first square the guard had kept, changing the positions of the punctuation marks. When that had failed, he altered his alphabet square, tried that, and reversed his punctuation marks once more. Patient and plodding the guard had formed this square:

,	.	;	"	:	
z	u	o	j	e	,
y	t	n	i	d	.
x	s	m	h	c	;
w	r	l	g	b	"
v	p	k	f	a	:

Without haste, he counted down under the semicolon and across from the side semicolon, stopping at "m". Gilroy followed him, nodding at the result. He was faster than the old guard at interpreting the semicolon and comma—"o". The period and semicolon, repeated twice, came to "ss". First word: "moss".

Gilroy straightened up and took a deep breath. He bent over again and counted down and across with the guard, through the whole message, which the old man had lined off between every two symbols. Completed, it read,

;;|;,|.|.;| ;,|.•|:,|.”|::|.•|:,|:.| ;,|;,| ..|”;|:,| :;|::|..|::|..|;,|.•|”.|:;|.;|
m o s s   o p e r a t e d   o n   t h e   c a t a t o n i c s

⠰⠤⠒⠒⠆⠆⠄⠶⠶⠄⠆⠄ ⠶⠄⠆⠄ ⠶⠒⠄⠶⠄⠆⠄⠒⠒⠆⠆⠄⠒⠆⠄⠶⠄⠒⠄⠶⠶⠶⠶ ⠶⠆⠄⠶⠄⠆⠆ ⠄⠄⠄⠶⠄⠶⠆⠄⠄⠄⠄⠆⠄⠄
t a l b o t   i s   f i n a n c i n g   h i m   p r o t e c t
⠆⠆⠄⠆⠄ ⠶⠆⠄⠶⠄⠶⠆⠄⠆⠆ ⠄⠄⠶⠆⠆⠄⠆⠆
m e   f r o m   t h e m

"Hmmm," the guard mused. "That makes sense, if I knew what it meant."

But Gilroy had snatched the papers out of his hand. The gate clanged shut after him.

Returning to the office in a taxi, Gilroy was not too joyful. He rapped on the inside window. "Speed it up! I've seen the sights."

He thought, if the dog's been bumped off, good-by catatonic story! The dog was his only link with the code writer.

Wood slunk along the black, narrow alleys behind the wholesale fruit markets on West Street. Battered cans and crates of rotting fruit made welcome obstacles and shelters if Talbot's gangsters were following him.

He knew that he had to get away from the river section. The gangsters must have definitely recognized him; they would call Talbot's headquarters for greater forces. With their speedy cars they could patrol the borders of the district he was operating in, and close their lines until he was trapped.

More important was the fact that reporters had been sent out to search for him. Whether or not his simple code had been deciphered did not matter very much; the main thing was that Gilroy at last knew he was trying to communicate with him.

Wood's unerring animal sense of direction led him through the maze of densely shadowed alleys to a point nearest the newspaper office. He peered around the corner, up and down the street. The black gang car was out of sight. But he had to make an unprotected dash of a hundred yards, in the full glare of the streetlights, to the building entrance.

His powerful leg muscles gathered. He sped over the hard cement sidewalk. The entrance drew nearer. His legs pumped more furiously, shortening the dangerous space more swiftly than a human being could; and for that he was grateful.

He glimpsed a man standing impatiently at the door. At the last possible moment, Wood checked his rush and flung himself toward the thick glass plate.

"There you are!" the editor cried. "Inside—quick!"

He thrust open the door. They scurried inside and commandeered an elevator, then ran through the newsroom to the editor's office.

"Boy, I hope you weren't seen! It'd be curtains for both of us."

The editor squirmed uneasily behind his desk, from time to time glancing disgruntledly at his watch and cursing Gilroy's long absence. Wood stretched out on the cold floor and panted. He had expected his note to be deciphered by then, and even hoped to be recognized as a human being in a dog's body. But he realized that Gilroy probably was still engaged in decoding it.

At any rate he was secure for a while. Before long, Gilroy would return; then his story would be known. Until then he had patience.

Wood raised his head and listened. He recognized Gilroy's characteristic pace that consumed at least four feet at a step. Then the door slammed open and shut behind the reporter.

"The dog's here, huh? Wait'll you take a look at what I got!"

He threw a square of paper before the editor. Wood scanned the editor's face as he eagerly read it. He ignored the vast hamburger that Gilroy unwrapped for him. He was bewildered by Gilroy's lack of more than ordinary interest in him; but perhaps the editor would understand.

"So that's it! Moss and Talbot, eh? It 's getting a lot clearer."

"I get Moss's angle," Gilroy said. "He's the only guy around here who could do an operation like that. But Talbot—I don't get his game. And who sent the note —how'd he get the dope—where is he?"

Wood almost went mad with frustration. He could explain; he knew all there was to be known about Talbot's interest in Moss's experiment. The problem of communication had been solved. Moss and Talbot were exposed; but he was as far as ever from regaining his own body.

He had to write another cipher message—longer, this time, and more explicit, answering the questions Gilroy raised. But to do that—he shivered. To do that, he would have to run the gang patrol; and his enciphering square was in the corner of a lot. It would be too dark. . . .

"We've got to get him to lead us to the one who wrote the message," Gilroy said determinedly. "That's the only way we can corner Moss and Talbot. Like this, all we have is an accusation and no legal proof."

"He must be around here somewhere."

Gilroy fastened his eyes on Wood. "That's what I think. The dog came here and barked, trying to get us to follow him. When we chased him out, he came back with a scrawled note about a half-hour later. Then he brought the code message within another hour. The writer must be pretty near here. After the dog eats, we'll—" He gulped audibly and raised his bewildered gaze to the editor. Swiftly, he slipped off the edge of the desk and fumbled in the long hair on Wood's neck. "Look at that, chief—a piece of surgical plaster. When the dog bent his head to eat, the hair fell away from it."

"And you think he's a catatonic." The editor smiled

pityingly and shook his head. "You're jumpy, Gilroy."

"Maybe I am. But I'd like to see what's under the plaster."

Wood's heart pumped furiously. He knew that his incision was the precise duplicate of the catatonics', and if Gilroy could see it, he would immediately understand. When Gilroy picked at the plaster, he tried to bear the stabbing pain; but he had to squirm away. The wound was raw and new, and the deeply rooted hair was firmly glued to the plaster. He permitted Gilroy to try again. The sensation was far too fierce; he was afraid the incision would rip wide open.

"Stop it," the editor said squeamishly. "He'll bite you."

Gilroy straightened up. "I could take it off with some ether."

"You don't really think he was operated on, do you? Moss doesn't operate on dogs. He probably got into a fight, or one of Talbot's torpedoes creased him with a bullet."

The telephone bell rang insistently. "I'd still like to see what's under it," Gilroy said as the editor removed the receiver. Wood's hopes died suddenly. He felt that he was to blame for resisting Gilroy.

"What's up, Blaine?" the editor asked. He listened absorbedly, his face darkening. "O.K. Stay away if you don't want to take a chance. Phone your story in to the rewrite desk." He replaced the receiver and said to Gilroy: "Trouble, plenty of it. Talbot's gang cars are cruising around this district. Blaine was afraid to run them. I don't know how you're going to get the dog through."

Wood was alarmed. He left his meal unfinished and agitated toward the door, whimpering involuntarily.

Gilroy glanced curiously at him. "I'd swear he understood what you said. Did you see the change that came over him?"

"That's the way they react to voices," the editor said.

"Well, we've got to get him to his master." Gilroy mused, biting the inside of his cheek. "I can do it—if you're in with me."

"Of course I am. How?"

"Follow me." Wood and the editor went through the newsroom on the cadaverous reporter's swift heels. In silence they waited for an elevator, then descended to the lobby. "Wait here beside the door," Gilroy said. "When I give the signal, come running."

"What signal?" the editor cried, but Gilroy had loped into the street and out of sight.

They waited tensely. In a few minutes a taxi drew up to the curb and Gilroy opened the door, sitting alertly inside. He watched the corner behind him. No one moved for a long while; then a black gang car rode slowly and vigilantly past the taxi. An automatic rifle barrel glinted in the yellow light. Gilroy waited until a moment after it turned into West Street. He waved his arms frantically.

"Step on it!" Gilroy ordered harshly. "Up West Street!"

The editor scooped Wood up in his arms, burst open the door, and darted across the sidewalk into the cab.

The taxi accelerated suddenly. Wood crouched on the floor, trembling, in despair. He had exhausted his ingenuity and he was as far as ever from regaining his body. They expected him to lead them to his master; they still did not realize that he had written the message. Where should he lead them—how could he convince them that he was the writer?

"I think this is far enough," Gilroy broke the silence. He tapped on the window. The driver stopped. Gilroy and the editor got out, Wood following indecisively.

Gilroy paid and waved the driver away. In the quiet isolation of the broad commercial highway, he bent his great height to Wood's level. "Come on, boy!" he urged. "Home!"

Wood was in a panic of dismay. He could think of only one place to lead them. He set off at a slow trot that did not tax them. Hugging the walls, sprinting across streets, he headed cautiously downtown.

They followed him behind the markets fronting the highway, over a hemmed-in lot. He picked his way around the deep, treacherous foundation of a building that had been torn down, up and across piles of rubbish, to a black-shadowed clearing at the lot's end. He halted passively.

Gilroy and the editor peered around into the blackness. "Come out!" Gilroy called hoarsely. "We're your friends. We want to help you."

When there was no response, they explored the lot, lighting matches to illuminate dark corners of the foundation. Wood watched them with confused emotions. By searching in the garbage heaps and the crumbling walls of the foundation, they were merely wasting time.

As closely as possible in the dark, he located the site of his enciphering square. He stood near it and barked clamorously. Gilroy and the editor hastily left their futile prodding.

"He must've seen something," the editor observed in a whisper.

Gilroy cupped a match in his hand and moved the light back and forth in the triangular corner of the cleared space. He shrugged.

"Not around there," the editor said. "He's pointing at the ground."

Gilroy lowered the match. Before its light struck the ground, he yelped and dropped it, waving his burned fingers in the cool air. The editor murmured sympathy and scratched another match.

"Is this what you're looking for—a lot of letters in a square?"

Wood and Gilroy crowded close. The reporter struck his own match. In its light he narrowly inspected the crudely scratched encoding square.

"Be back in a second," he said. It was too dark to see his face, but Wood heard his voice, harsh and strained. "Getting flashlight."

"What'll I do if the guy comes around?" the editor asked hastily.

"Nothing," Gilroy rasped. "He won't. Don't step on the square."

Gilroy vanished into the night. The editor struck another match and scrutinized the ground with Deerslayer thoroughness.

"What the hell did he see?" he pondered. "That guy—" He shook his head defeatedly and dropped the match.

Never in his life had Wood been so passionately excited. What *had* Gilroy discovered? Was it merely another circumstantial fact, like his realization that Talbot's gangsters were gunning for Wood; or was it a suspicion of Wood's identity? Gilroy had replied that the writer would not reappear, but that could have meant anything or nothing. Wood frantically searched for a way of finally demonstrating who he really was. He found only a negative plan—he would follow Gilroy's lead.

With every minute that passed, the editor grew angrier, shifting his leaning position against the brick wall, pacing around. When Gilroy came back, flashing a bright cone of light before him, the editor lashed out.

"Get it over with, Gilroy. I can't waste the whole

night. Even if we do find out what happened, we can't print it—"

Gilroy ignored him. He splashed the brilliant ray of his huge five-celled flashlight over the enciphering square.

"Now look at it," he said. He glanced intently at Wood, who also obeyed his order and stood at the editor's knee, searching the ground. "The guy who made that square was very cautious—he put his back to the wall and faced the lot, so he wouldn't be taken by surprise. The square is upside-down to us. No, wait!" he said sharply as the editor moved to look at the square from its base. "I don't want your footprints on it. Look at the bottom, where the writer must've stood."

The editor stared closely. "What do you see?" he asked puzzledly.

"Well, the ground is moist and fairly soft. There should be footprints. There are. *Only they're not human!*"

Raucously, the editor cleared his throat. "You're kidding."

"*Gestalt*," Gilroy said, almost to himself, "the whole is greater than the sum of its parts. You get a bunch of unconnected facts, all apparently unrelated to each other. Then suddenly one fact pops up—it doesn't seem any more important than the others—but all at once the others click into place, and you get a complete picture."

"What are you mumbling about?" the editor whispered anxiously.

Gilroy stooped his great height and picked up a yellow stump of pencil. He turned it over in his hand before passing it to the editor.

"That's the pencil this dog snatched before we threw him out. You can see his teethmarks on the sides, where he carried it. But there're teethmarks around the un-sharpened end. Maybe I'm nuts—" He took the dirty code message out of his inside breast pocket and smoothed it out. "I saw these smudges the minute I looked at the note, but they didn't mean anything to me then. What do you make of them?"

The editor obediently examined the note in the glare of the flash. "They could be palmprints."

"Sure—a baby's," Gilroy said witheringly. "Only they're not. We both know they're pawprints, the same as are at the bottom of the square. You know what I'm thinking. Look't the way the dog is listening."

Without raising his voice, he half turned his head and said quite casually, "Here comes the guy who wrote the note, right behind the dog."

Involuntarily, Wood spun around to face the dark lot. Even his keen animal eyes could detect no one in the gloom. When he lifted his gaze to Gilroy, he stared full into grim, frightened eyes.

"Put that in your pipe," Gilroy said tremulously. "That's his reaction to the pitch of my voice, eh? You can't get out of it, chief. We've got a werewolf on our hands, thanks to Moss and Talbot."

Wood barked and frisked happily around Gilroy's towering legs. He had been understood!

But the editor laughed, a perfectly normal, humorous, unconvinced laugh. "You're wasting your time writing for a newspaper, Gilroy—"

"O.K., smart guy," Gilroy replied savagely. "Stop your cackling and tell me the answer to this—

"The dog comes into the newsroom and starts barking. I thought he was just trying to get us to follow him; but I never heard a dog bark in long and short yelps before. He ran up the stairs, right past all the other floors—business office, advertising department, and so on—to the newsroom, because that's where he wanted to go. We chased him out. He came back with a scrawled note, saying: 'I am a man.' Those four words took up the whole page. Even a kid learning how to write wouldn't need so much space. But if you hold the pencil in your mouth and try to connect the bars of the letters, you'd have letters something like the ones on the note.

"He needed a smaller system of letters, so he made up a simple code. But he'd lost his pencil. He stole one of ours. Then he came back, watching out for Talbot's gang cars.

"There aren't any footprints at the bottom of this square—only a dog's pawprints. And there're two smudges on the message, where he put his paws to hold down the paper while he wrote on it. All along he's been listening to every word we said. When I said in a conversational tone that the writer was standing behind him, he whirled around. Well?"

The editor was still far from convinced. "Good job of training—"

"For a guy I used to respect, you certainly have the brain of a flea. Here—I don't know your name," he said to Wood. "What would you do if you had Moss here?"

Wood snarled.

"You're going to tell us where to find him. I don't know how, but you were smart enough to figure out a code, so you can figure out another way of communicating. Then you'll tell us what happened."

It was Wood's moment of supreme triumph. True, he didn't have his body yet, but now it was only a matter of time. His joy at Gilroy's words was violent enough to shake even the editor's literal, unimaginative mind.

"You still don't believe it," Gilroy accused.

"How can I?" the editor cried plaintively. "I don't even know why I'm talking to you as if it could be possible."

Gilroy probed in a pile of rubbish until he uncovered a short piece of wood. He quickly drew a single line of small alphabetical symbols. He threw the stick away, stepped back and flashed the light directly at the alphabet. "Now spell out what happened."

Wood sprang back and forth before the alphabet, stopping at the letters he required and indicating them by pointing his snout down.

"T-a-l-b-o-t w-a-n-t-e-d a y-o-u-n-g h-e-a-l-t-h-y b-o-d-y M-o-s-s s-a-i-d h-e c-o-u-l-d g-i-v-e i-t t-o h-i-m—"

"Well, I'll be damned!" the editor blurted.

After that exclamation there was silence. Only the almost inaudible padding of Wood's paws on the soft ground, his excited panting, and the hoarse breathing of the men could be heard. But Wood had won!

Gilroy sat at the typewriter in his apartment; Wood stood beside his chair and watched the swiftly leaping keys; but the editor stamped nervously up and down the floor.

"I've wasted half the night," he complained, "and if I print this story I'll be canned. Why, damn it, Gilroy—how do you think the public'll take it if I can't believe it myself?"

"Hmmm," Gilroy explained.

"You're sacrificing our job. You know that, don't you?"

"It doesn't mean that much to me," Gilroy said without glancing up. "Wood has to get back his body. He can't do it unless we help him."

"Doesn't that sound ridiculous to you? 'He has to get back his body.' Imagine what the other papers'll do to that sentence!"

Gilroy shifted impatiently. "They won't see it," he stated.

"Then why in hell are you writing the story?" the

editor asked, astounded. "Why don't you want me to go back to the office?"

"Quiet! I'll be through in a minute." He inserted another sheet of paper and his flying fingers covered it with black, accusing words. Wood's mouth opened in a canine grin when Gilroy smiled down at him and nodded his head confidently. "You're practically walking around on your own feet, pal. Let's go."

He flapped on his coat and carelessly dropped a battered hat on his craggy head. Wood braced himself to dart off. The editor lingered.

"Where're we going?" he asked cautiously.

"To Moss, naturally, unless you can think of a better place."

Wood could not tolerate the thought of delay. He tugged at the leg of the editor's pants.

"You bet I can think of a better place. Hey, cut it out, Wood—I'm coming along. But, hell, Gilroy! It's after ten. I haven't done a thing. Have a heart and make it short."

With Gilroy hastening him by the arm and Wood dragging at his leg, the editor had to accompany them, though he continued his protests. At the door, however, he covered Wood while Gilroy hailed a taxi. When Gilroy signaled that the street was clear, he ran across the sidewalk with Wood bundled in his arms.

Gilroy gave the address. At its sound, Wood's mouth opened in a silent snarl. He was only a short distance from Moss, with two eloquent spokesmen to articulate his demands, and, if necessary, to mobilize public opinion for him! What could Moss do against that power?

They rode up Seventh Avenue and along Central Park West. Only the editor felt that they were speeding. Gilroy and Wood fretted irritably at every stop signal.

At Moss's street, Gilroy cautioned the driver to proceed slowly. The surgeon's house was guarded by two loitering black cars.

"Let us out at the corner," Gilroy said.

They scurried into the entrance of a rooming house.

"Now what?" the editor demanded. "We can't fight past them."

"How about the back way, Wood?"

Wood shook his head negatively. There was no entrance through the rear.

"Then the only way is across the roofs," Gilroy determined. He put his head out and scanned the buildings between them and Moss. "This one is six stories, the next two five, the one right next to Moss's is six, and Moss's is three. We'll have to climb up and down fire escapes and get in through Moss's roof. Ready?"

"I suppose so," the editor said fatalistically.

Gilroy tried the door. It was locked. He chose a bell at random and rang it vigorously. There was a brief pause; then the tripper buzzed. He thrust open the door and burst up the stairs, four at a leap.

"Who's there?" a woman shouted down the stairwell. They galloped past her. "Sorry, lady," Gilroy called back. "We rang your bell by mistake."

She looked disappointed and rather frightened; but Gilroy anticipated her emotion. He smiled and gayly waved his hand as he loped by.

The roof door was locked with a stout hook that had rusted into its eye. Gilroy smashed it open with the heel of his palm. They broke out onto a tarred roof, chill and black in the overcast, threatening night.

Wood and Gilroy discovered the fire escape leading to the next roof. They dashed for it. Gilroy tucked Wood under his left arm and swung himself over the anchored ladder.

"This is insane!" the editor said hoarsely. "I've never

done such a crazy thing in my life. Why can't we be smart and call the cops?"

"Yeah?" Gilroy sneered without stopping. "What's your charge?"

"Against Moss? Why—"

"Think about it on the way."

Gilroy and Wood were on the next roof, waiting impatiently for the editor to descend. He came down quickly but his thoughts wandered.

"You can charge him with what he did. He made a man into a dog."

"That would sound swell in the indictment. Forget it. Just walk lightly. This damned roof creaks and lets out a noise like a drum."

They advanced over the tarred sheets of metal. Beneath them, they could hear their occasionally heavy tread resound through hollow rooms. Wood's claws tapped a rhythmic tattoo.

They straddled over a low wall dividing the two buildings. Wood sniffed the air for enemies lurking behind chimneys, vents and doors. At instants of suspicion, Gilroy briefly flashed his light ahead. They climbed up a steel ladder to the six-story building adjoining Moss's.

"How about a kidnap charge?" the editor asked as they stared down over the wall at the roof of Moss's building.

"Please don't annoy me. Wood's body is in the observation ward at the hospital. How're you going to prove that Moss kidnapped him?"

The editor nodded in the gloom and searched for another legal charge. Gilroy splashed his light over Moss's roof. It was unguarded.

"Come on, Wood," he said, inserting the flashlight in his belt. He picked up Wood under his left arm. In order to use his left hand in climbing, he had to squeeze Wood's middle in a stranglehold.

The only thing Wood was thankful for was that he could not look at the roof three stories below. Gilroy held him securely, tightly enough for his breath to struggle in whistling gasps. His throat knotted when Gilroy gashed his hand on a sharp sliver of dry paint scale.

"It's all right," Gilroy hissed reassuringly. "We're almost there."

Above them, he saw the editor clambering heavily down the insecurely bolted ladder. Between the anchoring plates it groaned and swayed away from the unclean brick wall. Rung by rung they descended warily, Gilroy clutching for each hold, Wood suspended in space and helpless—both feeling their hearts drop when the ladder jerked under their weight.

Then Gilroy lowered his foot and found the solid roof beneath it. He grinned impetuously in the dark. Wood writhed out of his hold. The editor cursed his way down to them.

He followed them to the rear fire escape. This time he offered to carry Wood down. Swinging out over the wall, Wood felt the editor's muscles quiver. Wood had nothing but a miserable animal life to lose, and yet even he was not entirely fearless in the face of the hidden dangers they were braving. He could sympathize with the editor, who had everything to lose and did not wholly believe that Wood was not a dog. Discovering a human identity in an apparently normal collie must have been a staggeringly hard fact for him to swallow.

He set Wood down on the iron bars. Gilroy quickly joined them, and yanked fiercely at the top window. It was locked.

"Need a jimmy to pry it open," Gilroy mused. He fingered the edges of the frame. "Got a knife on you?"

The editor fished absentmindedly through his pockets. He brought out a handful of keys, pencil stubs, scraps of paper, matches, and a cheap sheathed nail file. Gilroy snatched the file.

He picked at the putty in the ancient casement with the point. It chipped away easily. He loosened the top and sides.

"Now," he breathed. "Stand back a little and get ready to catch it."

He inserted the file at the top and levered the glass out of the frame. It stuck at the bottom and sides, refusing to fall. He caught the edges and lifted it out, laying it down noiselessly out of the way.

"Let's go." He backed in through the empty casement. "Hand Wood through."

They stood in the dark room, under the same roof with Moss. Wood exultantly sensed the proximity of the one man he hated—the one man who could return his body to him. "Now!" he thought. "*Now!*"

"Gilroy," the editor urged, "we can charge Moss with vivisection."

"That's right," Gilroy whispered. But they heard the doorknob rattle in his hand and turn cautiously.

"Then where're you going?" the editor rasped in a panic.

"We're here," Gilroy replied coolly. "So let's finish it."

The door swung back; pale weak light entered timidly. They stared down the long, narrow, dismal hall to the stairs at the center of the house. Down those stairs they would find Moss.

Wood's keen animal sense of smell detected Moss's personal odor. The surgeon had been there not long before.

He crouched around the stairhead and cautiously lowered himself from step to step. Gilroy and the editor clung to banister and wall, resting the bulk of their weight on their hands. They turned the narrow spiral where Clarence had fatally encountered the sharpness of Wood's fangs, down to the hall floor where his fat body had sprawled in blood.

Distantly, Wood heard a cane tap nervously, momentarily; then it stopped at a heated, hissed command that scarcely carried even to his ears. He glanced up triumphantly at Gilroy, his deep eyes glittering, his mouth grinning savagely, baring the red tongue lolling in the white, deadly trap of fangs. He had located and identified the sounds. Both Moss and Talbot were in a room at the back of the house.

He hunched his powerful shoulders and advanced slowly, stiff-legged, with the ominous air of all meat hunters stalking prey from ambush. Outside the closed door he crouched, muscles gathered for the lunge, his ears flat back along his pointed head to protect them from injury. But they heard muffled voices inaudible to men's dulled senses.

"Sit down, doc," Talbot said. "The truck'll be here soon."

"I'm not concerned with my personal safety," Moss replied tartly. "It's merely that I dislike inefficiency, especially when you claim—"

"Well, it's not Jake's fault. He's coming back from a job."

Wood could envision the faint sneer on Moss's scrubbed pink face. "You'll collapse any minute within the next six months, but the acquisitive nature is as strong as ever in you, isn't it, Talbot? You couldn't resist the chance of making a profit, and at a time like this!"

"Oh, don't lose your head. The cata-whatever-you-call-it can't talk and the dog is probably robbing garbage cans. What's the lam for?"

"I'm changing my residence purely as a matter of precaution. You underestimate human ingenuity, even

339

limited by a dog's inarticulateness."

Wood grinned up at his comrades. The editor was dough-faced, rigid with apprehension. Gilroy held a gun and his left hand snaked out at the doorknob. The editor began an involuntary motion to stop him. The door slammed inward before he completed it.

Wood and Gilroy stalked in, sinister in their grim silence. Talbot merely glanced at the gun. He had stared into too many black muzzles to be frightened by it. When his gaze traveled to Wood his jaw fell and hung open, trembling senilely. His constantly fighting lungs strangled. He screamed, a high, tortured wail, and tore frantically at his shirt, trying to release his chest from crushing pressure.

"An object lesson for you, Talbot," Moss said without emotion. "Do not underestimate an enemy."

Gilroy lost his frigid attitude. "Don't let him strangle. Help him."

"What can I do?" Moss shrugged. "It's angina pectoris. Either he pulls out of the convulsions by himself —or he doesn't. I can't help. But what did you want?"

No one answered him. Horrified, they were watching Talbot go purple in his death agony, lose the power of shrieking, and tear at his chest. Gilroy's gun hand was limp; yet Moss made no attempt to escape. The air rattled through Talbot's predatory nose. He fell in a contorted heap.

Wood felt sickened. He knew that in self-preservation doctors had to harden themselves, but only a monster of brutal callousness could have disregarded Talbot's frightful death as if it had not been going on.

"Oh, come now, it isn't as bad as all that," Moss said acidly.

Wood raised his shocked stare from the rag-doll body to Moss's hard, unfearful eyes. The surgeon had made no move to defend himself, to call for help from the squad of gangsters at the front of the house. He faced them with inhuman prepossession.

"It upsets your plans," Gilroy spat.

Moss lifted his shoulders, urbanely, delicately disdainful. "What difference should his death make to me? I never cared for his company."

"Maybe not, but his money seemed to smell O.K. to you. He's out of the picture. He can't keep us from printing this story now." Gilroy pulled a thin folded typescript from his inside breast pocket and shoved it out at Moss.

The surgeon read it interestedly, leaning casually against a wall. He came to the end of the short article and read the lead paragraph over again. Politely, he gave it back to Gilroy.

"It's very clear," he said. "I'm accused of exchanging the identities of a man and a dog. You even describe my alleged technique."

" 'Alleged'!" Gilroy roared savagely. "You mean you deny it?"

"Of course. Isn't it fantastic?" Moss smiled. "But that isn't the point. Even if I admitted it, how do you think I could be convicted on such evidence? The only witness seems to be the dog you call Wood. Are dogs allowed to testify in court? I don't remember, but I doubt it."

Wood was stunned. He had not expected Moss to brazen out the charge. An ordinary man would have broken down, confronted by their evidence.

Even the shrinking editor was stung into retorting: "We have proof of criminal vivisection!"

"But no proof that I was the surgeon."

"You're the only one in New York who could've done that operation."

"See how far that kind of evidence will get you."

Wood listened with growing anger. Somehow they

had permitted Moss to dominate the situation, and he parried their charges with cool, sarcastic deftness. No wonder he had not tried to escape! He felt himself to be perfectly safe. Wood growled, glowering hatred at Moss. The surgeon looked down contemptuously.

"All right, we can't convict you in court," Gilroy said. He hefted his gun, tightening his finger on the trigger. "That's not what we want, anyhow. This little scientific curiosity can make you operate on Wood and transfer his identity back to his own body."

Moss's expression of disdain did not alter. He watched Gilroy's tensing trigger finger with an astonishing lack of concern.

"Well, speak up," Gilroy rasped, waving the gun ominously.

"You can't force me to operate. All you can do is kill me, and I am as indifferent to my own death as I was to Talbot's." His smile broadened and twisted down at the corners, showing his teeth in a snarl that was the civilized, overrefined counterpart of Wood's. "Your alleged operation interests me, however. I'll operate for my customary fee."

The editor pushed Gilroy inside and hurriedly closed the door. "They're coming," he chattered. "Talbot's gangsters."

In two strides Gilroy put Moss between him and the door. His gun jabbed rudely into Moss's unflinching back. "Get over on the other side, you two, so the door'll hide you when it swings back," he ordered.

Wood and the editor retreated. Wood heard steps along the hall, then a pause, and a harsh voice shouted: "Hey, boss! Truck's here."

"Tell them to go away," Gilroy said in a low, suppressed tone.

Moss called, "I'm in the second room at the rear of the house."

Gilroy viciously stabbed him with the gun muzzle. "You're asking for it. I said tell them to go away!"

"You wouldn't dare to kill me until I've operated—"

"If you're not scared, why do you want them? What's the gag?"

The door flung open. A gangster started to enter. He stiffened, his keen, battle-trained eyes flashing from Talbot's twisted body to Moss, and to Gilroy, standing menacingly behind the surgeon. In a swift, smooth motion a gun leaped from his armpit holster.

"What happened to the boss?" he demanded hoarsely. "Who's he?"

"Put your gun away, Pinero. The boss died of a heart attack. That shouldn't surprise you—he was expecting it any day."

"Yeah, I know. But how'd that guy get in?"

Moss stirred impatiently. "He was here all along. Send the truck back. I'm not moving. I'll take care of Talbot."

The gangster looked uncertain, but, in lieu of another commander, he obeyed Moss's order. "Well, O.K. if you say so." He closed the door.

When Pinero had gone down the hall, Moss turned to face Gilroy.

"You're not scared—much!" Gilroy said.

Moss ignored his sarcastic outburst. "Where were we?" he asked. "Oh, yes. While you were standing there shivering, I had time to think over my offer. I'll operate for nothing."

"You bet you will!" Gilroy wagged his gun forcefully.

Moss sniffed at it. "That has nothing to do with my decision. I have no fear of death, and I'm not afraid of your evidence. If I do operate, it will be because of my interest in the experiment." Wood intercepted Moss's speculative gaze. It mocked, hardened, glittered sinisterly. "But of course," Moss added smoothly, "I will definitely operate. In fact, I insisted on it!"

His hidden threat did not escape Wood. Once he lay under Moss's knife it would be the end. A slip of the knife—a bit of careful carelessness in the gas mixture —a deliberately caused infection—and Moss would clear himself of the accusation by claiming he could not perform the operation, and therefore was not the vivisectionist. Wood recoiled, shaking his head violently from side to side.

"Wood's right," the editor said. "He knows Moss better. He wouldn't come out of the operation alive."

Gilroy's brow creased in an uneasy frown. The gun in his hand was a futile implement of force; even Moss knew he would not use it—could not, because the surgeon was only valuable to them alive. His purpose had been to make Moss operate. Well, he thought, he had accomplished that purpose. Moss offered to operate. But all four knew that under Moss's knife, Wood was doomed. Moss had cleverly turned the victory to utter rout.

"Then what the hell'll we do?" Gilroy exploded savagely. "What do you say, Wood? Want to take the chance, or keep on in a dog's body?"

Wood snarled, backing away.

"At least, he's still alive," the editor said fatalistically.

Moss smiled, protesting with silken mockery that he would do his best to return Wood's body.

"Barring accidents," Gilroy spat. "No soap, Moss. He'll get along the way he is, and you're going to get yours."

He looked grimly at Wood, jerking his head significantly in Moss's direction.

"Come on, chief," he said, guiding the editor through the door and closing it. "These old friends want to be alone—lot to talk over—"

Instantly, Wood leaped before the door and crouched there menacingly, glaring at Moss with blind, vicious hatred. For the first time, the surgeon dropped his pose of indifference. He inched cautiously around the wall toward the door. He realized suddenly that this was an animal. . . .

Wood advanced, cutting off his line of retreat. Mane bristling, head lowered ominously between blocky shoulders, bright gums showing above white curved fangs, Wood stalked over the floor, stiff-jointed, in a low, inexorably steady rhythm of approach.

Moss watched anxiously. He kept looking up at the door in an agony of longing. But Wood was there, closing the gap for the attack. He put up his hands to thrust away. . . .

And his nerve broke. He could not talk down mad animal eyes as he could a man holding a gun. He darted to the side and ran for the door.

Wood flung himself at the swiftly pumping legs. They crashed against him, tripped. Moss sprawled face down on the floor. He crossed his arms under his head to protect his throat.

Wood slashed at an ear. It tore, streaming red. Moss screeched and clapped his hands over his face, trying to rise without dropping his guard. But Wood ripped at his fingers.

The surgeon's hands clawed out. He was kneeling, defenseless, trying to fight off the rapid, aimed lunges —and those knifelike teeth. . . .

Wood gloated. A minute before, the scrubbed pink face had been aloof, sneering. Now it bobbed frantically at his eye level, contorted with overpowering fear, blood flowing brightly down the once scrupulously clean cheeks.

For an instant, the pale throat gleamed exposed at him. It was soft and helpless. He shot through the air.

His teeth struck at an angle and snatched—the white flesh parted easily. But a bony structure snapped between his jaws as he swooped by.

Moss knelt there after Wood had struck. His pain-twisted face gaped imbecilically, hands limp at his sides. His throat poured a red flood. Then his face drained to a ghastly lack of color and he pitched over.

He had lost, but he had also won. Wood was doomed to live out his life in a dog's body. He could not even expect to live his own life span. The average life of a dog is fifteen years. Wood could expect perhaps ten years more.

In his human body, Wood had found it difficult to find a job. He had been a code expert; but code experts, salesmen and apprentice workmen have no place in a world of shrinking markets. The employment agencies are glutted with an oversupply of normal human intelligences housed in strong, willing, expert human bodies.

The same normal human intelligence in a handsome collie's body had a greater market value. It was a rarity, a phenomenon to be gaped at after a ticket had been purchased for the privilege.

"Men've always had a fondness for freaks," Gilroy philosophized on their way to the theater where Wood had an engagement. "Mildly amusing freaks are paid to entertain. The really funny ones are given seats of honor and power. Figure it out, Wood. I can't. Once we get rid of our love of freaks and put them where they belong, we'll have a swell world."

The taxi stopped in a sidestreet, at the stage entrance. Lurid red-and-yellow posters, the size of cathedral murals, plastered the theater walls; and from them smirked prettified likenesses of Wood.

"Gosh!" their driver gasped. "Wait'll my kids hear

about this. I drove the Talkin' Dog! Gee, is that an honor, or ain't it?"

On all sides, pedestrians halted in awe, taxis stopped with a respectful screech of brakes; then an admiring swarm bore down on him.

"Isn't he *cute?*" women shrieked. "So *intelligent-looking!*"

"Sure," Wood heard their driver boast proudly, "I drove him down here. What's he like?" His voice lowered confidentially. "Well, the guy with him—his manager, I guess—he was talkin' to him just as intelligent as I'm talking' to you. Like he could understand ev'y word."

"Bet he could, too," a listener said definitely.

"G'on," another theorized. "He's just trained, like Rin-tin-tin, on'y better. But he's smart all right. Wisht I owned him."

The theater-district squad broke through the tangle of traffic and formed a lane to the stage door.

"Yawta be ashamed ayehselves," a cop said. "All this over a mutt!"

Wood bared his fangs at the speaker, who retreated defensively.

"Wise guy, huh?" the mob jeered. "Think he can't understand?"

It was a piece of showmanship that Wood and Gilroy had devised. It never failed to find a feeder in the form of an officious policeman and a response from the crowd.

Even in the theater, Wood was not safe from overly enthusiastic admiration. His fellow performers persisted in scratching his unitching back and ears, cooing and burbling in a singularly unintelligent manner.

The thriller that Wood had made in Hollywood was over; and while the opening acts went through their paces, Wood and Gilroy stood as far away from the wings as the theater construction would permit.

"Seven thousand bucks a week, pal," Gilroy mused over and over. "Just for doing something that any mug out in the audience can do twice as easily. Isn't that the payoff?"

In the year that had passed, neither was still able to accustom himself to the mounting figures in their bankbooks. Pictures, personal appearances, endorsements, highly fictionized articles in magazines—all at astronomical prices. . . .

But he could never have enough money to buy back the human body he had starved in.

"O.K., Wood," Gilroy whispered. "We're on."

They were drummed onto the stage with deafening applause. Wood went through his routine perfunctorily. He identified objects that had been named by the theater manager, picking them out of a heap of piled objects.

Ushers went through the aisles, collecting questions the audience had written on slips of paper. They passed them up to Gilroy.

Wood took a long pointer firmly in his mouth and stood before a huge lettered screen. Painfully, he pointed out, letter by letter, the answers to the audience's questions. Most of them asked about the future, market tips, racing information. A few seriously probed his mind.

White light stabbed down at him. Mechanically, he spelled out the simple answers. Most of his bitterness had evaporated; in its place was a dreary defeat, and dull acceptance of his dog's life. His bankbook had six figures to the left of the decimal—more than he had ever conceived of, even as a distant utopian possibility. But no surgeon could return his body to him, or increase his life expectancy of less than ten years.

Sharply, everything was washed out of sight: Gilroy, the vast alphabet screen, the heavy pointer in his mouth, the black space smeared with pale, gaping blobs of faces, even the white light staring down. . . .

He lay on a cot in a long ward. There was no dream-like quality of illusion in the feel of smooth sheets beneath and above him, or in the weight of blankets resting on his *outstretched* body.

And independently of the rest of his hand, his *finger* moved in response to his will. Its nail scratched at the sheet, loudly, victoriously.

An intern, walking through the ward, looked around for the source of the gloating sound. He engaged Wood's eyes that were glittering avidly, deep with intelligence. Then they watched the scratching finger.

"You're coming back," the intern said at last.

"I'm coming back." Wood spoke quietly, before the scene vanished and he heard Gilroy repeat a question he had missed.

He knew then that the body-mind was a unit. Moss had been wrong; there was more to identity than that small gland, something beyond the body. The forced division Moss had created was unnatural; the transplanted tissue was being absorbed, remodeled. Somehow, he knew these returns to his natural identity would recur, more and more—till it became permanent—till he became human once more.

NOSTALGIA

ALL IN COLOR FOR A DIME Ed. by Dick Lupoff and Don Thompson. The story of the great comic book heroes, told by the men who read and cherished them—with a 16 page color insert. (016253—$1.50)

THE GLORIOUS DECADE by Tedd Thomey. The story of television in the 1950's—with 32 pages of photos. (293753—95c)

THE GREAT RADIO HEROES by Jim Harmon. A recreation of the magic hours of radio, including original scripts. (302554—75c)

HOLLYWOOD AND THE ACADEMY AWARDS by Nathalie Fredrik. The illustrated entire history of the awards from 1927, with biographies of all winners. (342527—$1.50)

SO YOU THINK YOU KNOW TELEVISION by Donald Kennedy. Over 500 memory-teasing questions about television stars and shows. With 54 pages of photographs. (776809—75c)

WHATEVER BECAME OF . . .? #1, #2, and #3 by Richard Lamparski. The stories of what has happened to famous personalities of yesteryear—with hundreds of then-and-now photographs. (#1—880757, #2—880765, #3—880773—$1.25 each)

WHY DID THEY NAME IT? by Hannah Campbell. The story behind the stories of the brand names that have become household words. 40 illustrations of old-time ads. (886259—95c)

Available wherever paperbacks are sold or use this coupon.

26 B